The Antagonist's Prison

By DJ Jones

© 2024 Colloquy Publishing

DJ Jones
The Antagonist's Prison

All rights reserved. No part of this publication may be reproduced, stored in a retrieval system or transmitted in any form or by any means, electronic, mechanical, photocopying, recording, or otherwise without the prior permission of the publisher or author in accordance with the provisions of the Copyright, Designs, and Patents Act of 1988 or under the terms of any license permitting limited copying issued by the Copyright Licensing Agency.

Published by: Colloquy Publishing

Formatted by: Camille Jones

Cover Design by: Red Fox Illustration
jenniferbruceart.com

For Those Who Speak to Power

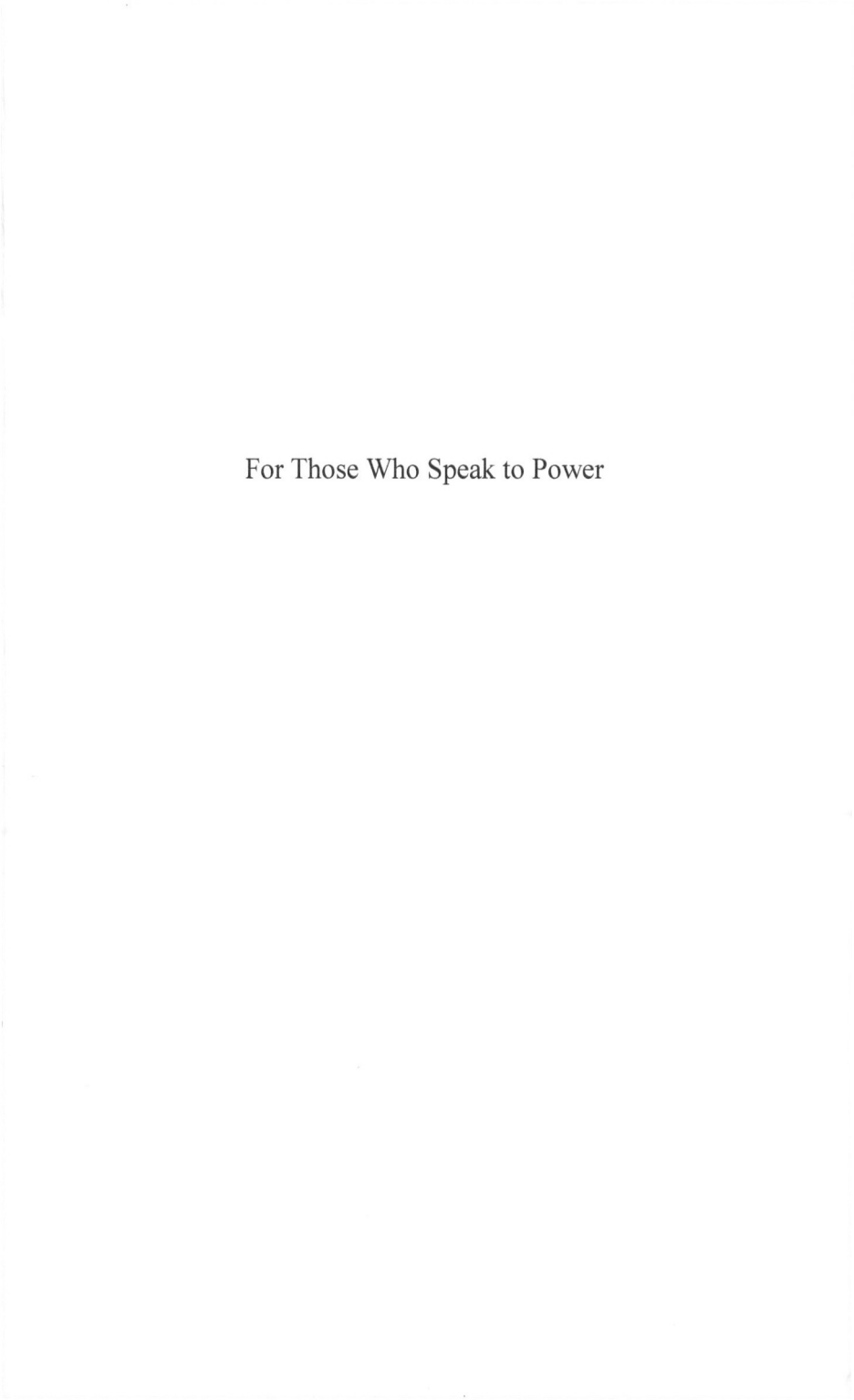

"No one deserves, Critch."
-A City Beneath Mantra

"I found your dark secret. I am the inquisitor. Critch is my weapon. The Antagonist is your reckoning. He is an Armageddon."
-The Widow in Yellow, Former Caretaker of Critch

"You don't talk about the Underground. You lie about it. You deny it. You perform all manner of subversion. If you stare into the black too long, it will stare back. If the Underground thinks you look tasty, it sends The Antagonist after you."
-Raile Trujillo, The Miscreant Queen

Drives
and a
Curious Woman

The moon meant to expose the countless scars carved into Aaron. Unsuccessful due to the veranda's dim. Legs crossed. Blanked out. Rocked on a crippled swing. A clove crackled loose in overly long fingers. Smoke hung about before it dissipated among the crabgrass and dirt beyond.

The calm white noise of gypsy jazz dropped. Caller ID flared through useful darkness and needy smoke. Adjusted into proper phone position. Body popped, cracked and ground like gravel disagreeing with the movement.

"Hey, Tyler," he said with a phlegmy garble. It had been quite a long time since he spoke. Cleared his throat.

"Yo, Aaron! How's your night?"

"Good, listening to someone named Django Reinhardt," Aaron said with mild implied threat. It wasn't his intention, just a certain force he spoke with. One he was not aware of.

"Cool, man, cool," Tyler was used to his friend and thought nothing of it. "He's just like the best fucking guitar player, like, Jesus, you don't even know."

"I don't. Just looked up guitar music and his name came up. Pretty good. Called gypsy jazz or some nonesuch."

"Dude, really? Your ignorance of music shocks, fucking shocks, I'm shocked." Aaron was certain Tyler was drunk and needed a ride.

The Antagonist's Prison

It was in the 'sh' sounds that were not intentional. A little flighty too.

"How can I help? What do you need?" Aaron said, ever the one not to say his assumptions aloud.

"Hey, can I pull a favor? You on your second bottle yet?"

"Not even halfway through the first," he said, shaking the mostly full bottle.

"Thank a god. Hey, dude, sorry, could you give me and Dot a ride? Dot and I, grammar...fuck. Wait, so, me and Dot...that's right, right? Shit, I'm sloshed all the way to shit, and she's rabid, fucking feral, know what I'm saying? Like, I should be afraid. But I'm not." Tyler's hiccup burp forebode through the receiver. His partner, Dot, distantly bitched in tempo with the far-off house music and STIs.

"No worries. Where are you?"

"Dude, I don't know, not a goddamn clue. We're in the hills by a super cool fire pit! That doesn't help much, huh? Here's Dot. Dot! Sweetheart, baby, darling, doll face, help me out. See what I did there, fucker? Album title or what?! Fuck yeah! Did you hear that, dude?"

"Just give me the fucking phone, asshole. Aaron?"

"How's it going, Dot?"

"Tyler's a goddamn asshole, that's how it's going. We're at 1016 Tea Avenue, up in the Forest District. Hey, could you give my cousin a ride too? She's staying with us. It shouldn't be a big deal."

"I'll be there in twenty." Aaron had not moved since sitting in proper phone-talking position. If there were witnesses, they might have found it off-putting.

"I'm so embarrassed," Dot said.

"I hear it. That's why I'm coming to get you," Aaron said in acknowledgement of her feeling. He was unaware his groaned-out voice made it sound chiding.

"You know, you don't need to be such a goddamned dick all the time. So sorry to disturb your nightly brood."

"Apologies?" Aaron said, baffled by the tone shift. Either way, Mr. Bennett let it go.

Drives and a Curious Woman

"Whatever, we'll be outside when you get here." She hung up.

In languid movements, a touch slower than one might expect, Aaron grabbed his leather jacket, turtleneck, keys, faded black fedora and humdrum if tasteful scarf. The toll of Critch's ultra-violence became obvious once pointed out. Redundant layers hid his lacerated appearance. Closer inspection raised theories no one wanted confirmed. He did *not* want to be known as the fabled monster of Indigo Bay.

Aaron drifted over patches of lawn shimmered in moonlight. The tall hedges always shaded at least a portion of the forsaken yard, especially at night. Crickets called.

Sitting on the porch before dinnertime, Mr. Bennett watched children sprint past the craven house as if it were haunted. The Victorian structure exposing more termite wood than pink paint.

The moon nervously peeked out behind quilted clouds as Aaron, no longer Critch, sighed in his little blue Civic. It was far too small for him. Had enough for a down payment for a new car, but this was all he needed. Radio always off. Flicked his spent butt away and lit another clove.

Indigo Bay curled, an exhausted dog around its little sea. Splayed out and happy and breathing deep with a big ol' grin. Once out of Downtown, the journey twisty-turned up through an insecure forest where affluence dwelled.

It didn't take long to drive through. Just another mid-sized bubble city along the mid-region of the west coast. People complained if they had to walk more than twenty minutes to get anywhere. Ten minutes by car was a commitment. The University was consistently third or fourth on lists of potential students.

Aaron turned on the brights as he drove up into the Forest District. Deer and lawbreakers abounded. A few switchbacks later, he stumbled onto Tea Avenue and followed the house numbers as his ancient phone's GPS twitched to catch up.

He mounted the lawn for closer access. Whatever property damage he caused at this point was moot. Lit yet another clove as his boots hit the fine-dewed lawn of some type of silly-named grass.

The Antagonist's Prison

Three semi-clothed bodies passed out just shy of a gaudy fountain. Not Critch Anymore nudged one with his boot. It groaned. He did the same to the others. No Tyler or Dot.

A broken window here, a beheaded lawn gnome there. Aaron righted it, but couldn't find its head. This trophy home of unused rooms should have smelled of museum musk. Pheromones, addictive substances, and transient piss overpowered. Followed the odors to find Tyler. The only discovery awaiting upstairs would be the clumsy mating rituals of whiskey dicks and unpleasured partners.

A couple raised their brows as Aaron turned into a wrecked kitchen of forgotten soldiers and wine spills. An unbelievable amount of dishes. Pizza boxes from several different pizzerias.

"Hey, your name's Aaron, right?" the taller one said.

"How's it?" he shook their hands. Aaron assumed his grip was firm. But New Acquaintances cradled their hands after, feeling bruised. Most resorted to fist bumping his mountain.

"Jason."

"Tiffany."

Jason was attractively tall. His workman's body in a pair of expensive skinny jeans, a button-up under a fancy vest which fit well. Tiffany's ginger hair taking up all the space it deserved. Discordant layered sweater covered in ostriches over Daisy Dukes, prismatic galaxy leggings, rounded off with sandals and leg warmers. The difference between Jason's height and Tiffany's dramatic stark.

"Sorry to bother you, man. You own Shirts with Words on Them, right?" Jason said.

"Yes," Aaron said with accidentally enough power to gut someone.

"Wow, Jesus, you've really got the seedy noir thing down pat, don'chu?" Tiffany said.

Her high-pitched, slightly nasal voice slurred. Too much happening about her. Mr. Bennett, Not At All Your Imminent Unforewarned Reckoning, would not be able to handle this conversation long. Too long since he'd been out of the Routine.

"Do shadows always fall on you like that?" she said.

Drives and a Curious Woman

"Maybe…Just be glad I shaved this morning, or you'd have to report a missing person," he said, shooting for funny. It was not. Menacing, in fact.

"Naw, your hair's too long for a hardboiled P.I. No self-respecting noir detective would have his hair all in his eyes like that. It'd screw with his vision."

"Sorry to disappoint. Looks like the party is dying out. Have you seen Tyler and Dot? Punk guy with blonde hair and a green canvas jacket. He's with a Rosie the Riveter thing."

"Uhh, yeah, Tyler's staring at the fire pit out back," Jason said. "So, umm, Amber works for you, right?"

"Indeed?" he said, drenched in peril. Aaron was, as always, oblivious to this.

"Jesus, Amber works for this guy? Help help! I'm being oppressed! Do you see his eyes, baby? I swear they're rotating." Tiffany cocked her head as she followed her maybe-not-hallucination.

Jason placated Tiffany's shoulder in front of Certainly Not His Unflinching Grin. "We invited her to a show at Last Chance, but she took off early. If you see her, tell her we're sorry if we offended her. I'm not sure what we did, but she's not answering any of our calls. I hope we didn't upset her or something…"

"I wouldn't worry about Amber. She probably thought she was a bother, or a third wheel, or she needed to get home to play a game. You have an excellent night. We'll worry about her if she doesn't show up for work tomorrow. If you want, give me your number. I'll text you if and when she comes in." Aaron truly attempted friendly. If only his tone wasn't so impending.

The two looked at each other and exchanged some sort of communication.

"That'd be cool, actually. Thanks, man." They shook hands again and exchanged numbers.

"Good to meet you all. Have a good night," he said. Their pupils dilated.

 "L-let us know what went down with Amber."

"Will do." His tone like a flood spilled off a cliff.

The Antagonist's Prison

The end of the acre backyard faded into a black forest. A small speaker belted out hip hop. The rapper said his name a lot. Aaron turned it down a touch.

Below the first brick patio, Tyler and Dot staked out one of several oversized outdoor couches encircling an ornate gas fire pit. The high, whipping flames masked anyone behind them. Tyler's normally perfect gelled hair had cowlicks. His green canvas jacket mostly on. No amount of drunk could remove those punk rock black jeans. He sailor-swayed on the edge of their couch while Dot snarled at Aaron. Aaron descended the stairs fluidly, with an unnerving grace. How a jellyfish might float down stairs. It was not okay.

"Finally! We could've walked home by now," Dot said.

"Apologetic." Aaron thought hard consonants were how to enunciate. "Do I need to carry him out?"

"Maybe. I don't know what got into him tonight. He normally doesn't drink like this."

"Eh, we all lose control from time to time," Aaron said.

"You're just saying that because you two are friends. Jazz! Come on, it's time to go. Aaron's here."

Jazz emerged around the flames as if waiting for her cue. Black hair, glistened from the fire, hung around her shoulders. She replaced her eyebrows with audacious spiderweb eyeliner, which ironically worked brilliantly. A silver spider pendant hung around her neck. Her pencil skirt fused with spiderweb fishnets. The fine-mesh long-sleeve shirt did little to hide her black bra, and was admittedly a bit much.

"Jazz, this is Aaron. He's Tyler's asshole business partner. He was talking about their bromance earlier."

"Cool," Jazz said. They shook hands. Jazz unfazed by Aaron's not-meant-to-be deathgrip. "Jaslynn, but everyone just calls me Jazz."

Aaron mentally scrolled through the myriad of names given to him in the past. None of them amiable. The One Who Will Make You Undone, in particular, was too far. But he did not choose it. C'est la vie.

Drives and a Curious Woman

"Aaron Bennett, pleasured. Which would you prefer, Jaslynn or Jazz?"

She made eye contact with hard, sea spray eyes and gave him a flirty smile. He never got those, and when both sides of him smiled back, she looked away. Though recoupled once she realized her nonverbal cue. "No one's asked that before. I guess if you're asking, Jaslynn."

Absolutely Not The Antagonist threw Tyler over his shoulders. Tyler smelled of over-indulgence and mumbled disagreements. Couldn't manage much more.

"Jesus, you'd think Tyler was a pool noodle," Jaslynn said.

"It's not my first time carrying a body."

"We jumped dark real quick, huh?" Jaslynn said.

"Not dark, that's on you. It's usually Dot I carry out."

"Hey!" Dot said.

"Apologies, that wasn't meant to offend, just a fact. Quick question, a bit out of the blue. Why are you garnished with spider-suggestive?"

"He has trouble with words, he thinks he's clever," Dot said.

"Sure," Aaron said. He did not consider himself a clever person. It wasn't so long ago that his mind was as broken as his body. He'd gotten fairly good at hiding that the persona of Aaron was only three years old. The only artifact left from the time before was his occasional speech impediment. He often used adjectives as nouns. It seemed efficient that way. His contextual vocabulary was fucked, along with numerous malapropisms. Aaron, who didn't know what any of that meant, was inclined to believe it.

"Dunno, I just like spiders," Jaslynn said without needing to comment on the odd word choices. "Most people are afraid of them. Maybe I like things people are afraid of. My friend Midge studies mythology. She told me that spiders are the creators and manipulators of the world. I've had to listen to a lot of her folklore bullshit, but the stories that stuck are about spiders, like Anansi."

"Clarified. Still odd."

"Lil' bit!" Dot said.

The Antagonist's Prison

Aaron lugged Tyler through the mansion, stepped over aftermath and struggled with the front exit. The girls didn't help, just watched as he threw open the dense front door with more force than he intended. Aaron stopped the bounce-back with his shoulder.

"So, Tyler mentioned your store earlier," Jaslynn said. "You know, drunkenly going on and on about it even though he buried the point, like, twenty paragraphs ago. I've been to the store, I get it. How would you describe it?"

"Think of it as a tattoo parlor where you donate your ink to Goodwill when you tire of it."

Jaslynn chuckled politely. Perhaps prodding more for no reason. Aaron did not respond to prods.

Even Aaron's little blue Civic was not sure how it fit Mr. Bennet inside. Aaron placed Tyler against the side of the car, holding his passed-out carcass with one hand as he unlocked the driver door. He reached in, unlocked the back door and dropped Tyler on the seat. Situated his head to face the window for the likely heave. Once he got in, he flipped open the passenger seat and rearranged to unlock the far back door. Dot sat in the back, lip snarling at her misbehaved slave. To her, Tyler should always be at the beck and call of her countless benders. He couldn't lift her, and she lashed out when forced to move.

It'd be hypocritical of Aaron to get frustrated with anyone. Not that Drunk Tyler was in any way comparable to He Who Stares Back From The Void. Tyler just needed to be put to bed.

"Can't you turn on some music?" Dot said.

He turned on the radio. She disapproved of all the presets.

"Don't you have Bluetooth for my iPhone?"

"Radio or nothing. Sorry, Dot. You know that."

"I could really go for some Chili Peppers." So she just blasted it from her phone.

He lit another clove as he hit the bottom of the Forest District. Offered them to the car, with the full expectation of universal turndown.

"Oh! Cloves! No one smokes these anymore," Jaslynn said. She lit hers by huddling into herself, licked her lips after her first drag. "I've been to your store a few times, but you're never there."

Drives and a Curious Woman

Dot sneered and coughed even though all the windows were down. Aaron didn't mind the silent judgments, but the comments on his health aggravated.

"Tyler and I don't always work at the same time. But I'm usually there for twelve hours most days. It's coincidence, probably, you'd have to ask Tyler why he never introduced me when I was there."

"There was a bit of talk about you at the party tonight," Jaslynn said, trying to get Aaron to talk. A surprisingly difficult task. "People kept saying you're a good dude, but also a dick. A few people even seemed to be afraid of you. Tyler didn't seem to have an opinion either way."

"I can't speak on that. Don't know, I hear most just find me a bit off." In a way, Mr. Bennett's self-oblivion was adorably ridiculous.

"Weird as fuck," Dot said. "Judgemental as all get-out, too."

"I don't mind anyone, Dot. I'm also very tired of saying that to you. I dislike being told I'm a liar when I am not."

"Whatevs, don't need to get all serious."

Jaslynn whipped around to give Dot the stank eye. Dot flipped a 'what?' hand signal. Jaslynn flipped her the middle finger then turned back to Aaron.

"So far, the only way you've been off is that you're taking us home at three in the morning just because it's the nice thing to do." Jaslynn punctuated nice-thing-to-do with a touch on the shoulder. Aaron didn't get touched a lot. He also didn't understand why she felt the need to do it. "Not a lot of people would do that. Certainly not any of the guys I've been with. They couldn't be bothered to put down their Xbox controller or their beer. Or their dick."

"Sounds like you're hanging out with the wrong attendants," Aaron said. She smiled kindly. Aaron assumed smiles were friendly attempts to end an interaction as quickly as possible. Just another random person on the street or another fucker behind the counter. Nor did he crave attention. Everyone was just more people.

"I'm inclined to acquiesce to that statement," Jaslynn said. Aaron shook his head at the sudden shift in vocabulary. Too many shifts in her speech. Backtracks and rearrangement of sentence construction.

The Antagonist's Prison

"You see, girls are programmed from birth to think they're ugly, blah, blah, blah, and we need validation from others to feel attractive." This sounded rehearsed to Mr. Bennett, also a little unnecessary. "But after a thousand people say, 'ohmygod, you're so pretty,' you kinda have to adjust your point of view. Who am I to disagree with everyone, you know?"

Aaron had an inclination she fished for a hook. A fruitless endeavor because he wouldn't remember her after tonight. "Don't let your psychosis affect your day to day."

"I've always considered appearances automatically false," Jaslynn said.

Aaron didn't know what to do with that, nor was it a subject he was interested in. Jaslynn sat back in the corner of her seat but leaned in toward Aaron.

"Wow, Jazz, your struggle is real." Dot coughed. "You guys are being way too thorough in this conversation. It's like listening to lawyers, or goddamn Shakespeare. Whereby, the aforementioned, now known as the proprietor. And Jazz, Aaron is a super fucked up dude. Don't let him talk you into anything."

Jaslynn twisted to glare at Dot again as he pulled up outside their apartment complex on the outskirts of Distillian. The kind of neighborhood where cars were scowled at past eleven. At this time of night? Right out!

"Are you really quoting Jim Gaffigan?" Jaslynn said. "And maybe his kind of fucked up is what I'm looking for. Hey, Aaron?"

"Hmm?"

"How fucked up are you?"

"That depends on your frame of reference." No blood on anyone's face.

"Uh...ok. Would you rape me?" Shockingly dark all of a sudden. But Aaron came from a place unfazed by the heinous.

"I support consent," he said. Certainly not thinking about all the rapists he'd killed. The Antagonist was no more.

They got out of the car. Aaron uprooted Tyler from his back seat and one-armed him onto his shoulder. Tyler whispered 'fuck off.'

Drives and a Curious Woman

Aaron smirked. It was too minute to recognize.

"What's the worst thing you've ever done?" Jaslynn said. She twisted her hair for some reason.

"I never pay parking tickets."

"I intend to find some dirt on you."

"Now you've leaned toward creepy. But go ahead, have fun."

Jaslynn's eyes checked off boxes on her mental list. Whether Aaron's answers were correct or not, he didn't care.

Dot unlocked their condo door and Aaron threw Tyler on their bed. He toppled back and forth. Without A Thought That Aaron Was Critch made it his mission to leave before Dot freaked over the long-delayed vomit. Aaron stepped into the hall past the tidy guestroom.

"What are you doing tomorrow?" Jaslynn said.

Apparently, she was interested in Aaron for no discernable reason. Aaron was tired and had to be at the store in four hours. "I work in the morning. Stop by, if you're curious."

"You work in the morning? What time?"

"Four hours."

"Jesus, why are you still awake?"

"I don't sleep much."

"I'm telling you, Jazz, don't fuck around with Aaron," Dot said. She faced away and tore off her corset. Jaslynn popped her ass out to grab a beer from the fridge. Aaron still wasn't sure what she was trying to communicate.

"Drea and I are going to be out and about shopping, we'll stop by at some point."

"Drea, the redhead who has a thing for Tyler? Flirts and fawns over him?" Aaron and tact were unacquainted.

"That hippie whore has nothing on me," Dot said. Tyler retched in their room.

"Well, we'll stop by tomorrow." Jaslynn took a long swig from her beer.

If she was flirting with Aaron, he appreciated it. Might as well be a comet sighting. "I look forward to it. You guys have a good

The Antagonist's Prison

night. Dot, do me a favor? Make sure Tyler comes in tomorrow."

"Wait, you're not going to help me clean up after Tyler? Some friend you are. You know Tyler. He loves your store more than me."

"No opinion. G'nite all."

"Selfish asshole. Why would you be into that, Jazz?" Dot said as Aaron shut the door.

"Shut up, Dot. You know very well why I might like Aaron," Jaslynn said, and anyone but Aaron would have said she stared at that door with thirst.

"Besides you being a whore for any man with dark hair and blue eyes?"

"Not to mention cheekbones that'd cut open my inner thighs. And besides, he drove us home! You called him an asshole like ten times. Goddamn, you can be such a bitch."

Dot lost her mind at Jaslynn as Aaron went down the stairs.

Reintegration was hard for him. He was fine with his existing construction and routines. Companionship was a thing, according to anyone but Critch. Aaron's psyche reeled back and brushed against The Antagonist's mangy fur. Our Relentless Shadow bristled instinctually, like Aaron was a fly landing on a dead god sleeping.

Sheets and a Game

A quarter before seven and Downtown Main was void. Employees stemmed from coffee franchises to work, ignored businesses not yet open. Shirts With Words On Them didn't open until eight and even then, there was no reason to be open that early. Business owners painted over graffiti from the night hours, cleaned their fronts, or made small talk with neighbors doing the same.

An elderly-looking man in a patchy gray suit crouched in front of Aaron's store entrance. His fumbled attempts to use his magic-shop picks laughable, somehow used the rake in the torque's position. Odd that he picked where everyone could see him. The shop was on the main drag and it was alarmed. Why not just break the window? If he asked nicely, Aaron would have just given him a few shirts. His hands shook as he failed again to pass the cheap lock. Aaron tapped his shoulder. He flinched, having somehow not noticed Mr. Bennett's silent approach.

"Everything going alright? According to plan? I have a key if you need one. I could also offer a hug."

The man put down his thievery and rose from the uncomfortable position he'd twisted himself into. Not old then, perhaps in his forties. The man smoothed out his much-repaired, besmirched suit, then bowed down without bending his legs to grab and dust

The Antagonist's Prison

off his gray fedora.

"Stay away from the Second Lust, she's mine," he said. His yellowed teeth chipped. He hadn't needed that suit for a time, but it did look comfortable.

"Noted," Aaron said like a dagger through the man's eye. The man wasn't under any substance that Aaron saw, sober enough, though it was never too early for that. He picked up his cane and skipped down Main Street to a jaunty tune only he could hear. Another random encounter with a strange one. Aaron thought that sort of occurrence was far in his odd past and not worth remembering.

Mr. Bennett scanned around to see if his employee Amber was about. She usually waited for him at the coffee shop across the way. It was unlike her to be late. Oh well.

The shopping floor had four small lazy susan racks filled with clever t-shirts ready and affordable for those who loved people staring at their chests and backs. At the front desk were two computers and a tablet for Tyler to draw on. Their custom shirts had taken off quite a bit, allowing Tyler and Aaron to pull themselves out of the poverty line in Indigo Bay and hire two lost youngsters, Amber and Jeff.

One Hundred Percent Not The Lady Made Of Dark's Bump In The Night, hung up his flannel-lined leather jacket and fedora in his office. Since no one was about, he pulled up his thermal sleeves to let his scarred arms bask in the blonde light weeping through the clouded windows. Aaron tried to de-yellow them, but old glass could only get so clean. He asked the property owner to reglass them, but landlords are the worst.

He started the heaters, booted up computers, tested chemicals. After fifteen minutes of work, he went out back. As Mr. Bennett lit the clove, a white van roared into the brick alley.

The sketchy-at-the-very-least van squealed along the wall. Scraped its paint. With his iconic blasé, Aaron stepped backward into the workshop as ski-masked men tossed an unconscious Amber out the back. Her lady bits barely covered by a sheet. With Aaron's arms out, he followed the van as it fishtailed. He knew it

Sheets and a Game

wouldn't stop to answer his questions.

Why did they come down the alley? Wouldn't it make more sense to come down the side street? If they knew where she worked, why not drop her off at her parents'? Not that that would've been a kindness. Mr. Bennett guessed he'd be the best choice if they thought about her well-being. They couldn't be, though. Best not to conjecture.

He hefted Amber into his arms with cigarette lodged in the corner of his mouth and placed her limpness on a workbench with little grace. Her bone-thin body well-muscled from obsessive workouts. Her white hair surprisingly clean as was the rest of her body. No dirt, no blood, no bruises. He assumed she'd be at least a little roughed up given her arrival method. If she was so clean, why did they drop her off naked? Again, best not to conclude without evidence.

Aaron grabbed a pair of pants from his car and a shirt from the rack. Cuffed them up significantly. Found the extra pair of cross trainers Amber kept at the shop, in case she needed to run on her breaks. While Aaron loomed and waited for the intense intake of consciousness, he smoked out the back.

Mr. Bennett didn't want to open with an unconscious girl on the workbench, she was in the way and stuffing her into a corner seemed insensitive. Finally, the breath. He sat down on a work stool. She squinted at the silkscreen equipment then rubbed her eyes.

"Amber?" Aaron said, hoping he sounded concerned. Too bad, he actually sounded deeply disappointed. Her glowered green eyes widened before narrowed again as she examined her hands.

"Something's wrong." Hands fluttered in her face.

"You're telling me. OK, where do we start? I know, let's talk about the van that just screeched down the alley and threw you out." She watched his hands move, seemed spooked, then searched around his face but couldn't find his eyes. "You wore only a sheet. Those pants are an extra pair I keep in my backpack, and that shirt is just a blank."

She immediately huddled as if she were still naked. Aaron understood her modesty and shame. However, her clothed or unclothed

The Antagonist's Prison

form meant little to him. She might as well have strolled up in her typical jeans and workout top. He'd seen every caliber of naked under Madam Ava's care.

"Umm, I'm sorry you had to deal with me."

Aaron immediately recognized the trauma speech, having definitely used it before. "Don't worry about it."

"Can you do me a weird favor?"

"Weird is the word of the morning."

"Can you turn on some music?"

"No problem. Do you want some coffee? Do you want to keep your sheet or should I throw it out?"

Her face reddened and her breathing shallow and rapid. Signaling panic, perhaps anxiety from Aaron's question. He understood, but wished Amber to feel comfortable. Not many felt comfortable around Aaron.

A local band played on Tyler's player. That's the only thing it ever played. Most of it acoustic folk, or folk punk as Tyler claimed. Aaron was sure it all sounded different to him. The coffee finished on cue. He grabbed each of them a mug.

"Music makes me sick," Amber said. She examined the mug from different angles.

"What?"

"Always made me sick and agitated."

"I have no idea what this has to do with your morning carpool."

"They said they were going to fix me..." Amber blinked hard. She might have been about to cry. It seemed appropriate, all things considered. Instead, she just glared at the printers and ink jugs.

"Are you able to work? You can go home if you want. I doubt customers will appreciate your acid trip." Trying to encourage her to approach this situation reasonably.

"I don't have anywhere to go. I've been away all night. I can't ever go home again."

"Your mom may be psycho, but chemically required to care about you."

"I'm not going home."

Sheets and a Game

"Well, do you have anywhere to go?"

The office phone went off. Money it was her mom. Aaron hung up on the woman many times. He didn't have to be nice to his employee's closest. As long as they worked effectively and professionally he didn't give a damn about their personal lives.

"Don't answer that," Amber said. She wandered around the room, angled desk lamps, shined them on his face, on her hands. She peered inquisitively at wherever the light went.

"Yeah, no worries. It's not my job to deal with your mom, it's your job and you suck at it. If you're choosing to stay, go open up." He handed her the petty pouch, and she went through the metal fire door.

Aaron texted Jason to let him know Amber came in and that he should probably talk to her about what happened last night. He would and thanked Irrevocably Not Our Imminent Unforwarned Reckoning.

Aaron sneered at the time, then down at his coffee. He woke up this morning wishing for normal before he visited Madam Ava. He contemplated his phone and wondered if he should warn the dominatrix of his impending advance. On second thought, she'd appreciate his showing up out of the blue.

Out front, Amber held her face on the sales counter, the aftermath of last night. Did she finally get over herself and drink? That didn't explain the van. Or the spooky hands.

"Can I get you anything? I'm sure coffee isn't going to help an upset stomach."

"I think more sore than upset. Can you do me another favor? I want to test something, can you put something more initial on?"

If Amber were a normal person, Aaron rightfully expected her to be freaking out over what happened to her. A normal person called the cops or holed up in their bedroom for weeks. Alas, the term normal in this room was mutable. As for Amber, she analyzed it. Aaron found that admirable, something he forced himself to do when confronting The Antagonist.

"More what? Sounds pretentious as hell," he said.

"I dunno, they played 'Initial' music last night," she said, with

The Antagonist's Prison

quote fingers. "Do you have any music that is more powerful than swishy sounds and gong noises?"

Ah, there's the cynicism Mr. Bennett hired her for.

"Look, I'm not the person to talk to about music. I just play whatever comes up on Tyler's player."

"Jason and Tiffany were talking about these bands like they were a greater form of music. Stupid phrasing, I know, but they talked about it like it was a higher power."

Since those two were at the party last night, Aaron assumed they were not the ones who kidnapped her, but he was inclined to believe they played a part.

"Met a couple last night, Jason and Tiffany. When I picked up Tyler from a house party. He was tall, dark, and well dressed, and she was a redhead in bad need of a straightener."

"They went to a party after I was kidnapped! What the fuck? Seriously?!" She squeaked mighty and loud.

"They thought you left the show early and were concerned you were angry with them. I wouldn't worry about it."

"You have no idea what they did to me last night!"

"Nope, and I'm sorry it did. Do you want to talk about it?"

"Not yet, I have to decompress first. Just put on some good music."

"I don't care, listen to whatever you want," Aaron said, handing her Tyler's player like a sword from a lake.

"No, it's not like that. The music these people chase after has a special quality to it...like, it strikes a chord deep within you."

"Music has never done that to me. Talk to Tyler, but this 'chord deep within' speak sounds like religious jargon. I'd stay away from fanaticism, a state of mind I do not hold highly. Jason and Tiffany seemed concerned about you, perhaps you should talk to them about it." Aaron needed another cigarette. "I'm expecting Drea to come in with an attractive woman in goth black. I'll be on the roof."

"How will I know it's her?"

"You'll know. There's no way you won't."

"Uh...ok? You know it's eight in the morning, right? Drea isn't

Sheets and a Game

even awake."

"Just letting you know for when, or if, it happens. I half-expect her not to show up."

"Right...Ok."

Up a wrought iron ladder bolted mostly to the brick, Aaron had a little smoking chair on the roof, one of those mesh deals with nylon flared in despair from the sun. Little else existed up there, about as remote as he could achieve while still in the thick of being a productive human. He took the first drag as Gradick and Raile's phone rang.

"Hello, Aaron, how are you?" Gradick said. The strange gravitas of his burly voice always built toward a crescendo that never arrived. No matter the subject, the room silenced against his charisma. Always about to stand and deliver a rallying speech to lead the revolution. Of course, it never got to that point and left you painfully aroused.

Machinery and giggles in the background. Raile must have been up to something. Gradick's magnificent counterpart a genius on all accounts. The pair made a terrific subterfuge engine.

"Good, always good. And you?"

"I'm well. I proposed to Raile the other night. We wanted to ask you if you'd be our best man."

"Congratulations. I'd be honored to be your best man. Though, it's about time you proposed."

"I suppose that's true. Raile's brother, Rudy, is in town showing off his new car. How's the store?"

"Have I met Rudy?"

"Yes you have, maybe all of us should go out tonight to celebrate. Tonight should be about our Circle," Gradick said.

"Thank you for considering me family, but I have a date tonight."

"That's amazing news, friend. Who's the lucky person? Can we help in any way?"

"I don't know, that's why I'm calling. It's been an odd morning. Amber showed up by way of creeper van, dressed in a sheet. And that was after I interrupted a homeless man picking the lock

The Antagonist's Prison

of my shop's front door."

"Don't question insanity."

"That was my thinking."

"Whatever we can offer. How's Amber?"

"Extremely off. She's in shock and not talking yet, but whatever happened, it wasn't pleasant. She keeps staring at her hands, blinks at me, baffled."

Aaron had to admit to himself that his fashion choices were occasionally poor. All the necessary layers made him on the verge of sweat at any given time. Especially up on the roof as the lacquered surface radiated heat.

"Peculiar," Gradick said.

"Do you know anything about a girl named Jaslynn, or Jazz?"

"What does Aaron want?" Raile yelled.

"Information. Come here and help, please." The sound changed to speakerphone echo.

"Hello, Aaron, long time no see. How is our favorite black heart of gold?" The smoke of Raile's voice trailed out of the receiver and covered Mr. Bennett in mist.

"I'm curious about a girl, Jaslynn."

"Jaslynn Phillips?"

"Yeah," Aaron said, not surprised at the familiarity.

"Tyler's rockabilly bitch of a girlfriend's cousin?" Raile said. "How is the Unappreciative treating the Deserves More, by the way?"

"They're still dysfunctional."

"No way!" Raile blared. "Okay, so Jaslynn, Jazz, is one of those girls who knows how fucking desirable she is and flaunts it. Which normally we'd lift up. Certainly do the same with myself. She showed up in Indigo Bay a few months ago and has since slept around every Circle she could find. A goddamned stud, or slut if you're still participating in connotative genders – more people she sleeps with, more sought-after she becomes. Which normally would be awesome. Unfortunately, she's a partner-eater. Broken up at least three Circles. She's ruthless. Everyone still loves her. Nobody considers her destructive, though she plays widowmaker

Sheets and a Game

every weekend. It's odd you hear nothing but nice things about her considering her path of ruin, don'cha think?"

"I don't know. That is why I'm inquiring," Aaron said, ripping out her entrails. Metaphorically. Unintentionally.

"Jaslynn, from what we've observed," Gradick said, "is searching for someone with specific qualifications. We're talking about more than just your standard likes-long-walks-on-the-beach, he-really-listens-to-me-and-makes-me-laugh personality traits. Whatever it is, she hasn't found it yet, despite her ever-growing population sample."

"Any idea what she's looking for?" Aaron, thinking of his own potential qualities, came up with nothing distinct beyond tearing people apart.

"We could theorize the hunt comes from abandonment issues, paternal concerns, or any of the problems children have," Gradick said. "But we think her pursuit is far more obsessive and desperate than casual dating or fucking for validation. She's looking hard for something nigh impossible to find."

The matrix of possible outcomes The Miscreant King presented overwhelmed Aaron and called for deeper deduction methods than he cared to implement. Even that thought was too much for him to think about. Yet he still thought it.

"She's twenty-four, getting her zoology degree at IBU, if you want the boring character framework about her. Crazy obsession with spiders, like E.B. White levels," Raile said.

"I do not know what that means," the Rather Uneducated Antagonist said.

"E.B. White, *Charlotte's Web*. He had an obsessive interest in spiders, too," Gradick said. "Look, despite the lack of negative press, we don't like her. Even if everyone thinks she's some sort of Dorian Gray. Which, if you know, is not a good thing."

A constant barrage of literary and philosophical topics they threw out as if it were common knowledge. It should be common knowledge, Aaron supposed. But Not Remotely His Unflinching Grin didn't need the references to understand their meaning.

The Antagonist's Prison

"Well, she's made her interest in me pretty clear. If she does come in today, the date tonight should go well. I'm getting her a gift to cement my memory into her bedpost."

"And what's that?" Gradick said.

"An affectionate spider from Madam Ava."

"Madam Ava? Should we know her?" Raile said.

"Friend from a few years ago."

"Like around the time when you strolled into town with no history, no nothing but your crazy blue eyes?" Raile said.

Here they went again with the Critch prods. They suspected hard. But like all good skeptics, they needed facts, not causal assumptions. "Around then, yeah."

"One day," Gradick said, happily frustrated. "You're going to tell us where you came from."

"Perhaps, but that day is not today. Thanks for your help."

"Anytime. Rudy is only in town for a few days. Maybe tomorrow we can have a barbecue?"

"We'll see. I think I can manage that."

"Sounds great, we'll text you to remind you," Raile said.

"Perfect. Catch you later," Aaron said.

"Oh, and Aaron," Raile said. "Watch your back with Jazz, she's really good at what she does."

"No worries, talk to you later. And thank you," Totally Not Your Unforwarned Reckoning said.

"Anytime, your circle is everything," Gradick said.

Aaron was glad for the information about Jaslynn, but he was certain that after seeing the absolute horror of the world, including himself, he could resist a little Topside manipulation.

Jaslynn and Drea hadn't come in yet, so Aaron started on the backlog. Inked the art and films from last night so they'd be ready for pick up. The detail consuming work and the priority task list reorganization shattered hours.

Aaron came up for air and the music played for only a few seconds, then skipped to the next song. How long had that been going on? He brought the finished shirts to the front and found

Sheets and a Game

Amber hunkered over Tyler's player. She frowned at the racks and garage art around the store as the song started. She shook her head and skipped the song.

"Amber, you're stressing out the customers. Commit." Despite there being no customers in the store, he was not wrong.

She handed Aaron an envelope with a loopy "Aaron Bennett" on the front.

Hello Mr. Bennett,
Do you remember me? Beware of Mr. Kinns.
Love, November

Hmmm, Aaron didn't remember you, November. He threw it away. Smelled violet.

"I'm sorry. I'm just trying to figure out what's going on with me," Amber said, voice shaking.

"So am I. Look, you can go home, or, hey, maybe call the police. Either way, please stop skipping songs."

"What music do you listen to?"

"Nothing in particular."

"Humor me! Just give me two songs." The outburst made Amber flinch. Aaron remained impassive. He sometimes wondered what it'd be like to be startled. He vaguely felt at one point maybe he did jump at loud noises. But not in his three-year lifespan.

"Hmm, I sometimes listen to Caspian, Pelican. God is an Astronaut. Heavy instrumental stuff I suppose."

"What do you know about The City Beneath The Bay?" Amber said as the pounding guitars of Pelican droned. If what happened to her last night had to do with the Underground, it was surprising she was still alive. Kidnapping was fairly typical in The City Beneath, but circumstantial evidence at best. Typically because the kidnapped disappeared from the world. Just because it's evil didn't mean it had to do with the Underground. Aaron barely thought that with a straight face.

"I wouldn't worry about a place that doesn't exist."

The Antagonist's Prison

"My friends at the bar last night seemed to think it was real."

"People always want to believe there is something else to this world. The degenerates of Indigo Bay believe that 'something else' to be this mystical City Beneath. Depending on who you talk to, they all blame the 'Underground.' You can write those people off."

He returned to the back to develop some film. There were inferences to be made when a man like Aaron fiddled with tubs of chemicals in a dark room lit by a red light. Terror, panic, horror would be an appropriate guide for these presumptions. Critch was the villain in quite a few nightmares.

Flipping the films and dipping them in the tubs, Aaron found soothing to his profound trauma. Something which took finesse and skill, something to be mastered. His other talent was not taught and did not need practice. Critch was already the best at what he did. Madam Ava used Critch like a firehose and men would disintegrate before him like balsa wood cutouts. He couldn't be touched.

That was a lie, the craggy shelved scars etched into his body were proof of that. He rubbed a bullet wound on his chest. Several of these grooves should have killed him.

Amber came into the dark room to interrupt his first brood of the day. He tried not to brood, but he was naturally inclined to do so.

"Jazz's here."

"Excellent, I'll be out inna sec." He put his hands on the counter and leaned as Amber closed the door. Let his head hang. Let's see if he could handle the frustration of the dating game. It'd be in the news tomorrow if he couldn't. Actually, it wouldn't, Madam Ava would handle the terrible, wipe it clean. Tie it up neat in a little black bag, burn it to ash and scatter it across the bay. He really hoped he liked Jaslynn regardless of Critch's opinion.

If Jaslynn noticed his entrance, she didn't show it. With each shift of her weight or readjustment of stance, she posed for the not present paparazzi ogles.

Drea's meek propositions were rephrased and recalibrated as she stumbled around her mulberry bush message. She continued to give more examples until her voice faded into the background.

Sheets and a Game

Around the time when she'd accuse you of not listening. The summation of her chewed-up clothes, grimied face, and dirty dreads hung about and smelled of mold.

"Ladies," he said.

Jaslynn turned slowly and gauged Aaron, hungry and feral through her hair. She dropped her default savage for a gleeful façade. "Still a pretty cool store, Aaron."

Amber glared at them, but missed the mark, slightly off their heads.

"Right? You wouldn't peg him as a clothing store owner, wouldya?" Drea said.

"What would you peg me as, then?" he said. Aaron had no idea how much power he had just by looking and sounding like himself. If he knew, he'd hate it. He didn't want to be special, he wanted more than anything to be no one in particular.

"I don't know. Autopsy examiner, grave digger, pedophile?" Drea said.

"Sounds about right, though fucking kids wouldn't be too hard a business to monetate, if you knew the correct people. What are you girls up to?"

Amber triple-took the area three feet behind Aaron. He shot her a what-the-hell. She stopped and squeezed her eyes shut harder than a child hiding from a closet monster. Aaron should thank her. Her odd behavior distracted the girls' rehearsed dialogue. This was Drea's go-to wingman approach, and Jaslynn looked entertained by his omission of play. 'Your Hand In Mine,' by Explosions in the Sky, skipped mid-song.

"Amber, what did we talk about?"

"Sorry, sorry."

"We were shopping, and, you know, thought we'd drop in," Drea said. "Is everything okay, Amber?"

"She's fine, doesn't want to talk about it. Where y'all walkin'?" Aaron said. He thought he sounded casual. He sounded judgemental and insistent.

"I'm running some errands before my friend Midge comes in

The Antagonist's Prison

tomorrow, that way we can hang out," Jaslynn said.

"Man, it's going to be epic having Midge back. Raile and Midge had a Cold War going, if you know what I'm talking about," Drea said.

Aaron didn't, but he was often out of his element when it came to what was going on. He enjoyed being oblivious. "Any plans for later tonight, then?"

"I gotta go to my internship in an hour or so, then I have a pole dancing class," Jaslynn said.

"I'm free after nine and I'm in the mood for sushi. Wondering if you ladies would like to join me?"

"You were going by yourself?" Drea said.

"Usually do, but company sounds nice," Aaron said, hard at Jaslynn. Trying to let her know that was a lie and he only invited Drea to be polite. He hoped she would step out like a considerate person might.

"What's your favorite sushi place?" Jaslynn asked.

"Sushi Rei, on the breakwater. Their spicy tuna roll is fantastic. Sashimi good too."

"Oh?"

"Yes. Come, it'll be my treat, I know the manager," Hopefully Not Critch said.

"Are you sure? We can pay. We don't need a man paying for us," Drea said.

Drea bothered Aaron because she identified so hard with an identity, any identity, as to be a checklist ticked off, not a jumping-off point.

"No worries, a nice date is worth anything monetary," he said.

"There's that word again. Odd," Drea said, maybe trying to protect Jaslynn from Aaron.

"You get used to it. 'Round ten?" Aaron said.

"Sounds great," Jaslynn said. She smirked, pleased.

They left whispering.

"Cute," Amber said. She did not seem impressed.

"Hmmm." The hum asked the question with no inflection.

Sheets and a Game

What that question was was up to interpretation.

"I met her at a bar the other night. She was super nice then. Dunno about now."

"How do you mean?"

"I don't know, she acted different, sort of. I don't know."

"I have a feeling she does that a lot."

"And that doesn't bother you at all?"

"I've met a lot of people who use different faces depending on their current predicament. There's always a common thread through all of them."

"What's hers?"

"Dunno yet. Gonna try to find that out tonight, me hopes."

"Where'd you find her?" Amber said

"At the party I picked up a blacked-out Tyler from last night. His girlfriend's cousin's former roommate or some shit."

"I didn't think you'd be attracted to girls like that."

"Why not? And don't you give me shit about reaching above my number."

"Well, maybe, but I didn't mean it like that. I just got a strange vibe off Jazz."

"Since when are you into crooked chakras?"

"Nevermind, I don't even know what to think about what I just saw," Amber said. Her eyes prepared themselves for tears.

"Tyler will be here in five minutes. Can you hold out till then? I gotta go get Jaslynn's gift."

"What are you getting her?" Amber said, kneading her eyes.

"She likes spiders, and an old friend of mine has some amazing buggers. Gonna see about getting one of those," Doubtfully Your Unforwarned Reckoning said as he drifted ghost-like to the back. Not ominously at all.

27

Caretakers and a Catastrophe

Cascade Riviera was a gated community for the well-to-do. Prerequisites included vast stores of vague wealth, along with passcodes, IDs, and chip cards. The HOA cost more than Aaron's rent. Most residents either reclusive or never home, out for weeks at a time making their money work for them. Meeting with the only ones who could relate to their plights. So much time on airplanes.

Aaron didn't have a guest pass. Even if he did, the guard at the front gate would profile his rags and laugh. The last few visits, he came chained in the back of a van. Six cattle prods pointed at his neck.

Critch – sorry, Aaron – parked his little blue Civic a mile away, outside of Breckberry, about three blocks from his best friends'. He followed a transient trail to the high walls behind the development.

Mr. Bennett shrugged with a too-old-for-this when he was too young to speak that way, and threw his backpack over the wall where it crunched and clanged on the other side. He jumped up and pushed off the wall with his foot, grabbing the ledge with one hand. He lifted himself up with his fingers, then jumped down with a little roll. Fixed his I'm-leaning-a-little-too-much-into-this-look fedora, straightened his heavy jacket, grabbed his pack, lit up, and calmly walked across the empty nine-hole golf course. No rich people used this waste of water. They had far

The Antagonist's Prison

more expensive ones to grace.

High-end cars judged him as he wandered through the empty opulence. The smallest mansion model contained five bedrooms and four baths. Half-acres with regulated lawn heights, separated property lines. Modern architecture predominated, but there were some in a ranch-style, and a good smattering of Spanish red-tile roofs, capping arched white walls and brick patios. Tract housing for the rich.

Each had a curved driveway. No one ever had to take precious extra moments to reverse out. Never go back, always forward. Most had pools with various uses.

A few years ago, A Faint Whiff Of The Antagonist would maniac through these backyards. He was no longer that person. Aaron could use sidewalks now, though these folk wouldn't be pleased to see a man like him decreasing the value of the cement. He passed parks of several different over-polished ethnic stylings and corporate art. Raile had been commissioned for several of the installations. Nannies watched neglected and forgotten children play. Moved closer to the adults when they saw Aaron sweep past. So Scary Aaron. The not-infants never with their parents who had them as a sort of check mark on the much stressed-over playbook of success.

About a mile into Cascade Riviera, a palace teemed on a small hill. Even in the richest neighborhood, it had the royal view of its domain. Its medieval European stone sat in grandeur with spires, arches, buttresses, and other terms that no longer mattered. Its windmill turned at a steady pace no matter the wind. The world held its breath when the windmill stopped.

Okay, Maybe A Little Bit Still Critch jumped the palace wall and waited for the dogs, old habit. They never came. He weaved up the stairs, in a tense silence radiating from the cameras hidden in the statues of owls and naked men. Each step took him further from a neighborhood and into a feudal time of serfs and baronies, which Madam Ava claimed we never left.

He ground out his latest clove on the porch and rang the bell. The door opened instantly to a man whose arms were sheathed and chained

Caretakers and a Catastrophe

behind his back. A cock and ball torture, the pin not far-twisted. Four hooks pinned open his mouth into a painful grin. Aaron didn't like the resemblance. His feet were red. Must be new. Next to the entrance a marble statue of Critch in full leathers, ripping another man's arm off. Distastefully avant garde. As was this whole fucking secret echelon.

"I'm here to see Madam Ava."

"Ymph whhh kaww hrrr lerrr."

In a quick gesture, Aaron Bennett unhooked his face.

"You will only...only refer to her...as The Lady Made of Dark," he said as his tongue thrashed around to moisten his arid mouth.

"Please ring your goddamn bell."

The slave smiled as if Not The Goddamned Antagonist didn't know what happened around here. He rang the bell with an innocent ting. Aaron's glacier-blue eyes on her entrance as she appeared. She would swear she didn't flinch. Only Aaron saw it, and he hated it. Her eyes knew he was here, followed him since he scaled the perimeter. Technically, always watched him. Critch snipped at the back of his brain and his vision skipped.

"Who disturbs my home?" Madam Ava said from the top of the stairs. Obsidian skin, black corset painted onto pointed curves. Her shaved head to a polished shine, not quite as tall as Aaron, much to her chagrin. Their presences sizzled against each other deliciously. Hidden watchers glued their eyes to the reunited friends.

"The Antagonist has returned. How glorious! Critch, please come in. Do I need to be worried?" Madam Ava said with an uncharacteristic hesitation mid-stair.

"No, everything's fine," Possibly The One Who Stares Back From The Void was happy to be able to say.

"Oh good," she said. "Please, join me for a cup of coffee."

The butler knelt before Aaron with a raised eyebrow.

"Please, call me Aaron," At One Point...Fine, Critch said.

"You will always be Critch to me, Mr. Aaron Bennett." Deadnaming someone always a fun way to annoy. "I understand why you chose that name, but my, my, it lacks the flare I prefer."

Madam Ava snapped her elegant fingers. Four slaves appeared

The Antagonist's Prison

out of the dim. She turned to one. "Brew some coffee for My Bump In The Night."

He bowed and disappeared. Madam Ava led Aaron to a drawing room instead of a cage, with red walls and light wood accents. Stone busts rested, candles burned, portraits on the walls of who knows who. The dominatrix motioned for Aaron to sit on a comfortable leather couch. She sat right next to him, to try to make him uneasy. She couldn't help it. And he didn't mind.

Above them, eight naked men, shaved shiny, hung in a spiral from their chandelier. Weights dangled from their cocks and their arms stretched into crucifixion. Candles burned from their wax-encased hands. Aaron didn't understand it, other than it was a sort of patient pain.

"I hear you have a shop in the city. Successful?"

"More than it should be."

"I'm glad to hear your integration has gone so well. Although, your departure still saddens me. Your replacements have been... less than spectacular."

"Should I be sorry to hear that?"

"Oh, My Executioner. Still feral, even in your projected persona."

"I am not Critch. Not anymore," Critch said with a holy-fuck tone.

The slave came in with a silver tray hung from a chain around his neck. His arms likewise bound and sheathed behind him. Shaved head to toe. His mouth gagged with a dildo. His gait in hobbled high heels showed excellent practice.

On his tray, two priceless Persian porcelain espresso cups, each filled with coffee made from individually chosen beans from an exclusive and violent plantation. Aaron grabbed the tiny coffee and tasted it. Notes and hints of flavors he couldn't identify with his naive tongue.

"What do you think of the coffee, Critch? Oh, my apologies, Aaron."

Critch had little desire to play her game and ignored the prod. "It's fantastic."

"I must disagree. It tastes burnt." She threw the thick contents of

Caretakers and a Catastrophe

the coffee at her slave, burning his face and naked chest. He barely reacted. "If you burn these beans again, I will punish you. This coffee is worth more than your son's monthly allowance. Now return with more."

The man disappeared, bowed in repeated ecstatic apology. Curious people watched unseen, possibly wondering why Madam Ava addressed a vagabond as an equal. The slaves paid her to be punished. The people she had in her employ were nonexistent until they were needed. Your Imminent Unforewarned Reckoning did not fill either position.

"I know you aren't here for a pleasant chat. Why the unannounced visit?"

"I met a girl. One I'm sure is used to sugar."

"Oh, would you like more advice on women?" The Antagonist greatly appreciated her practical advice.

"No, I understand women just fine, thanks to you. I just want to give her a present which cannot be bought, unless you know someone. I think it'll be better than flowers."

"And how might I help with that?"

"I want one of your red spiders."

"Finally, a girl of Critch's taste?" A stuttered suck-in of saliva. "One he thinks is deserving of one of my precious spiders." She hovered a hand near him then pulled back. "What is this girl's name? Jaslynn Phillips, yes? Do you think she'll find what she's looking for in you? And if she does, do you have the capacity to offer it to her?"

This confirmed for Aaron that Jaslynn was more than she presented. Sort of how The One Who Will Make You Undone forced Aaron's persona so hard on the world. "We'll find out. Either way, she doesn't belong in your world."

"I disagree. You know me better than that, My Dear Apocalypse. You should know there's nothing out there that can stop me, except maybe you. Have no worry, I have no need for her. My apprentice is doing well."

"Good to know," he said.

The Antagonist's Prison

"Now!" With a flourish of her elegant, gnarled hands. "If you wish for a spider, then you must do me a favor."

"I'm not going to show you Critch."

"No, no...no. I no longer have the manpower to handle Critch. I wish for you to meet Ramn, your current replacement." The slave came back with more espresso. Madam Ava tasted the coffee and seemed satisfied. The man's face dropped disappointed. He offered The Ending To Us All the new coffee. It tasted the same. Aaron thanked him, but he just moon-eyed him like a beaten dog. Mr. Bennett did not miss the expression.

Madam Ava rose and gestured for Aaron to follow her through the expensively adorned, crowded and low corridors. At least four dozen secret rooms and a maze of hallways hidden behind the fancy.

She directed to the windmill wing. Two men pushed posts on a pillar to slowly spin the windmill. Only white basketball shorts and their broad backs and calves rippled and shone with sweat from their constant job. These men were not slaves, slaves were not allowed in this wing. Aaron did not know how Madam Ava found the post pushers, or what she paid them. Their job would drive most mad. Aaron imagined the paychecks all they were here for. He thought briefly about their turnover rate.

The easy creak of the windmill comforted Aaron like a familiar sound from a childhood home. The smell of the wood and immaculate clean tingled. High above, the mechanism for the windmill churned. Yellow walls of stone loomed around the decahedron room. The vast vacancy of it was not right compared to the otherwise crowded, art-littered mansion.

When Madam Ava came in, the men stopped their pushing. They climbed on top of their posts and sat down. They untied blindfolds from their necks and covered their eyes, placed noise-canceling headphones on their ears which played painfully loud music of their choice. Planned isolation so they would have no idea what happened while the vault was open. No trauma from The Antagonist.

The Lady Made of Dark stuck a thin key into an invisible seam. A series of mechanical clinks and whirls sounded behind the walls

Caretakers and a Catastrophe

before an immense curved vault door swung slowly and silently open. Deep dents in the titanium from Aaron's fist blows cratered the other side.

Critch rumbled in his mind.

Pretty Close To Critch At This Point braced himself against the wall. Shouldn't have come here. His fingers splintered the masonry, turning it to sand. The Persian cup shattered on the ground.

"Aaron..." Madam Ava said, suddenly small and pressing. Her futile inquisition lost in Critch's ambush.

Madam Ava's finger shook violently as she missed the button on her ring. Her perfect posture now hunched as she backed against the stone wall. The second attempt made contact. Seven doors, not there before, snapped open. Thirty men rushed the room, their faces painted like mimes and armored in full fire fatigues. Their battle expressions melted before the struggle between Critch and Aaron. They gaped at Madam Ava as if she'd betrayed them.

"I think...I'd just like the spider, please," Aaron said through gritted teeth.

Every muscle in his body tightened and defined. Shoulders spread, ribs expanded, stomach convexed. Madam Ava reached for where his noose used to be. Her fear morphed to despair at the absence of the coil of aircraft cable. A cornered rabbit, she deflated as she accepted her fate.

His skin flushed to the red hue of glowing metal. Feared whispers and pleas scampered around the room.

"I am well aware!" Madam Ava said, her authoritative tone cracked. "Aaron Bennett!"

Tears streamed down one Firemime's face. Urine soaked several of their crotches. Shit perfumed the room.

Apocalyptically Close To His Unflinching Grin was timidly circled by those who knew if Critch emerged they'd fall in seconds. Thirty nooses spiraled. Many Firemimes fell into their iconic drunken stagger, others failed to shut down.

"Stop!" Aaron roared. The internal berserk stabilized. He took a long breath. "This is not my first time."

The Antagonist's Prison

Madam Ava plunged her hand into the pocket of a Firemime next to her, and pulled out his cigarettes. Only the slightest hesitation before she gave her former weapon the benefit of the doubt and lit one. The thirty Firemimes, who'd seen all manner of evil and gore, stared at her with self-abased horror.

She took a drag for herself before she approached with the nervous pace of a worshiper addressing the demon he was. She handed the cigarette over with wild vibrations from her core. Bricks of sweat fell from her defined jawline. He took a deep drag.

"Let's get you that spider," she said.

His skin returned to its natural pallor. Madam Ava whispered to a Firemime. He nodded and sprinted into the annals of the house, exuberant to get away from The One Who Will Make You Undone.

A tall woman made out of strong triangles with simple mime makeup strutted in like the concept of conclusion. She cupped something in her hands. Draped in a fancy version of the yellow firefighter canvas jacket over an elegant black dress with a long, beaded train. Like all of Madam Ava's compatriots, intense in their hale glamor. Her black, whole-sclera-lensed eyes did not break contact with Aaron's on approach. Unlike the rest, she did not stare him down like a wild animal. Her face conveyed nothing. The lack of expression was her only expression. She opened her hands and revealed a small, red tarantula.

"Hello, Aaron. Do you remember me?" she said in a flat drawl with no inflection. As if a computer read the words but no idea what the whole of the sentence meant.

"No," Aaron said. Neither of their faces did anything at all at this comment. Heartbreakingly so.

"Ah, Charlie. Meet Aaron," Madam Ava said. The spider raised its front legs at Critch. He swallowed his fear reflex. The Antagonist cupped his hands under The Widow In Yellow's. Charlie crawled up Aaron's arm to his shoulder where he curled his legs underneath and fell asleep. "As much as I enjoy your company, I think it is time for you to go."

"I understand."

Caretakers and a Catastrophe

The woman in black and yellow turned to leave with a runway gait, in heels uncomfortably high. "Maybe one day, Mr. Bennett, you will remember our time together."

"I'll be in the Underground for the next week or so. November will..." Madam Ava said to the retreating woman who was already half faded in the dim hallway. "Nova, please don't be rude to Mr. Bennett for no reason."

Without getting tangled up in her train, November pivoted.

"It was a pleasure to see you again, One Who Stares Back From The Void," she said empty. The corner of her black lips ticked. Then continued into the dark hall.

Aaron felt as if he should have remembered her.

"I apologize for her indignance. November has expressed interest in meeting with you since your departure. I don't know what has caused her sudden prudishness. You two used to talk for hours. Not that you'd remember those interactions. I'll send her by to check on you. I think she'd like that. The Arena starts the day after tomorrow. I would ask you to join me to spectate. However, now I think it would be better if you didn't."

"I don't need to be checked up on. I killed the last apprentice you sent to check up on me."

"Nova is not a part of The Fetishes. She sits at the table. Nor do I think Aaron Bennett would kill anyone."

"No, I wouldn't. But Critch would, and apparently, I'm not as far away from him as I thought." Each consonant a bite off of Madam Ava's persona.

"You never will be. Good luck with Jaslynn. Hopefully..." Madam Ava cringed as if she hadn't swallowed in quite awhile. "Hopefully, she can handle you."

"Good luck with the Arena." The house stared at him. The tentative acceptance, as always, shifted to familiar rejection.

Apologies For Lying, He's The Antagonist leaned on a lamppost

The Antagonist's Prison

at the harbor, his fedora tipped down in delectable drama. Came on time because he knew the girls would be late, as most were in this culture he fell into. Anticulture was quite inefficient, if he had to be honest with himself. No matter. Not easily bored, and he had cloves. Charlie on lap twenty-three around his feet.

Waves crashed on the water-break. The fog clung to the harbor like damaged goods to their current fling. Aaron's bisected brain argued that a relationship with a person like Jaslynn was a terrible idea. The other side suggested the seeking one could probably handle it. Maybe.

A black Mustang dropped the girls off, then proceeded to roar unmuffled down the boulevard. Aaron interrupted Charlie's fun and placed him under his jacket collar. He wiggled in mild protest.

Drea, costumed in a cut-up shirt, with a deep V down to the base of her navel, no sides, and nothing but a minuscule tether on the back. This shirt served no purpose. Her purple bra was in clear view. Just wear the bra. Her pierced navel infected, rejected sternum dermal and poorly tattooed back. She rubbed her arms. Had to be freezing.

Aaron didn't want to deal with that archetype, but if they're friends he didn't want to be rude. He assumed the partner was a bodyguard thing. Sad world we lived in.

Jaslynn's eyebrows drawn in black webs that traveled down her cheeks and morphed into her spiderweb earrings. Aaron appreciated the woman's skill and dedication to the theme, but the time-sink webbing was gonna be a problem. Unlike Drea, Jaslynn chose to cover herself completely, in a buttoned-up peacoat, black pants, and knee-high, black-heeled boots. Everyone involved was certain she wasn't wearing anything under the peacoat. Her smile hungry. Not tonight, eager one.

"Ladies?" Holy Shit It's The Antagonist Run Away! said. He pushed off the lamp post and flicked the butt into the harbor.

"Mr. Bennett," Drea said.

"Aaron," Jaslynn said through black lipstick. Just at the edge of the age when this ostentation took away from credibility instead

Caretakers and a Catastrophe

of adding to it. Still, her confidence was everything.

"Shall we?" he said as if leading them to the noose. Fortunately, Aaron was not their executioner today.

As they went inside, all turned to ogle Jaslynn. Some with disgust, some with appreciation, some with gross hunger. Aaron ignored it and caught Rei's eye. She glowed and bowed to him across the restaurant.

Rei contracted him to make all her employee's shirts, customized for each employee, which took awhile. A new custom stencil, filled with flowy traditional Japanese images, lots of different colors. But Pretty Far From Critch did it all with no markup, just the material cost. Rei repaid him by treating him like a VIP for his rare visits. Couldn't complain since Rei's really was the best sushi in town.

The TV played Celtic Woman on repeat, but the radio hooked up to the best of Michael Jackson. A long table dominated the main room, always crowded with a party of ten or more. To the right, a room reserved for tables of two. To the left, through silly rice white paper walls stabilized by brown gridwork, for parties of three to four. Past that room were VIP rooms where you had to remove your shoes to enter. Jaslynn and Aaron both sighed as their boots were laborious to remove, hers especially with the thirty-two eyelets.

Drea's tarred, paper-thin sandals cleaner than her blackened feet. Aaron knew there was a way to do that lifestyle. Raile's best friend, Pelican, personified the ideal of that outdoor living. Her feet were structured differently. Her skin cared for and hair sorted out despite experiencing houselessness on purpose. Drea was excusing laziness for hippieness. Rei led them into that back place. Within seconds sake and garlic chile edamame bowls on the table.

Aaron took Charlie off his shoulder and placed him in front of Jaslynn.

"Charlie, I want you to meet Jaslynn. She's your new master." Charlie crossed halfway, stopped, looked at Aaron with a sad spider face. He shooed him on. The oddly intelligent spider climbed onto her plate and waved. Jaslynn squealed and swore to whatever power. Charlie sighed. Or lowered between his legs a bit. Which was a spider

The Antagonist's Prison

sigh. Had to be.

"What the fuck is that shit?" Drea said.

Jaslynn scratched Charlie's front leg, he loved it.

"I know a gal."

"I have a feeling you know a lot of shady people," Drea said.

"He's wonderful," Jaslynn said. Then, with a smile, "The spider."

"How was your internship, Jaslynn?" Aaron said.

"Ugh, cleaning cages, washing instruments. My friend told me, you have to start at the bottom and weasel your way up. I'm willing to do that, but it still sucks, you know. I mean, that's probably how you got your own store, right?"

"That's Tyler's story. He did a bunch of retail managerial jobs before meeting my friend, Naomi. She knew I was looking into entrepreneurship, so she introduced us. I paid for the store and startup with the payoff from some investments."

Madam Ava put aside an enormous cut for each of his kills. She knew from the beginning he wouldn't be her unforgivable weapon forever. But he was deeply ashamed of that money. He paid for the start-up and hadn't touched the money since. It sat in an offshore bank account accumulating some ridiculous interest. The money was always available, but touching it sickened and angered the well-off Imminent Unforewarned Reckoning.

"Tyler does the art and I run the books, we both make the shirts. We expect it to burn to the ground at any time, but we're holding up for now. "

"Seems like a cynical way of running a business," Drea said.

"It's a realistic way of running your own small business. Think about it, there are a million online silkscreening businesses. The only reason we out-price them is because of the small markup and Tyler's custom art. Most of our profit comes from networking around town. We did the uniforms for a bunch of local businesses, which is good advertising in and of itself. Tyler says we're becoming the brand of Indigo Bay. Whatever that means."

"I hate that. You gotta know people to get anywhere, I can't just get by on my own merits," Drea said.

Caretakers and a Catastrophe

"No, that's not the way you look at it," Jaslynn said. "You should climb the ladder by yourself. However, you need someone with a ladder to climb, someone to hold the ladder, someone to show you where the ladder is, and someone to teach you how to climb."

"What, did you just read a self-help, *Starting Your Own Business for Dummies* before you came here tonight?" Drea said.

"I always look for advice. My parents certainly didn't teach me anything. You need help. Besides, you can't just have a good personality and work ethic, those qualities won't get you anywhere if no one knows about them. You have to show your strengths to others and hopefully you'll run into someone looking for what you've got."

Aaron thought that was meant for him, but he could just be all full of hope. Certainly couldn't assess how forward Jaslynn and her thirsty face were. It would make other folk uncomfortable with how forward she was behaving.

"You just have to be careful about who you owe favors to, especially in Indigo Bay. There are bad people working around here. There are higher authorities than the law. Like Critch..." Drea said, looking at literally Critch. Though she did not know this. "Also known by some as The Antagonist."

She hoped to get a reaction out of the table because a lot of people treated his name like Beetlejuice. She was all amped, must've just learned about him.

"Who?" Critch said.

"Why is this town so obsessed with Critch?" Jaslynn said. "I feel like I hear about this guy everywhere I go. I don't believe it. I mean, how can a guy like that exist without getting caught? How do the cops not know about him? There are too many plot holes. His story is so flimsy."

"I agree, Critch doesn't and couldn't exist," The Actual Thing™ said.

"I heard he's some sort of vigilante," Drea said, hunkered down, elbows braced on the table for the argument. Now that the party was in opposition to her, she would get the fiery debate she

The Antagonist's Prison

relished. "Like, if you do something really bad and get away with it, Critch finds you and kills you."

"That's news to me. I'm not sure vigilantes work outside of comic books," A Comic Book Character said. Straight out of the penny dreadfuls.

"My friend Neil saw him on the beach once. He's got some serious PTSD because of it," Drea said.

"What did he see?" Jaslynn said, intrigued.

"A guy in gimp leather tearing people apart," Drea said.

"Hot," Jaslynn said.

Some potential BDSM in his future. That was cool, you couldn't live with Madam Ava without learning a few things.

"No, dude, not like a fist fight, bar brawl. Naw, Critch literally tore arms off, then beat the men to death with their own limbs. He ripped organs out, crazy shit like that. I can barely believe it."

"But why was he wearing gimp leather?" The One Who Wore It asked.

"To be scary. Duh," Drea said.

"Sounds stupid and totally impossible," The Liar said.

Their rolls dropped. They never ordered. Rei remembered everyone's favorite dishes and then elaborated on them. She watched and kept careful records of what people liked and didn't. These eight rolls, sixteen nigiri, and twenty pieces of sashimi normally cost about two hundred dollars. Aaron wouldn't pay for half of that, but his tip would more than make up the difference.

"Do you have any idea how strong you'd have to be to rip off a human arm? Like did he hold the guy by the shoulder and pull?" Jaslynn said.

"Neil said he just grabbed the arm and pulled it off like a towel off the rack."

"You hear how ridiculous that sounds, right?" Jaslynn grabbed Drea's arm and pulled. Charlie redundantly mimicked her on Aaron's finger. "See how your body moved with you? The acceleration, the torque or whatever it's called, Midge would know, to just pull off an arm, is absurd."

Caretakers and a Catastrophe

With a not-eyeroll, Aaron changed the subject. Told them about Rei and her husband. They had become good friends. Gone to the market a few times. Gio was quite professional but had fun and joked with the fishermen. Aaron didn't understand a word of Italian, but Gio spoke some broken English and called Her Dear Apocalypse a humble American. Aaron said thanks. Said it was his best feature. He laughed and slapped him on the back.

Mr. Bennett told the women that story with read-the-room details. Strategic plot embellishments to impress. After the fourth tokkuri of sake, Drea leaned back and forth. She looked quite done. By tokkuri seven she was about to pass out. Jaslynn stopped drinking a while back, not wanting to lose composure on the first date. She knew how to do this.

After tokkuri twelve, Drea was face down on the table. Aaron was loose, feeling how most would after two beers. He really didn't have a frame of reference. Friends thought of it as an amazing gift. Aaron didn't think so.

His Unflinching Grin carried Drea out to his little blue Civic.

"You planned on getting her plastered, didn't you?" Jaslynn said.

"Of course. How else were we going to take a long walk along the waterfront by our lonesome?"

"You gonna tell me how you coulda been a contender now?"

"No, I'm going to shove your drunk friend in the back of my car and lock the door."

"Remind me not to fuck with you." He didn't hear the inflection in her voice.

"Keep in mind, you let me do it," Probably Best Not To Be Fucked With said, laying Drea down in his backseat.

"Of course, I did." Jaslynn winked. Aaron had never seen a wink as a flirtation tactic before, let alone on him. Ineffective.

Sushi Rei and all of its neighbors faded behind the fog until they became diffuse yellow dots. The yachts moaned in their stalls, many of them unused for months or years. Dusty trophies of wealth.

The breakwater was always a favored place of Aaron's. During the day, most people stopped halfway along the break, so the fur-

The Antagonist's Prison

ther one went, the less people. In that way, it felt like an accomplishment. Then he'd jump the fence and scurry across the rocks to the end, where pelicans rustled in the sun.

At night, nobody walked the break. It never felt safe. The waves swelled and burst skyward against the wet rocks and cement wall. Foreboding in the night hours.

Jaslynn spoke, without heed of silence or direction. Aaron didn't mind. She talked about her extensively researched and bleeding edge progressive world views, her entirely realistic yet still ambitious goals as a person. Aaron responded mechanically in one word questions or half-hearted groans, essentially allowing her to continue.

Aaron was not one to talk about himself. And if never asked, he'd never say anything. If he did, it was a lie or not very interesting.

"You seem lonely..." Jaslynn said.

"A little, but it hasn't bothered me until recently. Done everything American life expects of you, except have a relationship. I feel like I must be missing out on something."

"I couldn't tell you what it's like to be alone for a long time. I'm always surrounded by people. If I go to a bar, I'm ambushed by drunk, I-drink-a-whole-can-of-protein-powder-a-day guys. People stare at me everywhere, even if I'm just grocery shopping. It's exhausting and more than a little unnerving."

"Sounds as much. Though, a lot of people would love to live that life."

"But you don't?"

"Waste of time."

Our Relentless Shadow jumped the fence and helped Jaslynn down onto the rocks. Charlie cliff dove, legs splayed. Got good air. They found a large black one with less bird excrement on it than not and sat staring out into the bay. During the day, Mr. Bennett sat out here and stared at the city behind them. The peninsulas reaching out into the bay. The mansions cluttered up within the trees. Now, there were nothing but haunted movements in the mist. The floodlight made the fog opaque, creating a white room with dark flooring.

Caretakers and a Catastrophe

"You don't think you're lost at all?"

"I feel perfectly content with who I am."

"I want to hear about you, but you're not taking any of my prompts. Honestly, I'm reading you as disinterested. I'm trying really hard to express myself, yet I'm getting nothing from you."

"Apologetic, I didn't hear any of the prompts. I'm truly terrible at subtlety. What you see is what you get with me. I smoke. I drink. I don't have much in the way of goals. I'm happy. No want of change. I like my patch here."

The waves lost steam a hundred feet from where they sat. They hit rocks with a half-heartedness. They knew from this conversation, Jaslynn wanted more from life than The Antagonist did. That spelled doom for whatever relationship they were not mutually dreaming of. It could work for some, but not these two.

"By the way, I've met Raile, and I'm much prettier than her."

"Eh, good for you, certain angle, certain light nonsense. Again, I don't value appearances."

"Even so, Raile's got nothing on me. They call me the Second Lust, do you know what that means?" She straddled Aaron. He tried not to flinch in surprise. That didn't seem erotic. Not that he had any real intentions for her. "And it bothers me to hear such terrible things about you."

He was going to ask her more about this Second Lust tomfoolery, but she interrupted by kissing his neck long and stretched out. Critch's brain switched to a mode which hadn't been tapped in a while. He pulled her hips closer. Weaved hands into her hair. The makeout escalated. She unbuttoned her peacoat. We were right, she wasn't wearing anything underneath.

"I have a confession," Jaslynn said, without stopping. "Someone has been hunting me...for a very long time...well, when I saw you...I knew I finally found someone who could protect me." She reached for his belt. "Can you protect me, Aaron?"

He grabbed her hand, not even half hard from her gyrated efforts. They needed to talk about this without being punctuated by ellipses.

The Antagonist's Prison

The floodlight shut off with a heavy clunk and a rapid fade of light. Startled, they searched around, caught.

A giant person made of featureless clay, the mold of a person, emerged from the water. Jaslynn scrambled off the rock. The Antagonist pushed her behind him. The notion to run never occurred. The nightmare in his head never ran. Critch always held more sway than Aaron. His arms burned, hands trembled into weapons.

The creature was at least three feet taller than Critch, resembled a horrific Gumby. Gunk fell from fingers and chin, seaweed skin and debris hung about. It waited. Jaslynn screamed behind him. Not good for the cover story.

"I would not associate with the Second Lust!" The man from this morning launched over the railing. Tap danced in his gray suit over a few feet of rock. Pointed his cane at Jaslynn.

A head-sized fist haymakered. The One Who Will Make You Undone pushed Jaslynn back to the ground as he narrowly dodged underneath the slow blow. His heart ruptured, its beats per minute hitting the low thousands. Mist steamed into an aura. Shoulder blades split apart. Hands, now claws, dangled heavy. The blackout came and there was little Aaron could do. Critch wanted this and he had waited for a long time.

The monster's foot, as large as his torso, kicked him five feet backward. He didn't feel it. Caught himself in a skidded low crouch, his leg braced from behind.

Critch's smile larger than his mouth.

Alibis and a Suspicious Shortness

Aaron was a tiny being inside a floppy marionette. He pulled on strings and rods to flail limbs about. Squinted out his tiny pupils from three feet in. That floodlight seared frantic retinas.

In a fetal position, the light faded to tolerable. A red spider tapped on his nose with its one-inch leg. He jerked back, and it jumped away. The somehow personable arachnid raised its front legs and waved them to and fro in celebration.

Aaron Bennett's phone said one in the morning, meaning he'd been out for about fifteen minutes. In pain, but he knew how to deal with pain. He checked his face and gave his body a rubdown. No gashes, just a few bruises here and there. His knuckles hurt. The skin cracked but hadn't peeled. He stretched out his hands and they snapped their carpals back into place with pops and twitchy twists. He didn't come fully back to normal. Maybe it was his wizened age of twenty-five.

Every vertebra cracked as he sat up, sending a weird but familiar rush to his head. He dragged his depleted body up to a broken, teetered stance to better assess the breakwater. No Jaslynn, no gray-suited, dancing man. Blood on the ground, lots of slime and mucus blobs. Dozens of pieces from the dismantled clay thing on the rocks below where they dissolved bit by bit with

The Antagonist's Prison

every disgusting lap of harbor water.

Jaslynn was taken. As she had feared. But Aaron still did not know why. And he did not care. Callously so. He hoped for the best for her, knowing otherwise. He was well-versed in hardening his heart.

Thick metal railings on the harbor side of the breakwater were bent or sheared here and there. Five ten-foot craters shattered the reinforced cement wall. More than a few impact sites peppered the ground. That's why his knuckles hurt, he accurately presumed. A three-foot piece of rebar jutted from the ground. Blood slid down the shaft and pooled in its fissures. A bomb field of The Antagonist's fist blows.

Not Critch At The Moment picked up the still rejoicing Charlie and placed him on his shoulder. Aaron stumbled back to his little blue Civic. Drea drooled on the seat. That would stain. He quickly changed to one of his replacement black outfits and called Madam Ava.

"Mr. Bennett, you're only allowed to call this number if you have an emergency."

"Fuck, it's been years. I lost control and a gray-suited man took Jaslynn away, called her the Second Lust. He had a huge blank creature with him that trudged itself out of the fucking harbor." He cleared his throat, lit a clove with a palsy hand.

"Oh, that diminutive, cowardly motherfucker. You! Get over here! Find The Widow in Yellow," Madam Ava said, swallowing her commands. "November will handle it. I bet you gave that little cunt quite the scare. No one has beat a Knight yet. That's *my* fucking weapon." She primal growled. Proud like her sports team just made a goal point unit.

"Who is he?"

"Mr. Kinns. I can't imagine what his interest in Miss Phillips could be. What does November need to know?"

"It happened on the breakwater. Ate at Rei's, left the restaurant around midnight, went for a stroll with Jaslynn."

"Any witnesses?"

"Not that I know of, it's foggy as shit. I have Jaslynn's friend

Alibis and a Suspicious Shortness

passed in my car, I think she'll be out till tomorrow. There's some destruction. Jaslynn screamed. Hopefully, that won't cause problems."

"It shouldn't." She hung up.

Aaron's alibi would appear on his doorstep by the time he got Drea home. He thought he'd left this shit behind him. But it was never far enough. Never would be.

Hardly Critch Anymore knocked on the Compound's door. A few people answered. The Antagonist didn't remember the ride much. A slight shame crawled over him as he realized how a barely-lucid Aaron was not a responsible driver. He told the crunchy residents he had a passed-out Drea in the car. They laughed and helped get her into the squat. Aaron stayed for a mason jar of terrible boxed wine, then went on his merry.

Death always meant little to the three-year-old twenty-five-ish-year-old. He never saw the point in dreading inevitability. Nor did he perceive the value of his bag of matter as something that shouldn't end. He'd seen countless death parades. A spectacle in the majority of them. Watched with a braided metal aircraft cable noose around his neck until the point was made and his Deemed Useful Side was unleashed.

If he lost his best friends, Gradick or Raile, he'd feel. He didn't know about that, as those two were forces of nature who couldn't die. It'd be as if hope itself died. Jaslynn, on the other hand, no one would care much that she was gone, so long as it didn't interrupt anyone's life for very long. The notion of a relationship was a momentary judgment lapse. It was usually a matter of scope for The Antagonist. The same way a tree falling in the forest didn't ruin the forest. Objectively so. Only the trees adjacent cared. The forest did not.

November waited, stately rigid on The Antagonist's front porch. His guardian wore all her customary black: a long-sleeved, very tight dress, shaped like a simple, gothic champagne flute. A lace veil

The Antagonist's Prison

masking half her face. A too-wide black hat tilted low, shadowing her eyes, whose lenses and sclera matched the rest of her ensemble. Her leather-gloved fingers clinched hard on a classic, lengthy cigarette holder where a non-filter glowed bright. She was not wearing her firefighter jacket out in the open, but kept her face painted in mime. She watched Aaron's every movement. His noose coiled on her waist, thick as his wrist.

"Hello, Mr. Bennett, Your Unflinching Grin. Do you remember me?" She handed him an envelope, kissed his cheek, and walked away, leaving violet wafts in her wake. Aaron would be nonplussed if there was lipstick at the impact site. Fortunately, there was not. A habit of Aaron not bothering himself with people of her caliber. He was not of their concern, just a tool to further their wants.

He read the alibi: as they strolled through the harbor, they met a man named Captain Christopher Wallace, who invited them onto his boat for a few drinks. Aaron took Jaslynn home first, then Drea. Witnesses who saw Jaslynn get out of his car. No lost time.

Into the kitchen, The Lady Made of Dark's Bump In The Night chugged a glass of water. Took a shower. Went to bed. Charlie curled up on the pillow next to him. He slept like mountains.

A few hours later, Aaron walked back to his car. His body learned to recharge quickly. Took hour-long naps here and there when needed. Aaron turned around to see Charlie tailing him.

"Are you going to follow me around from now on?" The small red spider jumped in the air. "Is that a yes?" He jumped again. "That doesn't clarify the matter."

He skittered up to Aaron and raised his front legs at him. Mr. Bennett cupped his hands under Charlie and brought him up so they could speak face to face.

"I thought I gave you to Jaslynn. Shouldn't you be with her?" Charlie knelt down and swayed side to side. "Is that a no?" He jumped in the air. "I've to admit, Charlie. You are cute as hell."

Alibis and a Suspicious Shortness

He raised his legs, jubilant. The Antagonist put the jigging spider on his shoulder where he continued his many-legged dance.

When Aaron got to the store, he put Charlie on the desk and asked him to stay under his hat. The spider bowed cat-like, lifted up the grayed-out black fedora and disappeared underneath. Aaron murdered the morning paperwork. He slayed commissions, readied for Tyler and Jeff to complete when they got in. Executed the deposit for pick-up, been a good week. Eviscerated emails Amber forwarded to him. Aaron nodded, a nod so slight no witness would notice, pleased with his tiny store. It took a good deal of time to learn Aaron expressions, for all of them were micro. The office phone rang with a number The One Who Will Make You Undone didn't recognize.

"Hello, Shirts With Words On Them, this is Aaron Bennett."

"Are you the guy Jazz whored it up with last night?" A rather high-pitched child spoke.

"Indeed. Hi, who is this?"

"My name is Midge, a friend of Jaslynn Phillips. I haven't heard from her since yesterday afternoon, and Tyler and Dot said she never came home last night. So what happened, bud?"

"I dropped her off after dinner. Fuck if I know what she did with her night after that."

"You don't need to be a dick," the heliumed voice said.

"Reciprocal communication."

"Ok, fuck a god, I'm sorry. I'm just worried about her. You said Aaron Bennett, right?"

"Yeah."

"I've heard of you," Midge said.

"Congrats?" Critch really didn't need more odd. Today desperately needed to be routine.

"Look, this is going to sound weird. But, considering what I've heard about you, you're not Jazz's type. She usually goes for meatheads or sad, selfish sacks of human waste, so her sudden break in the pattern is concerning. What are you doing for lunch?"

"Meeting with you is my guess." He rubbed his forehead.

The Antagonist's Prison

Drivers cranked screws into his hands.

"I know, I know, it's just one of my proclivities. But I'm protective of her. She's kind of an idiot."

"Yeah, yeah, no worries. I'll meet you at Cataran's around one?"

"Cool. See you later, mister."

When Tyler came in, he told His Unflinching Grin that he looked haggard. Of course, Tyler looked immaculate in his business casual punk rock adopted from The Miscreant Royalty. Asked Aaron about how Jaslynn never showed up last night and bought the cover story with a shrug.

"Eh, Dot's worried but I'm not, you didn't fuck her, so she probably went out again for a booty call."

Aaron returned the shrug. As of right now, things would work out. Christopher Wallace was a real person, and Madam Ava trusted him, probably through extortion of some shockingly extreme measure, to back Her Dear Apocalypse up. If anyone inquired about Jaslynn's disappearance, he was more than covered.

Drea came in around noon. Her dreads fuzzed up under a bandana, headache screaming from swollen, bloodshot eyes. Cheeks a ruddy red. Aaron had never been hungover. A side effect of his oddness.

"You tricky fucker! You got me drunk so you could be alone with Jazz! What happened last night? Dot said she never came home!"

"You passed out. Jazz and I left you in the car and went for a walk along the breakwater. Met a guy named Christopher who asked us if we wanted a drink on his boat. Cool guy."

"And you accepted his invitation? Are you goddamned stupid? That's really fucking shady, Aaron."

"Meh, Jaslynn had mace," The Antagonist said.

Amber stormed in, looking like she hadn't slept for a week. The second day in a row she'd shown up in distress. At least this morning didn't involve ejection from a creepy rape van. Her celestial white hair frazzled in a rushed topknot, her posture lower than usual. Instead of her informal workout attire, she chose to don cut-off low rise

Alibis and a Suspicious Shortness

jean shorts and a white tank disturbingly not too small for her. Her arms now thinner than the bones that made them up. She went into the back without saying anything. Long night of video games would be anyone's guess, ignoring Amber's somber affect and no laundry. None of Aaron's business. Whose business was it to clock Amber's mental state? Because it seemed to be no one's.

Aaron guided the conversation toward Drea and Tyler, encouraging the flirting and sexual tension. When Drea forgot about He Who Smiles Back, the monster escaped to the back room, where Jeff and Amber found themselves in the middle of a tense conversation. Jeff's typical half-dapper, half-Hunter S. Thompson appearance abandoned for jeans and a sleeveless black band t-shirt. Did everyone but Tyler have a bad night? The young punk hyper-vigilant and coked out. His hands shook.

"Hey, Jeff, pay attention. Leave your last night's tribulations at home. You've got a job to do here."

"Fuck you, man! Gradick was goddamned killed last night!" he said, cracking over overwhelmed man sobs. Your Imminent Unforewarned Reckoning's head reeled back.

"How in the fuck?" Aaron said. The general consensus was nothing could kill a member of The Miscreant Royalty. In the same way a murdered object was just as much an object as an unmurdered one. "What the fuck were you fuckers doing?"

"We were in the Tunnels, a big group of us. He pushed us out of the way from those rainbow motherfuckers so we could escape..." Jeff got up to pace with hands orbiting his upset mind. He chose, like most men, to get angry in order to hide sorrow and desperate emotions. Tears still fell down his cheeks, his pitch higher. "I watched him get torn apart! And there was nothing we could do!"

"Fucking Christ, what were you doing messing with the Tunnels. Wait. What happened to Raile?"

Raile distressed couldn't be a good thing for collective society. The city should have burned to the ground at this point.

"I have no idea. I really don't know what stories to believe. There's a few going around!"

The Antagonist's Prison

"I saw her shooting a gun at her jacket in the woods last night," Amber said. "Heavily drugged and rambling nonsense. We tried to stop her, but she ran away."

"And what!? You couldn't catch her?" Jeff said, shaking Amber ineffectually. It was easy to look at Amber and see her as fragile. Jeff succumbed to sobs.

"Sorry, Jeff. She's really fast and left no trace."

"She was always really good at vanishing..."

"Sounds like everyone had an interesting night," Aaron said. Not knowing the full scope of the night before. Also, he had no tools to help with other's trauma. He barely contained his own. "We'll all have to grab a drink later, storytime. I'm leaving to meet up with somebody named Midge. Can you guys keep an eye on Tyler? Make sure he doesn't leave, he's clearly eager to go eat caramels with Drea instead of doing his job."

Aaron smuggled the red spider, who tried to nuzzle Aaron's neck, and left before they said anything more about the Tunnels. Not to incriminate himself any more than he probably already had.

The Miscreant Royalty and The Antagonist were supposed to have a barbecue tonight. The urge to cry overwhelmed Aaron, but his spent and shriveled ducts failed to turn over. He sat in his car and shook the wheel. There was a belief that one only had so many tears to shed. If that was the case, he used all his up in the care of Madam Ava. Always waking up in The Vault mid-sob, no idea what he'd done. Powerless against the smiling demon shaking his soul as a joke. Only coming to when he needed a nap.

Charlie crawled down to the seat and tapped on Aaron's leg. Then waved his legs at him. It cheered His Unflinching Grin up a bit.

Gradick was a man to be memorialized. Made drunken friends with every person in the bar, often getting the room to join him in a dance number or sing-along. He made life a happy musical. Although he never knew that Aaron was Critch, in tangential ways he helped him integrate through sheer understanding and patience.

And for fuck's sake, Raile. She'd be ruined. What did she do last night? He supposedly knew her brother, Rudy. That meant he

Alibis and a Suspicious Shortness

had his number. Critch called him.

"Aaron?"

"Yeah, Rudy?"

"You got it. Calling about Kat?" Raile's real name was Katarina Trujillo. "Don't worry man, I got her, she's alive. She's washing off last night right now."

"What happened?"

"So far, I got evidence for thirty-one break-ins, arson, theft, trespassing, reckless endangerment. That's not even a quarter of the stories. Dude, you need to get over here. She needs everyone, like, right now. Hold on, Pelican wants to talk to you."

"Mr. Bennett?" Gradick and Raile's other best friend said in her high-pitched husk. So much stank on his name it dripped. While Drea tried to do whatever she did, Pelican possessed actual anger toward him. Aaron was impressed with Pelican. She hated him.

"Pelican, what happened? What can I do?"

"Nothing. You stay the fuck away. Don't come over here. Raile doesn't need a motherfucker like you around."

"Fuck you. Raile is my best friend too, you child. Perhaps the last best friend I have now that Gradick has shuffled off."

"No. Because you're going to convince her to get revenge."

"No, I wouldn't, she needs to mourn and heal. "

A pause and a sigh. "Once I think I understand what you are, Aaron, you prove to be human after all."

"I don't give a fuck what you think about 'What I am.' But, if you think you can convince her of anything, you don't know Raile."

"Is that Aaron?" He heard Raile say from some distance away. Her voice shattered. "Can I talk to him?"

The beeps of the hang-up shot through the receiver. At a red light, The One Who Stares Back From The Void contemplated going to see this Midge versus helping his best friend. Not meeting with Midge would just raise more questions. If Pelican did her job, and she always did, Raile would be there when done with his luncheon subpoena.

Your Imminent Unforewarned Reckoning parallel parked a

The Antagonist's Prison

block from Cataran's. A coffee and sandwich shop split down the middle by a patio. Told Charlie to stay in the car, who gave Aaron a sad spider face. Critch told him it was for the greater good and that he'd be back soon. Charlie perked, crawled into the cup holder and curled up.

Cataran's was technically two businesses, owned by a man named Barry. A huge Haitian with a well-earned pot belly and pitted face. He used to be pretty dark before retiring. He never reached the echelon of Critch's past but was a good man to have in your network. The building's old, gray wood and cement patio were used and storied.

Mr. Bennett passed the sandwich shop employed exclusively by ex-cons and washed-out punk rockers smelling of vinegar and pickles. Aaron's nose burned from recently roasted coffee beans. Light came through the skylights but did little to pierce the constant dusk. College students, tattooed folk of the various clichés, and lower-middle-class moms discussed their trials over mugs of decent coffee. The line out the door. His Unflinching Grin waited for five minutes as the six happy hipster kids bustled to craft various caffeines.

Bootcamp-sore from last night, Aaron's muscles likely black and blue before night's end. Your Imminent Unforewarned Reckoning ordered an artisan pour-over coffee before realizing he had no idea what Midge looked like. With a name like that she could be short or tall, depending on humor. Looked for a woman who'd be friends with Jaslynn, but that was a dead end. Every person in Cataran's was a probable friend with the in-vogue woman.

"Hey Barry, how's it going?" Aaron said murderously.

"It's good, always good. Can I get you anything besides your coffee? Oh, and I want to talk to you and Tyler about some uniforms at some point."

"Of course, email me a good time for you and we'll make it happen. I'm meeting a woman called Midge. Know her?"

"Midge? Yeah, she's been coming here the last couple of days, working on school papers or something. She's over there."

Alibis and a Suspicious Shortness

He pointed to a dyed redhead with an a-line cut sitting in the corner. Light from the translucent window offered little reading power. A desk lamp with a green hood did all the work. She stared down at a thick book as her right hand scribbled automatically on a yellow legal pad. On either side of her were half a dozen tomes. Good, Jaslynn had a smart friend to look after her. A loose green sweater hung off a tattooed shoulder. A traditional flash swallow and a bright sugar skull adorned the backs of her hands. On her neck a flash rose with a banner which read "Tobin."

"Midge?" he said, in his most not-horrifying way. He startled her anyhow, sucking the blood from her face. She pulled down her neon green headset before she eyed The Antagonist up and down. He didn't get that look often. Looks of fear were standard. Instincts told people to cross the street.

"Aaron?" she said. Maybe he imagined the check-out because she quickly shut her Attracted off. Turned all Business. Extended her hand. "Hi, I'm sorry for the awkward phone call. I'm not articulate on the phone."

She paused her music on her tablet. 'Sparrow Falls.'

"Good song," he said.

"You like Wovenhand?"

He lowered as if into a grave across from her mountain of academia. "Don't really know many of their songs, but yeah, moody. And no worries, my recent phone calls only come in odd. So, what did you want to confirm?"

"You have a strange cadence when you talk, didja know?"

"Yeah, I get that. Just an affectation I've developed."

"Jazz can out-wit most men under the table. That sucks for her, and for me as her friend, because only guys with ginormous balls go for her. Unfortunately, such testicular enormity tends toward douchebags."

"Should I be going on the defensive? I'm not a douchebag, despite what the rumors might say."

Midge closed her book. Her scowl and green eyes ripped layers off The One Who Will Make You Undone's optic nerve.

The Antagonist's Prison

"Jazz always calls after a date. She loves to brag about her new guy, who is never different from the last one. I hate the ritual, but she never fails to call, no matter the hour. She'll call with him snoring in her ear after they've done the nasty. She claims she can't fall asleep without a load inside her. But she never called last night. So what happened?"

"We went out with Drea to Sushi Rei. We ate, were merry. Drea passed out. We had a lot of sake. Jaslynn and I went for a walk on the breakwater, met a chill dude named Christopher, and went onto his boat for a drink. 'Twas a good time. I drove Jaslynn home, then Drea. Stayed for a glass of welfare wine and chatted with her squat-mates for a bit."

Midge studied Mr. Bennett. His eyes watered from her Saint Peter assessment. "You're an amazing liar. Something doesn't add up. I know you're lying, so tell me what happened. Where is Jazz?"

"I don't know."

"See, that was an honest answer." With a snaking point of her finger, body mirroring the weave. "Here's some evidence that doesn't fit your alibi. Your knuckles are torn. And you're holding yourself like you just came back from your first Crossfit. Even though you look like you're a fitness guru under your layers. Did you beat the shit out of my friend?"

"I wouldn't be sore from beating Jaslynn. And even if I did, you're awfully calm about battery and murder."

"Because I know you didn't beat her. And I never said anything about murder," she said to the tempo of a hummingbird's wing. "Jazz's been increasingly paranoid ever since she moved back here, an out of character idiosyncrasy. You started lying when you mentioned that Christopher guy. Is he a real person?"

"Yeah."

"But you've never met him. Indigo Bay is full of secrets, I'm sure you know this quite well."

If she mentioned a Critch conspiracy, Critch was gonna flip the table.

"Yes, I've heard that," Aaron said.

Alibis and a Suspicious Shortness

"Careful now. If you did something bad last night, and continue to get away with it, you know what will happen, right?"

God fucking dammit. "I'd be wracked by guilt? Couldn't live with myself and my heinous crimes? Or maybe I'd just sleep like an exhausted cat after an intense laser chase?"

"Critch will come after you," she said, fishing for a reaction.

"Jesus Christ, why is everyone so obsessed with a goddamn fictional serial killer? Drea wouldn't shut up about him last night. I don't understand the sudden hype around an urban legend that's half a decade old."

"Over the course of two years, a man killed at least five dozen people around Indigo Bay, probably more. SIXTY!" Midge said. People looked over.

The Antagonist had no idea how many people he'd killed. Probably closer to a thousand. One had to account for bystanders.

"They were mostly corrupt shitheads, untouchable to the law. The Antagonist left his victims torn to shreds, as though they exploded. To this day, the cops have no leads, despite witnesses everywhere. He disappeared three years ago and hasn't been heard of since. What a story! Of course everyone talks about it! It was relevant and topical back then, but the fact that he was never caught immortalized him. He was an artist who died, sorry, 'disappeared,' which made him so much bigger. Think of all the rockstars who died young. Morrison, Hendrix, Lennon, Tupac, Biggie. Influential figures when they were alive and performing, but the tragedy and circumstances of their premature departures rocketed them to godhood," she said all in one breath.

Midge's hands finished stiff. Waited for The Real Deal to answer, slowly leaning across her books. Aaron waited until the lean became extreme enough to be silly.

"There's truth in that, yeah. And just so we're clear, you're equating The Antagonist with dead male rock stars? Who's to say Critch wasn't female?"

"No, definitely male, haven't you heard anything of the stories?"

"I just know people talk a bit too much about Critch. Especially

The Antagonist's Prison

when it suits their needs."

"Do you know what a berserker is?"

This set off a ping in The One Who Will Make You Undone's mind. Not meaning to, but also kind of meaning to change the topic at hand, he said, "Wait, Jaslynn said you were coming in today, but you've been in town for at least a week?"

"I had shit to do, you can't do anything with Jazz around. Anyways, you know, like a true berserker from Norse culture? The kind that sent the British and Romans running?"

So much for the subject change. "I know what berserking is, sure."

"Not like this you don't. I have a Ph.D. in Scandinavian history, and I'm almost done with a master's in evolutionary psychology, all because of Critch." She didn't look more than twenty-eight.

"You got your PhD in berserkergang? In an urban legend? Sounds like a book, not a thesis." Aaron banged on some weird wall we were ignoring.

"No, not entirely. I'm comparing Scandinavian and Roman History. My master's thesis is on the ideological differences and similarities between Norse and Roman war culture and mythological beliefs, and how their gods played a part in their warfare tactics. And berserkers are a part of that. Norse is based more on the balance of humanity interacting with nature than other creation myths. Which is odd for a war culture. Their gods make a lot of sense, reflecting the physical world, as opposed to the projected fantasy gods of Roman deities." She stopped for a moment. Took a casual sip of coffee. "You've manipulated the conversation away from yourself again. We're talking about what happened last night, remember?"

"What if I just cut to the chase, and confirmed your wildest dreams by telling you that I'm Critch." That typically shut people's suspicions down, though Aaron didn't think of himself as a manipulator.

"You're not Critch," she said.

She studied him again. Fuck, what had Critch done?

"Wait a minute," she said.

"I need a cigarette," he said hurriedly. Our Relentless Shadow

Alibis and a Suspicious Shortness

tried to escape outside. As if she wouldn't follow.

"I think I'm going to need one too."

They went outside and lit up. God fucking damn it. Midge lit a Kamel Red. She wasn't scared. She was relieved, mid-eureka.

Tyler and Drea sat down on the other side of the patio. Thank a god, a distraction. Your Imminent Unforwarned Reckoning narrowed his eyes, prepared to chew out his business partner. In a sad way, Aaron was proud of him for potentially cheating on Dot.

"Fuck a god! You really are Critch, aren't you?" Midge said, eyes so wide.

"It was nice to meet you, Midge. I have a business partner to murder now."

"No! You're not going anywhere! Especially after such an off-color joke. If you are Critch, then what really happened last night? Did you actually beat the hell out of Jazz?"

Her Dear Apocalypse turned around and let his height work its magic.

She shut the fuck up, but the five-foot redhead followed anyway. The Antagonist cast his shadow across Tyler from behind. He didn't notice until Drea looked up and gulped.

"Hello, Tyler."

He flinched as if Mr. Bennett had hit him on the back of his head.

"Oh, hey. What are you doing at Cataran's? It's kind of the last place I expected you to be..."

"Let's go for a walk," he said.

The patio paid attention to them. Tyler and Drea didn't say anything, just followed the tower of Aaron like the naughty children they were. Tyler hunched inward like a dog who shit the bed.

"What the hell, man? I really don't see what the big deal is? I mean, Amber and Jeff are solid. They've been around for a while. They're good, they know what to do, man. I trust them, you trust them...Don't worry about it."

"Of course you wouldn't see a problem leaving the store to be run by a twenty-year-old punk kid and a depressive who can't think, outside of trying to be nothing. Amber freaks if anything

The Antagonist's Prison

doesn't go according to dogma. Not to mention that both of them are distracted by some dire matter of what-not."

"Fuck a god, Aaron, have some faith, man. If there's a problem, they'll call."

"Let's poll the audience. Ladies, if there was a problem at work, what would you do? Call your boss, or try and fix it yourself?"

"Try and fix it," Drea said, her hand raised. She surprised the group by choosing Side Aaron.

"When would you call?"

"Only if it got really bad, like, I couldn't fix it. Or if I made the problem worse," Drea said.

"I should hire you," Her Dear Apocalypse said.

"Actually, I need a job if you've got one. The Co-Op isn't working out too well, you know, as a job. Like, I don't get paid to work there."

Midge shook her head. Aaron's phone rang. Everyone silenced as he looked at it. It wasn't the store.

"I need some good news, whoever this is. Don't let me down."

After a pause. "Am I speaking with Mr. Aaron Bennett?"

"Yes. What can I do for you?"

"This is Sergeant Williams with the Indigo Bay Fire Department. Do you lease the property at 802 Main Street, Indigo Bay?"

Tyler went white.

"I have a feeling this is not the good news I need," Aaron said, ego-strippingly to all involved.

"Mr. Bennett, there has been a fire at your place of business. We can discuss the details when you arrive."

"I'll be there in five minutes. Thank you, sir." He hung up and faced Tyler as his features relaxed down into purpose. "Fuck your mouth, Tyler."

Aaron Bennett tore at full speed. He beat cars to the store. The three others followed behind as best they could.

A plume of chemical-smelling smoke spun from the back of his shop, blackening the alleyway. After a brief chat with the fire-folk, a cop approached him for questioning. He asked about the

Alibis and a Suspicious Shortness

spray-painted message on the wall outside the office. 'Not even Critch can stop me.' The writing surprisingly neat, like they used a stencil. Critch told the officer the message meant nothing to him.

The fire started beneath the dryer. Someone cut the grating and threw a rag onto the heating component. The back a charred wreck, but the wall separating the front from the back, along with the door, was fireproof. When the cops asked if Aaron had any enemies with intent. He said no, he didn't, but Tyler might.

The Antagonist killed all his adversaries many years ago.

He wasn't worried about the store. Heavily insured. Madam Ava coached him to account for Murphy and his Law, and the destruction it could ensue given the opportunity. What concerned Mr. Bennett was how to maintain his employees financially until the store was back up and running.

Amber didn't seem to care about being temporarily unemployed. After questioning, she just climbed into an old red truck. Through the back window, Aaron saw a black beanie with blonde hair as they shifted into gear and cruised away. Not exactly the people anyone expected Amber to hang out with.

Jeff wasn't there when they arrived. Aaron needed to have a chat with him about accountability. But this was Tyler's fault, and he knew it. He could deal with the insurance company. The Lady Made Of Dark's Bump In The Night left him with the cops so he could answer questions. Aaron went back to his car. It was more efficient for him to walk to the store. Midge still tailed him in a brisk jog. Underneath the windshield wiper a small note written in elegant handwriting.

Hello Mr. Bennett,
Do you remember me? Twin is back.
Talk to him about the events of last night.
2048 Mission Pine Pass, Condo F.
See you soon.
Love, November

The Antagonist's Prison

More cryptic notes from the insane Widow.

Midge read the note and looked to Aaron like he knew what to do.

"Who's Twin?" she said. "And why does the letter smell like violet?"

"The Widow in Yellow, I guess, likes the smell."

"And who is The Widow in Yellow? You raise more questions than you answer."

"November, The Widow in Yellow, was a guardian of sorts. Look, I know you're super stoked about Critch, but you shouldn't be. The less you know about me the better."

"You can't tell me what to do. Besides, we're now tied together. I know more about berserking than most. If you want to understand it at all, I'm your best resource," Midge said. Her voice never got past adolescence and made her sound like a cartoon character. Aaron didn't mind it, but he saw how it could be irksome to some.

"I don't want to understand it. I want to ignore it." Period in black sharpie.

"That's dumb. So, who's Twin?"

"He's a hacktivist. Him and I have a history."

"Not a good one I take it. Did you kill him?"

"Yes."

"No one stays dead anymore!" she said with a toothy grin.

Aaron unlocked the driver-side door. The thing about having an old car with manual locks was that he had to reach across the way to unlock the other doors. Midge tried to get in but was shocked that it wasn't open. Unfortunately, Critch parallel parked tight. It was going to take some doing to get out. Midge took the opportunity to run around and stand in His Unflinching Grin's way. He sighed and rolled the window down. She leaned in to rest on the door, looking like an over-educated sex worker. Aaron didn't say anything.

"Look. I know you don't need me around. And I know that I'm just being selfish. I thought that I could say something along the lines of 'you need me' and all that. It's obvious that you don't."

Alibis and a Suspicious Shortness

"You're not doing a great job of convincing."

"I'm not. I'm asking politely. I really need to know more about Critch," she said with a sincerity twinge that plucked hard.

"If you knew anything about Critch. You'd know that could very well be the worst thing to know more about."

Midge's head fell. She stepped back. Aaron continued to pull out as she watched, halfway to tears. Critch was not done with this one. She was going to bug the fuck out of him until he gave in. She ran her hands through her fiery hair. Face red with disappointment.

While The One Who Stares Back didn't have much in the way of humanity left, her frantic curiosity did compel his interest. This girl had more than the academic journalistic quality The Antagonist usually associated with Critch prods.

He finished pulling out, stopped, waved her over. She jumped and made a child's noise. While she ran over, he lit a clove with the console's electric lighter. Half successful, but an ember stuck. It filled the car with acrid paper smoke trails.

"A few ground rules. Which you will break as soon as you can, I assume."

"Woah, sudden salt."

"Yeah, I'm allowing something truly stupid to happen."

Charlie appeared from his hiding place between the seats. He saw Midge and waved. Midge looked from the spider to Aaron.

"That's Charlie. Charlie, meet Midge."

"Umm, hi Charlie?" Midge said.

He poked her leg, left his leg extended, then looked up at her.

"He wants you to scratch it," Your Imminent Unforewarned Reckoning advised.

Midge raised her eyebrows but did it anyway. Charlie shuddered with pleasure then jumped on her thick legs and curled up next to her hip.

"He's really cute."

"Extremely. Back to what I was saying. You may pipe up with ideas, but you have no say in what happens from here on out. If you do, get off the ride. Second, keep the Critch prods to a minimum.

The Antagonist's Prison

Speakings of him bring him forth. Third, if you undermine me, legit make fun of me in front of someone we need to command respect from, I will push you off the ride. The people we will be talking to don't like their time wasted. They will already see us as a speck of dust on their bloody boots."

"I'm not sure I get it. I understand why you don't want a full discussion of Critch. But, I also don't want to tiptoe around your apparently fragile self-esteem."

"Not what I mean. Do you have a black heart of gold?"

"I once did, yeah, coming back into it. Do you?"

"Not intentionally. We will be meeting with dangerous folk to figure out what happened to Jaslynn and ultimately decide if she is lost to the world. While we talk to these people, we have to stand together. If you mock or question me during those moments, it will ruin everything. Critiques after or before are fine. During will not be helpful."

"Don't cut your balls off until we're in private, easy mode. Your circle is everything."

Dissociations and a Brother

Whenever Midge was about to talk, The One Who Stares Back From The Void told her it'd make more sense if she just waited.

"Okay, if we're not going to talk, can we at least turn on the radio? You must be the last person without a Bluetooth player in their car."

"Don't listen to a lot of music."

"Is that because you're insane, or because you don't know what good music is?"

"I know what I like. I'm exposed to lots of music at work all day because of Tyler. I prefer silence. I tend to read on my porch, sometimes I listen to music after the sun goes down and Miss Peach doesn't want to chat."

"Who's Miss Peach?"

"The woman I rent from. She keeps to the upstairs and leaves me with a mostly-empty old Victorian house to keep up with," Aaron said as if he cleared out ghosts and blood-stained carpets on the regular.

"So what do you listen to after the sun goes down?" Midge said.

"Is what I listen to that important?"

"Yes. And I will get out of this car right now if you say Metallica or Mumford and Sons."

The Antagonist's Prison

"Who? I tend to listen to Pelican. Red Sparrows. Explosions in the Sky. Caspian. I guess, progressive instrumental stuff?"

"Okay, post metal. So do you listen to Isis or Necrosis?"

"Neither. Never heard of them."

"Then how the fuck have you heard of those other bands? Oh no, you're not a Godspeed Black Emperor dude are you?"

"Not that I know of. I find bands whenever I go into Fallen Music, which is often, since Adam fires an employee every other week and needs a new custom shirt for his next hipster. If I like what's on, I'll buy that CD. Do you have a problem with those bands?"

"No, it's just not what I expected. I thought you'd be into Hardcore, or something thrashy. Bright Eyes, maybe? Whatever people who think they're complicated and misunderstood listen to."

"Nope. I don't feel I'm complicated. Everyone else seem to be the complicated ones. Are you recording this conversation?"

"I remember every conversation I've ever had."

"Sounds exhausting."

The sound of the world stopped as Midge said, "You have no idea."

Weird sensation to say the least.

Mission Pines was a backwoods route around the outskirts of Downtown and before the Forest District. The buffer of poor before the vertical climb to the places with an actual view. Apartment complexes and houses falling apart with their dead lawns. Narrow streets rammed with faded cars, gray asphalt Pollocked with black seam lines.

Cracks in the faded pink stucco wall of Mission Pines Condos exposed disfigured cement beneath them. Half-dead, sunburned plants draped neglected on patios. Condo F at the back. The tires of Mr. Bennett's Civic quite displeased with the cesspool potholes. This was not the expected result of Twin's sizable income. Part of the façade.

"I'm sorry to keep you in the dark about all this," Critch said.

"Are you kidding? I feel like I'm in a novel. Can I be the love interest?"

Dissociations and a Brother

"I thought Jaslynn was the love interest. That would make you...the plucky sidekick? Does that make me the protagonist? I'm not much of a hero."

"PLUCKY? Whatever. I guess I'm fairly plucky. I don't know, you seem like a good guy, diamond-in-the-rough sort of anti-hero," she said.

"You know people literally call me The Antagonist," Her Dear Apocalypse said, getting out of the car. With a flash of red, Charlie BASE jumped off the car seat. Aaron supposed he could come.

"That part of you is The Antagonist, what about the rest of you?"

"Doubt that I'm an anti-hero."

"Right. So, Mr. Not Hero or Anti-Hero, what's the plan? If you're not a protagonist or an antagonist, does that make you an agonist?" Her tone suggested an eye roll. But then with complete sincerity, "Holy crap, you're an agonist."

"Twin will recognize me, but he won't be able to resist a cute redhead with tattoos standing outside his door. You can do the knocking."

"Why? Is he some sort of rapist? Or just super personable."

"Twin is the embodiment of the worst stereotypes of nerd culture."

"Sadly, I know exactly what you're talking about. Still, what the fuck am I supposed to say? That I'm a Girl Scout selling cookies and tentacle porn?"

"Whatever you want, just get him to open the door," Aaron said breezily. Not like he was ready to murder Twin. That'd be ridiculous.

Critch hid to the side and Midge knocked. She got a little smile on her face.

"Pizza delivery."

"Just a minute," through nasaled gunk. The door unlocked and opened with more oomph than expected. Very tight shorts and a t-shirt with three wolves howling at the moon. The shirt not quite long enough to cover Twin's furry stomach. Frizzy black hair, grease-lined, and forever five o'clock shadow.

The Antagonist's Prison

He noticed Midge was not holding a pizza, then The Lady Made of Dark's Bump in the Night.

"OH FUCK!" He cocked his head to one side and said into his shoulder, "That's why you always check, you fucking fuckwad."

"She said pizza delivery!" he said, now facing straight ahead but not at either of them.

"Dumbass," he said, talking into his shoulder again. "You didn't even order a pizza. Who announces that they're delivering pizza anyway?"

Twin tried to slam the door, but Aaron's boot was in the way. The door bounced off. Twin ran into his condo and disappeared into the kitchen.

"Didn't you wear some crazy gimp suit out there?" Midge asked. "How does Twin recognize you?"

"The gimp suit was for spectacle's sake. Regular hits like Twin, where he'd be the only witness, I wore nothing. I tended to tear off clothing."

"A naked man beating the hell out of you would be just as scary as the leather shit."

"I suppose. Twin?" Mr. Bennett said into the apartment, hesitant to step on the coin-flip sticky-or-stiff carpet. The dark but roomy condo smelled of long-rotted food. Mold polyps floated. A narrow pass cut through hoarder levels of trash. The odor of the house slammed them backward.

"I need your help. I'm not going to hurt you," The Antagonist said in the same dire tones as one who might hurt you.

"Noooo..."

They found him in the kitchen cowered next to a stove holding up an oozing comal. The trash can existed within the overflow of used frozen food packages. Charlie poked at him, huddling ineffectual.

His thick, hairy arms mottled and old. The skin sagged like it wasn't his. It was, though taken from other parts of his body. The One Who Makes You Undone tore the skin off his arms last time, and Madam Ava provided the repair.

"No one deserves Critch. Twin, would that pan really do any-

Dissociations and a Brother

thing against The Antagonist?"

"Who are you?" Twin said to them and not to his mental condition.

"He's The Fucking Antagonist, cretin," he said into his shoulder.

"Shut up! He's not The One Who Stares Back From The Void, he's way too calm, not blood red. Not fucking smiling!" he said with his voice squeaking in the dog range. Charlie shrugged and ran away into the rest of the apartment to do spider stuff.

"Who's the girl, kinda cute, too fat, though. Two out of ten, would not bang," Twin's twin said into his shoulder.

"Fuck off, scumbag," Midge said.

"I'm sorry," Twin said.

"Damn right you are, asshole," Twin's twin said.

"You said it, not me," said Twin, raising the frying pan at himself, talking with spacey eyes.

"Get it?" Aaron said to Midge. "Twin. I can't take away your trauma. No apologies will help. But I'm not here to hurt you."

Twin placed the crusty pan on the stove. Made eye contact, Aaron looked away first. They were in agreement.

"So he talks to himself?" Midge said. "An asshole alter-ego? Although, aren't all alter-egos assholes?"

"Yup, except the asshole part is just his thoughts unfiltered. He has no mental block."

"I get it," Midge said, holding a stop sign hand. "I don't need things explained to me more than once."

"Noted," Critch said.

"You know how you have conversations with yourself in your head, well, I have those out loud," Twin said to an exasperated audience.

"The chick said she got it, dipshit," Twin's twin said with the disturbing tick to his shoulder.

"Well, some people say that but don't mean it!"

"I do," Midge said.

The microwave surface light the only light on in the condo. No TV, instead a massive desk with six monitors. One had a show

The Antagonist's Prison

playing, another a Japanese cartoon. The anime character basically dead on the ground with their leg twisted sideways and eye injured or gone. Two dollars said they were going to get up and win, even though they should have died from blood loss alone. A third monitor had a game with the character hovering actionless on a flying creature. One downloading a shit-ton of things, another on a website about kittens, and the last was a message board. Across all screens, random windows were obscured behind the primary programs. Including the colony of Bang cans, liter Coke bottles and Jack Daniel's handles lining the desk.

From somewhere in the room, a speaker played the same lyrics over and over again, "Warm...Leatherette," backed by a slow and boring beat. As soon as it was noticed, the song grated against their skins and minds. It started right up again. The music was going to be a problem.

Trash and foul clothes hid the couch. Most of the ground real estate devoted to towers of pizza boxes and a modern art installation of fast food trash. A closed blackout curtain hung behind the monitors. Under the desk, a massive computer tower chugged with a blue light. A weaving path of thread-worn between the bedroom, the computer, and the kitchen. It would be a good guess the rest of the hidden carpet was still flush.

"How do people live like this?" Midge said.

"They ignore it. The mess is progressive. It doesn't just appear, there's a slow build until it's a mountain," Twin said.

"True. They also keep saying they'll clean it up tomorrow. When they have free time. Tomorrow never comes, does it?" Twin's twin said.

"Are you done insulting me?" Twin asked, waiting.

"Twin, I need a favor," Aaron said when Twin's other side seemed finished.

"You can't afford me."

He technically could afford him, but Twin didn't know that. "Not that kind of favor. A real one."

"Like a Favor?" he said with evil hand twists.

Dissociations and a Brother

"Sure?"

"A Favor from Critch? Alright. What's up?" He weaved around his switchbacks to his computer and sat in a high-end swivel chair. He closed the movies and games and everything until it was just an image of an intricate, fantastical landscape broken up across the six screens.

"My shop was arsoned today. I think by the same guy who kidnapped a girl named Jaslynn last night at the harbor. Wondering what you could find?"

"Oh," Midge said. Opened and closed her mouth, eyes searching different corners of the room.

"K, give me a minute." Twin's hands floated above his keyboard and windows magically appeared and disappeared. Words were typed and programs booted. Midge and The One Who Will Make You Undone left the condo for a cigarette.

"'Warm Leatherette?' Fuck a god, I was going out of my fucking mind. Are all your friends that weird?"

"Twin is not a friend. I just know how to do this 'meeting with contacts' lifestyle. I spend my free time alone. I'd rather not do this."

"Nothing wrong with that. And you coulda warned me about his grafted arms."

"Truth be told, I forgot I tore the skin off his arms last we met."

"How do you tear just the skin off?"

"I assume quickly, like a tablecloth trick." Your Unforewarned Reckoning mimed the motion.

Midge cackled before they settled into awkwardness for a second. Midge just over five-foot, with a soft face contrasted by diamond-cutting fractal green eyes. Pear shaped with all her weight in her hips and legs. Midge took off her green sweater, leaving a gray tank top and purple bra straps. Tattoos of grape vines intertwined with a river flowing down both of her undefined arms.

"Where'd you get your tattoos?" His Unflinching Grin said, attempting conversation.

"Up north, I grew up on a vineyard with my parents. I have a

The Antagonist's Prison

lot of nice memories from there. Do you have any tattoos?"

"No, can't get any, too many scars."

"You must have an open area somewhere."

"If you saw me without a shirt on, you wouldn't say that."

"I don't believe that, not one bit. Although, that would explain why you're wearing a heavy jacket and turtleneck on a random spring day."

"I'm not going to take my shirt off."

"Take your shirt off."

"Why?"

"You don't strike me as the shy type."

"I'm not. I just don't want to make Twin jealous."

"See, you're lying again. Take your shirt off. Let's see that skinny body of yours."

He shrugged and handed her his Djarum. Took off his hat, jacket, and turtleneck. White scars of various severity latticed his entire chest and back. More scar tissue than regular skin. Some sealed with surgical precision, others jacked from self-healing avarice. A body not to be looked at.

"The bruises are from last night, I think."

Midge reached out, mesmerized, and felt down his chest. Her fingers bounced on the divots and raised edges. Her touch warm and alien. Critch disliked it.

"Fuck a god...at least you're ripped for a skinny guy."

The Antagonist laughed. It was unsettling.

Midge showed a remarkable ability to make light. "How are you still alive?"

"That's an excellent question."

"Imagine it during the flush...red and white skin."

Hm, he never told her the details of his berserk. She had done her research. Or maybe the flush was a thing. Aaron wasn't sure.

"Hey! I found something!" Twin yelled from inside. Your Imminent Unforewarned Reckoning put his shirt back on. Midge tied her sweater around her waist, and they went inside. Charlie waved a tiny spider arm as he left the apartment. Apparently to wait at the car.

Dissociations and a Brother

"It was hard as shit to find anything. All surveillance of the harbor last night was scrubbed. But I found some footage from a shame video uploaded an hour ago."

They flanked Twin and his newly cracked, fetid smelling Bang can, while his computer buffered a video. Three people on a tiny fishing boat. They were all hammered. The cameraman filmed a guy taking advantage of a college girl. Her lips drenching his neck between her giggles. The stoner laugh of the cameraman was not endearing. The unfortunate young.

Twin instructed to watch the background. In the distance, the waterfront blurred behind dense fog. They could barely make out Mr. Bennett's lank figure wailing on a large creature. Though just silhouettes, they could see the iconic alien bends, impossible contortions and ungodly flails of Critch. He flickered around, occupied space only as an afterthought. Still frames of strobed horror. Watching the video got The Antagonist heated. The rush sucked him into his head, overwhelmed his eyes, and ebbed his hearing.

He turned away and sat on the couch, crushing a bag of sharp chips. Midge came over and asked what was wrong. Something in her mind triggered, and she examined his devolving condition.

"You're the real thing aren't you?" she said with more pity than he'd ever heard from someone who learned what he was.

"I think you're pretty fucking dumb to be asking that question at this point."

"Shut up and breathe deep." She pulled up his sleeve and saw the hardened muscles and veins on his arm, his skin flushed beneath the scars.

"Seriously, guys, you're missing some carnage," Twin said.

He Who Smiles Back kicked the landfill table across the room into the back of Twin's chair. Twin dove under his desk with a thundering holler. It relieved the berserker's rush for a moment before it came on with renewed vigor. Papers and trash floated about the room. Bottles clanged and shattered.

"Shut the video off, Twin!" Midge said.

Aaron fell on the couch as Twin closed the windows with

The Antagonist's Prison

keystrokes. The blood in his neck and temples slowed and pulsed normally.

Twin frantically typed something into his computer.

"There was a man at the end of the video running away from you with a girl in tow. He got on a boat and sped off. I'm asking around."

"Let's have a cigarette, Aaron."

"Good plan."

Outside, his hands vibrated into uselessness. Trouble lighting the cigarette. Midge took the lighter and helped.

"So, what's the sign that I need to run? You held yourself through the flush. That's impressive," Midge said.

"You know a bit about berserking, huh?"

"I told you already, I know quite a lot about berserking. So, at what point do I need to run?"

"The smile."

"Uh, what kind of smile?"

"Dunno, it always happens right before I black out. My face rips in half and I'm gone."

Midge blinked twice, recorded for later. "You don't hulk out, you stay skinny..."

"All I know is that my body rearranges. I don't get bigger or anything."

"Rearrange? In what way?"

"No clue, but it's painful."

Twin peaked outside, looking for a bomb. "Someone found the video just like I did and deleted it. I saved most of it, but I can't ask around until interest in the video wanes. The man was Mr. Kinns, and he's out of reach. Sorry."

That confirmed Madam Ava's prediction, also The Firemimes' efficacy in hiding Critch.

"What do you mean?" Midge said.

"He's a Faction Head in The Underground. So unless you know how to get down there, that girl is gone."

Alarms went off from inside the condo.

Dissociations and a Brother

"Holy shit!" Twin locked the door.

They got back into the car. Midge collected Charlie asleep on the hood.

"So now what are we gonna do?" Midge asked.

"This will soon become completely fucked. I'm going to The Underground. Stay away, Midge."

"Fuck your mouth. I'm coming too."

"Bad idea. Suit yourself."

Midge steeled. Hopefully strong enough.

"I need to go see Raile first."

"Why?" Midge said as Aaron sped back and forth to get out of the complex as fast as possible. "And what's with the hurry?"

"The Firemimes are coming..."

"With that kind of tone, yeah, get the fuck out."

As they sped along Mission Pine Pass, they passed a large blacked-out luxury car speeding equally fast in the opposite direction. It was followed by a large black van that Aaron had never seen the outside of until now. Poor Twin.

"I take it those were The Firemimes by the way your face dropped."

"They looked more suspicious than I thought they would."

"A blacked-out car that size would get double takes no matter the circumstances. So what's next for our adventure?"

"Drea said you and Raile had a cold war going, or some such."

"Not really, we had completely separate contacts before I left for Europe four years ago. When I left, she and Gradick absorbed my people into their fold. Why?"

"Gradick was killed last night."

"The...WHAT!?" Midge shrieked.

"They were in The Tunnels for some reason. And shit went bad. I don't know the whole story, but I do know Raile went on a rampage across Indigo Bay last night. She's being taken care of by her brother and Pelican. I'm going to see how much condolence I can offer."

"Fuck...Gradick just proposed, didn't he?" Midge said. Her

The Antagonist's Prison

lips quivered and tears surged.

"Yeah, I was going to be his best man."

"How does that make you feel?"

"I was a little broken up earlier. Better now. Death means a little less to me."

"Don't you dare say because you've seen so much of it."

"I wasn't planning on it. Something like that."

"Poor Raile...I'm going to miss Gradick," Midge said, a quarter away from tears.

"The world has lost a remarkable human being," The Antagonist said. Even his voice quivered if Midge gained the ear for it.

Aaron turned into Breckberry and Irgon Circle, before pulling off a stemming street. Midge staved her grief as Critch parked in front of a beautiful Dutch-inspired two story. Gradick's old Sportster Volvo in the driveway. That's gotta be a bitter reminder. Out front, a huge black Escalade with a white car trailer. Two ancient Jacaranda trees reached out over the street, shading not only Gradick and Raile's house but the one across the way. Browning petals on the asphalt, purple blossoms falling.

Aaron parked in the driveway, then walked to the front door with Midge following. There was another letter in The Widow in Yellow's cursive waiting, wedged in the front door.

"Not what I expected from The Miscreant King and Queen," Midge said.

"It's a nice house, huh?"

"Adorable."

No one answered. The One Who Will Make You Undone peeked into the window. No one in the living room. Damn it, Pelican, you had one job.

"Where is everyone?" Midge asked.

"I told them you couldn't stop Raile from doing anything."

"Stop Raile? Are you fucking kidding me? You think she's going back?"

"I hope not."

Aaron pulled out The Widow in Yellow's letter. Charlie jumped

Dissociations and a Brother

and landed on his back. He squirmed there out of boredom.

Hello Aaron,
Do you remember me? I'm sorry about what needs to
happen to Twin. You must be protected.
I look forward to seeing you in The Underground.
Love, November

From under Aaron's elbow Midge said, "Scary shit."
"You have no idea."
"It also still smells like violet. Why does she start these with 'Do you remember me?'"
"I don't remember her. So I can't answer that."
"How did she know you'd be here?"
"Probably knows how I think. Can't say."
"And she told you to go see Twin, knowing you would, only to attack him afterward. That's fucked up."
"No one said she was a good person. Everyone in that world is unapologetically evil."
Midge growl scoffed.
A bright reflection blinded as a silver BMW appeared in front of the driveway. A tall, chiseled man of Latino descent stepped out of the car. He immediately pulled a joint out of his black three-piece suit with a thin purple tie and took a massive drag. He held it for a long while.
"Fucking Christ," he whispered when he finally let the smoke free. He hadn't noticed the couple yet.
Aaron remembered the man's *iconics* from previous interactions.
"Rudy?" Your Imminent Unforewarned Reckoning said, still cautiously tentative in case he remembered incorrectly.
The man jumped back and reached inside his suit, perhaps for a knife. "Jesus Christ, Aaron! You are not the sort of man you want to sneak up on you."
"Sorry. Rudy, this is Midge, Midge this is Raile's brother, Rudy."
"Cool," Rudy said.

The Antagonist's Prison

"Hi. My condolences."

"You weren't able to keep her down were you?" Aaron said.

"No shit, brah. Not at all. Have you met my sister?"

"How was she holding up?"

"Not well, dude." They smoked for a minute. Him on his high-end pot, Aaron on his clove. Rudy offered the joint to them. Midge took a puff.

"How are *you* holding up?" Rudy asked Aaron. "I know you and Gradick were brothers."

"I'm fine with it. Did my mourning earlier."

"Naw, fuck you, man. I know how close you two were. Raile loves you too. I love you. How can you be so careless with that?"

"I guess I just have a different point of view on death."

"Alright, dark wisdom dispenser. Gimme something. Now is as good a time as any."

"I dunno. Never saw the use in worrying about my life. I see a bit of freedom in how inconsequential we are," One Of The Most Consequential People said.

"We care about you, bro." Six-foot Rudy brought Aaron down in an awkward dude, back of the neck grab, despite the ten-inch difference. "No need to feel so cynical, you've got family right here. We need each other right now."

"Don't mistake my cynical views and values as calls for help. My esteem is high and all that. Gradick understood that," Critch said.

"Man, Gradick understood everyone. Kat's going to The Underground. Do you know what that means?" Rudy said.

"I do. I'm sure she'll be fine." That wasn't remotely true. But you gotta lie to people sometimes.

"The fuck kind of life do you live?" Midge asked, gesturing to the house, the car, the bro, the One Who Stares Back, the world in passing.

"What do you know of The Underground, brah? I've been there. Most surreal and dangerous time of my life. I can't tell you what that means. It was fucked, man."

"I know."

Dissociations and a Brother

"Okay, dude, real talk. Who are you?"

"My name is Aaron. I own a silkscreen store."

"Alright, spin that yarn. Pelican hates you, why? You always seemed cool to me."

"Pelican hates you?" Midge said with scrunched but also raised eyebrows. Impressive. "Pelican doesn't hate anyone."

"You know damn well why Pelican hates me," Her Dear Apocalypse said.

"She knows?" Midge said.

"She knows everything."

"Player, I know you. I respect you. But apparently you've been hiding something from me, my sister, and her man. Enough to make a fly-ass chick like Pelican spit your name out of her mouth. So what's going on?" Rudy said as he ground the joint into the driveway. "I've known Pelican for years. Man, does she hate you."

Rudy leaned forward and spread his chest. Squared up to fight The Antagonist. Behind Rudy, Charlie's back legs played the world's smallest violin.

"No comment."

"What did you do to her?"

"Nothing personally. Her and I just exist for different reasons."

"What the hell does that mean?" Rudy said, with upped arms exasperated. "And how much do you know about The Underground?"

"Okay, fine. Check this out," The Antagonist said, passing The Widow in Yellow's letter.

Midge flicked her hand up frustratingly. Aaron didn't react. He knew what he was doing.

"What does this mean? Who's November?"

"As in Nova, the leader of The Firemimes."

"The Widow in Yellow?! Dude, why did you show me this? This is a threat on my life, seeing this." Rudy looked around for minders. There probably were some.

"You weren't kidding about that powerful people nonsense,"

The Antagonist's Prison

Midge said.

"And why are you on such familiar terms with the leader of The Firemimes?"

"I was once very close with The Lady Made of Dark."

Rudy took a step back and scanned around paranoid. The blood in his handsome face drained. He breathed in too long. The hand holding the letter trembled before he dropped it. Charlie pounced on the paper as it hit the ground. Stamped on it twice for good measure. Rudy still had not seen the large red tarantula.

"Shhhh! You can't just say that name like that, brah. Even divulge her name beyond just saying Her. Dude, in certain circles, if I referred to Her at all, I'd be tortured to death. I don't want to know. I'm gonna be killed by the end of the night now. Fuck!"

"No, you won't."

"And why the fuck not?"

"Because you're talking to me. I gave her the name."

"Shit." Rudy leaned heavy against his car. "I'm way beyond my caste."

"Yes, you are. Let me know if you hear anything about Raile."

"For certain."

They went over to Aaron's car and watched as Rudy loaded the BMW into the trailer. His Unflinching Grin waved goodbye, clove in hand. Rudy sat on the curb as the trailer lowered its gate. Gripped his gelled hair, crying.

"You are truly a spymaster," Midge said.

"Is that sarcasm?"

"Halfway. Instead of lying, you just increased the shroud of mystery around you, which only raised more questions. I can't say it's not effective, but I can say it's not the most effective way of dissuading people from looking into you."

"I've found the shroud to be more useful. When someone who looks like me says there's nothing special about him, people don't accept it. But, if I'm a man with a past who says he doesn't want to discuss it, people are more or less agreeable to that."

"Hard line to balance."

Dissociations and a Brother

"It's gotten easier with practice. Plus, it's fun to watch them struggle with the spiderwebs unfolding from the mists of my past."

"One, I hate that metaphor. Two, you sound like Jazz. Three, how complex is your spiderweb?"

Aaron loved that she followed through. Most people never made it to two. "Densely. You wonder why I don't put more effort into fixing myself? It's because all my mental capacities are devoted to maintaining a lie. One that must stay hidden."

Midge sighed. "I sadly can't disagree on any particular point. Your struggle is real. I mean that truthfully."

Her Unflinching Grin was rarely sympathized with. He could get used to it. But knew it would leave soon.

Doctorates and a Homunculi

A cute elderly couple waved at Midge as Aaron pulled into the driveway. They held smoking pipes and stood content with weight sunk into their hips, a state of relaxation Aaron envied. New life goal. The Antagonist normally walked as loose as he could, but when he wanted, the world moved around him like a river around a rock.

Midge lived in the attic-turned-studio of the orange and green Victorian house. Two blocks from Cataran's, on Trinity Street, one of the parallel streets to Main. The partners out front spent their days watching the constant stream of cars trying to avoid the traffic jam of Main. A separate stairway led up from the gardened backyard of bulbous succulents. Aaron parked next to an old, blue Prius.

Aaron took the stairway slow, heavy on the railing. Beneath it, an outdoor shower. American-written Indian music played from the older couple's floor. Midge's studio was small and a bit warm. A bookcase overflowed across the floor. A laptop on a comfy looking couch, which Aaron assumed was a futon, no tv, an empty kitchen, and a fixed gear bike.

She removed her gray tank top as she stepped inside. Grabbed a backpack and went over to her dresser. Aaron listed off a jacket, some comfy clothes, and good shoes. Then he turned around as she grabbed a sports bra and unhooked the one she was wearing.

The Antagonist's Prison

Waited until she said it was okay to turn around. She changed into baggy camo pants, newish red high top Cons, and a white tank with a maroon leather jacket.

"No weapons, tools, or anything?" Midge said.

"I've got that covered." She glared at him with a questioning tone.

At the trunk of his car where he kept that ancient oiled canvas backpack. Took out the books, notebooks, and various chargers from its bowels. Put in two cans of mace, a hammer ax used for camping, duct tape, zip ties, bandages, and superglue. Lighters, fuel, twine, protein bars, water, and a flask of moonshine.

"It looks like you're putting together a rape kit."

"I know what to expect. You've heard of The City Beneath The Bay, what do you think about the stories?"

"I think you're testing me."

"Yes."

"I've heard a lot of things. It mostly sounds like anarchy. Do what you want, no repercussions. Sounded cool at first, until I realized who'd be able to thrive in that environment."

"That's the right kind of thinking. All the stories you've heard are true."

Besides Gradick and Raile, Midge was the first person who Aaron had met who rightly assessed the wretched City Beneath.

"There's a boat that takes people there around ten, most nights." It was three. Time flies when you're busy. Her Dear Apocalypse didn't like it.

After a pause. "A boat...? Uh, we have some time to kill. Dinner?"

"Sounds like a plan." Aaron missed Midge's fear twitch.

Before the Canyon District off the highway was Springwood Avenue, a three-block shopping street. Couture shops sat empty of customers. Consignment stores equally void lined the street. Women adorned with shawls and strange shoes, boys in polos and cargos or sharp suits with identical haircuts. They strolled with cof-

Doctorates and a Homunculi

fee cups talking about subjects Mr. Bennett couldn't understand or relate to. No one went into the stores, just windowed it in, pointed occasionally. The places didn't need to make any money, just pet projects for bored spouses, paid for by their actual moneymaker partners.

The Miscreant Royalty looked down on this culture. Amber was terrified of Springwood. The way folks seemed to know you're poor on sight. The Antagonist had seen more wealth and power than these folks could fathom. At the end of the night, he saw it as a different scene. Just owned different values and motives. Neither correct nor wrong.

Both of the restaurants glut with the public. The line to the sandwich counter five deep. The old man behind the counter moved like he died years prior. After ten minutes, they ordered from the choices of turkey, roast beef, pastrami, or chicken. Coffee on the side, to go.

The old man put the paper-wrapped sandwiches on a wicker plate with a pickle and napkins. Twenty dollars each. Midge grabbed a tiny bottle of champagne from the sliding door fridge. Aaron asked her to grab him one too. People greeted her like a friend. Many of them recognized Aaron, but not for being The Antagonist, and agreed the two should be hanging out together. Their approval encouraged The One Who Stares Back for some reason. They found a tiny table in the corner of the crowded patio. Critch opened the sandwich paper and furrowed. White bread smothered in mayo and turkey.

"Why is this twenty dollars? I could make this for a buck."

"I like it. It tastes like the sandwiches my mom used to pack for me when I went to school."

"Exactly. This is a lunchbox sandwich," Aaron said.

Midge took a big bite and smiled.

"It tastes like nostalgia," she said, sandwich stuffed into her cheek. "I hate to treat you like a test subject, but I'm curious about something. Would you consider yourself a nervous person?"

No umbrellas. Indigo Bay's afternoon sun burned Mr. Bennett's layered shoulders. He chose to sit facing the sun so Midge wouldn't

The Antagonist's Prison

have to. He put sunglasses back on. Midge never took off her green-rimmed heart-shaped ones.

Charlie crawled out on the table from Midge's purse. Grabbed a chip and danced with it. Midge giggled.

"You don't have to be like this," Our Relentless Shadow said to Charlie. He hunkered and swayed. "Do as you wish. I can't recall ever being exceptionally nervous."

"I'm just curious what quality makes you a natural berserker. Do you know how it works?"

"No, when I think about it too much, I usually stir up Critch. Never dwelled on it long."

"So, most people have a switch in their heads," Midge said. "Yes, I'm ignoring your passively vague warning. As long as that switch works, it prevents us from doing anything physically damaging to ourselves, a self-preservation mechanism. It's why even though breaking a finger is only slightly harder than breaking a carrot, you can't do it to yourself." Midge downed the champagne with an alcoholic swig. Impressive way to treat champagne, The Antagonist supposed. "People who fight a lot have a faulty switch. Nervous people or people with anxiety problems, get overwhelmed and that switches the switch off as well. Fuck, how awkward was that sentence? And because drugs affect brain chemistry, users often have faulty switches. But berserkers are people without a switch entirely. So, in a fight, they go all the way."

"I know plenty of people who get violent while drunk and don't remember anything the next day. But their rage tantrums, nothing like Critch." At least the pickle was good. Aaron struggled to find the nerve to eat the mayo sandwich.

"Do you always speak so oddly?"

"Sometimes the words come out weird. I don't do it intentionally. By all accounts I used to speak nonsense. A sort of permanent word salad. It helps if you don't remark on it."

"KK. Interesting. But that's what's so cool about you. Sorry, *interesting* about you. Or intriguing. You're a myth! Have you heard the tales about the Roman soldiers with horror stories of

Doctorates and a Homunculi

these crazy fighters who took on ten men with their teeth and didn't stop until they bled out?"

This talk caused no rattle in Critch's cage. Curious. "Sure, it seems to be all anyone knows about berserkers. They're Irish or whatever."

"There are berserkers in every culture. Most people just assume the Romans were doing what most people do while storytelling, exaggerate, embellish the details. You know, 'the fish they caught was this big!' bullshit." Aaron never met someone who could string together words so effortlessly. "Most people just excused those soldiers for making their shameful retreat less shameful. However, while I think most of those stories are exaggerations, I do think that there were a few legendary berserkers that really did do all of those things. That's why I've been looking for more information on Critch. He's, well, you are one of those legendary berserkers. But there's no real information on him. Just stories."

"To go on a tangent, we can come back to talking monsters later, possibly even encouraging Critch to have a romp in the hay in the scary way. My turn for questions. Why are you interested in berserkers?"

"Because I want to know what the female version of berserking is."

Critch had deemed the sandwich inedible. "Wouldn't it be the same as male? Get pissy, kill things. Lift cars to save babies."

"In traditional mythology, male and female trait spectrums are contradictory. What is the opposite of berserking?"

"Enlightenment? Becoming one with the force like some sort of Jedi?"

"No, see the Dark Side and berserking are the same, but very different in manifestation. Both from wrath, but one uses lightning, the other makes a rage beast. And the Jedi are peaceful and balanced, not good. Enlightenment is not berserking. I'm not looking for the opposite of berserking, I'm looking for it in its feminine form."

"Can't women berserk?"

"Of course, male and female qualities in stories refer to what's

The Antagonist's Prison

typical for a strawman version of male or female. Either gender can have each other's qualities."

"Don't talk to me like a student. Just tell me what you think the mirror of berserking is."

Midge took off her sunglasses, her emerald eyes flickered and The One Who Will Make You Undone understood.

"Ah, you have the female version of berserking. You think you berserk, but not in the usual way."

"Yeah," she said, smaller than normally projected.

"It's cool, we don't need to talk about it. I understand."

Her eyes flooded to bloodshot. "That's the goddamned problem, though. You're the only one who could possibly understand what happens to me."

Charlie ran over and tried to lift her hand to crawl beneath it but wasn't strong enough. Midge cupped her hand on top of him.

"Midge, I really don't think this is the place for your berserk. So enjoy your excellent overpriced coffee."

Midge smiled. "Are you some coffee aficionado?"

"I had some with an old friend yesterday. She had it priced per bean, corvette coffee or some such."

"Civet?" Midge said.

"Civet?"

"Yeah, civet. It's a small animal from Indonesia who eats coffee and shits out the beans, which are collected and sold to rich people. They're kept in small cages and force-fed coffee all day. It's pretty fucked up."

"Reasonably sure these civets were free range. It was very good. That was the best coffee I've ever had. The coffee I make at work is terrible. This coffee is on the higher end of that experience spectrum."

Midge laughed. "Experience spectrum? You're full of it."

"Maybe, but what would you call it?"

"Something less stupid-sounding. The coffee you make at work is terrible?"

"I have no idea. I'm just not good at making coffee. I've come to accept my shit coffee."

Doctorates and a Homunculi

Flogging Molly from a few blocks away and approaching fast. The sandwich shop turned to face a speeding flatbed truck weaving around, horns blared. On the bed, a band played 'Devil's Dance Floor.' Contraptions affixed the members to the bed as the driver gave no regard to laws. Amber in the passenger seat.

The One Who Stares Back From The Void made eye contact with her over the rim of his glasses. Amber pointed left and up, to the peripheries of the Canyon District. Aaron cocked his head and her eyes widened in embarrassment. Amber's face reddened as the strange crew passed.

Their music faded as the song switched to 'What's Left of the Flag.'

"That was Neil and Didds, right?" Mr. Bennett said.

"Yeah, who was the girl in the passenger seat? Really caught off guard when she saw you."

"Amber, one of my employees."

"I thought you said not all your friends were weird."

"I didn't think I was lying, mayhaps I was. Anyway, we were talking coffee."

Not a poor person here, and possibly none with an idea what it was like to be uncomfortable in life. Men wore button-up shirts and classy ties. Showed no signs of stress. No wonder a bagel here cost ten dollars. Good bagels, from Wick's Bake Shop over on Buckfields Drive. On a side note, a bagel from Wicks cost four dollars. Almost triple the price. Bold move, old man.

"Oh yeah, I've spent my whole life in academia." Apparently abandoning coffee. "In some ways I hate it. I love education and I can deal with the politics. It's the other students I have a problem with." Midge chuckled. "I was going out with this one dude named Josh for a while. Like a year. We were at a party once, with my friends, not his, because his circle considered me a moron. They made sure to point out my 'idiocy.' Defined their personality as knowing more than you. Everything had to be followed by an exception. Fucking infuriating. Anyhow, there was a guy at my party. Zach, I think, yeah. I would have thrown myself at him had I not

The Antagonist's Prison

been dating Josh. Zach, Josh, and I went outside. I think Zach knew I was unintentionally flirting with him. Zach and Josh were the only ones not drunk at this point. I was pretty intoxicated myself, much to Joshua's chagrin. Zach was sipping on a full tall glass of Glenfiddich, taking his time. He knew how to drink. Josh didn't have a drink. They began talking about high-end liquor. Josh only drank at parties where they busted out their finest for guests. He would have two fingers. And that's it."

The Lady Made Of Dark's Bump In The Night had no idea where this bubbly fast talk story was going or how it pertained to anything.

"It was supposed to be a power play. Josh used this ploy effectively before, but Zach didn't take it that way. Josh, in an attempt to show up Zach, and everyone else at the party, explained that he only drank at parties when it was polite. However, he only ever gave that speech at parties where everyone was hammered, so he could show how respectable he was. Zach nodded along and waited for Josh to conclude his speech slash argument slash gloat.

"Then Zach said, 'However you want to drink is fine. There's no wrong way to drink, except when you're doing it because you have to, or if you're drinking to make a point.' Less articulated, of course, but that's the gist. I realized that although Josh was very smart, he could still be shut down by some random dude at a party. I broke up with him two weeks later. Dated Zach for a month, then dropped him because as smart as he was, he had no ambition. He was cool, able to relax and listen to the silence, which was admirable, but not what I wanted. I haven't dated since then."

"That's nice, I guess. But what does this have to do with coffee? I'm usually pretty good at following bullshit stream of consciousness. Lost on this one."

"I dunno. I just realized you took coffee and made it a metaphor for how you live your life. And it made perfect sense to me because that's how I like to live my life. And you did that off the top of your head! Something neither Josh nor Zach could ever do, because they'd risk sounding stupid. And that analogy was stupid."

"That was the point of your story?"

Doctorates and a Homunculi

"Hey, I'm saying you're smart! See that's the other thing, you're not afraid of looking stupid. You don't need power plays, or anything. Do you know why?"

"Because at the end of the day I can rip them apart."

"Umm..." Midge, dejected at that remark.

"I guess I live my life on two mottos: Be interesting and be yourself. If you have a goal, you shouldn't change who you are to try and achieve those goals. You know, you should become a better version of yourself."

"You can't just be the same *you* always," Midge said, not quite getting there.

"Except you can, I mean, I like to think of a personality as a sphere," Aaron said, using his hands to make a sphere between them, as if she didn't know what a sphere was. "This is a personality. You can put shit on that sphere. Shit that makes you interesting, because all of our personalities are basically the same. You can't really change a sphere much. You can put shit on your sphere that other people like. Be happy because folk like your accessories. Or you can put shit on your sphere that you're proud of, and be happy regardless of what other people like. Finding out the difference is like the difference between Zach and Josh."

They left to get drinks Downtown. In pauses, as he drank whiskey and her a mojito, Critch and Midge's alter egos whispered to each other behind their smoke on the patio. Their elephants in the room eventually compelled every other conversation to brush against their ballooning presence. Eventually had to stop talking altogether. Or they'd have to acknowledge elephantine rumbles.

At a liquor store, Midge bought a pack of menthols and Aaron bought his fourth pack of Djarum Blacks for the day. He already coughed up blood that morning. Fiberglass cigarettes did that sort of thing. Considering the state of his body, he was not gonna live past 30, so who gave a fuck? He once had an old man tell him that's what all young people believed.

On the way to the harbor, they stopped by The Antagonist's bank. If watched all day long, no one came in or out of the lot.

The Antagonist's Prison

Indeed, no one worked there. The building empty save for a lone ATM, clean and shiny compared to the ruined parking lot covered in pine needles and the occasional palm frond. The side of the building had Indigo Bay Mutual in faded blue letters. Aaron pulled out a few grand. Called a number and wired that money back into that account.

"So, do you have a secret offshore account filled with millions of dollars you refuse to use?" Midge asked.

"Yes."

"How much money are we talking?"

"I'd rather not."

"Are we talking Cheryl Tunt from Archer, or like middle class life savings?"

"Who's that? I don't want to say, drop it."

"But I really want to know, now."

"That's good for you. But you will never know."

"Dick."

"Sorry, but to me, that money barely exists. I never want to touch it."

"But you just did."

"Yeah, because we're going to need at least a grand each down there, and I don't know about you, but I don't have a few grand of unallocated funds." He put the money in the inside pocket of his jacket and zipped it closed.

"I guess we need to stop by my bank, too."

Midge pulled out two grand, but they still needed more. Aaron sighed as he pulled up outside Miss Peach's house. Midge followed him to the base of the stairs. His Unflinching Grin crouched down and ripped a plank off.

He pulled up a small black box with chrome edges from beneath the stairs. Inside were maybe two hundred black obsidian coins about the size of a quarter. Featureless, somewhat easy to counterfeit, though it wouldn't be wise to do so. He grabbed thirty, more than enough.

"What am I looking at here?"

Doctorates and a Homunculi

"These are called Favors. You wanted to know how wealthy I am. These are wealth beyond measure. You can pay cash down there for most things, but some places only run with these because regular currency down there means very little."

"So how much are those equivalent to?"

"Not a clue. But Madam Ava paid me in these and claims that this amount of them makes me historically rich. They're more symbolic than anything."

With money hidden, they arrived at the harbor. Charlie found a happy corner in Midge's purse. The Antagonist mad-dogged the dock and found five people standing outside a yacht with no business being next to each other. Two wore expensive suits, one man guarding his craven boss. The other three were deviant to the point of hilarity, two boys and a girl with half-shaved heads, mohawks, and rejected, yellow-scabbed piercings.

Addressed the more important, suited man. He was old, and his depraved wrinkles with bulging knuckles suggested he was the sort of man who would wink at his partner and a week later Aaron would be killed in his sleep.

"Sir," because men like that needed to be recognized with a little title, otherwise they wouldn't talk to you. "How much longer until we depart?"

The less important man checked Your Imminent Unforewarned Reckoning out, then nodded. The old one turned to face Aaron and smiled.

"Any minute now, my son. This Captain always leaves on time."

The three punks examined Midge and Aaron. How did he get the wherewithal to talk to men of the like of that? The answer was unpretentious confidence.

"How's goes it, guys?" he said to the little punk rockers.

"What's it to you?"

"Quite a lot."

"Pssh. If you and that bastard over there can talk as friends. You and I are not friends."

"Did you hear what happened to The Miscreant Royalty?"

The Antagonist's Prison

"I live with Jeff. His stories, what they've done with Gradick and Raile. Fuck."

"First off, Jeff is my employee. Second off, I was going to be Gradick's best man before he was killed last night."

The punker suddenly didn't know what to do with Our Relentless Shadow. "Who killed the Miscreant King?"

The captain a young man with a patchy beard, Woody Allen glasses, of medium build and flannel shirt. He jumped off the ramp and looked at the seven.

"Welcome to my ship, *Daphne*," he said, fast and clipped, with weird salesmanship. Always about to pitch an idea. "My name is Christopher Wallace. I'll be taking you to The Underground tonight. Come aboard, have your payment ready."

The important men handed Wallace a lottery ticket. The kids came on next and handed Wallace a silver box. The Captain peeked in, nodded with glee, and let them aboard.

"Are you 'the' Captain Wallace?" Aaron said conspicuously.

"The only one I know of, if you're trying to talk your way on, it won't work."

"Did you get a call from The Widow in Yellow last night?" he said. More to confirm a suspicion than as an intimidation tactic. Worked both ways.

Wallace narrowed his eyes at Critch, sized him up, then evaluated Midge. She waved. "Who are you?"

"My name is Aaron Bennett. I'm a close friend of the Lady Made of Dark."

"I did receive a call from that wretched woman last night. I'm an alibi for your murder. That doesn't get you on my ship."

"The Lady Made of Dark would love it if I were to join her down there. She'd hate it if you prevented our visit."

"How do you know Her? And what gives you the right to call her anything but, Her?"

"Fine." Her Dear Apocalypse reached into his jacket pocket and pulled out a Favor. "How about one of these?"

Christopher looked sideways and drew back a bit from the

Doctorates and a Homunculi

black coin. He'd probably never seen one before.

"Where'd you get that?" he shock whispered.

"Will it get us on the boat?"

"Ahem, yes, welcome aboard."

Mr. Wallace gave the group a tour of the yacht. All the while he eyed Aaron, which led everyone else to eye him, too. Finally, Wallace showed them the drinks and went up to the helm. They grabbed a six-dollar bottle of wine each, no glasses, and went to the upper deck. Midge was twitchy. Her hands never let go of the railings.

"Sharing time," she said, lighting a menthol. "I think you should go first. Who the fuck is The Lady Made of Dark? Why did that guy take Jazz last night?"

"Fair questions. Second answer, I have no idea why Mr. Kinns took Jaslynn. He called her the Second Lust. I'm more pissed that he awoke Critch from hibernation. First answer is a little more complicated. What stories do you actually know about Critch? Got 'em? Every single one is true. The stories you haven't heard are worse. The Lady Made of Dark is a powerful oligarch named Madam Ava. She found me four to five years ago, that period in my life is gone. All I have are fleeting glimpses and terrible dreams. Though I do know I gave her that title.

"Something you need to understand about her, any person with that much power always seeks to garner more. I showed up at her mansion, and she was compassionate with me until I wrecked half her house. Then, she was elated with her newfound investment. I paid off in spades. She kept me as a hidden, gruesome weapon. Those I killed were bad, those who could escape the law. I remember very little from that time. Then, three years ago, I came out of the haze of Critch. I rented my place from Miss Peach, and with her understanding, along with The Miscreant Royalty's friendship, I slowly reintegrated. That's my story."

"So you're a murderer?"

The One Who Will Make You Undone raised an eyebrow at her.

"Sorry, blonde moment." Roots confirmed blonde.

The Antagonist's Prison

"I'm a peaceful person. I have no desire to kill people. I'm not remotely violent. Critch loves it, though. Until last night, hadn't had an incident for years."

Mr. Bennett always imagined when he finally told it to someone they'd run away, or cry, or call him a liar. Midge thought about it. If he were to guess, corroborating both her berserker education and the stories she'd heard of Critch. He felt relieved to finally pop his elephant in the room. Now it was time for Midge to pop hers.

"Not to interrupt your analytical," Your Unflinching Grin said. The corners of their vision dimmed. "But you haven't said anything about your dark side."

"I dunno, it's hard to explain. In all honesty, it's impossible."

"I don't give a fuck about impossible."

"True. Alright, you know how the brain ignores about ninety percent of what we see. It registers our surroundings as normal and inconsequential, it only processes what we focus on, or what seems out of the ordinary."

"Sure, makes sense to me." He took a long swig of the bad wine. Midge put her bottle between her red Cons.

"That's not how my brain works. I have a photographic memory, and hyperthemesia. My brain is a computer. If I run too many programs at once, my brain slows down as it attempts to process everything. And by everything, I mean I start noticing every detail of my environment: how many leaves are on the tree, all the pebbles on the side of the road, a catalog of every freckle on someone's face, the number of threads in my carpet (10 million). I'll stand there watching the world slow until time stops entirely, during which my brain records everything."

"So your berserk stops time?"

"Sort of. From my perspective at least. Time is a relative thing, depending on how active your brain is. A few seconds for most people can seem like hours for me during an Episode. Processing that much information at once is so overwhelming it hurts. I have seizures. My eyes bleed. I come out of it a bloody and exhausted wreck. The pain...I don't want to come up with a metaphor. I don't

Doctorates and a Homunculi

want to think about it, even now the world is slowing. Can we talk about something else?"

Midge's tether, coupling the two, shortened, pulling Aaron's longer. He shivered as the atmosphere slowed.

"Yeah, you said you grew up on a vineyard?"

"Good call. My name is Samantha Estire, but that's a horrible name, especially for the lifestyle I chose. When I was younger I went by Sammi, but when everyone had their growth spurt, I didn't, so everyone just started calling me Midge. I've been five foot for forever. My dad owns Estire Winery, and his wine regularly gets points in the high nineties, making my family pretty rich. I hate having money. I like the stress of a budget, so I cut myself off and paid my way through school."

She looked around the boat at the water and scooted closer to Our Relentless Shadow. Put his arm around her. Rare for him to conceptualize how large he was, but in this compassionate movement, he could consume all of Midge in his embrace.

"Why do we have to take a boat? Where is The Underground?" Midge said. Her body stone hard beneath him.

"You can take The Tunnels, but by boat is the best way."

"If it's under the bay, how can a boat take you there? Do we jump into a Super Mario tube, and pass through everything until the music changes, and we're in a new world? Will Toadstool appear just to inform us Jazz is in another castle?"

"Could be," he said.

"You have no idea what's going to happen, do you?"

"I generally go along with the people who seem to know what's going on."

"Then what happens when something goes wrong?"

"I leave them and make my own way."

"Harsh."

"The way you're phrasing questions makes me feel like you don't trust me. Life isn't about planning everything out, it's adapting, and assigning priorities. You're making me feel like an idiot."

"I just like to have a plan for when things go bad."

The Antagonist's Prison

"Seems like a waste of time. Murphy has laughed at me too many times for me to pretend to know what's gonna happen."

"Run riot. I don't like boats," Midge said, giving up.

"Is that a conversation grab? What the hell am I supposed to say to that? 'Why do you hate boats, little damaged person?' Or 'I totally hate boats too, fuck boats.'"

"My brother died on a boat and I almost drowned trying to save him."

"Seems like a valid reason for hating boats," Aaron said, not at a loss for words. Swallowing his own hesitation.

Midge's eyes total bloodshot. A drop of blood hit the white deck.

"Let's go inside," Mr. Bennett said.

The boat engines stopped. The yacht became an enemy. Aaron took Midge inside. Situated her on the couch. The suited men rushed by angry. Oh good, that confirmed this was not where they were supposed to stop.

"Did you hear that?" Midge said.

She jumped up and ran out to the back deck. Aaron smelled harbor steep. A squared hand gripped the back railing. Then three more. Two monsters this time. Critch thumped his chest out. Midge turned toward him with her cheeks covered in bloody tears.

"Aaron..." she said with a small voice.

His skin flushed. His smile creaked across his face. Midge's face dropped in horror. She stood erect, arms out. Spraying the air with crimson droplets. Her feet lifted off the ground, metaphorically right?

Mr. Aaron Bennett disappeared behind Critch's black reaches.

Corollaries and an Elevator

First step, open eyes. Okay, that was painful, now turn head. Aaron willed himself to sit up. Clenched his fists. Knuckles broken and purple.

"Are you Aaron?" Midge asked Wasn't Aaron Recently. In just her bra and underwear. A fire dried out their clothes. Cool, he was basically naked, not a state he was fond of. There was a towel over his bathroom mirror at home. He didn't like seeing all the damage. Charlie ran around the small fire to stop in front of the berserker. He rose up, as if assessing, then waved his whole front half at Aaron.

"Yeah," he said.

"Sorry, stupid question. If me stripping you is a problem, it shouldn't be. I liked what I saw."

Not exactly the reaction he expected. Surprised she was even talking to him.

"How're you?" Mr. Bennett said, almost accusatory. Though he did not feel he accused her of anything.

"I've had enough excitement for today." She sat cross-legged. Both her legs shook like she needed to pee. Her voice reserved. Charlie skittered over and reached out with a leg. Midge slowly eagle-clawed down to scratch it. It calmed her a bit.

"Where are we?" Not Grinning said.

"I saw Critch kill everyone on the boat..." Two bloody tears ran

The Antagonist's Prison

down her cheeks. She shook her head and swallowed tears and fear. "How the fucking hell do you think I'd be after seeing that Old God, Elder Thing spawn?! I refuse to think about what I saw, and yet my brain can't handle it and it's gnawing at the memory."

She grabbed a stick to probe the fire. So much for networking with those on the boat.

"Can I be honest with you, Midge?"

"Yeah."

"I admire strong women, it's something I'm attracted to. But there is no reason to be strong after what you've seen."

Midge scooted closer. Sobbed into his chest. "That...smile... you took so much, so much glee in killing them. I've never heard the sound of ripping flesh before. Their screams! Red hot, save for the white scars. The impossible spread of his lank torso. How you twitched around, barely a part of the world. Snapshots of terrible configurations. You don't have to hear their screams! I haven't slept...I never knew what it'd be like to see your berserk. I thought I'd be thrilled by the gore, like a slasher flick. The legends make it sound so glorious. Fuck that smile..."

"I know," He Fucking Didn't! said.

She stopped and became angry. The stages of acceptance. "No! No, you fucking don't! You don't know anything. *You* blackout! I saw it! And that's the thing...you're great. Well, Aaron is great. But what you harbor...goddamn, I mean, look at what you've done to your body! And you don't even know what I've seen, and what I can never unsee because of my stupid head. Critch's goddamn movements had no order, followed no logic. Blows hit before they started. Bounced around in a frothed bloody holocaust. They say in literary classes once you see the monster, it becomes less scary because it is now material. Critch is not like that...Nothing..."

Midge was near seizure now, vibrations upsetting her stomach, her eyes shut so hard her cheeks flushed.

The Antagonist wasn't sure how to comfort someone who'd seen him, there were rarely spectators aside from the Firemimes. If there were survivors, it's because Madam Ava stopped him and

Corollaries and an Elevator

meant for the witnesses to tell tales.

"Wait. Why are you still alive?" Our Resident Murderer said.

"That is not the right thing to say!"

"Perhaps not. But seriously, why aren't you dead?"

The switch in Midge's head was nearly audible, her education held her emotions under water, watched them bubble. "That's actually a really good question. Critch defended me. Possibly due to the recognition of our common plight? Perhaps the splintered berserker aspects reacted to each other?"

"A potentiality." It took some time for Critch to stand. He did a few stretches. New cuts on his body. One pretty nasty. "Was I stabbed?"

"Three times."

He felt his clothing, dry enough. They dressed. He picked up Charlie and placed him under his jacket's collar. "How did we get here?"

"You really were out the whole time, huh? You swam us here."

"How far?"

"Does it matter?"

"I guess not."

Indigo Bay's islands were already a heavy traffic zone. These privately owned land masses were the dirty secret everyone was okay keeping, whether affiliated with The Underground or not. The islands where foxes ran and the rich escaped their busy lives were actually tributaries to the City Beneath. You'd think the few who knew of The Underground and didn't support its function would protest its existence. There were enough passionate people in Indigo Bay for them to rally against the hedonism. However, there were people and places evil enough that you should just ignore them. If you did bring attention to the madness, it would swallow you. And if you stared into the void too long, Aaron stared back.

The Underground thrummed under them. Now it was just a matter of finding the entrance. It was possible he'd been here before. If he hadn't been berserking every time, he'd probably be an

The Antagonist's Prison

expert at getting into The Underground. As it was, they'd have to find their way around. A fence fuzzed. Obscured in the fog. Not much of a barrier. He moved to unsling his backpack when he realized that he had no backpack.

"My backpack is at the bottom of the ocean isn't it?"

"Yup."

"Mother fucker. I had cigarettes in a plastic bag in there. So much for being prepared. Murphy is a clever god. There were protein bars in there, too. At least Critch didn't take off my jacket."

"Why'd you have to mention food? Now I'm starving. Do you hear that?"

"No?"

"I hear a calliope," Midge said.

Our Relentless Shadow jumped for a superficial glance over the fence. A nicely groomed lawn with some wispy trees and a pond. Up a hill, a bunker. He hopped up and over the fence onto the top bracing, where he teetered. Crouched, he grabbed the fence and reached down far enough for Midge to grab his hand and pulled her up. She scaled the fence and jumped into the foot-high grass. There were speakers on the trees and on posts throughout the fairgrounds playing circus music. A rusted rollercoaster waited in the fog.

"What the hell is this? Is this it? You realize that The Underground is just a stupid conspiracy to me, right?" Midge said.

"No, this is an entrance, probably privately owned by the powers that be down there."

"Down where?"

"Beneath us."

"Like below this pedophile ranch?"

"Like beneath the bay. Let's role play for a minute. You're a pedophile and you're a sex addict. You need your kid ass to get off, and it's driving you crazy, consuming your every thought. But you don't want to go to jail. You're trying to be honest, and fucking kids is bad. Then, you hear of a place where, for the right price, they supply kids for you to fuck. For the right price, they'll even find kids who want you back. That's The Underground. Suicide

Corollaries and an Elevator

by murder? Check. Torture for both ends, check. Rape? You have no idea how many types of rape there are. There's a shop for everything. I remember one place where you could shake a baby to death. Sometimes a businessman says straight-faced to his family that he's going on a business trip, then comes down here to kill someone, gory meticulous."

"A purely evil society can't exist, it's like anarchy. There have to be safe places, leaders, sanctuaries, rules."

"Of course. In fact, there are seven Powers, each leading their own fanatic cause. Not everything in The Underground is evil, the whole point is to provide a tolerant place for odd people to go and be odd. Each Power can decorate their island entrance however they see fit. I'm thankful this one's pleasant."

Dawn streamed streaks of orange and yellow, only casting deeper shadows on the morning.

"I assume there's competition to become a Power," Midge said.

"Yeah, but it's hard to do. You need a neutral party to go meet each of the leaders and ask permission to move in on an established Power, usually by passing a test of some kind."

"That's surprisingly civil."

"The tests tend not to be. And we're going to need to pass them if we want to make a move on Mr. Kinns, or the whole city will turn on us, including Madam Ava. We don't want that."

They came out of the grass primed for an ambush. The mist circled, unconcerned with their anxiety. Perhaps the fog turned a blind eye to the foreboding. The calliope music cut out and a singsong voice spoke to them through the misty curls.

"Mr. Bennett. Ms. Estire," said the loudspeakers. "You survived two of my knights on the boat. But, how about all of them!"

Nothing happened. The calliope music came back on, quiet surroundings. Midge watched. Critch swallowed himself, burning the underside of his skin.

"What the hell!?" Mr. Kinns said.

"I think Mr. Kinns is fucking with us," Midge said, after a few minutes standing ready. "And why do you know more about The

The Antagonist's Prison

Underground than literally anyone else in Indigo Bay? I mean, you talk about it like you grew up there."

"There are quite a few people very knowledgeable about The Underground, they just know how to keep their mouths shut. Madam Ava loved explaining it to me in my half lucid moments."

Midge shut up after that. Before witnessing Critch firsthand, she wanted nothing but to soak up Critch lore. After experiencing him, she wanted to ignore him, just as Aaron did. Safer to pretend his constant threat wasn't an issue. It could all be over at any moment. You just needed to get on with your life. Pretend his atom bomb could never happen to you.

The path turned into a bridge across a pond. Fish came up to the surface and begged for food.

"You okay?" The Wrong Person To Ask That Question asked.

"No! Fuck this, I hate this feeling. I feel hunted, I feel like I need to save myself from the bogeyman of Indigo Bay. It's ridiculous."

"I'm not asking you to."

"Yeah, well, that doesn't change the fact that I feel like I have to, like it's some kind of fucking courtesy."

Still nothing, no signs of movement other than the greedy fish, who disappeared when they got off the bridge, poor fish. Aaron, For Now At Least, needed a cigarette.

Midge sighed at the edge of the bridge. "The tales of Critch, along with my own baggage, inspired my research as an academic. I loved hearing about a modern day legend. I desperately wanted to witness or meet him, because think about how much credence a firsthand account would give my research. I also wanted to see if Critch's eyes matched mine. If we'd recognize each other as sibling aberrations. But I don't know what to do with your violence."

Midge's voice started to crack as her smothered anxiety seeped out.

"I saw what Critch did, how you did it. I heard the bones snap, the sound of flesh tearing. His languid, ebullient movements as he rushed in a blur around the ship. Powerful men sprayed across that spreading smile as they fell in a circle. Innocent people's blood

Corollaries and an Elevator

dripped from your mouth and across your clothes. I'm surprised you can't smell it."

"I think it's time for me to make a funny joke."

"No. I don't know what to do about Critch's crush on me! Should I be relieved, or worried? I mean, I wish I could say that I survived Critch. I didn't. Instead of attacking me like everyone else, he rushed around me leaving bloody froths and buckled, dismantled bodies, all the while, his grin checked up on me and made sure I was ok. Maybe he did recognize my condition, and he liked it, a lot. But that goddamn Cheshire Cat visage is what I'll never forget! I'll get over the gore and chaos, but the animal, instinctual lust..."

The veins in Midge's eyes burst. She toe-tipped and her arms stretched out crucified. Until then, Aaron didn't know what a still world looked like. He'd been in empty, windowless rooms, been in deserted alleyways, accompanied only by corpses, but those were only quiet environments.

Now, the ripples in the water and the wisps of fog stopped, the world suddenly a photograph. Yet, Aaron wasn't frozen along with the rest of it. He could think just fine and could move, though not well. He no longer belonged and could never go back.

The veins and muscles on Midge's neck froze mid-seizure. She begged with red bleeding eyes. The grip of this motionless world bolted Your Imminent Unforewarned Reckoning's feet to the ground. He was aware of his arms' weight.

Midge's eyes pleaded. With his considerable might he was able to drag his back leg forward an inch. His neck cramped. His groin pinched with a potential hernia. The simple movement sapped his strength after one step. Aaron knew that Critch could move in Midge's berserk, but this was for Aaron and Midge. He let out a growl and a grunt, which helped a little, now she was only a foot away, not that it mattered. The temperature rapidly fell toward absolute zero, the sweat on his body froze. He reached out with the force of an angry god, pushing on his forearm, and as soon as he placed his hand on her rockhard torso, she collapsed. The noise of the world deafened.

The Antagonist's Prison

He knelt down to check on her. Midge grabbed him. She wanted to cry, but held it back. Her body trembled. Now was a good time to say something funny.

"At least labor pains will be a breeze, assuming you want a child."

A buffet of humored air shot. "That, or I'll freak out, and an eighty hour labor will become fifty times longer."

She grabbed hold and he lifted her to standing. He guessed that she'd never had someone else experience her time freeze, let alone help her out of it.

"I'm glad I met you. It seems my brain doesn't know what to do with you."

"Hope it stays that way. If that's what allows me to release you."

The bunker seemed haunted and abandoned. The Antagonist didn't remember any of this. He remembered being on a boat and lowered down through a tunnel or some sort of a ventilation shaft. This island chain had many entrances to The City Beneath. On second thought, this did seem vaguely familiar. Yes, this bunker belonged to The Smuggler Confederacy. Hopefully, Luciana remembered him in good graces.

"Do you think we can enter through that World War II bunker? Or do we have to spelunk down a pit, dodging punji traps?" Midge asked.

"This entrance was controlled by The Smuggler Confederacy," he said, hesitating at the door. If Mr. Kinns was going to ambush, it'd be here.

"I kinda want to spelunk," Midge said, her head sunk into a pout. "Aaron, I don't like this. I'd rather be trusting my own knots, dangling precariously above a cliff of horrors."

Midge grabbed a hold of an invisible rope and pretended to swing above an abyss. Charlie swayed his front legs next to her.

"Alright, enough of that, both of you," Aaron said.

"Okay!"

Charlie ran up and swayed in defiance.

"What are you? Four?" He raised two legs. "Two?" He jumped.

Corollaries and an Elevator

"It doesn't bother you that Charlie is really smart?"

"Hadn't given it much a thought."

The door opened in a burst as he reached to knock. Midge clung to The Lady Made of Dark's Bump In The Night's arm as if she hung above a sinkhole.

Goddamnit, now she had everyone doing it.

Nothing beyond. He switched on a light. Whoever owned this bunker was not present. Scuffs on the walls and the smell of bleach stung. A battle recently cleaned up.

"Do you know what a will-o'-wisp is?" Midge said.

She's one of those nervous talkers. Oh well, whatever got her through this.

"Nope." He went into a control room. Shattered camera screens.

"How about a jack-o'-lantern?" Midge said. She went over to an old lever made of wood. The carvings told a story Aaron couldn't decipher due to ignorance of symbolism and just plain old wear.

"Not in the way you are thinking of," he said.

"A will-o'-wisp is a swamp spirit. A jack-o'-lantern is a murderer of the swamp. This is Indigenous by the way." Indicating the carvings on the lever. "Not sure which Nation. Tells a basic story of Creation."

"Are you sure you want to tell those stories now? You might spook yourself."

"Too late! Anyway, there's a folk tale about a murderer in the swamps. When he died he came back and led people traveling through the swamps to their deaths. Lost travelers would chase after the light thinking it was a hut, with someone inside who might be able to help. But, there was a man who didn't fall for Jack o' Lantern's trap."

"You're not making this story very scary. Pull the switch," he said.

She did. The lever slowly started rising. They left the room and entered the main room with a hole about twenty feet across.

"I'm a scholar, not a storyteller. Anyhow, a lost traveler chased after this light, so he wouldn't die in the swamp. He

The Antagonist's Prison

stopped just short of a cliff edge and noticed that the light was still in the distance off the edge of the cliff. That's when Jack turned around to reveal he was just a skeleton holding a lantern! It makes you think of all the people who fell off that cliff. Fell for his trick in desperation to be saved."

"That doesn't explain why he's called Jack, or why there's a lantern involved." The Antagonist didn't see any point to her story, other than filling silence.

"You really aren't that smart, are you?" Midge said, frustrated.

"You can go fuck yourself."

"Maybe later. He carried a lantern to lead people astray, and his name was Jack because that was his fucking name. Jack of the lantern. Jack lantern. Get it?"

"So, is Jack an inherently evil name?" Everyone involved was getting frustrated.

"Fuck a god, really?"

"Like, Jack the Ripper. Evil. Or Jack Johnson. Fuck that guy."

"Actually, this is a lecture I plan on using next year," Midge said, slipping into academic. "Jack is just a nickname for John and John is a common name in Western culture. Everyone knows a John, so a John in a story becomes instantly relatable. But there are also a lot of Jacks in Western mythology, like Jack and the Beanstalk, or Jack Sparrow. So, while John is a common hero, Jack is a trickster character. Heroes in folklore need a special trick that makes them better than the average person, like a sword or weapon. Jack's trick is typically being a clever guy who is lazy and gets by on his luck and wit."

"So the worst kind of person."

"I suppose. But all cultures have a trickster character. My favorite has always been Coyote."

"Pick a damn culture. We're talking about Western mythology, but you are a Norse scholar. And all the while your favorite is fucking Indigenous."

Midge ignored The Lady Made Of Dark's Bump In The Night's exasperation. "I'm shocked you know Coyote. Loki is such a bor-

Corollaries and an Elevator

ing trickster. I mean, in early myths, Odin and Loki are the same fucking guy. It'd be like if Jack and John were the same person. I like that idea. Jack and John being the same person. You got a wise warrior, skilled in magic, who is also clever and likes to manipulate people instead of doing it by his own might. Think about it. A guy who makes other people do his work, but would do it better than anyone else if he had to. That's the dichotomy of the Norse I can get behind. Not the watered-down Catholic interpretations."

"Alright, Jesus, this doesn't affect our current situation."

"How about a sweet story?"

"As long as it's a story and not something you're gonna read off like a Wikipedia article."

Scrub marks on the stone. The unique acrid smell of water used for pressure washing. The evidence wiped clean while the evidence of the clean was just as damning.

"Hey, some of us are trying really hard to make Wikipedia legitimate. So, this is my favorite story. There was a small norse tribe. Though small, they were strong, with plenty of great warriors. They also had a secret weapon, a berserker, like you. And like a true berserker, he couldn't control himself. He'd kill friend or foe alike. He was banished to the wilderness even though he won many battles for his people.

"But, of course, there was a woman. She hated seeing such a mighty man live on his own without anyone. So once a month on the new moon, she'd go into the forests and check up on the man by lighting a torch. They fell in love. The leader of the tribe found out...oh shit, I forgot about something! The girl happened to be the witch of the tribe. Chances are she wasn't a witch at all and was just schizophrenic. That's why there's still schizophrenics around, by the way. Sorry, getting off track.

"The woman had a vision of the small tribe falling to an invading tribe unless they sacrificed the deep secret they'd been keeping. She interpreted her vision to mean that the tribe would be destroyed unless the banished berserker was allowed back in. Sure enough, another tribe came and attacked the small tribe. The small tribe realized they

The Antagonist's Prison

couldn't win without the berserker. Tribe, tribe, tribe, tribe, tribe. Fuck.

"At first, the berserker refused to come to the aid of the people that banished him. But because he was a noble person, and because he loved the witch, the girl was able to persuade him to help. Before he arrived, they were being decimated by the bigger tribe. But, in the true good timing of a myth, the battle shifted as soon as the berserker arrived. The berserker pushed them back because the invaders weren't used to a fighter of such strength, who couldn't be killed. With the help of the berserker, the tribe survived. What was that, eleven tribes?

"But here's the part that kills me, the romantic part. During the battle, the berserker survived off adrenaline. However, when his rage ended, he bled out on the beach, dying in his lover's arms. As far as Norse stories go, that one is extremely romantic."

"Well, are you pleased with yourself? Now I'm freaked out," Aaron said. Wood from the Mesozoic Era emerged from the black hole.

"Yes, very pleased. I'm freaked out too."

"Sad story, by the way."

"I know, right?"

"That's how I figured I'd go."

"Really? Death by defending a loved one?"

"That'd be a bonus. No, by bleeding out after Critch left me to die."

Midge frowned at his response. "I got this, I'll pull the lever again, be right back. You got us on the boat, after all. We'll trade off. Eventually, someone will kill us, then we won't have to keep tally any longer."

Midge swaggered forward, giving Aaron a chance to check her out from behind, without getting caught. She threw her hips out when she walked.

Raile could get anyone she wanted. However, everyone's first reaction to her choice in Gradick was 'what the fuck?' Gradick was a man better suited for coal mines, or war. He was not known for his handsome appearance. So why did she choose Gradick?

Corollaries and an Elevator

They certainly weren't a cute couple.

When asked about him, she smiled. That smile was one everyone knew, it's the look of a partner who did not question their choice.

Midge glanced back to see if he was ready and caught him checking her out. He didn't get it. In that moment, the way she held herself, the way a few strands of her red hair misplaced, and her adventurous smirk, should have meant something. Instead, he smelled smoke.

Critch stepped on the elevator. It didn't groan, how disappointing. It lowered. Midge ran into the room and jumped down the five feet it'd gone in the meantime.

Expanses
and a
White Wolf

"Warm. Leatherette," Midge whispered at some pitch black distance from the surface. Aaron jumped, Charlie hissed. She was closer to him than he expected. Charlie fell off his shoulder in surprise.

"What?" Critch said.

"Fucking song is stuck in my head. So what the hell was that?"

"I don't know."

"Where are the portal guardians?"

"What?"

"There's usually a Portal Guardian at this point."

"Explain."

"So, let me just clarify this. We are literally going underground to get to The Underground. We are literally going into an Underworld. That's fucking called The Underground. I mean, really? The name is one root away from its definition! Whoever is writing your hero's journey is a lazy fuck."

"Wait...what the fuck are we talking about?" The constant ambient clunking of gears became their slow jazz elevator music.

"Joseph Campbell? George Lucas, The Empire Strikes Back?"

"Never seen Star Wars." But he knew the sequel title somehow.

"Fuck a god, what's wrong with you? You know what, never mind. If I don't stop I'm going to predict the rest of your journey

The Antagonist's Prison

and that seems like a dick move. And you made a Star Wars reference yesterday."

"Eh, colloquial stuff."

"At least you have a vocabulary."

"You're an odd one, Midge."

"Thank you?"

After that followed what normal people called an awkward silence. Mechanical noise excluded.

"What's my protagonist thinking?" Midge asked.

"Enough, you're ruining the joke."

"Alright, then. Aaron, what's on your mind?"

He shuffled up, turned away. Then turned broad toward her, which she puffed up toward, ready. "I was thinking about the berserker story you told. And why you found it romantic that a woman would love and take care of an insane person. It seems the more independent the woman, the more extreme the person they want to take care of needs to be."

"Alright, I'm following, and I don't like where it's going," Midge said, surely crossing her arms. The scuff of her jacket heard but the actual gesticulation unseen.

"I dunno. What if a partner wants companionship but doesn't want a caretaker? Do they wait for a partner who can take care of them without the partner knowing? Or do they try to believe there is a partner out there without that compulsion? And what does it mean for a partner if they don't want to take care of someone?"

"I've never heard you speak so much. That was like, equivalent to a paragraph. You're a single sentence man."

"Midge, I hear something crumbling...Shh."

"Ok, fine, I see what you're getting at. It's not necessary for me to elaborate on the times when you need to be taken care of, like when you're sick and unable to do things by yourself. I don't enter a relationship consciously wanting to play caretaker to my partner. I mean, maybe that's why partners like bad gender iconography, they think nurturing will change the person. I'm not like that, I've learned my lesson. But I do like showing that I care. That means looking out for

Expanses and a White Wolf

them, seeing them from a different perspective and helping them see things they wouldn't see by themselves, like when someone comes up and fixes the solitaire you're stuck on. That's taking care of someone."

Critch rumbled out of the darkness, "But do you think you need to take care of your partner? Like, is it an innate compulsion? All I've ever seen is one partner controlling the other. Telling them how to act, how to think. When they're out of line, treating them like a moron."

"First off, what you're doing right now is why being alone for too long isn't healthy. You're saying stupid things that you probably came up with sitting on your porch, after a bottle of whiskey. Aaron, you need to show you care, otherwise, you just fuck. Friends with benefits relationships miss out on that deep connection bullshit that we all pretend to not want."

His shoulders dropped, and he took a huge step forward. She didn't budge other than to assume a neutral stance pressed up against him. "That's still not what I'm trying to address."

"Fuck a god! What's your damage? Quite a lot actually, sorry. The willingness to be attached to someone is what separates friends from partners. We worry that something might happen to them, something that we can't do anything about. I want to help my partner in times of need. While it's a desire to help, I'm not compelled to do it, as you're failing to articulate. I want to be attached to someone, Aaron. Physical affection isn't enough, because I know that's where you're going next. Emotions need to be played with and built on. I want a partner emotionally, physically, and spiritually," Midge said, changing her voice to be like a flamboyant therapist.

The Antagonist wished it wasn't so far down to The Underground when the descent slowed, potentially signaling the bottom.

"Hey, you're the one who wanted to know what I was thinking about. This escalated quickly."

"You know what, this is a good thing. I appreciate that you're trying to talk about your feelings."

"That wasn't the intention." He adjusted his clothing for how he wished to walk through The City Beneath. Murderous

The Antagonist's Prison

glare to the street corner.

The elevator doors opened to a shoddy bridge which cracked and skittered when stepped on. He had faith in the bridge, but that didn't stop Midge from stepping on the same places he did. The Underground was in a cave some odd distance beneath Indigo Bay. The tiny village on an island in the middle of a lake, enveloped by an enormous cavern. Scattered drops fell from stalactites hidden within the void. The spotty rain made everything a shimmered damp. One hit Midge on the head.

"It's called the Drip," Aaron said.

"Why is everything so literal in your world...?" Midge said, faded out in awe of the place.

The buildings carved from porous blue stone. Gas lamps barely pierced the darkness. If the black was stared at long enough, it might cause unfortunate thoughts.

In the center of the city was a proportionally huge coliseum. The streets between were empty, most petitioners inside businesses. There wasn't a lot of foot traffic in the Underground. The still cave water was slightly salty, becoming more so with every boat that came through the locks. The bridge was not lit and Midge concentrated on her steps. Midge stomped in a puddle then spun around with arms out in a what-the-fuck.

The One Who Stares Back from the Void thought about The Underground's reaction to his return.

"Fuck a god. It's a fucking anachronism," Midge said, cautiously petting the rough blue stone like it was a frenetic bipolar cat. "Is this made out of coral?"

"Dunno what it is."

"Maybe it's lava. So, all these buildings are evil businesses?" Midge asked.

"No, that's not really how to talk about it. All these stores are places you can purchase goods and services mostly illegal topside. Yeah, most are evil, but some are just weird."

He scanned the surrounding businesses and couldn't find one Her Dear Apocalypse deemed safe enough for food and drinks.

Expanses and a White Wolf

Almost all businesses were dual-purposed, bar and murder, trinket and sex. There were ones who specialized in only one niche, but not in their immediate vicinity.

"And look at the coliseum."

"The Arena," he nomenclatured.

"Here I thought it'd be called 'The Battle Place.' So in order to tell the history of a place you have to study the monuments, art, and architecture. Like, take the buildings, the doors are thinner and taller than our standard doors. Let me guess, there's a name for the normal world."

"Topside," he said, vocalizing the sound of infinity.

"Of course that's what this place calls it. So that tells us that whoever built this was tall and thin, compared to normal humans."

Definitely aliens. For certain.

"So people who look like me? Doesn't that depend on a lot of things?" he said.

"And it's vaguely Middle Eastern in style," Midge continued in spite of Aaron's subjective questions. "Why would that be over in the west of North America? Weird."

From above, a flash of blue, the brilliance of the sun blinded the entirety of The Underground for a few pupil-strained seconds. A terrible groan trembled down the walls and shook the ground.

"Look!" Midge said. She pointed up into the black of The Underground's ceiling. A sheet of water hit, drenching The Underground in a heavy, painful splat. Knocked Midge down.

Out of the dim, three figures emerged. They controlled their out of whack spirals with parachutes. Another figure swung upside down, on what looked like a rope.

"They're coming down rather fast, don't you think," Midge said as she stood up.

"And they're aiming for us for some reason."

As they sped down, Aaron recognized the one dangling from the fifty-foot rope as.... "Amber!"

In mid-sprint to her approximate impact site. Her arms out and moving in a calculated way, eventually leading to a cease of her spin.

The Antagonist's Prison

She was still coming down at a dangerous pace.

"Who?" Midge said a fair distance behind with no hope of catching up at Aaron's full speed. "Your employee!?"

The Antagonist was now ahead of Amber. He pivoted round as he skidded across the cobbles with his slick boots. Long ago had lost all traction. She let go and sailed toward him. He caught her with the air in his lungs disgusted by his heroism. He set her down. Reinflating his lungs proved difficult. That didn't stop her from grabbing him in a bear hug. He tapped out on her shoulder. She didn't know what tapping out was. She squeezed him and ruined the notion once again that Amber was feeble. Her strength shifted ribs.

"Amber, you're suffocating him," Midge said.

Amber dropped him and he coughed out the blue in his face.

"Sorry," she said.

"I'm good, always good," The One Who Stares Back From The Void said. "You've got a talent for unlikely entrances. Has anyone told you that?"

"And you have a knack for being there when I need it."

"Hands off, big girl," Midge said. With no reason to be defensive. Either way, to Aaron, Amber never mentioned anyone she was interested in. It was as if the desire to have relationships wasn't in her coding.

"Oh no, sorry. It's not like that," Amber said. She pleaded him with desperate green eyes. Her skin covered in gnarly red, green, and blue-scabbed irritation. A horrible reaction to poison oak. She idly itched.

"I'll always be there for you Amber, whenever I can. I guess it's good that I'm down here at the moment. And stop saying 'sorry.'"

Amber took a step back and held her withered arms across her chest. Still in her tiny, dirty white tank top and torn jean shorts clutching bone legs. Her hunched-inward posture despondent.

As if Aaron had given permission without either of them realizing she needed the release of posture, she collapsed. Midge sank with her, holding her so she wouldn't scrape her knees. She didn't cry or make a sound. Her attenuated limbs done functioning.

Expanses and a White Wolf

From beneath Midge's nurture, "We fell when the melody rejected us...Why did it reject us?"

"Absolutely no idea what that means," Mr. Bennett said, so straightforward it sounded dismissive. "Are you okay?"

Those who knew Aaron could recognize his care. He did not present as caring. He presented as a royal upset that a peasant died at his feet.

"I don't have time to be okay," Amber said. Her body reviving itself.

"You'll figure that out later," Midge said. She stood up to give Amber room.

"And you always have time to be okay," Aaron said, soapbox appearing out of nowhere. He deigned not to step on the imaginary thing. "It's always the case that you never have time to become okay. You gotta make time anyway. Regain control and all that."

Amber stood. Wiped her splotchy legs off. More colors, as if the pigmentation came from within. Aaron saw it as the reality of the moment and made no reference to it.

"What are you doing down here?" Amber asked.

"Revenge for the man who burned down my shop."

"The person who burned down the store is down here?"

"It's a long story. Well, not so long, but not one that matters. Same question back at you. By the by, got any cigarettes?"

"How did you know I smoked?"

"I smell it." And it was horrifying.

"Yeah, here, it's the same brand you smoke."

Between frames he grabbed the pack missing only two cloves. He took out four. "Do you mind?"

"Not at all, take the pack. I shouldn't be smoking anyway."

"You're right." He pocketed the pack. Besides, he was sure she could find somewhere down here where she could get more. He read her devastation. Handed the pack back. "You need a vice. Smoking's a good one for folks like us."

He sucked in a bottom of the lung drag. He breathed out the headache, and his irritation fell like the clove's ash. He pocketed

The Antagonist's Prison

the other three.

"What're you doing here, Amber?" Midge said.

"Amber Collins," Amber said, extending her hand.

"Midge Estire, nice to meet you properly, didn't know if we were going to do the introduction thing or not." Midge shook her hand and held her forearm with the other hand. For what reason? We will never know.

"Same. So good to see you, Aaron. The Seekers are hard to deal with. I don't feel like my life is mine right now."

"Don't fuck with the Seekers," Aaron said with great solemnity. "They're fanatic, and that's not a quality I respect highly."

"You're with the Seekers? Fuck Zo!" Midge said.

"How do you know about the Seekers?" Amber said. "You told me two days ago the Underground wasn't real, and...look at this place!"

"I lied. I actually know quite a bit about the Underground."

"Why? And don't you dare tell me that you were only trying to protect me."

"Oh, I will dare, I was protecting you."

"So much for that."

"Hey, Amber. Check yourself," Midge said. "Do not forget where you are and how people react to that behavior."

"Or what? The Antagonist will get me? No one will tell me what that means."

"And I won't either," The Antagonist said.

"You really don't want to know," Midge said.

"I'm tired of people intentionally not telling me things out of secrecy and because they don't trust that I can handle it. Like they don't want to hurt my innocence."

"You *are* innocent, Amber," Aaron said. Her fire died with that.

"Look, I'm all for the jump-into-the-deep-end lifestyle," Midge said. She put her palm on Amber's chest. "But Amber, you're not jumping in the deep end here. The air locks have ruptured. Now is not the time to learn to swim. Now is the time to be crushed under the ocean's weight."

Expanses and a White Wolf

"The Miscreant Queen and her Proteges said something similar in the Tunnels." Amber stood elongated. Broad but away and down. Ready for the back blow.

"You saw Raile?" Her Dear Apocalypse said.

"Yeah, she was a freaking firestorm. Scariest person I've ever met."

Raile was alive in the Tunnels. Mr. Bennett crossed his fingers that she was still alive. "I'm sorry Amber. You know I like to be honest with you, with everyone. But I hide truths and horrors in a world you do not need to know, witness, or understand. I will tell you, now that you're down here, in this place of all-encompassing, subtle evil. All you need to know is – I've got your back, as best I can."

Amber's face flickered around contemplations until her sandy brown eyes rested on the realization. "Oh...Okay. Got it."

"Is Zo still leading the Seekers?" Midge said.

"Yeah, she and Peter and the band should be here any moment."

"Listen to me, Amber," Midge said. "Aaron seems to respect you quite a bit. He respects me too. So listen to me. Zo is the devil. Keep your wits about you."

Amber was about to respond, but a little redhead hippie in a patterned short dress and a Burning Man shawl with cleaner dreads than Aaron's hair approached. If she was older, the outfit would morph into fashionable richie woman, a sort of split between professional comfort and a Coachella dancer.

She was followed by a man with a fighter's body, a Hawaiian shirt unbuttoned halfway, and white bucket hat, old calloused skin, black knuckles from so much brutality. He walked with a limp from a recent injury. More a black eye than a healed scar. Midge raised a shut-the-fuck-up hand. From around the corner, three folks jogged to catch up.

"I hear the flutter of wings," Midge said, hand cupped around her ear.

"I'm assuming they're devil wings," Zo said. "I said I was sorry so many times, Sammie, what more do you want?"

Zo had a CEO demeanor, all business and cold narcissist.

The Antagonist's Prison

"Some betrayals are unforgivable. And you never meant any of those perfunctory apologies. You stole all our research, discredited all of us, bought out the board. You buried us, ruined their careers. Mondo killed himself!"

"What is it Raile says? 'Be savage in your pursuits?'"

"Be ruthless in the pursuit of truth," Midge said. "And you can't use their Colloquies. You are everything The Miscreant Royalty stand against. Believe me when I say, your reckoning cometh."

"From who? You?"

"The children are bickering," the large tourist fighter said to Critch.

"Aaron," Your Imminent Unforwarned Reckoning said, shaking the Antagonist Hunter's hand.

"Peter," he said, shaking as hard as he could. The intimidation ritual fell flat as His Unflinching Grin barely felt his remarkable yet ineffectual crush. He held the handshake for too long then let go with bafflement painted.

"Pleasured," Mr. Bennett said. "I can tell you're protecting them well, please continue to do so. For all our benefit."

"No one is more qualified. I've been trained to take on Critch," Peter said.

"That's quite the accomplishment. Have you ever fought him?"

"No, but I hope to soon. He has finally come out of hiding. I hear he's already killed The Divorce's Arena fighter."

"Critch is back?" Critch said, not displaying as much terror as he hoped. Never been much of an actor. The Divorce would need a fighter for the Arena. He could curry favor from them by offering his services.

"It's still a rumor," Peter said, still rational but Aaron heard the excitement he tamped down.

"The Widow in Yellow told us, and she is a snake in the grass," Zo said.

"Then you two have a lot in common," Midge said.

"Shut the fuck up Midge," Her Dear Apocalypse said.

"You're right, sorry." She remembered the agreement.

Expanses and a White Wolf

"Either way," Aaron said. "The Divorce are out of the Arena if they can't find a fighter. If Critch is back I wish you luck for your fateful fight. Zo, I'm sorry for any defamation Midge may have implied. Amber seems to look to you for assistance with whatever plagues her. I hope that continues, with her best interest in mind."

"Thank you, Aaron. I will try my best."

"I'd appreciate it."

Zo did not look anywhere near The Antagonist. She hard-looked at Amber and when she did acknowledge him, it was a quick side glance and back to anywhere but his direction.

Aaron nodded to Amber, then went on their merry before the other three could join in the conversation. No need to confirm the theory brewing.

"Do you think Amber is okay in Zo's protection?" Midge said once they were out of range.

"I don't know, Peter is trained to fight Crtich single-handedly, that's gotta mean something."

"You know you're Critch."

"Oh, I think Peter might've picked that up. Even if he didn't, Zo knows."

"Oh, I know Zo well enough. I've never seen her address anyone like she did with you."

"So yeah, safe-ish. And I think I'm slowly learning not to underestimate Amber."

"Amber? Yeah, she's fine. She's awesome, in the literal sense. I'm filled with awe from her. Did you see her eyes changing colors?"

"Didn't notice, no."

"And her skin covered in those thick scabs?"

"Saw that. But we got shit to do."

Midge flung out her arms and shook some of the excess water. "So, the walls trembled after the blue flash. Then what? Almost ten seconds later the water fell. So, the ceiling is about five hundred meters up?"

"Sure, however you came up with that number. Sounds about as accurate as any number I've ever heard."

The Antagonist's Prison

"Distance is equal to Gravity times Time squared divided by two. Gravity, to make it easy, is ten meters per second per second. Time was ten seconds. Do the math and you get roughly five hundred meters give or take, what, twenty? And the deepest point in the bay is six hundred meters. So that means we're... um, a kilometer or so beneath sea level?"

"Sure."

"Why don't you care about the infrastructure?"

"Don't see why it's relevant."

"You don't see much as relevant do you?"

"Few things are. You're obsessed with details. Forest remark here." Passed several A-frames offering a variety of selective goods and services, most of them specialized in ways not okay Topside. "It's also where the monsters are. I don't care about the details when I am a detail."

"Details are where I live, and while I agree that I may be a little too conscious of them, not paying attention at all is not something I can get behind either."

Charlie launched off Aaron's shoulder to spin three times to the damp ground where he did not like the damp. Shook his legs frantically.

Aaron picked Charlie up cradled at his chest. "The Divorce need a fighter. Let's start currying these favor shenanigans."

"Why?"

"The Arena happens every three months. A way to judge how well the Powers can keep order. If they don't fight, they lose their status and others can contest their dominance. Otherwise, the only way one can make a move on the Heads is through a neutral party. If any power doesn't follow protocol, the entire Underground turns against them."

"Awesome. No sarcasm. That's just fucking awesome. So we, the neutral party, will get the permission of The Divorce, by making sure their status as a Head is still established. Not a bad plan."

"Thank you," The Enemy Of This Place said.

Expanses and a White Wolf

A man and a woman stood on opposite sides of the door to The Divorce's headquarters. The woman silently glared at Aaron from on high, impeding their entrance.

"I understand you might be in need of a fighter for the Arena. I'm here to offer my services."

The woman sized him up, then stepped aside. They walked past her.

"You realize fear is a healthy thing, Aaron?" Midge said. "You can't just walk up to everyone like they're tiny mortals in comparison, especially down here."

"I don't do that."

"It certainly looked like you went up to that woman like she should get the fuck out of your way."

"I'll show fear when an appropriate."

"How was that not an appropriate? Fuck, I'm starting to parrot you."

"When a swift kick in the balls will take care of the problem, I don't fear them."

Midge laughed and shook her head.

"Do we need to revisit our agreement?" Aaron said.

"No, sorry."

Chairs were torn and mismatched and the assembled seemed to have pulled every variety of style off the rack. Down the middle of the tavern woodgrain, a void of furniture between the two overhangs on either side rammed with people. On the raised floor at the back, a blonde woman sat on an outdoor camping chair of high quality as a sort of throne. Flanking her were a lumberjack, flannel-and-beanie man and a neo-twenties flapper woman.

The Divorce were heterophobic, though Aaron didn't realize the segregation was so extreme as to put ten feet of nothing between either gender. The leader seemed to be waiting for the light of recognition to cross their faces, guys on the left, girls on the right. Midge and Aaron switched sides.

The Antagonist's Prison

"How do they handle trans people?" Midge said into his ribs.

"My guess," he said down into Midge's ear. "They don't tolerate trans until post-op."

"Bisexual?"

"Not welcome? Leader's name is Isabel. Last I know."

Possibly Isabel in down-home southern belle dress with a flower in her curly autumn hair. A silly parasol to shade her from the brilliant sun of her tavern. Lipstick lesbian to whatever degree.

"Greetings, my lord and lady." She curtsied at Midge, checking out her tattoos and a-line hair. She squinted at The Antagonist, working out if she recognized him. He tipped his hat in greeting but also to hide his face.

"Isabel, I presume?" Midge said.

"Indeed," she said.

"Where the fuck are we, in a royal palace after the nukes?" He Who Smiles Back whispered into the back of Midge's head. She held the laugh back.

"I'm sorry, but I must ask. Are you two together?"

"Only in an official capacity," Aaron said.

Midge looked at him with a slight confusion then remembered where she was and sneered, shaking her head in effective false disgust.

"We have had a tragic accident. As you know, the Arena is tonight and our fighter was killed by Critch."

"What happened?" Midge said. Good, she knew how to do this.

"The boat bringing him to The Underground sank seven hours ago. Unfortunately, rumor has it that The Antagonist was on it. Which means Madam Ava has brought her pet out of retirement. You stand no chance against her horrific champion, no offense."

Critch was going to tell her he thought he'd be alright against Critch, but Midge placed her hand on Critch's forearm. "Mr. Kinns has taken a friend of ours and burned down Aaron's business. Well, his store, Topside, that's what you call it, right? We've come down here for revenge. I understand that you need tokens of favor to move against Powers here. What do we need to do to get your permission?"

"We have no special appreciation for Mr. Kinns. He is a

Expanses and a White Wolf

maniac. Our normal task for initiation is not appropriate for the times. If you compete in tonight's Arena and survive, I believe we can make an accord."

"Then I'll see you afterward," Aaron said in professional business response.

Isabel scoffed at him and the whole house gave a professional giggle.

Not Normally This Petty let Critch out, just a bit, as he glared at Isabel, letting his irises spin 'round, the smile creep. She stopped laughing and her panic shamed him. It took a moment for the rest of the house to see their leader's pallor. Her eyes teared up, and she left the room.

A tight-shirted man came up to them in her absence. "Favor will be given if you are menacing in the Arena. The Divorce aim to show The Underground we are not to be trifled with, we are on edge as it is. Sadly, if Critch is indeed back, you cannot win. Survive and don't be pathetic."

Aaron left. The Divorce down-nosed at him like the monster he was.

"We won't disappoint," Midge said before turning to catch up to Aaron.

He paced outside, Critch in his throat. If he focused on him in any way, he might break his binds. He tried to find something else, but everything in sight brought up latent memories.

Seeing his distress, Midge sat down calmly. "I don't think agreeing to those terms is such a good idea."

"No shit. I don't need another lecture, not now."

"Are you okay?"

"I don't know yet."

Midge put on a serious face. Her academics struggled against the real-world experience this berserker put her through. "What's it like?"

Midge might as well have flipped out a reporter's notepad. She should know better. Her curiosity would be the death of her.

"It's like being an alcoholic at a bar, and someone just poured cognac over my face. It's better I don't think about it, ignore the

The Antagonist's Prison

compulsion."

"Well, I'm fucking starving, let's get some food. We have about an hour to get back here."

"I have to hold off on berserking for an hour?"

"You could try fighting without raging. You said you didn't berserk for three years."

"I doubt that will happen. There was a reason I spent all that time alone. I rarely went out. I didn't want to risk someone having a problem with me and throwing a punch."

"Hate to break it to you, but most social experiences, if not all, don't end in fists."

"Not so in my memories."

Midge stopped in front of a store and sniffed.

"German," she said, before heading inside.

Not sure why that was the selling point for her, then again, Critch didn't know much about German food beyond the notion of sausages. Her senses far better than his. His five senses gone. He could blame smoking for notable memory of some of them, but his eyes were average at best and a selective sense of touch. Beyond physical pressure, his skin was largely numb.

She found a booth and sat down. The Antagonist waved his arms to keep from falling into Critch's maw. Charlie crawled down his arm and explored the space. Pushed a decorative candle over.

Three clouded windows behind the bar. On the other side were scared young children who, if they ever escaped, would have their minds nullified into a pile of drug mush. No amount of therapy could save them from their trauma.

Most of the patrons sat by themselves waiting for their turn to walk up and see what was behind door number three. There was a premium window with a virgin behind it.

"This is what's hard about The Underground," Aaron said.

"I know. I can't say anything, can't do anything....just let the

Expanses and a White Wolf

horror happen. Wow, enabling rape. I try to be tolerant, but I've always had a hard time finding where to draw the line. Rape was always a good place, but it appears you can't draw lines down here. Jump into the deep end is my philosophy. I once read an article on rape versus murder and why rape is worse than murder."

"I don't think there needed to be a study to prove that."

Food arrived at the table. It was fried chicken in a red sauce with french fries.

"Ah, German food. Someone has a sense of humor."

He Who Smiles Back laughed.

A Firemime sat at their table. Aaron bristled. His face freshly painted white, preparing to look his best for the Arena. Charlie hissed at him.

"Is that one of Her spiders?"

"What do you want, man?" The Subject Of His Profession said.

"I thought you looked familiar and I didn't want to be rude and not say hello."

"I get that often. But why sit with us, us sitting alone, us off to the side where people won't bother us?"

"Would you want to talk to anyone in here?" the Firemime said.

"No," Midge said. "I wouldn't want to talk to anyone, except the person I came in here with."

"Hey, no need to be a bitch. I swear I've seen you before, man."

It was bittersweet luck that this kid was wet behind the ears. If he were a real Firemime, he'd have walked out, then come back with fifteen of his friends. Thirty likely.

Firemimes were found by The Widow in Yellow. They started fighting young, became prodigies. Their greatest hope was to be contacted by organizations like the Widow's. They're trained to fight berserkers, how to hogtie a man, how to fight lions and bears. No tigers, it'd be cliché. How to pull elephants from their foundations. Life as a Firemime when Aaron was The Widow in Yellow's weapon was short and expendable.

A woman walked up to the bar and pointed to door number two. The clouds flicked off and there was a little boy cowering,

The Antagonist's Prison

no more than ten. The back of his little prison rose, giving him the hope of escape. The patron strolled through the doors to give chase. Guess that was part of it.

Food hit the table for the Firemime, who shoveled greasy tubes into his mouth like a starved orphan. He stopped eating as he put pieces together, eyed The Antagonist with confliction.

"Get out of here," Aaron said. "And leave the lasso."

He rocketed out of his chair, knocking his plate around and spilling the water. He took out his lasso and staggered back and forth.

"Look, man," Aaron said. "Get out of here before you tout him out of his cage. You won't be a hero, you'll be dead and everyone in this restaurant will be dead."

He left his messy plate half finished and sprinted out of the bar screaming "The Antagonist has returned! He's back! He's here!"

The rapists in the bar starried.

"That was good. See, you can control yourself if you want."

"Pretty sure Critch just saw him as a waste of time."

"Way to be all negative. So let me guess. There's a lot of powerful people down here. And you've never heard of these people and they like it that way."

"More or less."

"God, I love and hate this place," Midge said.

"Back when I was more Critch..."

"Do me a favor, Critch is you, just a nonthinking, completely impulsive you. If you keep thinking that part of you is someone else then how are you going to get rid of it?"

"That part of me is stronger. Madam Ava used to say, there are wolves in the world, and they go after sheep led by a shepherd who protects them. But how does a shepherd protect against wolves? With a stick? A fence?"

"There are three things that protect from wolves," Midge said, answering the questions he meant to be rhetoracle. "Bigger wolves, moose, and the cold hard winter. You have to choose which you are. Then, of course, there's the man without a stick, but has a sword and all those fighter instincts. I think you know how to de-

Expanses and a White Wolf

fend against wolves. And it isn't speaking softly and carrying a big stick, that's for people. The people down here don't act like humans so you need to be a predator they can't comprehend."

"Like Critch?"

"No, Critch is a wolf." Midge sighed. "Look, I think you know people don't need shepherds or sheep, they need training and discipline. Leaders don't work, unique individuals are what make stories and heroes. Let me tell you a proverb. It's usually told using Cherokee Peoples, I don't know why. But it goes that there are two wolves inside us. One who lives off hate and bad emotions, one who lives off love and good stuff. They fight with each other all the time, and the one who wins is the one you feed."

"So I should feed love and not hate?" Aaron dismissed with cigarette flick.

"I'm going to blame that quip on you being defensive about yourself. No, this proverb works for you for another reason. The hate wolf already won and it is goddamned Fenrir. But your other wolf never died. It's healed. You've been feeding that one, or at least focusing on that one, protecting it. But you never weakened Fenrir, so your lovey wolf is stronger than it was back then, but not strong enough."

"Alright with your extended metaphor, if that's what it is. What should I do?" If he could fade out from a conversation now he would. Unfortunately, part of him was hyper-vigilant and didn't allow him to space out.

"Fight and feed. Oh, I should write that down, that's a really good general statement. Fuck, I could teach a class on that nonsense. But this is about you. We have to get some bullshit tokens from these craven people, to keep peace and balance or whatever bullshit in a bullshit evil society. Isabel wants you to fight in the Arena. Try not to berserk, feed your white wolf."

"I'm going to bet you a dollar that's impossible."

"Maybe, but try anyway."

Battles and an Emporium

This room was a cell beneath the Arena. The doors would open and Critch would maim or kill the person on the other side. It's old hat at this point, really. A bench and a metal water pitcher. No glass. The crowd cheered as the current fight ended. Its roar had never charged His Unflinching Grin.

He was losing moments again. That used to be normal. Madam Ava had a name for it, but The One Who Stares Back could not remember. His knuckles didn't have new scabs, though he did not remember going back to the Divorce. He did remember walking with them toward the Arena. That was it. The One Who Will Make You Undone panicked for a moment, thinking about Midge. She was probably fine. To the right of Isabel. It's what he must believe.

The door opened and the sound of the crowd and the door's creak spun him. A titanic cauldron burned above the Arena floor. Its heat radiated down in incessant waves. The yellow light reflected off the white sawdust and scorched Her Dear Apocalypse's eyes so used to the umbra of the Underground.

A large man greeted the crowd, arms raised up, egging them on as they chanted his incoherent name. He focused on Critch as he ambled out of his cell. The crowd booed. Peter unbuttoned his Hawaiian shirt, showing several pretty impressive scars. Mr. Bennett was a decent fighter, but the normal reaction in a fight was to berserk.

The Antagonist's Prison

Critch skittered behind the trees at the edge of Aaron's vision.

The Antagonist took off his hat. Pulled off his jacket and shirt indolently to showcase his fractured skin. The Powers sat in their own sections along with an upper general admission area. Perhaps two hundred people, up to five hundred. Either way, there was plenty of unused space. The second level unpopulated.

As soon as he stepped on the floor, dozens and dozens of Firemimes stood within the masses to approach.

"Alright skinny," Peter said. "Why didn't you tell me you were competing?"

"Didn't see it prudent." Critch strafed behind Aaron like a tattered crow torturing a cat. Each pass busted a hole in his skull a little larger each time. "Good to see you again, how goes the search for Critch?" The Actual Thing said. He didn't like lying in this way.

"Ongoing. Answer the question."

"The Divorce needed a fighter, like you said. I volunteered."

"It is a shame that your first fight will be against me."

"I suppose so," His Imminent Unforewarned Reckoning said.

"You should be more afraid. I am the Seeker's enforcer. Guardian of the Prismatic Orthodoxy." Oh looky, other people could have titles. "I'm one of the few who can stand before Critch. I have already defeated many of Madam Ava's berserkers. I intend to beat Ramn today and I will win the Arena again. I have made The Seekers a power not to be fucked with."

"You said you've never faced Critch before?" Critch stood like a hulking giant behind The Antagonist. Confusingly. He flicked the back of his head with fingers as thick as his neck. "What makes you think you can stand before him?"

"Let me show you. "

He punched. Not The Antagonist Yet spun to dodge and he slammed a cross hammer into his ribs. Never spin. Aaron ducked beneath his kick and returned the rib shot. It hurt his hand. Peter didn't react.

"Well, I wish you the best of luck against The Antagonist."

"What...?" Peter said. The rim of the Arena floor was lined

Battles and an Emporium

with Firemime's lassos swirling 'round.

Critch grabbed His Unflinching Grin's head, ripped it off and squeezed into his body like a tight pair of jeans. Peter's face slacked to wide-eyed, pale-faced horrific.

Blood dripped from his hands and forearms. This was another reason he wore black. His neck, wrists, torso, and ankles raw from rope burn. The water pitcher bent and sheared, made useless. He followed the trail of water around the room where it ricocheted. Did that make you feel better, Critch? No, he supposed he couldn't separate anymore. Did that make him feel better? That really did change the tone of it. Throwing a tantrum, something a child would do. It didn't solve anything. The One Who Stares Back got angry with themself then found their zen place. No cheering from the crowd above. Typical after one of his performances.

He peeked out of his holding cell. A heavy gauge chain prevented it from opening far. Aaron squeezed the pitcher out. There were two Firemimes standing guard. One was maybe thirty, the other much younger. The green one jumped back and tried to get his lasso spinning. He was so nervous he couldn't get the rhythm right.

"Hello, Antagonist. What can we do for you?" the older Firemime said.

"Hey, I destroyed my water pitcher. Can I get some more water? And maybe a rag, if possible."

"Yeah." He took the pitcher and disappeared out of view. The eyes of the younger one when he saw that pitcher did not help Her Dear Apocalypse's self-esteem. Charlie huddled in the corner.

"Sorry, buddy," Aaron said.

Charlie didn't move. Guilt flushed out of Aaron.

The door opened behind him. A man perhaps ten feet tall breathed heavy in the middle of the Arena.

Ramn.

The Antagonist's Prison

His Unflinching Grin slammed into Critch and before the smile finished forming, he was already flying over the mountain range of Ramn, ten feet off the ground, fifty feet from where he stood a moment before. He saw himself still in his cell. Smile not finished with its grin. It never would be.

His fingers covered in bite marks. He squeezed out the blood onto the floor, his briny depths backpack had super glue in it for this. Critch knelt in despair for just a moment. Goddamnit. He growled at his fingers.

Aaron knew Critch was not the real him. He once thought of him like that, of course he did. Yet Mr. Bennett still didn't know how to function without him. He occasionally wondered what it'd be like to gander at the black woods of his mind and think, hey, they're only trees, not the hunting grounds of a Wendigo.

The door opened and yet another colossal man stood, hands behind his back, somehow mocking militaristic at ease. This was not the situation where he should be dealing with Critch, might as well quit smoking in a Las Vegas Casino. Jump into the deep end, as Midge said.

Aaron came out on the floor, still not wearing his shirt. Where did the shirt go? The crowd was silent and far less numerous than the first bout. The faces His Unflinching Grin could make out were unpleasant ruined expressions. They huddled in tightly packed herds. A line of forty Firemimes swirled their lassos on the wall above the Arena Floor. Vain of them to think that was enough.

The man in front of The Antagonist did not look healthy. Heavy bags under his eyes, wet blood patches made his shirt stick to his barrel chest. It wasn't until he was five feet away that Aaron recognized him as Gradick.

"Not a place I'd expect to see you, old friend, " The One Who Will Make You Undone said. "And certainly not in this condition. I heard you died."

Battles and an Emporium

Seeing someone he recognized in the Arena pleased He Who Smiles Back greatly. Then, Not Currently Critch remembered that they had to fight each other, and the sad determination in Gradick's eyes suggested he had something to fight for. Making him dangerous, at least more so than Current Antagonist. Aaron was fighting for other people, not himself.

"Believe me, I've died several times, in several ways, in the last day or more," the Miscreant King said. "We both have stories to tell."

"You look terrible, better than being dead, I suppose," Aaron said.

"You look the same as you've always looked, but your mind is unraveled. That makes you more unpredictable than my best man."

"Doubt it."

"Well, at the moment, Aaron, you are struggling. I hope Aaron wins and not Critch. I can't beat The Antagonist." Gradick slammed Aaron's face with a biker punch. Easily blocked, but your guard meant nothing against the force and angle.

Critch rose up. He swallowed him down.

"Keep your cool, Aaron."

"It's a little difficult to do that right now!"

"If I ever want to see my darling Raile again, you, and Critch, are in my way. I can't beat you if you're Critch, but if you're Aaron, I have a better chance. Make them afraid to be your enemy. Have a black heart of gold. Run riot. Raise hell."

Critch ducked underneath Gradick's next punch, couldn't stop it, avoid it. Your Imminent Unforewarned Reckoning elbowed The Miscreant King's side with all Aaron's weight, pushing through to the other side.

"You can't expect me to be the martyr," Our Relentless Shadow said.

"You must be the martyr. You've always been the martyr, my old friend. A societal scapegoat. Take the sins of this place and then be killed for donning that mantle."

The crowd got itself together, and their eerie whispered chant whistled around. 'No one deserves Critch' from everywhere. Aaron's

The Antagonist's Prison

skin flushed and muscles tensed. Hopeful the Miscreant King might save them.

"Keep it together, friend."

"Not for much longer."

He imagined Midge in the crowd, praying to a god she didn't believe in. His vision faded.

"Aaron! Pay attention. You and I can work through this. Your circle is everything!"

"You'll do anything to win and get your precious love back."

"This is true, and I also believe you can control yourself."

"You're not the only one."

Heartbreak shrieked across the Arena floor. Cut out all sound to the world. Utterly decimating Critch's ascent. In a crowd of white shirts, a woman in black reached out with both arms.

"GRADICK!" Raile screamed. Again muting the world with her desperate plea. The Miscreant Queen's anguished face seared into Critch's mind.

Definitively And Completely Aaron Bennett took his chance and sucker punched Gradick to the ground. Left the floor, middle fingers raised to the almost gracious crowd. Back in his cell, he prevented himself from defragmenting. There would be time for that later. At least he hoped so. Ghost bits of himself tousled up by current events.

The doors opened to the halls beneath the Arena and the veteran Firemime asked if it was safe. The One Who Stares Back said he was fine. The Firemime opened the gate all the way. Isabel stood there with her entourage. Aaron picked up Charlie and placed him on his shoulder. The delightful spider scratched his neck. Three men and three women split on either side of Isabel. It must be hard to keep that arrangement.

Isabel resentfully held out a necklace for Aaron, half the links male symbols and the other half female symbols, and in the middle, a square ruby separated the sides.

"I don't know what you want with Mr. Kinns, Critch. We want nothing to do with The Antagonist and wish you'd told us who

Battles and an Emporium

you were so we could have rejected your proposition. However, in thanks for winning the Arena, here is our token of permission." Isabel and hers moved to the side and let Critch pass.

Weird days getting weirder. It took him a while to find his way out. It didn't help that he didn't remember how he got into his cell. Not A Lick Of Critch desperately needed a cigarette.

Midge leaned cross-armed against a lamp post, waiting for His Unflinching Grin. He thought she was angry, until she recognized his silent stalking pursuit. She pushed off the post. They hugged for a long time.

"I knew you could do it," she said, pressed against him. She released, a little flustered and went to her lamppost and handed him a new black shirt and his treasured and still a tish damp jacket. Then handed him the last clove he stole from Amber.

"Thanks." He lit the clove, immediately felt better. Midge jumped at him. Caught her, dropping the clove into a puddle. He didn't mind.

"I was so...watched you...that thing. It...It hasn't gotten easier. It gets worse every time. Each time that smile seems to cut another slice into my brain. Still shots of you in impossible twists and unwinds. You killed forty people!" Midge gulped as her body shuddered. She cleared her throat and said, "But then you held yourself together against Gradick. I'm proud of you. So what now?"

Didn't Always Have to be Critch nodded three times with proud lips stuck out. "Thank you. We find another Power. I know which one."

"Come on, I found a place that might sell cigarettes."

Not far from the Arena, a store with a standing sign read, 'Flowering Existential.' Inside the small pharmacy stood a fine wood bar with mirrors built into it. Midge rang the bell. A match lit. Your Imminent Unforewarned Reckoning leaned across the counter as a plume of rosemary and lavender smoke bombed them from below. Within the smoke a hag rose, dressed in rags, but the hump didn't move right and the makeup was exaggerated with highlights, more like stage makeup to be seen from the back rows rather than two feet away.

The Antagonist's Prison

"Drop the act please," Mr. Bennett said with no love of pageantry.

"Aye, I know not what you speak, man shrouded by the pagan lords."

"No really, please, before I can't help but be rude."

The woman stood up, letting the raggy costume slough off in a mound of fakery. The actual woman was tall and thin. An extra typical of Indigo Bay, maybe even a little soccer mom splashed in for flavor. Short cropped red hair of one who would like to speak with the manager.

"Oh, hey. Let's just not address what happened."

"I'd think lots of people would like a witch to come with their Underground apothecary," Midge said.

"Some do, some don't. That's why I made it with quick catches. The costume is easy to put on and take off. What can I do for you?" The caked-on makeup had yet to be removed.

"I'd like some cloves please."

"Real ones or fake ones."

"Real ones if you got 'em," Our Relentless Shadow said, fairly giddy for him.

She knelt down out of view. After a minute or two she stood with some celebration and presented a Ziploc with fifty odd non-filter cloves.

"Careful, those are pure. Can't get them in the United States, they hit hard. That'll be a hundred." He took one out and lit up. Put the money on the counter. He assumed if it were someone else they would hit him hard. As it was, it just got rid of the headache faster.

"So, what else? Anything for you?" The apothecary said.

"Can I get some Vicodin, Valium, some hardcore styptic glue. Also, as much Silphium as I can afford. Quaaludes if you've got' em. Appalachian Moonshine. Oh, and some filtered Lucky Strikes."

The woman turned to collect the order.

"I don't know what half of that is," The Antagonist said.

"Some of it is for your pain and your wounds. Some of it is for me."

"What's Silphium?"

Battles and an Emporium

"It's an extinct form of birth control used by the Greeks. I figure, if we're in a place that could possibly offer it, I'll take it. It was so effective they consumed it to extinction. It's a sort of morning-after pill. Just because it's extinct doesn't mean it's not still around. And we are in the Underground."

The woman placed several baggies on the wood. "Alright, I can see what you're shooting for, and while these are a good bit more expensive, I think they're what you're looking for. I got your Silphium. However, I've got these bandages here soaked in a Lock Operator resin. Warm them up and they'll not only shut off all bleeding but also infuse the body with white blood cells and promote healing, kinda like a styptic saniderm on steroids. I also have a limited stock of Mind Eraser, it'll knock you out for eight hours with pleasant dreams, you'll wake up refreshed, at least until you remember what you did. If you want a total Mind Eraser, I've got a neuralizer that'll make a week of your life disappear. I also put in a complete analgesic. It lasts for a few hours, but it has a brutal cut off once it leaves your system. But if you need a few hours of no pain, it'll do just that, just be careful not to bite off your tongue. Seven hundred for this, five for what you asked. Sorry, Silphium is expensive."

"Competitive rates," Mr. Bennett said.

Midge counted out the twenties on the wood.

"Huge profit margins on some of these, not on others," the apothecary said. "Business, you know. Charge a lot for what everyone comes in for. Not a lot for what's in low demand. Erasers aren't a huge market down here. Same with medical supplies."

"Well, I'm not one to haggle," Critch said. "Thank you for your time. Sorry, never did get your name."

"Abby."

"Aaron. This is Midge."

"Pleasure, come back anytime." A slight pause. "I swear I know you from somewhere."

"I doubt it. I'm no player," the Lying Enemy to This Whole Place said.

The Antagonist's Prison

"You look in bad shape for a nonplayer." She started strapping her costume back on. Leaned down to grab her book. There was a cushioned place for her to sit and wait for customers out of view.

"I just participated in the Arena. Got the shit kicked out of me," Aaron said.

"Did you face Critch?" Eager oohs and aahs from the now re-garbed Abby.

"If I did, do you think I'd be walking, much less talking?"

"I guess not. Be careful. With Critch back, we all have to be on guard."

"On the up and up," Mr. Bennett said with a tip of his hat.

"More than ever. Come again if you need anything. Have a good day."

"You as well," he said.

Outside, Your Imminent Unforewarned Reckoning lit another Indian clove. It ripped through his lungs in the best of unhealthy ways.

"That was nice of you not telling her you're Critch."

"She didn't need to know. Those who need it, know, those who don't, don't."

"Fuck a god, you suck at talking."

"I had to relearn how to speak. I lack a lot of the nuances." He headed off around the Arena's circle before taking a street he knew to take with no memory of it.

"Dude, you speak in Esperanto as if it was English."

"No idea what that means."

"Actually, you speak like a newspaper feature from Firefly."

"No idea what that means either."

"I have so much to teach you. I'm so excited."

"Can't reciprocate that affection."

"The most infamous thing I've heard of The Underground is Suicide Alley. Do you think we have time for that?"

"I have no idea what our time schedule is. If you want to visit Suicide Alley. I suppose we could do that."

"Do you know anything about suicide or depression?"

Battles and an Emporium

"No, I know Amber has depression. That's about it. When she's depressed at work I don't hold it to much of a candle. It decreases her work output. I usually send her home until she has a handle on it."

"Not exactly how you should approach her."

"I'm a boss. Cordial is how I approach my employees. Any more than that and I sacrifice the integrity of the business. I treat them well, but they are not my friends. Everything I have ever read says so."

"Do you think Amber needs help?"

"I have no idea. Probably. I'm not one to go to with heart issues."

"It's just...I'd think you'd understand how it feels to be distant and detached from the general populace."

"Never felt detached or attached. Just me."

The first building from the Arena started the three-block avenue of Suicide Alley. All main streets ran at rays from the Arena, with curved side streets connecting the voids between the main avenues. Chaotic alleys weaved stupid within the triangular blocks of The Underground. A starburst originating from the Arena.

"What's the fascination?" genocidic Critch said.

"Dark? I dunno. To run a business you need repeat customers. Suicide Alley has no repeats. So that means they have to charge immense rates for their chosen ways of killing people."

"That assumes they have bills to pay. Also, who says they stay dead?"

"They've got to have material costs, and rent to pay."

"I'm not sure if they have to pay rent."

"What? How? Why wouldn't they?"

"The Underground caters to services. If your service is deemed necessary, they keep you around. I'd venture, if you don't offer anything new, you can't establish a place."

"True market economy? Sounds weird and impossible. Preposterous Ayn Rand shit."

"Either way, we are doing something of some import. And wasting time exploring an action I do not support or believe in

The Antagonist's Prison

is not effective use of our time."

"Alright, then I'm fucking starving. I barely ate at the rape place."

"Are you looking for a restaurant that doesn't dual purpose?"

"That would be a plus."

"I gotcha. I know where we can go."

About three blocks from Suicide Alley, off one of the ten Mainways, Our Relentless Shadow lead Midge to a street crammed with tables full with customers. The most densely populated portion of The Underground. The line to the counter forty-thick.

"What is this?"

"This is A Slice of Heaven. The best bakery in the world. Three Michelin Star bakery you won't see on any list. If this society had their own rating system, this place still would have the highest ratings."

"I know I said this before, but I still love and hate this place. Euphoria is what you're looking for. I heard my dad say he got an Euphoria for Samantha Stones. The wine he named after me. He'd never been more proud of himself. Nor had he ever been so drunk. He actually passed out in the pool and my mom had to fish him out, laughing all the way."

"A Slice of Heaven has several Euphorias I would assume."

"Fuck yeah. I'm stoked to try the best bread in the world, whatever that means."

Behind the counter, dozens of bakers worked in a flurry of complexity and absolute mastery. Mastery Critch would have totally expected, save for the shame it brought upon him all of a sudden. Mr. Bennett was fairly good at his job. Skilled enough to have a name for himself in Indigo Bay. He made mistakes but few would consider him an amateur at this point. Amber said many times, watching him work was mesmerizing because he tended to do multiple orders with both hands.

There's a song, something something about the sound of the chain gang. Hope it did not get stuck in anyone's head. How their bangs made a rhythm that could be music. The pots banging, the paper ripping, the hands kneading, the dings of ovens and scootches

Battles and an Emporium

of bread, down to the hands doming the bread and even the sound of people crunching and moaning as they ate their croissants and slices. Most should understand the music of work. How, with just the right mind, everything could be music.

"And as they stirred, Heaven and Earth, they combined to one, and everything was everyone, and each one was all," Midge said.

"Soapmakers, Clutch," The! What! said.

"How do you know about them for someone so musically disinclined?"

"Disinclined? I'm starting to rub off on you."

"Shut it, I have a terrible parroting problem. I'm told that those who have that problem are more empathetic than others."

"Probably why I still talk the way I do."

"It'd offer at least one explanation. Back to how you know about Clutch."

"Gradick listened almost exclusively to seventies and eighties Arena rock. But Raile enjoyed modern punk and rock acts. Clutch was one of them. Raile and Gradick knew most of their songs by heart and they'd quote lyrics to each other at times when the lyrics matched the situation."

"What did you think of their relationship?"

Two plates appeared on the counter, each with four slices of white bread and two croissants. They were fifteen dollars total. Stoked for a normal price down here, Midge handed the waiter a twenty. They chose a place outside with a little table you might find outside a cafe in swank country. The black umbrella shielded them from The Drip, but not the chairs. They sat on the metal chairs with scattered droplets and little regard to wet corduroys.

"Honestly?"

"Yeah," Midge said. "Of course, I dislike half truths because I can tell that the person is lying every time. Micro expressions and all that."

"Well, honestly, I think Gradick settled for Raile."

"That's a first." They took a bite of the plain white bread. Chewed and swallowed then made eye contact. Neither spoke as

The Antagonist's Prison

they took another bite and another.

"Fuck me," Midge said.

"Innuendo," Your Imminent Unforewarned Reckoning said.

"No, seriously. Make this into a dildo and fuck me raw with it."

"Yeah, how the hell do you describe this?"

"Ooo, ooo, the winemaker's daughter to the rescue, what can I pull out of thin air? It's simple with a depth that cannot be explored enough. Structurally fluffy with enough substance to leave each bite enough to remember. The crust is firm but far from dry with an earthiness which compliments the skyward reaches of the core."

"That's impressive," The Antagonist said, looking around at the patrons of the Slice of Heaven. Some of them stared and whispered about him.

"Thank you. What's your problem?" Midge said, looking around as well. "Forget them. I want to try the croissant."

Midge shoved the whole thing in her mouth. "I should be thinking about carbs, huh?"

"Doubt it. This place bothers me, we should go soon."

"I said forget about them, or is it something else. It's something else, huh?"

"I think I like my job because, while I'm good at it, I'm always improving at it in minor ways everyday."

"Kaizen. Got it."

"What?"

"Continual, gradual improvement every day." Midge rolled up a slice of bread into a ball and took a chunk out of it, she sat back in relishment. After a moment, "Japanese word."

"Sure. But then I look at these bakers, taste this bread and it fills me with shame and hope."

"Finding someone better than you at something should be an inspiration, yeah. You're mature enough to know that. Everyone is better than you, you better than everyone."

"Oh, believe I understand that. It's one of my mottos."

"I know, that's something I like about you. You're mostly respectful of everyone, and you listen to everyone to improve

Battles and an Emporium

yourself. You're really good at it, too. So what's the issue?"

"I think I like a skilled labor job because I can improve at it. Because Critch was born the best. And it's one of the aspects I hate about him..."

"You! Come on, we talked about this."

"Me, I was the perfect killer. Fuck, that really does put a lot more weight to that. Saying it aloud."

"It really does. But the situation hasn't changed. What can you learn from that aspect of you?"

"I don't know. I guess I'd need to know more about that aspect of myself to explore it any."

"Exactly. Unfortunately, I can't help you with that. My mind can't register what Critch is. Other than it's an unthinkable creature from realms we are not meant to know."

"Cryptic."

"YOU HAVEN'T SEEN WHAT I'VE SEEN, AARON!" Midge said. Now everyone side-eyed them. "Sorry...I can't think about you like that. The sight of him maddens."

"Maddens?"

"Shut the fuck up, you malapropistic hypocrite."

"Sorry," Critch said with a chuckle. Lit a clove. Midge lit one of her filtered Lucky Strikes. Charlie scuttled out of Midge's purse. He raised his arms at her. Was he asking her to calm down? Shouldn't project onto a spider.

"Change of subject," Aaron said as a king might, though he meant it out of insecurity. "You said it was a first, that I think Gradick settled with Raile."

"Yeah, usually it's the other way around."

"Then you don't know Gradick how I did. He's very harsh, don't get me wrong, but he does it out of hope and critique. Raile just slams on you for everything you could be doing better. Raile acts from war. Gradick acts from peace."

"Is Raile really that way now? She used to be like Gradick."

"No. It's complicated. Gradick and Raile are brutally, uncomfortably honest. But Raile has gotten more ruthless. Gradick a bit

The Antagonist's Prison

more pressured-patient."

"But, Gradick isn't like that. He was a heartless, unforgiving taskmaster."

"Gradick and Raile only ever have a problem with authority. The outcome of their trials are for you. If you take offense it saddens them, because their intentions are just to show another way."

"Exactly. I'm glad we see eye to eye on that," Midge said very carefully. Aaron's opinions matching her own was very important to her, for some reason. Aaron said his opinion whether or not the other person shared it. And he was completely fine with the disagreement, because he was fine with being the one in the wrong and needing improvement.

"I saw Gradick and Raile as pin cushions," Midge said. "No matter what you did to them, still kept their shape. The happiest people ever despite all the violent jabs directed at them."

"It saddens me greatly that Gradick is elsewhere. Poor Raile lost her everything."

"But you said Gradick settled for Raile...?"

"I dunno. It's hard for me to articulate. There are no two people better suited for each other. But there is something I can't conceptualize that makes Raile not quite on Gradick's level."

"I can sort of see where you're coming from. Come on, eat a croissant. It'll cheer you up."

He did and it did cheer up The One Who Stares Back From The Void.

Old Men
and an
Exquisite Fur

About a block away from A Slice of Heaven, a girl, perhaps fifteen, in a sheer white dress sprinted out of the alleyway. She stopped to greet them before screeching bloody fucking murder, then ran down the street. Not a minute later, two men in mid-level business suits appeared, looked both ways, saw the growing-smaller girl, then saw the Strictly Friends. They nodded and were about to continue down the street.

Critch's smile spread awful.

Mr. Bennett came out crouched on the ground. Who knew how long later. Not very, he suspected. At least he was not in fetal this time. His vision untunneled. The two men dead on the ground. Two red smears on the wall led from about eight feet up where the mush of their heads first impacted. Their headless bodies next to each other. Skull fragments in a ten-foot radius. Must have smashed with a good deal of force to get that distance. Midge leaned casual against the wall, smoking a safe distance away. He stumbled at first, as his body remembered how to walk in this form.

"Well, I can't say that I enjoyed that. But you ending their rape hunt was satisfying in a schadenfreude sort of way. That's the Critch

The Antagonist's Prison

I heard about."

"No one deserves Critch."

"If anyone did, that scum did."

"I never was okay with the rape hunts."

"Isn't that...a good thing?" Midge said with more than a sprinkle of no shit.

"Think about it like this. With all the awful things we're likely to see down here, I have a reasonable amount of confidence that I won't berserk at the sights. But the rape hunts get me every time."

"So what do you think that means?" Midge said, following after, hesitating as she passed bodies.

"I don't know. Do you think it's significant?" Aaron said as if he were describing the end of the world.

"Probably. This is good, you're thinking about Critch and what he represents. Or, at least occasionally represents."

"Not going to get very far with it, I'm afraid."

"Maybe, but you know, baby steps."

The Brotherhood of Einingar, or however you said that shit, weren't hard to find. Old Norse on the cover of metal albums, fording a river that's rougher than any river could be. They tucked their well-kept beards into their belts. If they were Topside, could confuse them with a motorcycle gang, and it wouldn't surprise any involved if some of them were wild, free and ungoverned, or other bullshit outlaw claims.

These men and women followed Norse heathenry in the most old-school way they could manage. His Unflinching Grin thought Midge would have a good time.

The guard outside held himself ready like he begged you to speak so he could twist them words into fightin' ones. Muscled arms out and taut with dry skin and faded, cheap tattoos with words long illegible. Bare hands cracked and held in coked-out fists.

"Sir," Your Imminent Unforewarned Reckoning said. "We'd like

Old Men and an Exquisite Fur

to speak with Oscar if you don't mind."

"I doubt he wants to speak with a scrawny motherfucker, or his tiny wench," the man said, looking up and up at Aaron.

"I'm a little fireball in bed, though. A tiny one with a blue flame you're afraid to put out with your fingers." She mimed the gesture.

"I'm sure you are, little one, but you're going to have to wait. Oscar hasn't come back from The Arena. I hear rumors The Antagonist is back. What an exciting time. Oscar has always wanted to speak with The True Rager. I know he'll be seeking him out."

The True Rager would never be one of his titles.

"Well, his time has come," Never Be Called The True Rager, To Reiterate, said.

The guard's energy refracted through Aaron's energy and left him confused.

Midge looked at him with a teacher's disapproval.

"What? I've got to own up to it if I'm going to get over it."

"Can I talk to you over here, Aaron?" Midge said with a pivoted finger.

They crossed the street and sat on a damp bench, lit by a hooded lamp. A postcard scene for The Underground, and an iconically heavy spot for a terse scolding.

"Let's roleplay here for a minute. I'm an empowered psychopath, I come up to you like Patrick Bateman and I'm like, hey bro, I hear you've always wanted to meet a murderer, check this shit out," Midge said, caressing her body.

Charlie skittered down to Aaron's lap, curled up, and noped out of this conversation.

"I think we need to revisit the deal we made yesterday."

"That's why we're over here."

"Tip-toes the line. Oh, this is fun, can I be the self-empowered biker who'd love to beat the shit out of a child toucher?"

"So you get it. Why the fuck did you tell him that you're The Antagonist? What good would that do?"

"Oh, he may want to beat me, show me his manhood. But he can't because Oscar wants to meet me, so he has to hold his breath."

The Antagonist's Prison

"So you think telling him that you're a berserker will be your VIP ticket in? I don't understand you, Aaron. You act like an idiot, but you're smart, and you think fast. It's going to get you in trouble."

"Dunno if I act like an idiot ever. Seems like your impression of me is flawed if that's the case. And it has landed me face down in the past. I've taken my bruises and lumps for it. I've learned when shit is about to hit the fan and when to move out of the way. More importantly, I know when whoever threw the shit isn't strong enough to lob the shit all the way to the shit, so everyone who thinks they know when to dodge the shit runs the fuck away, and I stand there laughing at the shit who threw the shit."

"That last shit was for good measure wasn't it?"

"Most likely." The One Who Stares Back from the Void smirked.

Rambunction came around the corner. The Norse Men swung wide. Some of them not handling the change in momentum well. But Oscar strut with a determination The Antagonist recognized in his own gait.

"Well, besides your pretentious little speech that fell apart toward the end," Midge said. "You've shown remarkable restraint in the past on who you tell. I disagree with your decision to tell the guard."

"It's going to grease the wheels with these guys. I hope."

"My goodness, if prayers don't come true," Oscar said. His smile turned up his whole face, causing his forehead to smile. He came up to Aaron with a bear hug, consuming him in mulled wine clothing and hard muscle. "If it isn't the one and true berserker, come inside. We shall feast. I will have my wife see to your hands."

They stepped into an anachronistic bubble. Retrofitted the blue stone building into a mess hall straight from Beowulf. Two long tables and benches. Full-bodied women erupted out of the backrooms and collided with their full-bodied men like penguins come home, finding their mate despite each looking the exact same.

"When is this going to turn bad?" Midge said, watching the happy spectacle.

"Don't know yet."

Old Men and an Exquisite Fur

A woman made like a dam sat next to Aaron and tortured his hand, wrapping it up in medical gauze, then took out some super glue and closed some of the wounds on his face. She asked him to take off his shirt to stitch other wounds.

"Welcome to my house. My name is Oscar," he said sitting next to them, making both feel like children.

"Pleasured," Midge said. "Goddamnit. Pleased to meet you, Oscar. The Antagonist. Fuck! Aaron is rubbing off on me."

"Before I ask why you've finally graced us with your presence. I need to know. What is it like? Believe you me, I've tried. I've tried the berserkergang, done the herbs. But seeing you again. I've seen nothing like that. That horrible sight, worse than I remember it, more terrible each time." The rowdy welcome home stopped to listen as Oscar described Aaron's shenanigans. "The glimpses I managed. I could not look, nor could I look away. The twitching, stop motion, strobe-like movements which started further than your arm, the strikes which never seemed to end their arches, or start..."

His face caved in on itself as he dissolved into the memory. His description turned to mutters, aging him as he spoke. His wife stopped fixing He Who Smiles Back and consoled her partner. Several of the masculine figures cried.

"I apologize," Critch said.

Oscar sniffed back man snot. "No, no need. It was a terrible honor. Thank you, Critch, for reminding us of the power of the Gods. For sometimes they are kind and sometimes terrible. The latter of which we must see from time to time. It is not often we have a chance to converse with mortal gods among men, or vail my cohorts with your talents."

He pat The Antagonist on the back and he about spit up from the force. His eyes widened and body twitched.

"First, don't do that." Aaron gripped the table, broke wood off, but the pain from his treated hands made it worse. Midge held his leg. Rubbed his back. Mr. Bennett calmed down. "It feels like someone stepping into me from behind."

The Antagonist's Prison

"You make it sound unpleasant," Oscar said as if he were about to HoHoHo afterward.

"It isn't pleasant."

"From my position, it sounds glorious. A feeling of divine intervention."

"It might be if I didn't come out with blood on my hands and torn bodies beneath me. The dread that comes with it is what makes it unpleasant. The feeling itself might not be so bad if someone else controlling my actions released me."

"Ah, so you feel as if it is a possession. That isn't the way I'd interpret it. Because it is still you, just a relocation of your head, so to speak. Alright, son, you two came here for a reason. How may I help you? Do you wish to join our ranks? Sounds as though you'd benefit from what we teach about the push and pull of life."

"Mr. Kinns has stolen our friend," Midge said. "And burned Aaron's shop. We're here to show him what for."

"Ah ha, you need a token to show our approval. That means you must go through our Initiation. To the backyard everyone! Bring the chains," Oscar said giddy.

Everyone rose at once and headed out the back.

"What do your shit smarts say about this?"

"They're telling me to go fuck yourself."

"That's not what I have planned for you."

"You're quite good at that."

"I know, right?"

Out back was a training courtyard. Old-school wooden dummies cut to shit. Metal practice weapons hung on racks. The Drip made them shine slick. The men practicing stopped and the courtyard quieted.

At the back was a stage with two, ten-foot wooden poles a foot thick. Men threaded heavy-gauged chains through the eyebolts on the top. At the end of each chain was a manacle. Strong enough to hold a ship in a storm.

"To join the Order of Einingar, you must show knowledge of our culture and be able to take a hit. You can take a hit better than

Old Men and an Exquisite Fur

the rest of us. But your nature makes this a special occasion. Critch, if you would please chain yourself up."

At the mention of his name, the courtyard somehow quieted more.

"Please, everyone grab a chain. Just in case The Antagonist comes."

The entire order dusted their hands with talcum powder before grabbing a section of chain. A double tug of war against The Antagonist, and they knew they would lose. Aaron sighed and climbed on the stage, put his wrists in the manacles. His arms drawn up for the hundredth time. He waited for the questions he had no idea how to answer. The old wood speckled with blood brought waves of ancient buried shame. Thirty huge men and women per chain gripped with their sixty flexed bodies.

Oscar's wife came out with a whip, and two grabbed Midge. She panicked and screamed.

"Midge!" Our Relentless Shadow yelled. "Look at me."

But The Antagonist could already feel Critch coming on. Who felt who is kind of the point.

"I'm sorry, Missy, I don't like doing this to softer people. Pronounce the world tree to me," Oscar's wife said.

"Uh, Yggdrasil?" The whip cracked across her back, spraying blood. She yelped. Critch punted Aaron away for a fifty-yard field goal.

The warped metal of defunct manacles sliced deep into his wrists. The twelve-inch poles left scrambled trails in his wake. The entire Order collapsed across the yard. Titanic people on their backs, out of breath and shiny from sweat. Their palms bled onto the dusty ground. The chains must have slipped link by link through their fingers.

Oscar slumped against the fence. A weapon rack toppled and its contents strewn about. His wife checked for vitals. His face in pieces.

The Antagonist's Prison

Midge cried on the ground, her white shirt in tatters. Blood flowed from six welts across her back and soaked into her shirt.

"I'm sorry," The One Who Stares Back said.

"Are you okay," she said, through her stigmata tears.

"Did you berserk?"

"No, the whips came too quickly for me to focus." She pulled apart the useless shackles dug into his wrists and held seeping gougings.

"Are you sure you're okay?" Midge said as blood pulsed around her fingers.

"I'm going to need a transfusion if this vacation keeps going like this."

Midge laughed. "What's wrong with you?"

He stood up, bringing her up with him. "Many specific things."

"Fuck you."

"Later."

"See, you can do it too."

"How long was I out?"

"About two minutes. They could barely slow you down. You collapsed after you hit Oscar. Out for about a minute after."

With the help of his wife, Oscar came over. Gaia herself was shocked he was alive, much less awake.

"You were right about your lot taking a hit," Aaron said, trying to pull a Midge and make light.

It worked and Oscar snorted. A few teeth fell out. He unclipped a hatchet from his belt. Into the blade and handle was etched an ornate tree design. He handed it to Midge.

"You know more about our culture than you let on, little one. You have my permission. And if you do enter battle with Mr. Kinns. My Order would be honored to fight alongside a one true berserker, Critch."

Not even the one who came up with the title, which will not be mentioned, could continue using it.

"Let's go find a place where they sell shirts. If this keeps going like this, we're gonna need a stash," Midge said, wincing as she walked.

Old Men and an Exquisite Fur

Midge found a shop, as the idea of buying a shirt in any context was beyond Aaron. If he needed a new shirt, The Antagonist just grabbed a blank. Perk of owning his store and didn't pay much attention to shrink. Also, it tripped Mr. Bennett out that he normally ran a clothing store, this current life was not the norm and he reminded himself to keep this in mind.

Ms. Estire didn't seem to mind much that her back showed bloody welts. She didn't seem to mind her body at all. He mostly knew those obsessed with their "shameful" flaws down to tidbits in their armpits. Except for Raile. Raile's pride in her body, her pride in everything about herself, her whole world, her everything, inspired.

The Platonic Companion did make adjustments to look how her inner mind perceived herself, of course, she dyed her hair red and she had full tattoo sleeves. But as far as normal things children obsessed about, she accepted and moved on. That sort of perspective was a rare quality, one that should be sought. It should be heralded.

Most of the store's merchandise was hide and fur. Midge grabbed a white tank, first guess was cotton, but we all knew better. Rough hewn tables showcased the skeletons of several animals, made into a variety of scrimshaw, carving decorations and accessories of various capacities.

"Holy shit, this is soft," Midge said.

Charlie leapt onto the fur then immediately bounced off. He shook his legs, flicked his fur off. He did not seem to appreciate the softness.

Midge giggled. "So, like you said, what's the terrible thing about this place."

"How much you wanna bet that's polar bear fur."

"Jesus."

"I'm sure it was killed humanely, too."

Critch went to the counter and rang the little bone chimes made from bald eagle or something. A small-but-done-some-

The Antagonist's Prison

gnarly-ass-shit kid came out of the back.

"What's this made out of?" Midge said.

"Baby seal, clubbed them myself. About four."

Midge swallowed. "How much?"

"Twenty four."

"Thousand? Fuck my mouth," Midge said.

Your Imminent Unforewarned Reckoning put a Favor on the counter and the boy gaped at it.

"Are those things really that valuable?" Midge said.

"Yes, I could buy the bar with one of these. There weren't too many when I received them. That's kinda how value works, right? What's your name, man?"

He didn't answer. His world fell apart in the presence of a Favor.

"Hey, look at me," The Antagonist said, strangely demanding for him.

"What?"

"What's your name?"

"Sean, sir."

"My name is Aaron, this is Midge. Don't need to call me sir."

"You have how many of those again?" Midge said

"Around two hundred."

"WHAT THE FLYING FUCK?!" the boy said as he fell backward. "I've only seen these in the hands of the people who run our society. They hand them out like they're handing off a piece of their soul! How in the hell do you have TWO HUNDRED FAVORS?!"

"No need to yell. I was paid with them for awhile."

"YOU WERE PAID WITH FAVORS! TWO HUNDRED!"

"I think the exclamation points were redundant," Midge said. "So, wait, let me put this together, only people outside of Topside society know what these are. And only the top rung of these people actually own them and they treat them like heirloom jewelry, right?"

"More or less."

"So the only way you could have these is if you killed some of the people who run this society. Right?"

"Madam Ava made room for herself using me."

Old Men and an Exquisite Fur

"So you killed at least how many to get paid that much."
"No clue."
"You're saying you killed untouchable, unknowable oligarchs," Sean said. "Should I even be talking to you. Who the fuck are you?!"
"Use your head," Aaron said.
"The only person I know who could have done that...There's no way..."

Tinkling bone chimes over the entrance announced her arrival. The Widow in Yellow emanated once again in her finery. The dress a straight rectangle to the ground, but her powerful hips popped out of the ridiculously high slit. The neckline to her waist. Enormous black hat tilted low over her mime-painted face. Midge flushed with jealousy or attraction, His Unflinching Grin couldn't tell.

Nova clicked over on black sky-high heels. Neatly folded her lacy black parasol on her approach. Charlie mocked her with each raised side of his body to match her heel clicks.

The Widow's face done up minimalist, with the upper half white, the bottom half down to her cleavage black. A yellow half-fire jacket, black aircraft cable tied around her waist, and noose head thrown over her square shoulders.

She knelt in front of Charlie and said, "I've never appreciated your insolence." She stood to address Aaron. "Hello, Our Imminent Unforewarned Reckoning. Do you remember me?"

Her black whole eye lenses locked with Aaron's grayed-out irises. She handed him a note and kissed him on the cheek in that awkward cultured greeting sort of way. Her hands touched his and she held them there for a moment longer than needed before retracting.

"Hello Midge, my name is November, it is nice to meet you."

Midge, pissed, stuck her hand out. The Widow in Yellow shook it.

"It was good to see you again, Aaron." The Widow in Yellow left. Aaron and Midge stayed in their photographed positions. Charlie hissed.

"The fuck was that? That was November? That was your 'guardian' of sorts? Fuck me," Midge said, failing to rip the note

The Antagonist's Prison

from Aaron's hands.

Hello Aaron,
Do you remember me? I am pleased you have returned. Madam Ava wishes to meet Samantha 'Midge' Estire. Her champion is, as always, on the forefront of The Lady Made of Dark's mind. Mine as well. At your earliest convenience, please come to The Lounge for your token of Favor.
Love, November

"We need to pay Madam Ava a visit. She wants to talk to you," Aaron said.

"Me? Don't know how I feel about that."

"Neither do I."

Midge slowly took off her shirt, flinching as the welts burned. They used all the styptic bandages to seal her up. She eased the baby seal fur shirt on.

"Liked what you saw?" she said.

"It's turning out to be a fantastic day."

"Holy shit, all this shit is happening in one day. Now I'm tired."

"It was good to meet you, Sean. Don't spend that Favor all in one place."

Sean said nothing. Aaron broke him. They left the fur store and walked down the block.

"Alright, so two Heads down," Midge said. "Madam Ava will give it to you no problem probably."

"Hopefully."

"Who's left?"

"The Smuggler Confederacy, The Seekers, The Lock Operators, and The Cultists."

"No problem. Easy as pie. Let's go. To The Smugglers, then Madam Ava's and take a nap there."

"Sounds like a plan," he said.

All the buildings they passed the same height, same fronts, same catalog appearance. Nothing to betray the debauchery inside.

Old Men and an Exquisite Fur

Who knew how big or what the layout of the inside of the buildings were. Which were all one, and which were separate businesses.

Midge yawned and stretched. "You seem fine. You know, beyond the wounds and blood loss."

"'Live in the moment' line."

"I don't get it, Aaron. You have crazy baggage. So I see why you live like a hermit. But you've gone a step further. You don't have close friends, no family, no support, just you. I like that, but that's a hard life to live. You ignore all your problems completely, not caring if they go away or not."

"I guess." Aaron didn't notice the sudden quiet in the street. No one about. "But that's partly out of necessity, partly my own fault for keeping people so far away. I'm used to being alone. Dealing with my problems myself. I kinda like it because, since I have no one to complain to, I can't complain. Just accept things as they are and try to make it a little better when I can."

"Don't you get lonely? I mean, I live by myself and usually keep to myself. But I had Jazz as a close friend. I visit my family often. Support groups are good just to have another perspective. I mean, you can only shadowbox with yourself for so long."

"Sure, I get lonely. Been about three years, I guess. It comes and goes. I mean, the whole reason I went on that date with Jaslynn was because I sit in my house at night and sometimes I wish there was someone there with me." The One Who Stares Back From The Void left a black hole from where he paused. "But it's strange. I have Tyler, he's a good guy. Gradick and Raile would love to have me as a close friend. But they see friendship in a way I don't like. Tyler has close friends and they talk about bullshit problems that I don't see as applicable to me. I don't see why they'd care, or understand my problems, they don't want to think like me, which is fine, but I can't view them as close if that's their prerogative. I should be closer to Frank. I want a friend who I don't have to be worried about being me with."

No one but Midge noted how people crossed the street as they approached. Or turned around, remembering where they could

The Antagonist's Prison

supposedly be going. Gave Aaron a wide berth.

"So, if I was younger," Midge said. "I'd say that you could talk to me. But I know what you're talking about. You need a friend who shares your ideas and complements you. That's fine. Everyone is better than you, you better than everyone. I know you respect me. And you make me laugh. I'm down for hanging out with a dick that has those qualities."

"Did you just come up with that?"

"What?"

"That we are all dicks, but you gotta find the person with a dick that you like."

"Uhhh...No, but when we speak of this again, I am that brilliant. Fuck, I should write that down."

Kinships and a Pollutant

The Lady Made Of Dark's Bump In The Night hadn't gone too far into his mind. They said people had fantasies. For the life of him, Aaron didn't know what his were. He had them, according to everything. The ability to imagine the future and how it could be better or worse was the basis for all human culture. Entire religions established to only exist in what was happening now. That concept was alien to him. He had no plans for the future until he decided to meet with The Second Lust. Completely content with his rigid routine.

The people down here had so many things they wanted, they couldn't get all of them fulfilled.

"How much darker can we go?" Midge said.

"What do you want? Sex with a baby?"

"What the fuck? No! Fuck a god! No! This place is truly fucked."

"You're starting to get The Underground."

"Not fucking babies, but I think something sexual. I don't think we've done anything sexual yet. That's the most depraved seed I can come up with."

"I think when we visit Madam Ava's that quota will be fulfilled sufficiently."

"BDSM is so boring. Power exchange might be the most basic

The Antagonist's Prison

definition of the sexual impulses. Fuck the last generation, that's probably why Madam Ava has so much influence down here. Her brand of fantasy is so common. Not to mention, I suspect her level of power exchange is marketed as exclusive. No, I require darker."

That would be hard. The lamps were pathetic, the Drip overbearing. The patrons avoiding the two were now uncomfortably obvious.

"You're going to have to come up with something on your own, little one."

"Don't call me that. How about a peeping tom theme?"

"Still need to be more specific."

Midge made a 'p' sound at the beginning of her sigh. "Is there a block we can peruse to get a sense? I suspect there is."

"Well, let's go for a walk. If there was a cluster of sex shops, it'd be around Madam Ava's. And as dark as you want, it'd be around the outskirts of her territory."

"Let's test my tolerance."

An explosion sounded in the distance, followed by a plume of smoke. The few denizens close around them turned down and away from the sound. Only concerned themselves with themselves.

"Raile?" Midge said with a yeah-of-course-shrug.

"Most likely."

"We're going to run into her at some point aren't we?"

"I hope not."

"What? Isn't she your best friend?"

"She was. I don't know if she still is my best friend or has finally fallen into the agent of chaos she's destined to become."

"If that's true, she needs you to ground her."

"I don't want to be a rock. People have always treated me one of three ways. As a fool, a refuge, or a tool. I can't be someone's refuge right now, especially against the caliber of storm Raile embodies at the moment."

"You know nothing of what it is to be in a relationship. You have all these fears and assumptions. Yet you've never been in one. So how could you even comprehend your role in a relationship? You know what my favorite definition of a hipster is?"

Kinships and a Pollutant

"Are you really calling me, of all people, a hipster?" Aaron said with the thunder of Xerxes' army.

"Let me finish. You're the one wearing a fedora. And I'm the one with dyed red hair and tattoos. Listen a sec. Hipsters don't know what they are. They just know what they don't want to be. So yeah, you're a relationship hipster. You don't know what relationship you want, but you certainly know what you don't want."

"I don't see the problem in that." Our Relentless Shadow stopped and lit a clove. Leaned over her. Maybe intimidating, but she got that he was trying to be receptive.

"Of course you don't. Let's say you've never had a sandwich. But you know what you don't want in a sandwich. You also know that a sandwich is basically meat in between bread, sometimes with cheese, occasionally mustard and mayo. Oh, you might say, I don't like mustard or mayo, and I refuse to eat a sandwich with turkey. Great, that's three things you don't want on a sandwich. You have no idea what a great sandwich can be. Literally hundreds of toppings to choose from. That's experience. The toppings. But since you've never had a relationship, how could you possibly know what you want? You learn what you want by trying all the toppings. You may discover you really like hummus on a sandwich, maybe not. Until you try it, how the fuck do you know?"

"I'm following." Aaron's smoke concealed the space between him and Midge.

"Good. The bread and meat of a relationship are easy. You know, thrust thrust bang bang. You have loyalty, companionship, and support. That's a decent structure for a relationship. But you have no idea what my toppings are."

"What happens when I find one of your toppings displeasing?" Our Unflinching Grin said. Violence was never implied.

"Well, that depends. There are toppings you can tolerate and toppings that will ruin the sandwich just by their presence. For example, I despise raw onions. Even if I take them off the sandwich I can still taste them. However, I love grilled onions on a sandwich."

"If I'm following, you like a flawed topping transformed into

The Antagonist's Prison

something you like?"

"Umm, sure. Let's say that's what I was going for. Fuck a god, Aaron, you have an amazing mind. Why don't you ever use it?"

Aaron's flicked clove sizzled in a puddle. Each boot step made a tiny splash. "Never seen use. My career has more to do with craftsmanship than intelligence. I prefer it that way."

"Then that is my intention. My raw onion with you is your misuse of the intellect you are clearly afraid of. Grill that shit."

"And what am I supposed to do with it? My life doesn't need smarts."

"To improve. To fight and feed. The creature you harbor is instinct only. You can't beat an expert on instinct by trying to catch up to him. You have to beat him with something else."

"It'd be a fool's errand to think of Critch as unintelligent."

"You're entirely missing the point." Midge pressed her index finger against her thumb and repeatedly pointed the circle at him. "If you are outmatched, change tactics to take the advantage away from the enemy."

"You're suggesting some Sun Tzu shit on the fucking Antagonist?"

"Dude, Aaron, how do you know nothing but seem to know things written by those who know a lot?"

"What?"

"I know, sorry. I don't even know what that meant. You know Sun Tzu? Critch is an enemy with better supply lines, better positioning and better tactics. What do you do?"

"Run away?"

"Partially. I believe the term is baiting. If I were to venture a guess, Critch doesn't like you. He will pursue you if you run. Stretch his strengths until you can snap one or more of his advantages." Midge gestured in a direction. "To the Fetishes?"

"The Smugglers first, then satiate your groin appetites."

The weight of the black grew heavy. If he survived this, the brightness of Topside would be unbearable. The Drip never let Critch spend too long in his head as random drops hit shoulders or

Kinships and a Pollutant

hands. This was why most who spent a good deal of time in this awful place wore hats or some kind of umbrella.

Rare groups of people watched them as they watched them back. He Who Smiles Back's dulled senses were stretched raw. The mistrust of his surroundings thinned him out, which allowed the features of Critch to press closer to the world.

"Where do all these people, willing or otherwise, come from? I can't imagine they find their way down here on a leisurely stroll that just took too long."

"There are dozens of ways to The Underground. Usually for a price. Sometimes you express interest on the internet and people like Twin find you. If you're unlucky, The Smuggler Confederacy just plain kidnaps you."

"Oh good, and we're going to curry favor with them?" Midge said.

"It shouldn't be so bad."

"Our definition of 'so bad' is quite skewed at this point."

"To be fair, mine has always been at a pretty strange standard deviation."

On the east side of The Underground, at least as far as one could tell when below, were The Docks. Until you calibrated and cured your confused sense of direction, finding your way was mostly done by judging where you were in relation to The Arena.

The Docks were for the rich beyond GDPs. The yachts were not only fancy as hell, but were teched out beyond any military. Some stalls had elegant roomy submarines. Unlike the harbor in Indigo Bay, these ships never stayed long. One of the primary ways into The Underground was through one of two Locks. From the top of the ramp, Your Imminent Unforewarned Reckoning saw *The Adumbration*, Madam Ava's black yacht with red trim hidden in the dusk of the lake.

Inside the Smuggler's Confederacy, a room filled with desks upon desks of people wearing headphones tapping away on steampunk morse code tablets. Green and purple text fell down their screens.

A woman approached in librarian conservative. "Can I help you?"

The Antagonist's Prison

"They're not using Morse Code," Midge said.

"No, we use our own encryption and shadow network. Who are you two? We don't handle walk-ins."

"I thought we needed to schedule a lock trip," Aaron said.

"The locks haven't worked in two months, sorry."

"We are planning on moving on Mr. Kinns and would like to get Permission from your Head to do so."

"Luciana is busy...Do I know you?"

"My name is Aaron Bennett. This is Midge Estire. How long have you worked for the Smuggler Confederacy?"

"Twenty years." Matter of fact.

"Then you'll know me as Critch."

The din of the taps in the room stopped. The silence unsettled.

"Get back to work." The business resumed, though remarkably slower. "Yes. You look good, Critch...It's good to see you again and finally on your own volition."

"Are you kidding me? He looks wrecked," Midge said.

"My dear, you have seen nothing of the damage to this man's body that I have seen. Mrs. Luciana would love to meet with you."

"I barely remember her, to be honest."

"I believe you. Please follow me." Stuttered giggle with no eye contact. Her shoulders hunched away from Her Dear Apocalypse.

They weaved around desks, all of which starkered terror at Our Relentless Shadow. A zone of silence in a four-desk radius.

A manual lift down a level to a warehouse filled with dark stone cubes. Those willing to be here stood in a queue to explain to the ambassadors why they were here. They were directed to wherever they were useful. The loading dock lay empty. A vague memory spoke of being unloaded.

Into the office at the back, Luciana. A woman Aaron trusted, though this was a first impression deja vu. Luciana studied two tablets, shuffled things between them or within the individual tablets themselves. Her black, thick-rimmed glasses and strong jaw clenched as she sorted whatever was in front of her. Blue hair pulled back into a practical bun. An intricate braid along the left

Kinships and a Pollutant

side of her head.

"Ma'am?" the escort said.

Luciana stood and smiled warmly. "Oh, The Antagonist has returned. How are you?"

Luciana was a matronly woman of genuine congeniality. A sort of mama bear. Like Midge, her body had heft to it. Her and Madam Ava had a long, storied history. They ran their businesses in similar fashions. Never owed debts, respectful of everyone they met, and never let anyone assume their friendliness should be excused for naivety or weakness.

The mama bear description fit Luciana well. She would ruin your whole world with a smile. Being on the other side of The Smuggler Confederacy was not where you wanted to be. The extent of her blacklist was far-reaching and weaved its influence into even the most basic of Topside amenities.

"I've been better, as you can see. It's good to see you again," Mr. Bennett said.

"No one deserves Critch. It's good to have a discussion with you when you are not on the inside of a titanium sarcophagus. Please have a seat. And who might you be?"

"My apologies, this is Midge Estire."

"Pleasure to meet you, Midge. It's nice to meet someone Critch admires." Luciana poured some foul-smelling tea from a steaming pot. "'Tis a rare leaf. I had a moment to myself and decided to have a proper moment."

Somewhere in Aaron's gory past he heard of the theory that productive people on this echelon didn't have time to relax. What they got were moments. And they treated them as precious. It was an honor for Luciana to use her moment on them, and they both knew it.

Luciana locked eyes with Charlie. He stretched up and waved. "Hello, you rapscallion. I see Madam Ava finally offloaded this one onto you, Aaron."

"I don't mind."

Charlie settled back down onto his shoulder.

The Antagonist's Prison

Luciana smiled. "Join me, if you would. I'm glad for your visit. I've enjoyed your company in the past, though I doubt you remember many of our encounters. That sometimes feral brain of yours was often enlightening in its recklessness. Whilst Madam Ava gathered your entourage to bring you to The Lounge, we'd often have long discussions of our shared afflictions."

"You're a berserker?" Midge said.

"Not in the traditional sense, Miss Estire. My berserk acts more as a stillness that emits from my body."

"So it is a berserk?" Midge said with a sweet hunger.

Luciana judged Midge for a minute. "We are a rare kind, yes. I've met very few feminine iterations of the berserk. Maybe two men and two women, a few along the spectrum. All with varying levels of extremity. The male version is far more common, though I think the three of us know Critch is something else entirely. My study of him helped me understand more of myself, yet it didn't shine any light whatsoever on the Antagonist. Not even *my* Stills seemed to affect him. And usually my Stills kill everyone in line of sight."

"Kills? Mine doesn't kill. Everyone just stops moving for hours and I seizure."

"Interesting. My Stills last for an agonizing minute, then everyone's bodily functions cease. It has been a useful tool in the past against those who might jeopardize my operations. I've never heard of one lasting longer than half an hour. Are you sure it doesn't just feel like hours?"

"With heed of patronization. That seems like a silly question."

"I suppose. What does Critch do during your Stills? His emergences are some of the few times since I gained control of the Still that it's happened involuntarily. It did nothing to him. Other than frustrate him that he couldn't kill anyone. Gut-wrenchingly terrible."

"Gut-wrenching! Perfect. The Antagonist is gut-wrenching. Sometimes literally! Sorry. As to address your question. Critch loves acting in my Stills. His normal glee spreads into exhilaration."

"Critch wanted to be contained. With The Widow in Yellow's

Kinships and a Pollutant

money, I devised a way to contain you to your satisfaction. Placed them around the world at several Waypoints." Luciana ignited the tablet. Without too much searching, she opened a sheet and began scrolling down. Dates, timestamps and codenames of the people Aaron had killed. She kept scrolling to make the point but got nowhere near the bottom.

"It is an impressive list." She shuddered. "Over a thousand confirmed kills, not to mention collateral not taken into account."

"Wait," Midge said, stopping the scroll. "The time stamps on these don't make sense."

Luciana smiled an oh-you-noticed-an-inconsistency-isn't-that-fun. "Why not?"

"Two same day hits in South Africa and Delhi, five hours apart."

"Do you think they are inaccurate?"

"As all get out. I've made that flight."

"Who said November flew?" Luciana smiled again and powered down the tablet, signaling the end of the conversation. "Come! Let me give you a tour of the facilities as we speak on our shared conditions."

Luciana stood for the first time with a purposeful grace. "Some call this Port Underground. Unfortunately, the only lock in operation right now has gone rogue and refuses to help anyone save for The Prismatic Orthodoxy and The Grand Innovator. The Scientists split by gender when Brooke and her husband... divorced for some reason. Now, Sam, once a long time friend, only works for Mr. Kinns and Ms. Hopper. Brooke has not been able to fix her lock, and as such, the dock has been rather dry, as we now must rely on the Tunnels to ferry in our goods."

Hundreds of workers moved in the darkness with electric torches blinking in and out, stretching for several blocks. Perhaps a few hundred yards away was a bright beacon. The Lady Made of Dark's Bump In The Night didn't know what it was, but part of him knew the place. He spent quite a long time within that light.

"This is one of several Ossuaries, as they're called, located

The Antagonist's Prison

around this Underground," Luciana said.

"Ha! I knew there was more than one," Midge said.

"Of course, there are several. That is the main function of The Smuggler Confederacy, to transport goods to the various Undergrounds."

The librarian from earlier came up with a tablet. They glanced over. Luciana smiled and showed them the scrolling green, blue and purple patterns on the screen.

"Go ahead and read it," she said, then laughed. Her eyes did not scan as she read. They spread apart. Read on her inside peripheral vision. Both briefly tried to spread their eyes out so they looked in opposite directions. Would snap a muscle before any progress.

"Who fixed it?" Luciana said.

"The Trujillo sister is in The Underground." The librarian eyed Aaron, ready for retribution. For what, only she knew.

"Find her before Madam Ava does. Bring her here."

"Raile?" Aaron said.

"Yes. Rudy works for me and makes all my engines. Though I've never met the man, he does good work. No one knows how to recreate his engines, but he has yet to improve upon the design. I concluded a long time ago that he was not the inventor. With the Rumormill's help, I found he has a sister. That sister just fixed the lock and is now in The Underground."

"Good luck with Raile," Aaron said.

"You know her?"

"Yes, I was to be the best man at her wedding. Before the Cultists killed Gradick. Now I suspect she is on the warpath."

"Gradick Hatch?"

"Yes..."

"Interesting, very interesting. Which means Madam Ava already knows about her. Fuck." To the Librarian, "Find Carly. Aaron, might I ask you a favor?"

"Whatever I'm willing to offer."

"Still as savage as always. Raile. Where would you suspect that she would rest down here?"

Kinships and a Pollutant

"The Scientists or Madam Ava's. I don't know who she might deem acceptable."

"The Scientists? Have you not been listening? They have been shunned to the operation of the locks. The Heathens have taken over their power structure."

"Who are the Heathens?"

"An anarchist collective, led by the enigmatic Asher."

"That's where she'll end up."

A tall girl with an innocent face appeared next to them. Her sudden existence didn't sit with His Unflinching Grin. Both Midge and Luciana rose to their toes as the smile stretched. Aaron stopped it.

"Aaron..." Midge said.

"Sorry."

"Your control is, as always...impressive," The Hider of Tragic said.

"And Midge stopped her Still as well," Aaron said.

"Yes, well done, Miss Estire."

"Ummm," Carly said, braced against the railing. Her knuckles white and thin arms shaking.

"I want you to take one of The Scientist batteries to the Heathen House." Luciana's calm orders soothed the nervous girl. "Tell Asher to give it to Raile when she shows up. Then inform him that The Smuggler Confederacy has a better offer than Madam Ava as regards to her employment."

"For certain," Carly said. She covered the distance out of the loading dock with a world-record-paced stride.

"Here's the horrific part. Had you berserked. No amount of speed can outrun Critch. I've witnessed you appear in front of cars. Half the reason we started using Trujillian engines is because of The Antagonist. We don't know if they're fast enough."

"Numbers and distance never matter."

"That's the mantra Madam Ava passed around," Luciana said. The three sighed.

"No one deserves Critch," both Luciana and Critch said.

"Cheers to that," Midge said with her teacup raised.

The Antagonist's Prison

They descended the stairs and turned into the dark warehouse. Luciana grabbed a chemical torch and lit it. Moved into the blackness of dark storage containers. "Do you know the difference between what we do, versus what Critch does?"

"I understand the biomechanics better than most. If Aaron and I get through this I would love to interview you for my paper."

They passed rows and rows of shipping containers stacked three high for a few blocks in all directions. Horrors ranged from crying to screaming to laughing. Animal growls and tiny howls. Heard fighting. Smelled urine, blood, shit, and fear. Workers with brooms, mops, and water sprays to clean.

"I think we can come to some sort of accord, Midge. We have a variety of packages to be delivered to the various shops around or to other Undergrounds. I pride myself on a fast turnaround with the exception of a few very rare requests. Either way, anything under our care is given the utmost quality of caregiving, as far as the participants are willing. Our staff is the best of the best when dealing with all matters. We do our best to treat our packages as well as we can."

They came upon a clearing around the middle of the Ossuary. A plastic cell in the middle of a column of light. Surrounding The Antagonist Prison were bars, upon electrical wires, upon cables, upon abandoned watchtowers. The walls of his cell six feet thick.

"The Widow in Yellow still uses this as a holding place for her berserkers. None of them have been able to get past your cell."

"I remember conversations with you in that cell."

They climbed to a raised staging area to witness the intricacy, set up to somehow stop Critch. The complex weaves of bars, cables, and trip hazards.

"The Critch I've seen, the warzone this place once was, hundreds of militia lost their minds as they struggled to track you when you attempted to escape. He would only succumb to his noose..." Luciana shuddered as her face retraced the erratic path from a memory.

"I'm sorry," The One Who Caused The Trauma said.

"YOU'RE FUCKING USELESS, AARON," Midge said.

Kinships and a Pollutant

"The agreement, Midge," Aaron said.

Midge screamed. Pulled her hair. "What the fuck am I looking at! All this! All for you!"

"Miss Estire, if you'd allow – the persona of Aaron has a great control over The Antagonist. Better than I've seen anyone control that aspect of him. I would focus not where he is now but making sure he doesn't return to being primarily The Antagonist."

"I'm looking at a cage to contain a god. You're telling me the absolute shit-inducing thing I've seen is not the full Antagonist."

"The Antagonist is always the full Antagonist. I was relieved it only took thirty Firemimes to contain him, and that only twelve of them died."

"It was me. Critch is me. The Antagonist is me."

"No, it isn't. Aaron Bennett is a benevolent figure. Yes, Critch did need this amount of security. The burn marks on your body. They're from the cables you snapped by moving through the ten thousand volts."

"TEN THOUSAND!" Midge said. "Ten thousand..."

They walked back to the loading dock. A fishing boat arrived. Out of its bowels came several cubes with various persons meant for the supply of The Underground. A line formed quickly. They were apparently waiting a long time to take the locks down here.

"Do you know the distinction between berserkers and witches?" Luciana said,

"A witch?" Midge said.

"Berserker is male. Witch is female. It has nothing to do with gender as I'm sure you're aware. More of a tendency than anything."

"Needless distinction given the current company," Your Imminent Unforewarned Reckoning said.

"Berserking has to do with containment and wanting freedom. Witching, or sorcery, has to do with control and wanting power over everything you know, not what you don't know. They're born from the same desire, to get past what's inhibiting you, control or freedom. Why are you trying to control your world? Why are you trying to break free from your world? That's the crux of our

The Antagonist's Prison

conditions."

Forklifts glided electrically silent past. The darkness of this Ossuary bothered. No one wanted to see what's held down here.

"Although I'm sure other cultures appropriated other terms. Repression is the source of everything. Hiding from ourselves is the source of everything the human race does. But yes, generally to have these abilities, it comes from a terrible trauma. How it manifests also coincides with the nature of the trauma."

"So there's a literary trope that I hate," Midge said. "In general, the hero always has a massively sad thing happen to him. Otherwise, he's an everyman character. I've always wondered why. Why does the hero have to have a death or a genocide happen to him?"

"Motivation is my guess," The Villain To Many said. "Something to propel them to greatness, probably to stop whatever happened to them from happening to anyone else. You twisted that question to make me explore Critch more, didn't you?"

"Yes, sorry, that was mean."

"You realize that you just equated The Antagonist to a hero," Luciana said.

"Well, going with the analogy just for the sake of my argument, Aaron has no trauma, right, because Aaron is only, what? Maybe three years old. Whoever he was before had the trauma and became Critch. That person had such an awful thing happen to him that he became The Antagonist. Hence the hero analogy. And maybe what motivates that aberration is stopping the evil that happened to him."

"Can't put a fire out with fire," Woefully Misunderstanding The Scope Of How He Was Used said.

They arrived at the loading dock and got a look at the black water around The Underground. Light blasted out and across the lake, fighting the dark until it was consumed before reaching the cave wall.

A trio of black prison cubes rolled down to the docks as girthy workers controlled their descent with ropes. They stopped right in front of the trio. Aaron peeked inside out of morbid curiosity. Two

Kinships and a Pollutant

children per small cage.

His lip snarled and turned to face Luciana with his relentless grin. It'd be a decent title, if it weren't redundant with the other titles.

Kneeling with his head down and his fists in a crater. Critch had hit...*he* hit the sheet metal so hard it buckled and exposed the blue stone beneath. Midge stood in front of Luciana. Her bloody tears ran. Luciana huddled comic behind Midge. Her eyes also bled.

Unlike Midge's two solid streams down her face, Luciana's blood spattered as if it burst from her tear ducts.

Twenty lay dead, clutching their throats and stomachs. Yet none of them seemed injured.

"What happened?" Aaron said.

"Critch came for me..." Luciana said, still out of breath. "Midge stepped in front of me and we both had an Episode..." Luciana cleared her throat. "Like I said before, my Still kills people. Their organs seize and they die. Critch stood there...unaffected by our Stills. He vibrated for some time, knowing that Midge didn't want him to kill me. My god, I've never seen Critch out of containment...off leash...unmoving. The sight of his static anger crawled into my eyes. Pried open my mind to tickle me slow, until, out of frustration, he slammed the ground and gave up."

"I'm sorry," Mr. Bennett said.

"God, I hadn't forgotten him. You can't forget him...It's... He's...You're worse every time. Exponentially more every time."

Luciana cried normal tears.

"It's getting harder to resist," he said.

"Perhaps he's feeling attacked," Midge said.

His sight convulsed at the edges.

"It has to do with children and rape then, huh?" Aaron said.

"If it does, whatever happened to you. Whatever made Critch. Fuck."

Luciana brushed herself off, wiped the blood off her

The Antagonist's Prison

face."Alright everyone!"

The workers who survived continued working as if this happened all the time. None of them looked over.

"Clean this mess up," Luciana said. "As much as I enjoy your company, Critch. Do not take this the wrong way, I have a business to run and my employees are unsettled by you."

"I understand. Thank you for your time, Luciana. I hope to see you again soon."

"You will. Midge, next time I am Topside, I will make contact and we will have that interview over a nice dinner. It is relieving to meet another witch. Good luck overthrowing Mr. Kinns. I wish I could offer something beyond my easy allowance of your siege. You, of course, have my permission."

"Thank you, apologies for disrupting your establishment," he said. Midge and Aaron exchanged cheek kisses with her and went up the loading dock and headed toward Madam Ava's.

The blue cobblestones stretched down one of the main thoroughfares toward the towering Arena. The roads left and right curved around out of sight. No one moved. The Underground gave a constant sense of eerie abandonment. You were not alone and you knew it, but where was everyone? What were they doing?

"Okay, you said it wasn't all dark down here. What's down here that isn't dark? At this point, I don't believe anything but evil can happen down here."

"Well, there are lifestyle centers. Also tastings, some mystical places."

"Elaborate."

"Vampires who actually drink the blood of different animals and humans, have thralls and such. Also full-time cosplay people, furries and all, people who are elves, or dragons. A jerky place for endangered animals or thought-to-be extinct animals. Never been to any of the mystical places. Don't know what they're about."

"So we probably couldn't visit the lifestyle places."

"Not really."

"And since I have no desire to figure out how folk can subsist

Kinships and a Pollutant

off blood alone..."

"Additives."

"Don't know, don't care, probably. I'm curious what counts as mystical in this place. Hopefully not just smoke-and-mirror tea leaf shenanigans."

"You want a reading?"

"Oh fuck yeah, let's get our chakras read. I need a break."

Madam Ava often got herself read at a place not far from The Lounge called 'Intrinsic Effluvium.' Inside, some sort of smelly resin burned which no one actually enjoyed, despite protestations. Multiple patrons sat at stainless steel tables with capped vials and tinctures corked. They breathed in smoke, held it, then breathed it out, and the apprentices carefully assessed what happened. Occasionally, the smoke came out in different colors and more excited notes were jotted down.

The smoky room had a dojo feel, people practicing a craft. An Indigenous person in charge, dressed in black and purple religious-looking wraps and jewelry. "Hello, and welcome to Intrinsic Effluvium. Would you like a reading today? I'm sure one of my apprentices would love to help you."

"A reading would be great," The One Who Will Make You Undone said, tipping his hat down. "The Lady Made of Dark has spoken quite highly of your establishment in the past."

"Oh yes, The Lady Made of Dark comes in once a month to check on herself and the directions her body is heading. How do you know Her?"

"I was once a close associate of Hers. We've kept in close contact since those days. Circumstances have required my return to The Underground."

"Well, a friend of Her is a friend of mine. A wonderful woman, if a little domineering."

They laughed professionally at the not-great joke.

The Antagonist's Prison

"How does it work?" Midge said.

"Some things you cannot know, my dear. Oh, my apologies. My name is Deria, Mist Reading has been in my family beyond record."

"My name is Aaron Bennett and this is Midge Estire."

"Estire? Of Estire Wines?"

"Yeah!"

"I once went to a release party at your winery. You have an exquisite Cab Franc. The Samantha Stones, I believe it was called."

"My father always did enjoy naming his wines after family."

"Do you think your father still has a bottle of Tobin's Memory?"

"He does, though I think he'd probably not be too keen on letting one go. I can talk to him about it, I guess depending on what happens here."

"That would be wonderful. Thank you. Now please follow me. We shall use my table."

Just beyond the main counter through a thick veil of mist, the air cleared around a redwood table crafted crude and ancient. Black greases covered it in layers and layers of stain and sealant. It was never stained, the smoke and mists of centuries layered its tar over the wood.

"We shall start with some informational readings." She reached into an equally ancient cabinet and pulled four vials from the top shelf, six from the middle shelf, and a box made from the same special wood as the rest of her furniture from the bottom shelf.

With care but memorized practice, she placed the vials. Two in the front, three in the following row. Then, with a brief prayer, she opened the antediluvian box and pulled two more vials from it. Put one of each in the last row. Although they all had different functions, the corked vials were the same size and whiteness inside.

"We shall do a full reading today. A rare honor. Let us see what we can discover about ourselves. Please take the first mist to your left, uncork the vials and breathe in as much of the mist as you can, hold it for as long as you can then breathe out through your nose."

With smoker lungs, they could hold it in for less than twenty seconds before slowly letting out.

Kinships and a Pollutant

"Good. Perfect form. That determined your relative health. Miss Estire. Happily, you are in remarkable health, despite the whipping you received earlier, although the amount of whiskey and Bloody Marys you drink may become an issue for you later on. You also have cancer to look forward to. It also assessed your relative mental capacities. You are remarkably intelligent, more so than most I've come across. Yet, you have little control over your emotions. This means you often blame others for how you feel.

"Mr. Bennett. You should be dead. Your entire physical form has been destroyed multiple times. You have maybe five years of life left. And not from your five packs of cloves a day habit. You've exhausted your body's capability to heal. Soon we'll figure out why this is. Don't tell me anything yet, it causes a bias in the readings. You, Mr. Bennett, are also quite smart. Moreover, you have a perfect grasp on your emotions. The best I've ever seen. Curious. That amount of control means that you've had to regulate yourself in the past for a significant reason. I thought that amount of emotional control was extinct. Take the next vial, please."

So far, this woman had not convinced them that this was anything but cold reads. However, Madam Ava was a master cold reader and you couldn't con a con. They breathed out. Midge's was red mist. Aaron's was purple.

"Excellent, that surmised your driving emotion. Midge, as you've probably determined, your driving force is anger. Red, of course, anger rooted in a surrender you know you conceded too soon. This makes you prone to help beyond the scope of what you can offer, never giving up, because of the anger of what giving up did to you before."

"This is becoming hard to take," Midge said. Her eyes red and the barest tremble in her lip. She wiped her nose.

"Yes, the reads can be harmfully honest."

"Have a black heart of gold," Midge said, referring to another story.

"I understand the torment well, Miss Estire, believe me. Mr. Bennett, your driving emotion is sadness, rooted in anguish.

The Antagonist's Prison

Strangely, anguish rooted in helplessness. Something in your past has caused a great grief. One you feel guilty for, yet you are conflicted about because it happened before you could feel that emotion. Who are you?"

"No answers yet, right?"

"Sorry, lapse of duty. You show so many qualities that I've only heard in theory." Deria started to predict things about him even as she tried not to. "Now we shall discover more of who you are. Take the next vial on the right. This one is more personal."

Midge brought the vial to her lips, took a second before sucking it in. Without innuendo.

"This one is simple. What do you smell? The first two you can describe."

"Ocean and wine," Midge said, clipped.

"Violet and copper," Aaron said.

"The first smell is what you love, the second is your most significant memory."

"Violet, huh?" Midge said, leaking anger.

"What?" If she referred to The Widow in Yellow and her predilection toward that smell, then she was more insecure than Aaron desired. "Are you angry about The Widow in Yellow? Seems like a bold jump to me. Why are you so in love with the ocean, then? Is someone from your past a sailor you secretly love?"

"No, it refers to Tobin, my dead brother."

"Oh," the Antagonist stumbled. Any conflict came from overlooked details.

"Although I didn't know so much of my personality was driven by his death."

"The readings often provoke confrontations. I prefer to do them individually. However, we have several more readings."

"Apologies," Your Imminent Unforewarned Reckoning said.

"Sorry," Midge said.

"Next please."

Midge breathed out. Smoke clouded the otherwise clear area around the table, crackled like neurons, before it coalesced into a

Kinships and a Pollutant

tight ball and dissipated naturally. Critch's came out and swirled in an increasingly complex hurricane, the eye always clear, despite the crackling energy sparking about.

"My dear Samantha, you are Sherlock Holmesian in observance, but you have trouble assessing what you see. You claim to be scientific, but your humanity gets in the way, so you don't know what you see, just that you see it. Aaron, though, you have constructed a perfect matrix, a disturbingly perfect veil around an aspect of yourself. Usually when that happens, there are strands of mist venturing forth into the eye, typically from other people's observations. Yours is completely clear of probes. What is it that you hide, that no one wants to look into?"

"We have two vials left. Then answers?" Now Aaron was interested when she'd figure out who he was. Then went ahead and hated him.

"Right, my apologies. I've just never read mists like the two of yours. The next vial please."

Midge breathed out a searching mist. Tendrils hit surfaces and the borders of the mist room where they shriveled and died. Mr. Bennett's formed an immense tree with titanic branches falling on what looked like tiny villages as a frame of reference. The tree made the tiny huts almost microscopic. The branches fell larger than whales.

"That was uncomplicated. You both are falling apart, failing at what you do best. The last, please. However, one at a time. This one is always a heavy one. Miss Estire, you first."

Midge held it for almost a minute, then, red faced, coughed as it came out. Blue and purple mist hands reached for Deria and Critch. The hand closed and withered a foot from his face. The other gripped Deria's skull where she sat undeterred. Then Midge's many hands grabbed at the opaque smoke surrounding them. They flashed an electric yellow, sparking erratically before the hands disintegrated the veil, exposing several apprentices observing.

"You feel cornered, so you're trying to reveal the world as only someone like you can, by breaking the structure of it, to show its

The Antagonist's Prison

nuts and bolts."

Deria muttered something. The mists vanished in spirals.

"Aaron, if you would."

The twenty or so people awaited his demonstration.

He breathed out a glistening, inky slime of black pollution. The ooze landed on the ancient wood table with a thud, which the floor hated. The creature sprouted innumerable tentacles and chewing maws, each of which chittered on the edge of hearing. Charlie retreated to the farthest edge of Aaron's lapel, shaking and huddled.

Grasping like dozens of spiders meshed together, the creature made of smoke rushed toward Deria. It leaped for her. She took a frantic drag from a pipe as it was about to grasp the entirety of her head and torso. She blew out a blue cloud of spikes. They stabbed The Antagonist's exhalation.

It spasmed then grew to the size of the room. Deria and all her apprentices dragged on pipes and, with all their talents combined, the frothing black tentacles and mouths, now speaking in subsonics, shaking them like organ pipes, twitched and popped in a swirl of foul smoke.

"Get out, you monster!" Deria said. "You toxic abomination! Plague upon this planet! Get out! Before you corrupt our home any longer! Our kind has been decimated by yours!"

Deria and house grabbed them and forced them out with little effort to resist on their part.

"As always, tentative acceptance shifts to familiar rejection," Aaron said. More to himself than to anyone in particular.

"Wait," Deria called after her eighty-sixers. "You are correct. Come back here."

They were let go and led back to Deria and her table.

"Everyone except for my apprentices, out!"

The few rubberneckers left with sad ceremony.

"Surround The Antagonist," Deria said. Instead, the apprentices made for the walls. They whispered his names and shook in his presence. "Do as I say!"

Aaron sat in a chair and they did as they were told. He lit a

Kinships and a Pollutant

clove. Charlie sought the safety of the inside pocket. The acolytes all pulled out their pipes and held them in their mouths, sweating and shaking, refusing to make eye contact.

"You know, if I do berserk, blowing smoke at me isn't going to do a damn thing."

"Shut up. You've desecrated this holy place for long enough. You may stay while I analyze the witch." She resettled into professional like a preening bird. "Miss Estire. Despite the fact that you have feelings for that aberration, here's my assessment of you: You have two unhealthy obsessions. The death of a sibling and an affliction I cannot ascertain. You have hit a wall with both of these, and the wall is tearing you apart. If you do not come to terms with your afflictions, you will start taking your frustrations out on others. As far as what you must do to break through the wall you've encountered, I recommend, as I always do, forgiveness of self, dream therapy, and thought-net skimming. I can't tell you how to do any of those things, for you must discover your own procedures for doing so, but they must be done before you ruin everything in your life. Including your collusion with The Antagonist."

So much stank on the end of that sentence.

"Believe it or not, my 'collusion' with Critch has been most healing. What is within him cannot be denied, but the man he is beyond that, his undeniable integrity, his complete acceptances. That's what people should be concerned with."

"My dear. You are wrong. It is only the darkness within ourselves we should be concerned about. You are listing the same attributes an abuse victim might, choosing to ignore the terrible characteristics of this man."

"May I speak?" His Unflinching Grin said. Ironically the only one with smoke about him.

"No," Deria said. "You revenant."

"Fair enough."

"Please let him speak," Midge said.

"Keep it brief, Critch," Deria said with so much disgust the figurative loogie dried on his face.

The Antagonist's Prison

"If I am to learn anything from Midge and her lectures, it is that acceptance of what is wrong with me is what I should be doing. Not nuke it, but hug it and dissipate its influence on my ingratiation of that part of me which has been shunned." Aaron had to go over that sentence again in his mind. He didn't like it. He preferred to speak simpler than that.

"You are a fool to even begin against that which you hold."

"You're fucking insane to think someone can't gain hold of their mind," Midge said. "Dammit! I'm parroting again. I think the mists have given all they can, Aaron. Let's go to Madam Ava."

"At least her reverence for me will balance the disdain of this wise leader."

"Do not dare accuse me of discrimination," Deria spat.

"There is not a single person on this planet who should not be examined, understood, and healed," Aaron said. "You speak as if you know better. Come on Midge, we are in the realm of the uninitiated."

Midge jumped up, and he carried her out piggyback. His joints twanged but worth it. Deria and her apprentices took long drags on their pipes and flooded the room with fog.

Outside, Aaron dropped Midge and lit a clove. Down aways, a man with a cart filled with trash and debris. Did he just throw it away, or did he have a dark purpose for the waste? This place made every innocuous thing have some other sinister gutter purpose. Hopefully, he was just collecting trash.

Charlie shook his butt at the building and stamped his back legs. He then ran to Aaron and lept behind his boot. Embarrassed by his mockery.

"She called you a revenant. Do you know what that means?"

"No clue."

"A revenant is an undead creature who cannot rest until it has resolved its anger against that which killed it."

"I'm not a zombie."

"No, but if she thinks berserkers are out for revenge, what do you think you have to avenge?"

Kinships and a Pollutant

"I'd imagine something pretty fucking awful."

"Fuck the last generation, what happened to you? Someone did something truly terrible. Maybe so much that you've entirely blocked it?"

"I wouldn't know it then."

"Oh, fuck you."

"Keep your pants on for a bit longer."

"Strange note. I suddenly understand the word awful. But does the etymology come from awe full, with an e, as in full of awe, or does it come from all full, as in can't take anymore so it spills out." She escaped the terrible by sinking into her education. "Probably full of awe. Either way, I don't think it matters. Also, an observation, there are no seams between building and ground. There's also no seam between cobblestone and street. Does that mean the whole place was carved out of one stone? What made this place? Fucking Lizardfolk or the fuck like that?"

Madam Ava's Lounge was only a few blocks away.

"Aaron?"

"Hmm?"

"You stopped and started humming, low and sing-song. I didn't like it."

"Huh?"

Midge hugged him for a long time, enclosed him with her whole body. "This place is taking a toll on both of us. Please keep it together."

"It's hard when I don't know that I've faded."

"I know, I really do. So did Luciana. How about a conversation to keep you here?"

"Shoot."

Midge sat on a bench. Again with iconic heavy conversation imagery. He sat next to her.

"Are you a virgin, Aaron?"

"No, and why is that important?"

"Oh, it's not, well I guess it's kind of important. I'm not in the stage of life to teach someone how to fuck."

The Antagonist's Prison

"I wouldn't worry about that. Nor did I have much a plan to fuck you. I'm not an exceptionally sexual fellow. Madam Ava believes in the healing power of sex. She often sent women to me in my lucid moments. According to her accounts, I'm proficient, not that it matters to me."

"Uh, wow, Aaron. Not normal. Ok...when was the last time you had sex? It's been like six months for me."

"Once again, your sexual past means nothing to me. I don't care. But I guess it's been three years. Naomi and I had a brief relationship before I realized I wasn't ready. She understood and we've been close ever since, but just as friends. My past is a black hole. There's a reason I don't talk about myself to anyone."

Midge's face twitched with at least seven emotions. Dropped them and hugged Aaron with his arms pressed into his side. An embrace for her. He rested his cheek on the top of her head, and she cooed.

Hierarchies and a Revolutionary

The Not Breeder Couple approached three Firemimes stationed outside of Madam Ava's blue stone building. They tensed at the presence of Aaron. At the drop of a hat, there could be another six Firemimes, if another hat dropped, twenty-five would burst from the cracks in the stone. The Firemimes were trained to fend Aaron off. At their most skilled it only took The Widow in Yellow and six to subdue him. It was highly doubtful these guards were a part of that entourage. Though The Antagonist's recent antics might have incited increased security.

The Firemime Organization was the supplement to Critch. They mitigated collateral. One of the countless ventures ultimately controlled by the Lady Made of Dark. She owned the entire city of Indigo Bay, perhaps all of California, perhaps more.

Aaron nodded to the three Firemimes, as if a knowing greet. They judged The Don't Get Your Hopes Up couple. Our Relentless Shadow fully expected them to know who he was. They didn't let the two through. The leather and heat from inside washed nostalgia over Mr. Bennett. Midge saw his demeanor change and held his hand to prevent the rush from going too far. Critch clawed at the inside of his skull. From every direction. Anxious to return home.

"Really, guys?" The One Who Stares Back said.

"No one gets in without The Lady Made of Dark's express

The Antagonist's Prison

permission."

"Go tell Madam Ava, Aaron and Midge are here."

"You dare speak her name? She wouldn't speak to you, I doubt she'd even notice you dying on the street. She'd step over you. Sneer at the mess you made."

The Antagonist rolled his entire head. "Doesn't that mean she'd notice me?"

This obscurity worked well outside of The Underground, where Madam Ava was a shadowed hand delicately influencing everything. However, just beyond The Lady Made of Dark's main lodging in this evil city of blood and treachery, the secrecy seemed pretty silly.

Midge fished out the crumpled up note from The Widow in Yellow. The man read it and threw it on the ground. Midge jerked her palms up in confusion.

"Where did you get that? Stole it, I bet. Get out of here, you are not a Fetish, no matter how much you want to be."

"I certainly don't want to be a Fetish," Midge said.

The pathetic Firemime guards drew their batons. This should have been easy. Just them seeing Critch, The Antagonist, the weapon The Lady Made of Dark used to get her power, should have been enough for them to not even speak to him. Not that he missed that fucked-up moon-eyed expression. The collapse of despair folk had when they recognized His Unflinching Grin.

"Go. Now." His voice shook the air. Dimmed the gas lamps. Shrunk the Firemimes into huddled messes. He asked Midge with eyebrows if she would stop him from going too far. He knew she didn't want to prevent berserks for the rest of their time together, that wasn't her burden to bear. She sighed. Made sad eye contact with fractal green eyes beneath her bright red hair. She sighed and nodded.

Critch pounced, ready and happy to be called. The three Firemimes loosened their stances and faded into their vacant drunken style of fighting. Grabbed their lassos. Aaron emulated Critch's smile. The smile became real and his vision tunneled back

Hierarchies and a Revolutionary

to a prick of light.

Came out two seconds later, Midge's lips on his cheek. Critch blinked out. Sweat oozed out of every pore, body desperate to extinguish the flush.

"Can I go in now?" he growled at the Firemimes.

"Who are you?" said the one with dry pants. Their lassos spiraled, but their enormous pupils showed their naivety. These had not been a part of Critch's entourage. They're just guards.

"Aaron Bennett," he said. "I told you that already. But since you're all about your silly titles, I'm also known as Critch, The Antagonist, The Lady Made of Dark's Bump in the Night. Our Relentless Shadow. Her Dear Apocalypse. The One Who Stares Back From The Void. The One Who Will Make You Undone. Your Imminent Unforewarned Reckoning."

One Of Those Titles pushed through their flaccid blockade. Madam Ava would know they're here soon enough.

Most of the sexual escapades happened in the red-lit auditorium. The Lounge. At the rear of the room, up steps and behind a heavy red curtain, Madam Ava and her closest relaxed beneath a dim blue light. The air was cooler behind the lush curtain. The smell of pheromones and latex no longer burnt frontal cortices.

The Lounge's walls painted a bruised, engorged red, with Italian black leather trimming. Fifteen or so booths scattered across the pit beneath the stage. The booths were often pushed together, sticky. They could be veiled, though most chose not to. Exhibition rampant. The patrons, men, women, but mostly a blurring between the two poles, wore matte or shiny black leather of varying immodesty extremes. Some walked twirling ropes. Letting subs know their expertise. Midge and Aaron sat down at the slick black bar.

The rules of engagement in these situations dizzied Her Dear Apocalypse. It stressed him not knowing when The Lady Made Of Dark's Bump In The Night broke etiquette. Or didn't break it enough. Part of this sadomasochistic nonsense was structure and gatekeeping, following a strict set of rules. He just didn't have that type of mind.

The Antagonist's Prison

All this pomp and circumstance for what should be the easiest request to move on Mr. Kinns. Midge's back bled from her recent whipping. Aaron bled from everywhere.

Over the speakers played 'Warm Leatherette.'

"Oh my god, why is this song in my life!" Midge shook her head and called the bartender. He was a short, extremely thin man with offensive tattoos down his arms and across his chest, seen under a black, deep V-neck shirt.

"How many nicknames do you have?" Midge said.

"I don't know. Quite a few. His Unflinching Grin?"

"That's an appropriate one," Midge said.

"These people like to have their names be their achievements. Madam Ava is a little obsessed and gave herself and hers dozens."

The bartender finished a drink and brought over a tumbler with a dark liquid and orange peel garnish. Gave it to Midge, then reached down and handed Aaron an IPA with a label he didn't recognize.

Midge took a sip. Her eyes widened as she savored. "What the fuck is this? Because it's the best drink I've ever had."

"Cognac with black walnut liqueur, bitters and a splash of vodka. A Nocino old-fashioned, interpreted."

"How the fuck does that work? And how did you know I like cognac? I want another sip, but that means more of it will be gone and that'll be a tragedy."

"I have a talent for this sort of thing. My name is Jeb. And thank fucking God you showed up. I'm tired as hell of waiting on these nitpicking folk. Y'all look normal."

"In varying degrees." Our Relentless Shadow took a sip of the IPA and almost spit up on the bitter. It was fantastic. He took another sip.

"It's good, right?" Jeb said.

"It's fantastic." Making descriptions redundant.

"Yeah, and it's 25 ABV. 200 IBU. Can't even tell, huh? Not a lot of people can handle that beer."

"Thank you for believing I could," Aaron said genuinely. It came across as a threat.

Hierarchies and a Revolutionary

"Naw, it's not like that, man. I saw you and was like, he likes his shit bitter as fuck. Aged in expensive Highland Scotch barrels, too."

"Any idea when Madam Ava can see us?" Midge said.

"Eh, she makes people wait a bit. But you see that timer behind me?" A big neon clock counting down, thirty minutes left.

"Every three hours is BDSM time and shit goes weird, know what I'm saying? I'm pretty numb to it now. But I'd skedaddle before that timer runs out, guests get absorbed, you know? Most enjoy it after a time."

Jeb broke two ice cubes, and eye-balled some portions, then placed it on the bar with a flamed, peeled garnish. Thirty seconds later a curved-the-fuck-out person wearing black thigh-high boots, a garter belt and nothing else, came up and grabbed the drink. Did they have a rib removed to look like that?

"You can't be fooled, is that right?" they said.

"Eh, it's difficult," Jeb said.

They went back to their booth and grabbed the meat next to them. Placed their head between their legs. They sipped casually as the other went to town.

"That damn client changes what they want each time, it's a power play thing. I don't mind much, they're just being in their nature. Assumes I couldn't possibly know what they want. That same old routine. So I can't get angry. You guys aren't into this stuff, right? I'm not offending you?"

"No, not at all. Actually, it seems like you're the first non-atypical person we've met down here," Midge said. "It's fucking with my head. I kinda just want to go to a family dinner at this point."

"Refreshing, no? Now, not to be rude, but I've met dudes like you before, Aaron. Greyed-out eyes, rough appearance, scabbed over with broken hands. Yet, you're not like any murderers I've met so far."

"I'm The Antagonist."

"I highly doubt that," Jeb said.

"That's your prerogative."

The Antagonist's Prison

"Jeb's lying," Midge said. She eyed Jeb. "You're a good liar, too."

"Part of the job. But that misses the point. When I see you I see murderer. Not Critch. Not terrifying, not all the other things people have said about you. Just someone I wouldn't want to be locked in a room with. You have the same look as The Widow in Yellow back there. You've done terrible things, often without believing in them."

"Great, they have the same eyes too," Midge said with sass.

"Green is a terrible color on anyone, Midge," The One Who Stares Back said.

"Back to what I was saying. Midge, here, has a problem with Critch, and I'm pretty sure you do too. I'm sure you know that you can't just remove him from your psyche. Which, props to you for understanding that. You can't remove him but you can affect him."

"Unneeded advice. I need a cigarette." As he got up to go outside, Jeb yelled that he could smoke in here. He missed the point. 'I need a cigarette,' was a roundabout way of saying whoever needed to step away for a minute. To smokers, they're synonymous. What Jeb said was too close to what Critch was and that was dangerous. Acceptance wasn't the solution, though. Aaron tried it, failed. Time to try something new.

Midge came out to join Your Imminent Unforewarned Reckoning. She lit her cigarette.

"I'm no psychologist, I just study the biology of the human brain. Even so, I've been thinking, like your parents beat you and you have an anti-social disorder, or something. That'd explain why you don't think about your family."

"Doubt I'm a sociopath." A drop from above landed on his cherry, putting it out. He flicked the cigarette away and lit another one. He smoked it reversed, ember toward the palm. "After coming out of my berserking haze, after my old roommate Naomi and Ms. Peach took me in and helped me become functional. I still don't know. I don't remember my past, just feelings. No concrete imagery."

"You did need other people Aaron, and still do...wait, how old are you?"

Hierarchies and a Revolutionary

"Around twenty-five, not sure."

"Shit...I thought you were older than me...like *a lot* older."

A Firemime timidly poked his head out the door, informed them Madam Ava was ready for their audience. Inside and up the stairs onto the stage. Patrons watched them wistfully.

They broke through the soft red of the Grand Curtain in the middle of the stage. The stark coolness behind refreshing. The lighting was natural with red and blue lights blending together. The colors broke from time to time, illuminating someone's face red or blue. Everyone twisted awkwardly toward the Grand to view Madam Ava's weird guests. The prime slaves, the ones wearing solid crystal collars, recognized The One Who Will Make You Undone. They stopped their serving and stared. Minute traces of nervous shaking rattled the fancy plateware on their trays. On the small of their backs were branded demonic eyes. Across their ass cheeks branded enormous smiles.

As they weaved around tiny tables, priority patrons and Firemimes judged with prying eyes. Two chairs sat vacant in front of Madam Ava's table. Proper etiquette was mandatory, so they stood behind the comfy stools and waited for an invitation to sit. Madam Ava smirked, awaiting the optimal level of tension to breach their faces. She was well aware that this could take a while. Midge memorized the room.

The dark tower of Madam Ava relaxed back in her lush chair. A glass of priceless wine in her overly long fingers. Skin so dark she blared out from the claret leather of her throne. Brutal blue eyes happy to see Her Dear Apocalypse. Polished shaved head. Six four and a hundred and thirty pounds of absolute methodical power. Her custom leather dress caressed her emaciated curves.

Midge had no desire to participate in any sort of staring contest. She made eye contact with guests, waved excited toward them. Or she'd slouch low, letting her arms hang, then sporadically jerk them up high with lazy jazz hands. Madam Ava knew this game, soon the tension would break Midge. The room was willing to wait. Madam Ava's attention wasn't on Midge. Her

The Antagonist's Prison

eyes were on Aaron. Neither blinked during their connection.

A painting hung behind Madam Ava. In it, she looked much the same. Madam Ava's former apprentice stood to the left, looking far more like a dominatrix's number two compared to The Widow in Yellow's porcelain doll. Critch loomed behind and to the right of Madam Ava, so tense he shuddered the frame. Holographic amongst the thick acrylic of the rest of the painting. Yet, the painter drew him messy in Ralph Steadman caricature to the rest of the painting's stunning photo realism. And even more so, his facial features muddy except for the cubist smile of molars.

Beneath the painting, a table of idyllic women of all shapes, sizes, colors, and fashions waited for the trial to conclude. Normally, her current champion and her apprentice would stand behind Madam Ava to the right. Ramn wasn't present, nor was her apprentice. Instead, The Widow in Yellow stood to her left in a long black gown with a yellow overcoat, styled like the Firemime uniform only fancified. Beneath her wide-brimmed black hat, her black eyes flit about the room, assessing. November would stare at Aaron occasionally with an intention lost.

Madam Ava smiled, volunteering to break the tension. Odd jibbers scampered around the room like a clumsy puppy. Why would ragamuffins like them have the honor of Madam Ava's forfeit?

Stupid, stupid bullshit.

"I know why you're here, Mr. Bennett. Otherwise known as Critch." The room scooted back at the mention. Twenty Firemimes stood. They knew that wasn't enough. "You wish to attack Mr. Kinns. You've come seeking my approval. As my alum champion, you, of course, have my approval. Although, formalities are here for a reason, so I must ask two things of you. First, I want Samantha Estire to hear a story about Critch. And second, I would like to witness Samantha's berserk."

Midge looked at Aaron, eyebrows peaked.

"My research was correct, was it not? Rumor said a witch accompanied Critch into The Underground. I entered the Mill, and now I know everything about you. It took no time at all, really."

Hierarchies and a Revolutionary

Madam Ava softly cackled. "I did try to learn from your Topside ways. I became frustrated with your rudimentary understanding of Rumor. Some people are simply not cut out to be Rumormongers."

Midge mouthed a what-the-fuck to Aaron who remained an ominous tower of awe. He thought he stood casually. Mr. Bennett shrugged because nonsense. He couldn't listen to the enigmas these people spewed.

Clients in codpieces and high-heeled horseshoe boots lowered a curvy, red-haired person in front of them, followed by a platter of sashimi across their back. That was all Madam Ava would feed him. Michelin Star sushi. You'd think he'd get tired of it, but he never did. Midge stiffened at the choice of table.

"Your Father's wine is excellent, Samantha. Or do you prefer Midge? Apologies, the name Midge has no elegance. Has Aaron told you how our time together began?"

"I've seen what he's capable of," Midge said. Her defiance on the edge of its patience. If Madam Ava kept up the derogatory, Midge would snap. It was all part of the plan. Madam Ava loved to break people. It somehow gave light to their true selves. At least that's what she told everyone who'd listen. She was never able to break Aaron.

"Ah, but the devil is in the details. And he is most certainly a devil. In his present form, he's a scapegoat. He never had a chance to learn to speak naturally. So he constructs what he's going to say days beforehand with backups and disaster tracts. In his other form he is a destructor, the invincible wrath of a fallen alien god."

"I can tell when he's speaking naturally and when he's pontificating," Midge said. "You haven't seen him in a few years, and in that time he's learned quite a bit. I don't think it's fair to judge someone on their dark pasts. Especially when, in the present, they are a completely different person."

"That is until their past seeps out, as it always does, and has it not? Past aside, your short time together has been tinged with the sublime. Your interpersonal experience has been limited to an otherworldly environment, one which is more magnificent and

The Antagonist's Prison

stimulating than your native bough. With Aaron, you've learned of, and waded through, a world you could not comprehend before. How will you react when you find out he's incredibly dull Topside?"

"That's what I want. Boring. I never wanted to have to go through this bullshit. I never had a need to be whipped, tortured, a need to witness the atrocity people are capable of with encouraged debauchery. The City Beneath disgusts me."

Madam Ava's derisive smile buried Midge's self-righteous proclamation. Even better than Gradick and Raile's knowing smirk.

"I had a representative, employed on an on-call basis. I used him to recruit pit fighters. He had a knack for scouting talent and was lucrative. However, I was already in a position where money was not a consideration. The real benefit of his employment was his assistance in my ascension into my current status. My representative showed me a new and dark world, heard through only sinister whispers. The Underground's bellow resonated within me the night he sent Aaron to my doorstep."

Aaron, at this moment, chose to move for once and ate the obscene variety of art fish on the platter. Savoring each piece accordingly. He treated the human table as the garish set-piece that they were. He did not, for the safety of others, listen to the story again.

"He stood rigid, extremities spread, as if his skin was made of needles. Inside this ravaged body something waited. Hunched. His back spread in an attempt to house a being threatening to erupt out of his flesh. His clothes rags. His skin scabbed and infected. He didn't know his own name. Oddly, though he was starved, he looked strong enough to laugh at a bomb's gale. I was terrified. A primal fear, one I can only describe as a prey instinct, took me. My sympathetic nervous system told me to shut the door. To run! Although, beyond the fear, I was overcome by an insane intrigue. Where did this creature come from? Could I harness his power?

"He handed me the token from my representative. I led him to a secure room. I ran to my own and shoved an armoire in front of the

Hierarchies and a Revolutionary

door. I lay awake wondering where my representative discovered this boogeyman. That night I was awoken by the sound of horror. It lasted perhaps a minute. I found him in my living room, crying on a cushion, drenched in blood. Pieces of my bodyguards lay scattered around my house. Up the walls..." Madam Ava said, faded out, staring-gesturing to all the blood drenching her living room.

"My staircase and its railings in ruin. My fine leather couches torn into sections and thrown through walls. A wrecking ball crashed through my home and the only person standing was this scrawny conifer of a man, dripping with the blood of my decimated accomplices and his own gashes.

"I sat next to him. I knew this would happen again. With shaking hands I made him some tea. Dropped a few sleeping pills in his cup. This failed to sedate him. He remained awake after calmly drinking his tea. He never said a word. At that point I didn't know if he could speak. His mind dismantled as my house."

Madam Ava drained her wine. A slave in time poured the wine as she placed the glass on the coaster.

"I eventually poured the entire bottle of pills into a protein shake, fearing that if I didn't tranquilize him soon, I would become his next target. Thankfully, he gulped the shake down, desperate for calories. Critch fell asleep. The amount of pills in the shake would've killed a normal man, but he curled up with a grin, happy to be tired. I carried him into my basement. He slept for days. I contracted a crew and created a cage I hoped would contain him. Titanium bars bolted deep into the ground and into the framework of my home, strong enough to stop a plane. I placed a drain in the floor, and poured cement, polishing it for easy cleanup. He slept through it all, slept like he hadn't for years. Or had never slept.

"One night, my representative came seeking refuge from a woman who was going to kill him. Keep in mind, for one to track my representative, one would need talents from another tier of this world. A tier I wanted to be a part of. I led my representative into my basement because I knew I couldn't bluff this bounty hunter away and I valued my life more than my employee. I knew that

The Antagonist's Prison

if I attempted to fool this woman, she would kill me. Within the hour the bounty hunter rang my doorbell. Though we exchanged no words, she looked as evil as any person I've met. She was quite cordial. I showed her where she could find my representative, left the basement lights off and waited. Soon came sounds of muffled butchery."

"I've seen the butchery unmuffled," Midge said, drinking straight from the sake bottle. Careful not to touch the table. Or person, depending on how one thought about it.

Madam Ava gave a sideways nod of recognition. "I cautiously entered the basement to find the remains of my representative and the bounty hunter splattered. No surface didn't drip. The rawboned man crying again. When he heard my approach, he stopped crying, assuming his berserking persona. He shot forward, as though he'd been fired from a cannon, too fast to see. The distance folded and unfolded, placing him in both places at once. Imagine my surprise when he slammed the gate shut, separating me from him. Critch's mind has always been his most terrible feature. Many believe he's mindless, that when he's berserking he has no control over his actions or who he kills. No, he picks and chooses his targets, as well as the individual methods of murder. He chooses tactics that will sow the greatest fear in his prey.

"I fell against the stairwell wall. Oh, his smile...it cuts deep, does it not? His smile brands your nightmares like a fading Cheshire Cat. I stayed until the berserk ended, he never stopped shaking the bars. Shook the entire house. As I watched in absolute despair I had an epiphany. I knew if I could draw the reins of this gift, I would ascend to the bounty hunter's tier of power.

"The man sunk down as the rage ended, using the bars for support. He said in an unused and terrible voice, 'Critch in side. Maintenance potential. Appreciative.' Critch passed out on the floor."

Aaron swallowed his last bite of ahi and leaned forward in his chair, hand on elbow. Dared Madam Ava to continue.

"It is a good story, is it not?" She winked at Her Unflinching Grin. "From there, I used him as my weapon, a deterrent to

Hierarchies and a Revolutionary

those so evil and so skilled they couldn't be caught. Your body count, Mr. Bennett, is legendary. Many believe that Critch is a centralized phenomenon around Indigo Bay. No, I took him around the world. He's killed so many unknown horrors. Aaron, the most boring name next to John or Jacob, or any other biblical name. The amount of money he has and has not touched, staggers. The interest alone puts him in the category of those who still have old money, if you know the term. Of course, I'm at a tier where money means nothing, just influence. *Aaron* has never asked for a balance, when he took out the starting costs for his business. By the time he had gotten home he had already remade the withdrawal. Aaron is a simple man. I quite like his middle class idea of wealth. On my level, there are no countries. Just a few people making the globalized decisions for everyone."

Madam Ava's story did not have the usual effect. Midge's eyes watered with pity. She grabbed Aaron's hand. Maybe details were a good thing when one wanted to see them.

"Samantha 'Midge' Estire, you're an odd child. You do not appear to be troubled by your present environment. Now, tell me, what allows you to understand Aaron so well?"

Midge sighed a here again. "I'm very observant, I try not to be, but like you said, the devil is in the details. If I start panicking, I tend to move in bullet time, if you know the term. From my perspective, the world stops, and I archive everything within sight. Everything from the number of leaves on a tree, the current number of raindrops in the air, to how many freckles are on your face. Not that you have any."

"I know. Do not worry Midge, I am aware of my elegance."

"Ummm, sure. I find freckles attractive. My brain speeds up to collect all the details until my mind is moving faster than normal time. My eyes bleed, I'm paralyzed. I've been stuck like that for hours, in unbearable pain. But to the rest of the world it's only for a second. From the research I found there's, long story short, a correlation between berserking and my Episodes. Basically, it's a gross overreaction to a stressor. Aaron's berserk stems from a

The Antagonist's Prison

staggering release of noradrenaline, whereas mine stems from a surge of dopamine agonists. For my thesis, I am attempting to find a strong correlation between our overreactions. Hopefully, this will convince future scientists to study the biopsychological causes of these overreactions. What we do is not normal behavior. Mutation is the only way to explain how Aaron and I do what we do. To be honest, I am really only concerned with qualifying the cause of my condition."

"Smart kiddo," Madam Ava said, drumming her fingernails on the well of her wine glass.

"Thank you...? You know what? No, I'm not going to take anything you say as a compliment. You are passive aggressive and cryptically condescending."

Madam Ava calmly raised an eyebrow.

"I used my credentials to study both the myths and physiology behind berserking. There's plenty of lore that explains berserking, yet in all my years studying human biomechanics, there is nothing that can explain what Aaron and I can do. The human body is not capable of such epic feats. I digress. I knew Aaron as Critch from the moment I met him at Cataran's. Everything about him, the keloid-scarred skin, the prowl of a walk, and the caged animal eyes indicated that he was the modern day legendary savage. This began as a case study."

This conversation made Our Relentless Shadow uncomfortable, so he shifted and took a piece of ginger. He knew of Midge's academic obsession with Critch when they began, but case study reductive was another thing. He didn't know he was being studied when they first met, but he guessed that's why she was so adamant about following.

If Aaron were a child, he'd be offended, angry she characterized him like that. And he did feel compelled to see it like a betrayal. His rational mind screamed that this knee-jerk reaction was not appropriate, so he dropped it. Whatever the feeling, it was novel, and he didn't want to lump it into an old emotion like betrayal. Gotta keep 'em separated.

Hierarchies and a Revolutionary

"I like his fuck-the-coloring-book-I'll-draw-however-the-fuck-I want approach to life, his character affectations. Except for the Critch portion, of course, nobody likes seeing...Also, he isn't affected by my Episodes. While everyone else is motionless, he remains in normal time. Except his movements are labored, like he's fighting against my world that's trying to freeze him but can't." Midge smiled and rubbed his back. Awkward as all get-out.

"That's it, then. I wish to see that for myself. Midge, I require you to berserk. If I'm impressed with your presentation, I will give my permission."

"You will also gain access to my Firemimes to assist in your cause," November said. Her sudden input broke the verisimilitude of the conversation. A drop of sanity in an otherwise staged world.

"I can't just call on it the way Aaron does."

Charlie raced down Aaron's arm to run circles around Midge's feet. In encouragement?

"Samantha, Aaron was unable to control it in the beginning. As you can see, he still has trouble controlling Critch. As I said before, and I don't like repeating myself, he came into my care feral. I conditioned his behavior to fit my needs. However, somewhat to my displeasure, he was smart enough to find the human buried beneath The Antagonist. If he can do it, so can you." Madam Ava gauged her, a heavy scrutiny like Midge put Aaron through back at Cataran's. "You lost Tobin and foolishly feel responsible."

"I'd rather you not do this," Midge said.

Madam Ava looked at her watch counting down. "I know, but you must understand. I have other things I must tend to. How did Tobin die?"

Midge sighed, accepting her fate. "On our family yacht. My little brother was complaining about his itchy life vest. I thought it'd be okay for him to take it off, you know, just for a few minutes." Midge sniffed back tears of absolute guilt. "He fell over the edge. He had to wear braces on his legs, and always had trouble stabilizing himself when the ocean was choppy."

"And you failed to save him." Madam Ava made shame fingers

The Antagonist's Prison

at her, tsk-tsking.

"I–I couldn't save him. I couldn't swim fast enough. He sank like...like he was wearing cement boots." Midge giggled, trying to save herself with gallows humor. Her eyes went bloodshot, no white left, just green irises and red corneas.

"Don't run from this, Midge. There's no point in running, dear. If I can't get you to open up on your own volition, I have other techniques."

"I watched him sink into the black, sending bubbles up to me as I kicked like mad to reach him. Finally, the features of his face, warped in despair and horror, faded and the world stopped. Do you know what it's like to be waterboarded?"

"Yes. One of my specialties."

"Eh. Right, well, so do I. I drowned for hours...Couldn't breathe! Move. Dying forever..."

Midge broke and rose out of her chair up to the tips of her painful toes to the furthest reach of her arms. Almost dislocated her shoulders. Madam Ava smiled and leaned back in her chair. Proud of what she caused.

Aaron stood to save Midge when the wave of Still erupted out of her. Knowing Madam Ava, she'd want proof he could break through the Still. The closest person to him was a Firemime. He needed his jacket. Midge's attention bored into Critch like he'd been walking around in the dark his whole life and she just turned a spotlight on him. Her blazing form ripped His Unflinching Grin apart, particles flicked off him like shitty stucco in a tornado. Mr. Bennett swallowed Critch.

His feet buried in sand. He pulled and grunted to leave furrows in the floor. Midge's blistering sun pressed against his neck. Yet the Still was Siberian. Two steps. Limbs didn't work. Used his whole body to throw arms and legs. The Antagonist felt suppressed, shuffling feet with all his strength just to go forth with life.

He got to the Firemime, smelled his coat, the blood on his body, the wafts of an evil odor. He Who Stares Back faded out in that stench. He blinked. The other murderer floated through the air.

Hierarchies and a Revolutionary

His dense jacket in Aaron's hands.

Aaron fell around to face Midge. Her white shirt seared the room. Midge's light glared divine in the void temperature. When Critch came again, Aaron had no idea where his driving emotions came from or where they directed. They could've been for Midge, himself, or maybe for both. In a deep sweat, he reached out with marathon exhaustion. He'd been less wet in a downpour. Midge collapsed into his sticky arms and he struggled with her weight.

Madam Ava stopped mid sentence. The Firemime slammed against the wall thirty feet away. Shattered the picture frames before falling ten feet on his head. No use thinking about it.

Midge wiped her bloody into his shirt.

"Thank you," Midge said. She sobbed into him.

Madam Ava started to say something, stopped, tried again, failed. She smiled and broke into a clap. Those on the stage started to clap slowly, then faster. Not sure if they should be clapping at all. The Widow in Yellow deigned not to participate.

"Oh, my dear Critch, you always left me speechless. And Miss Estire, you are equally impressive. We are in the presence of gods, my compatriots."

"I hate this woman," Midge whispered while she collected herself.

"Are you happy now?" Aaron said to Madam Ava. His voice shook the air. His first words in however-long knocked those on pedestals off.

"It was a perfect display," Madam Ava sighed. "You have my support. Nova, if you will."

The Widow in Yellow left the stage and disappeared into the wings. Her dress didn't sway as it should have, she slid forward with strings holding her aloft. Her heels clicked hard on the stage floor.

Draped over her arms, like a prized sword, a braided black metal cord, tied into a noose hung heavy. She stepped down and presented the rope one-handed to Midge. Midge examined the ornate matte black aircraft cable capable of landing a jet. Midge's features tersed at the noose with a what-the-fuck face. She grabbed the cord, and her arm fell to the ground.

The Antagonist's Prison

"Be a good Caretaker for my weapon, Miss Estire, Only Witch for Our Relentless Shadow," November said on one knee level with the petite Midge. Her powerful reek of violet and cigarette smoke drenched them. Their eye contact so intense Your Imminent Unforewarned Reckoning felt intrusive. November tied the noose around Midge's hips like a gaudy belt.

"It was the one thing Critch couldn't snap. The noose shut him off. As if pulled by tethers from the past." The Widow in Yellow rose and boasted with her long stride off the stage and into the mist of The Underground.

Madam Ava came down and placed her slender, long, and incredibly strong fingers on Midge's comfortable shoulders. "I've been waiting for this day for a long time, Samantha. Critch is your responsibility now. If your fledgling companionship hits the rocks and sinks into the sea among all the fish and the black struggling all the while, I request you call this number and November will pick up Critch's leash."

She handed Midge a card. Midge held the rope around her waist with dread.

"Can I say something?" Midge said.

"I didn't take you as someone who asked permission to speak. Perhaps I misjudged you, Miss Estire."

"Just shut up, you aloof cunt."

The stage took a breath and held it. Madam Ava smiled, awaiting the scorn.

"I'll take your token of permission, or whatever you freaks call it. But I won't take this goddamn analogy of a relationship as its implication. That's not what a relationship is to me, and I will not control or contain Aaron. I'll take this noose and use it as an acceptance of what Aaron is, and never expect him to be more or less. I like him exactly how he is, Critch and all." Midge took out her Bic and lit the business card on fire. She dropped it, letting it burn on the stage floor. "He's a goddamn forest fire and I'm here to slash hoses and break gas lines."

Critch appreciated the speech, but he didn't think he was a fire.

Hierarchies and a Revolutionary

He could be the forest maybe.

"A darling speech, really. However, I have no faith in relationships. Humans are polyamorous creatures, monogamy is not natural. Please, don't let me stop you from trying," Madam Ava said.

"Who said this had anything to do with sex?" Midge said.

A slave came by with a silver stopwatch open on a tray.

"I feel obliged to tell you that you may not want to be here within the minutes to come." Madam Ava's attention shifted to the stage.

Midge and Critch nodded to each other. They rushed from behind the curtain and down the stairs. They gave Jeb a side five and fist bump. If such an exchange had some name, no one knew it. The door shut rudely behind them. The building wanted to watch without being worried about non-participants.

Midge slid to the ground against Madam Ava's building, pulled out her Lucky Strikes and took a long drag. She sighed, releasing blue smoke and stress. A clove had not left Aaron's fingers since the Arena. It's the same way on his days off. He sat on his porch all day with coffee or tea and watched the sun cross the sky.

"Aaron!"

"What?"

"You disappeared there for a second. His smile was spreading."

"Sorry."

They sat on the cobblestones until Midge was done with her cigarette. Midge watched The One Who Stares Back with a desperate emotion on her face he couldn't identify. Instead, he listened to the little sounds of his world, the drops of water hitting ancient puddles, the flicker of the lamps. There was a slight heartbeat thrum in the ground he never noticed before. He probably missed a lot of things. His numb senses not made for this world.

"How about the Heathens next? If they are an anarchist collective, then we shouldn't have much trouble getting their permission."

"Sounds good enough to me. Though, I thought the same for Madam Ava and look how that turned out."

"What was the token Madam Ava's dude gave you?"

"Huh?"

The Antagonist's Prison

"Her representative. He gave you something?"
"It was a Cracker Jack box."
"Was it empty?"
"No."
"So, did you eat the Cracker Jacks? What was the prize? That's the whole reason to eat Cracker Jacks, the shitty magnifying glass or whatever the fuck that didn't work but you felt triumphant."

Her Dear Apocalypse raised an eyebrow. "I honestly don't remember."

Midge, with an eye roll, accepted that His Unflinching Grin didn't remember something so insignificant. Even if she found it oddly significant.

Instead of the huge Tesla coils which used to harass anyone who passed, a broad water tank of a man intimidated in front of the door to The Heathens. His body suggested a past of protein enthusiast, or football player, but he had since stopped his regimen. He could lift a car given the motivation. His bald head and the thick X's tattooed on the back of his hands put him in the once dangerous Straight Edge phenomena.

Midge and Aaron refugees from war. Walked miles in the desert before seeking asylum at some foreign motel where the tenants were suspiciously nice. Mr. Straight Edge judged them.

"How do you want to handle this?" Your Imminent Unforewarned Reckoning asked him. Over all this shit, ready for a bed.

"My name is Hoss. This is the Heathen household. Should I know you people?"

"I'm Midge, this is Aaron."

"Never heard of you. And if I haven't heard of you, can't let you in. Sorry."

"How often are you down here, Hoss?" Aaron asked.

"I've been here since we took over this House from the Scientists. About a year. But I know where you're going. I hear a lot of

Hierarchies and a Revolutionary

stories and rumors."

"You've really never heard of her? Midge Estire?" His Exasperated said with a fake sigh, hoping that all the evidence from Topside fell through the cracks to Hoss here.

"I remember a woman who went by that name, three or four years ago. But then her kid brother kicked it or some shit, she cracked and shipped off to Europe. Haven't heard anything about her since."

"How about me, Aaron Bennett? I own Shirts with Words on Them."

"Store rings a bell, and I know Tyler. Hmmm, Aaron? Must be that creepy, recluse co-owner. You're not creepy enough to be that guy."

"You've heard about Critch, I reckon?" The Antagonist said.

"Pffft. I doubt you're Critch."

Her Bump in the Night asked Midge, with his manner, if he should prove it to him. She shook her head and hung from his arm.

"Alright, fine," His Unflinching Grin said. "We need to talk to your leader. We're here to overthrow Mr. Kinns. He destroyed my shop, and stole a friend of ours named Jaslynn."

"Now that's a name I know. I dated her years ago. She was a wonderful woman. If Mr. Kinns is after her, she never had a chance. That fucker, he plans years...up, up to a decade ahead. He carefully sets up all his dominos, then makes them fall into his own gruesome designs. Have you seen his territory? If you haven't, I suggest you go take a look, it will dishearten you."

"So how do we get into your House, or is your house a VIP club?" Aaron asked.

"A simple question. How do you make anarchy work?"

"Anarchy doesn't work, because..." Midge began a lecture.

"That is not what I asked, Ms. Estire. We are the exception that proves the rule."

"Each citizen in an anarchist society must be completely independent, and cannot rely on anyone else," Aaron said blankly because he'd been asked this question too many times.

The Antagonist's Prison

Hoss raised his eyebrow. "That is the most concise, correct answer I've ever heard."

"My business partner, Tyler, and I have had this bullshit argument too many times, and that's basically what it comes down to. It's a cute summation of all those arguments. Whipping out that line makes for drama from time to time, because people love the idea of anarchy but have no idea what it'd take."

"You are correct. You answered my next question. I kind of like it." Hoss gave a knowing nod. "Come on in."

It smelled of permanent grime no amount of cleaning would release. On the couch were some crashed-out punks, beer rusting their livers.

A man with burbling black hair, a recently clean wife beater, and thin blue jeans came heavy down the stairs. He was a handsome man, sans the beer gut. He could have been an actor or at minimum someone famous for their face.

Midge flicked her hair back and scratched her nose, little signs of attraction.

"More visitors," he said coming over to greet them, "And hey, they looked fucked up, too. I'd offer you a drink, but I've had enough already. Stay sharp, feet on the ground, know what I'm saying?"

He knew how to act when hammered. Aaron liked that awareness in a person.

"So, you're Midge and Aaron," the man said. "I shan't say your other name. You look completely unhinged. The both of you. Y'all have been making a lot of people angry down here. Not the best idea. Fucking love it, though."

He shook their hands and flopped on the couch. They sat on another of the five couches and chairs circling the main floor. In between were the Passed Out. A normal thing in this sort of household.

"Whatever, I do what I want!" Midge said, cocking her head back and forth with sass, snapping in the proper Z pattern.

"Psshh. I'm not in the mood for this," the leader, presumably Asher, said. "Don't care, and I don't think any of us are in a state

Hierarchies and a Revolutionary

to have this conversation, I know I'm not. You know, Aaron, there are people here who know you. They couldn't stop talking about you. They respect you."

"They shouldn't."

"Regardless, they do. They kept talking about your ass-tearing rants, how valuable your wisdom has been."

"It's not, though."

"Perhaps you don't get what wisdom is? I know you guys are in the right, sorry, our collective mindset. I'm sure you want to get down to business. Defeat the Huns. I don't want to go through all this initiation stuff tonight, rules, rules, rules. Combine. Dark side of the moon. Really? None of you were going to finish that?" He two-finger ping-ponged between Midge and Aaron. Blank faces. "You look tired, and I'm done. The dorms upstairs are full, but the ones downstairs are empty. We'll talk tomorrow."

He unceremoniously rolled over, cuddled with a ratty pillow, and snored. A foot explored his hair.

Midge and Critch exchanged confusion, shrugged and headed downstairs. The second door on the left. Inside was little more than a bed and a chest that didn't lock. The door didn't have a lock either, or even a catch to make sure the door stayed shut. No sense of privacy here, but that left them to trust those in the house. Which was the point, if any involved were to venture.

Midge sat on the bed and untied her red cons. Then tore off her baby seal shirt. Blood peeked out of tiger stripes across her back. Aaron sat on the bed next to her and undid the laces to his thin soled boots. His hands were purple and shaking. He'd have trouble closing them tomorrow, at least until he broke the scabs and warmed the carpals.

"This insanity is about to hit me," Midge said, grabbing his sunset-colored hands.

"I know the feeling."

"I'll be right back," Midge said. She headed upstairs topless, concealed only by her ripped and dirty camo pants.

Midge was suddenly holding Aaron tight. His hand through the

The Antagonist's Prison

wall. Claw marks crosshatched the area.

"Aaron...Please?"

He slowly withdrew his hands from the wall, blue breadcrumbs falling behind him.

Midge came back with rolls and rolls of tape and gauze, dumped them on the bed, looked at the medical rubbish, cursed, then ran back upstairs. She came back with a bottle of vodka and a piece of cloth.

Aaron Bennett sat on the bed and finally started crying. Midge held him, crying as well.

"I'm losing moments. I'm trying to focus. I swear," His Imminent Unforwarned Reckoning sobbed.

"I know. We'll get through this together. I swear. If it's the last thing I do. It just might be, right?"

"I guess all we have left is gallows humor."

"Hey! Keep the optimism I admire about you. I don't want broody Aaron." She sniffed. "Though I think gallows noir is exactly how our lives look at this very brief moment."

"You're right."

"I know." Midge perked on up as she fisted away her tears. "I couldn't find any rubbing alcohol or peroxide. Did you know peroxide doesn't do anything to sanitize? Vodka will have to do."

Aaron nodded.

"Take off your shirt," she said, kneeling behind him on the bed.

He took off his ten-pound jacket and peeled off his shirt, the thermal cloth catching and sticking on wounds he didn't know he had. Midge unscrewed the cheap vodka, took a quick sip and poured it onto the cloth, getting more than enough on the bed. She cleaned with mercy, but the sting rushed through him. She applied bandages, wrapped wrists, knuckles, and torso until he was mummified.

"My turn," she said.

He unwrapped her wounds. Placed the gauze across her whippings. Tight and precise. One had to get pretty good when there wasn't anyone else to bandage one's broken body. Mirroring that precision onto someone else took a change of perspective.

Hierarchies and a Revolutionary

He sat next to the topless woman. Midge snuggled up and rested her head on his chest. He felt her cheeks curl into a smile. She readjusted, so her arm was free. She stretched across him and nudged him backward so he would lay on his back. Then straddled him. She came down, placed her cheek on his chest again. He rubbed her sides, careful not to touch her wounds. Charlie settled on the pillow, nestled up against Aaron's forehead.

It did not take long to fall asleep. A quiet embrace to feel safe beneath the bay.

Black Hearts of Gold and an Unlikely Rant

Our Relentless Shadow couldn't sleep. Too much pain. He grabbed the cheap vodka and went upstairs to drain the bottle, futilely hoping it might numb him out. It wouldn't, but seemed a better location than in bed.

All the lights out, save for a weak candle on the central table. Bodies had moved on. Someone sat on the couch and smoked distantly. They timed the drags just as the cherry was about to burn out.

She had scary accurate timing, considering the woman didn't look at the cigarette at any point. The Antagonist sat across from her messy, long dark hair, floating like the smoke of her barely lit cigarette. He knew that hair. The Miscreant Queen had a bottle of Grant's whiskey leaned against her thigh and torn-to-shreds black skinny jeans. As he sat, she looked up with pained yellow eyes before falling back against the couch, leaving a vague sensual silhouette. Arms across the back like the wings of an Erinyes.

"Hello, Aaron. How is my favorite black heart of gold? Would you like a chat?" Raile said. She drew out her words. She had every right to be under some substances.

"Works for me. Sorry about what I did to Gradick."

"Never seek redemption." She started fast and then finished the sentence slow. "I get it. I'm glad you didn't become your Hyde. I'd have to kill you, and I don't want to kill friends. I'm losing

The Antagonist's Prison

them right quick," she said. Snapped her fingers like each loud, echoed crack was a friend leaving in the wake of her personality.

"Shit happens. Nor could you lose me as a friend. I'm too loyal."

"Did you come alone, or bring friends? My circle is out upstairs. They almost killed me earlier, not their fault, but still. Hell is for freezers. Fuck the shit out of this place. Hell, at least it makes for a good story. Possibly a happy ending. Though it remains to be seen."

Raile's babbles fizzled and broke as she finished. She made no attempt to stop the tears.

"Fuck!" Raile screamed.

"What?"

"Your face. What's happening?"

"Sorry. I'm losing moments."

"They weren't kidding about that smile. Fuck a god. You know the worst part. The worst part about all this. People who used to like how I act are all of a sudden displeased with my demeanor. What happened? What changed? Whatever, doesn't matter, right? Gradick is the only person able to deal with me. Someone like me, the piece of shit I am, my pool is fucking small," she said leaned forward aggressive, pinching her fingers together until it looked painful. "I squandered my relationship. That's the worst part."

"I don't know if that's an accurate perspective."

"Finally, someone without some pithy piece of advice, or a weak attempt at flirting with me. Thank you."

"I appreciate your savagery. Always admired you two's total candor. To answer your question. I came down here with Midge."

"Really? Midge Estire? That's an odd match."

"So far, it's working out. Although, you are the first person to disagree with my companion."

"Figures that, huh? Guess that's why we're best friends." Raile took a big swig off the bottle and cringed as the shit whiskey ruined her scratched throat. "I'm so tired of talking about the fucking nature of relationships, friends, buddies, countrymen. Can we talk about something else, something interesting."

"So long as it's not about berserking."

Black Hearts of Gold and an Unlikely Rant

"I don't give a good goddamn about Critch. That fucking smirk you were getting. Nope, hm hmn. Fuck you and fuck that. I know, I know, can we talk about..lost it. I don't know, co-rumination or, you know, I don't care about your weekend. I've always cared about character, what makes you the person you are."

"That's an easy one for me to answer."

"Yeah, yeah. Critch, I get it. Who am I? I'm a savage shaman pointing and laughing at the comforts we all don't see us cozying up with. That's me in a sentence. That shit is easy and boring. Everyone is better than you, you better than everyone. You're an alien-demeanored hermit. Whoop Dee Gosh. That ain't you. That ain't surface shit even. And I can drone on and on about all our flaws. Yet people admire us, they, meaning those fuckheads upstairs, look up at us. I can't figure out why."

This was a conversation requiring a certain skill of handling one's liquor and remembering a train of thought and finishing it. "Don't ask me, people shouldn't listen to me."

"They maybe should listen to me. But they don't. They fight back, which is what I taught them to do. Promises are for the trustworthy. Be ruthless in the pursuit of truth. It's frustrating. You know what? We'll have to continue this conversation another time. I'm not going to remember it tomorrow."

"Have a good night, old friend."

She braced herself on the armrest and struggled to remember how to walk. "You too, my final friend, actually, fuck Bechtel. I'm doing all of this, endangering my Circle, myself, everything, for a partner I don't deserve!"

"Well, my only and oldest friend. Doing something for someone who loves you and you don't deserve, that sounds like the most noble thing you can do."

"I can't do this right now."

"Well, maybe, but something in you will understand my dark wisdom, as you call it," The Lady Made Of Dark's Bump In The Night said.

"Do you feel that way about Midge? Do you feel so much

The Antagonist's Prison

love? Yet not deserve it?!" There's the firestorm. Her truthful rage blew Critch back. Her hands loud on the table. Her beautiful face inches from his.

"Honestly? No, I don't. Should I? Seems like ships passing in the night, at this point."

"Six years, Aaron! Six fucking years with Gradick! What? You've known that worthless cunt for less than a week?! If you're going to give any fucking advice, maybe you should know what the fuck you're talking about. Promises are for the fucking trustworthy. Because your spouting falls on drunk, deaf ears. Validation is toxic."

She dropped the now half-smoked cigarette to stumble up the stairs. Aaron shrugged her off. The Miscreant Royalty were like that, killed your perception of yourself. She wasn't wrong. She so rarely was. It just was always such a brutal way of telling the truth. Aaron reminded himself that he was not as small as Raile momentarily made him feel. He lit another cigarette to think and continued to drink until he had drained the handle. He was pretty sure Asher wouldn't mind.

The grains of the last few days scratched The One Who Will Make You Undone's eyes. The torn muscles, down-to-the-bone bruises had shut the majority of his body down. Made him heavy and dormant. It was typically at this point that he'd have to berserk to move. To his horror, he didn't remember the walk down to the room.

Midge yawned with foul smoker's breath and slowly sat up, showing off the whipped curves of her back. Sometimes he was aware that his mouth tasted like burning tobacco, roasted cloves and the alcohol from the night before. The subtle relaxation of the clove was worth the momentary notion that his mouth tasted like an oddly specific farm set aflame.

Midge's eyes turned inside out. He rubbed his eyes and grunted to bend rigor mortis into a sitting position. Popped the top verte-

Black Hearts of Gold and an Unlikely Rant

brae between the shoulder blades. Harder to do every day. Briefly, he thought this would be rough if he were hungover. He often wondered what hungover felt like.

"I'm confused, Aaron."

"About what?"

"What your plot is about?"

"Really? Goddamnit."

"Sorry. No, let me have my fun. I was thinking about plots, you know. At first, I thought this could be a save-the-damsel plot, but then I realized neither of us care about..."

"We're down here to do the right thing!" Critch raised his voice so rarely, it stopped Midge in her tracks for a moment. "What's wrong with getting Jaslynn back?"

"Do you think it's your fault she's down here?" Midge's voice small. "Do you think it's your duty to get her back?"

"Yes. She asked me to do so." Aaron was the type of person who would wait thousands of years until the right moment presented itself, and act on that moment.

Midge nodded. "Okay, then. Understood. So maybe this is an Alice in Wonderland type tale. That also doesn't fit, at least I hope it doesn't because that means you'd have to leave the dream world without your mate, which is me. Or maybe your mate is supposed to be Jazz, which is disappointing."

"Doubt it." He fell back down, exhausted by Midge's tenacity. "Is this going somewhere or is this one of those times I just listen to the ramble? Also if Jaslynn is the mate, you could leave with me. The original structure still stands. This would be the twist."

"It's a ramble, I'm telling you what I'm thinking, nodding along is all the validation I'll need. Anyhoo, then I tackled it from a lateral approach. Tragedy! You are the villain to a lot of people down here. But if this is a tragedy, you're going to die, according to the classic plot. I won't let that happen."

"This is real life, Midge. The chips are gonna fall wherever they may. Life is not going to happen A, B, C, D. You keep saying if this happens, then that will happen. And say it does happen to

The Antagonist's Prison

turn out exactly like your plot? Are you going to be pleased with yourself? Is this how you make sense out of life? Because I can't get behind that."

Someone knocked on the door. It opened a bit under the light rap.

"You can look if you want, but I don't want to hurt your virgin eyes," Critch said.

"Come up to the living room when you're done," Raile said with her weird innuendo drawl. She left their nude and went up the stairs.

"I'm a person, Midge, not a protagonist, nor a hero. I don't stand on hills overlooking armies with a costume and a big billowing red cape."

"You can't just come out of this experience without changing and becoming mature. In the literary sense, not in actual maturity. I think you're plenty mature already. I don't think anybody could come out of an experience like this and not change in some way."

"I have a feeling this leads to a Critch discussion."

Midge didn't say anything. He nailed her ambush. Aaron threw himself out of bed and stretched. Pulled on black corduroys, black shirt, and black hat. As he laced his boots, Midge was suddenly fully clothed. The Antagonist's eyebrow asked the question.

"What? It's a college thing to get ready in under a minute," Midge said as she tied Critch's noose around her waist. He threw his dense jacket over his shoulder to hang from his mutilated hand. He even winced. The world was proud of this facial display.

His body took a good half hour to warm up before he stopped moving like a half forgotten Lovecraftian nightmare. He let Midge go up first because it was gonna take a long second to ascend each step. Five grooves adorned the blue stone walls of the staircase. Critch got Mr. Bennett to bed. Midge glanced at the grooves and sniffed back a quavered, broken sob.

The Miscreant Queen leaned back against the kitchen counter, her right shoulder heavily bandaged. She clutched a large yellow mug filled with shit coffee. Like Jaslynn, Raile did not stand. She posed. Her face aged from the tragedy of her recents. Her yellow

Black Hearts of Gold and an Unlikely Rant

eyes full of a fractured mind. Fired in a kiln and left ashen.

Under her cliché leather jacket, a body toned by purposeful action. Her torn jeans low on her hips with no compunction on her part to pull them up and cover her pronounced V-muscle. Those shredded jeans still managed to squeeze thick-with-three-c's muscled legs designers could only dream of instead of the twigs of prepubescent girls. Her knotted black hair framed a ferocious face.

When she saw her best friend, her smirk curled up into a deviousness that made her feral and untrustworthy. Aaron lit a clove. This would be rough. Only Gradick could deal with her pungent piss and vinegar, and that singularity of a man was gone. He failed the Arena, that's the general fate, like damaged greyhounds.

Raile's posse tumbled down the stairs. Jeff was there, along with his frumped, punk rock chic girlfriend in her dark green pleated skirt proud with stains, and gray spaghetti strap. The couple tied dark green bandanas around their necks. Gold hearts silk screened by Aaron himself. Stylized like long-exposure sparkler hearts.

A lank nerd with stubble sat next to his full-bodied girl, no nothing beneath her little sister cute. Their dark blue bandanas with matte black hearts slashed and oozed gold blood.

In Raile's back pocket was her black bandana. Two curved gold lines in the shape of a heart.

"Fancy seeing you here, Raile." Aaron always felt compelled to address her as an untouchable royalty. He glanced at the black stone engagement ring. It roiled almost on fire. Her red hangover corneas eyed Aaron with pity.

"Likewise, Aaron," she said, her voice low and pornographic. "Seems odd you'd be here with Jazz's best friend."

Your Imminent Unforewarned Reckoning wasn't sure if she remembered their conversation last night or played a clever façade for Midge's sake.

"It was an accidental meeting. I assume you've heard what happened to Jaslynn?"

"Asher told us. I'm glad you're as gallant as ever."

Mr. Bennett wasn't sure what she meant by that. Like always,

The Antagonist's Prison

Raile spoke as if she were trying to convey thirty things at the same time. Every carefully chosen word after curated word had so much to be read between the lines, it left The Antagonist baffled.

Midge studied Aaron as he talked to Raile, assessing how protective to be. No need.

"Run riot," Midge said.

"Raise hell," Raile said.

Was this some sort of greeting? Midge said she was friends with Raile awhile back. So maybe she knew all the silly phrases Gradick and Raile habitually recited.

"Have a black heart of gold," Midge said.

"I can only be me," Aaron said. He wasn't sure what was being discussed, so he went back to the original conversation.

Raile's head fell as a tear of situational gravitas rolled down her embattled face. She collided with Critch. The power he'd always admired. Her shock of life dissolved as he felt her ribs through her thick leather jacket. Holes punctured her motorcycle jacket like she shot it. Sounded like something Raile would do.

Off his chest, Raile said, "I'll destroy her, everything she is will be undone."

How tiny she'd become. Our Relentless Shadow didn't know what to say. He was not the comforting sort. Gradick was still alive. Aaron doubted she'd be this put together otherwise. The one bitter thread anchoring her to this world.

"You need my help, don't you?" Aaron said.

Raile gathered herself and let go. Not six days ago her yellow eyes shimmered vibrant. Now jaundiced. "I need to get to the leader of The Cult. But there's no way for us to get that far in. I need shock troops. I need The Antagonist...There's a lot of them."

"Numbers never mattered." He smiled for her and it was not received well. He'd have to berserk again, which, at this point, neither Midge nor anyone really approved of. Mr. Bennett hoped it wouldn't offend Midge that he berserked for another.

"I'm sorry to ask you to become your shadow." Leave it to the Miscreant Queen to point out the obvious symbolism.

Black Hearts of Gold and an Unlikely Rant

"You won't be the last, and if one of us gets out of here with a semblance of life, I beg the fates that it's you."

Midge stared upset at the base of his spine. She knew this was a moment to be shared between friends. Her rolling commentary was not appropriate for the awkward moment.

"I don't deserve the friends I have," Raile said, staring at the couch of deviants then back at Aaron.

He never was able to follow Raile's thoughts. She was too sovereign and outcast for him. In general, her demeanor changed rapidly.

"This face doesn't suit you," he said.

"I don't know what face to have any more. Which face would you prefer to see? Lately, people miss my giddy princess."

"You're only allowed to have one face, old friend."

Raile's well-oiled mind froze and struggled against his wrench. He knew she prided herself on being whoever she needed to be based on the situation. That worked when you were young, or in politics, but not in your own issues, where authenticity was everything.

Asher stepped up to Raile's rescue. "If you help The Miscreant Queen, I'll give you my favor."

Aaron barely knew this Asher guy but liked him as if he were a brother.

"Yay! Hooray for when it all comes together," Midge said, clapping her hands together once. Shook a fist in the air. It broke the drama and the room felt better.

Raile cleared her throat. "Fuck a god, did a toddler wrap you up?"

"Midge did."

"Well, no offense to you, Miss Estire, but you shouldn't be a doctor. Take off your shirt. Asher, get me some gauze and bandages."

"Yes, ma'am."

Raile pointed at a mason jar filled with deeply golden liquid with three tea bags steeped. Asher nodded. He went into the kitchen and brewed more tea. They seemed to know why, so Her Dear Apocalypse went with it.

Aaron took off his shirt and the room gasped. The bloody ban-

The Antagonist's Prison

dages hung loose to show scars and gashes with polka dot bruises scattered nonsensically. Raile carefully undid the useless bandages and started to clean and fix. Placed tea bags strategically.

"I gotta get something off my chest," the wet-eared co-ed of Raile's posse said, lounging all over the couch. She stood up to say something dramatic and biting, and it took a good fraction of everyone's being not to shut her down. This wasn't her place to interject. They were in an emotional moment and she stood up to give her two cents like a drunk uncle. "Why is she mothering that scary motherfucker when all she's done is scold and mock us?"

"Raile's French in her actions, Cassie," Jeff said.

"Stop using all these goddamn references, say it simply, please," Cassie said.

Revel in the pent-up bitter.

"You should read more," Midge said. "Conversation becomes easier after you're educated."

"Fuck a god, are all of Raile's friends total assholes?" Cassie cried to Wren. Jeff cocked his head at The Antagonist like he'd waited for someone to put Cassie's face deep into her apple pie until the bubbles stopped.

"Sit down, Cassie," Aaron said. Raile focused on wrapping. She knew anything she said would only make things worse. The Miscreant Royalty's direct way of speaking pissed off almost everyone. Critch appreciated it a lot. He didn't need to read into her remarks. She always said exactly what she meant.

Cassie tried to stand her ground and resist The One Who Will Make You Undone. He did not want to deal with a self-righteous, shallow, cheepy-cheepy young woman while he stood here wounded beyond anything she'd ever seen.

"I said sit the fuck down!" His Unflinching Grin said with a rumble from deep inside Critch's throat. The room sank deep within their fragile shells. Raile dropped the bandage. It rolled away. She terror stepped back. The dread of his peers cut him deep. Midge grabbed his arm. Cassie crumpled. "Sorry."

"Never seek redemption," Midge said. "I know, but your

Black Hearts of Gold and an Unlikely Rant

friends want you to be the mean blast of reality. Just get it done,"

"Cassie, you are not Raile's friend. Can't you see that my best friend is trying to bandage me up while we bearing? Can't you feel the gravity of the situation?"

"What do you mean? How am I not Raile's friend?"

"Because I can tell, based on how this entire room regards you, and how you regard one of the most generous, supportive people I know. You're a student. Friends with Raile? You can't comprehend her. You should respect her. Once you understand her, then maybe you can be her friend. Contrary to popular belief, Raile has few friends. And that is a good thing. The fewer the friends, the better."

"That doesn't mean she has to talk down to us," Wren said. She stared at her coffee. No one in the room even moon-eyed Mr. Bennett.

"And how patient do you demand a person be. She teaches, sees if you prove yourself. How many times have you been taught the same lesson? How patient do you demand a person be?" Okay haiku murderer.

"I shouldn't have to prove myself," Cassie said.

"What?! Why not?" Asher said.

"Because people should just be nice to everyone."

Cassie smelled like resignation.

"Fuck that," The Antagonist said. "Yeah sure, be nice, be courteous. Whatever, respect people. How long do you expect people to just put up with your shit when you refuse to make yourself better? You have to earn someone's respect, not just expect to receive it. Wren, remember when Raile took you to the hospital after your dad beat the shit out of you, then housed and cared for you for three weeks?"

Wren didn't say anything, just looked away. Guilt crawled around her features. Raile sobbed against the counter.

"What's the matter?" Aaron said. Completely unaware of how cathartic he was being for Raile, who really wanted to finally have someone on her side.

"How the fuck do you do that?" she said before hugging him

The Antagonist's Prison

again. This time, stronger than before.

"I'm not sure what I did?"

"It doesn't matter, thank you. Your circle is everything."

"You're welcome?"

"You're trying too hard," Midge said. "And, not to sound cold, or ruin Aaron being an Atonement with the Father figure in someone else's plot. Because he really, really shouldn't be. Though this is the first time he's given his opinion on someone's behavior. However, I want to see Mr. Kinns, save my skank whore friend, and get the fuck out of here."

Asher and Raile nodded.

"I've gotta warn you, Aaron, Mr. Kinns is a paranoid motherfucker. The guard is lax on most houses, most of the guards patrol small areas. I'm sure you've noticed how easy it is to avoid the patrols," Asher said.

"We didn't know there were patrols," Midge said.

Raile and Midge engaged in a nonverbal. Midge won. But then Raile smirked, mocking beyond reproach. Her and Gradick's resting face was, 'Yes, thank you for doing exactly what I thought you'd do.'

"My point exactly. It's like Topside, you could go a week and never see a pig," Asher said. "Then they rain upon you. I mean, the only real threat you see are The Widow in Yellow's Firemimes, you know those guys wearing firemen clothes and painted white faces. But they only mess with you if you get in their way."

"Led by November?" Raile said. Somehow she knew The Widow in Yellow's name. She was an information sponge. Remembered everyone she'd ever met and what they did together.

"Yes," Asher and Critch said.

"That isn't the case with Mr. Kinns," Asher continued. "There's always an army around. I'll take you, Midge and Raile to scout it out."

"Fuck that! Why only them?" Jeff said.

"Because we could die, and I need someone to stay back and run the fort, just in case." Asher used a favor to shut him up.

"Fuck, we've fought all the way down here," Wren said. "Now I have to sit and watch Roger stroke his fucking ego?"

Black Hearts of Gold and an Unlikely Rant

"This isn't your fight. No use dying for somebody else," The One Who Stares Back said a little hypocritically. And lit another clove, usually took two to get rid of the headache. He left the house and let the others follow.

Our Relentless Shadow stopped when he saw white hair blazing like a beacon from inside a shop called 'Eventual Cognizant.'

"Before we go any further and now that we're away from them, let's stop and have a chat," Aaron said.

Amber sat at a table with her head in her hands. Out of all the named people present, she was the last person who belonged down here, and was not handling it well. Her red, infected scabs birthed horrible watercolor smudges across her skin. Her face hardened even under her puffed-teared eyes.

Also amiss, her fashion had been upped to business-punk-rock-adjacent. White button-up with quarter length sleeves. Thin black suspenders. Irritated cyan, magenta and yellow blemishes over her slightly exposed chest. Black jeans with black boots. Gone was the practicality of before, replaced with clothing of specific purpose. A middle finger to a system she wanted to belong to for so long, now a separated professional.

The place harmless, no people waiting to tackle customers and show them what they did best. Raile noticed Amber and understood why Aaron came in here. Raile and Midge dragged another table over. Asher grabbed a chair. Aaron sat down across from yet another person with an 'A' name. She looked up like she was about to get gangbanged, then her expression changed to sudden hope. Like the rest of them, her mind only sort of around. Midge sat next to Aaron, Raile sat next to Amber, and Asher sat at the head of the table.

"Everyone I know down in The Underground, all at the same time. Does anyone else think this is fucked up?" The Antagonist said.

Raile ordered five of whatever. Critch tried to make eye contact with Amber, but she couldn't look at him. She must now know the

The Antagonist's Prison

horror he was. That saddened Her Dear Apocalypse. Amber should never have been exposed to this world of Aaron's.

"Yeah, happens," Asher said.

"The only times in my life when I came down here is when I was truly fucked up. Here I am again. So my question, for all of us, is why are we down here?" His Unflinching Grin said.

"What are you suggesting?" Raile said.

"Why are we in an underworld?" Midge said.

"Underground?" Asher corrected.

"You know nothing, Jon Snow," Midge said. "No, this is an underworld, we're all here to receive a boon to bring back to the realm of the mortals."

"Wow, your education astounds, Midge," Raile said. "Equating what we're doing to Campbell, does doing that make you feel better about your fate?"

"Maybe you *are* a bitch, Raile," Midge said.

Raile half smiled again at Midge. Aaron watched casually amused as Raile mocked Midge's lobbed tennis balls.

"Rather be a pig than a fascist," Amber said.

"What?" Midge said.

"Never mind," Amber said.

"Did you just make a Miyazaki reference?" Asher said.

"Yeah," Amber said.

Asher and Amber high fived.

"Hell yeah, though I'm curious. Why?"

"You were talking about mythological studies, specifically points on the Hero's Journey. I remembered the ridiculous fight at the end and its war symbolism and related it back to this conversation as a nod to the archetypes presented."

"Amber," Midge said. "I don't say this often, and I want you to understand what I mean when I say it. I have no idea who any of those characters are, but you just might be the smartest person in the room. You might just want to find a better room."

"You know what I've noticed about the people who come down here?" Asher said. "They only come here when they have a

Black Hearts of Gold and an Unlikely Rant

dire need to alleviate their core fantasies."

"That's very helpful," Amber said. She was evolving into a bitter sack of shit. No one liked that evolution.

"I'm Asher, by the way," he said to shake Amber's hand. "Wow, that's quite the handshake you've got there."

Amber blushed. "I've got pretty strong hands."

"What are you getting at, Asher?" Midge said.

"Be ruthless in the pursuit of truth. Anticipate the wrench," Raile said.

"It's not you versus me, it's us versus power," Midge said.

"Everyone down here, including myself, has something to work out," Asher said. "Most of them indulge in sick things, hedonism the rule here, experience what they yearn to have, but the people at this table are different. I can't find the words."

"Pelican said she doesn't come down here because she doesn't want to deal with the people," Raile said. "Same with Frank. There's no reason to come to The Underground if you're mentally healthy because there's no void you can't fill Topside."

"Then what am I down here for?" Amber said.

The entire cafe stared at her. She understood her misjudgment.

"Perhaps our boon is to get rid of something to *not* bring back Topside," Midge said.

"To help us focus?" Amber said.

"What's with this meta talk?" Raile said. "It has nothing to do with reality or what we are actually doing here. Talking structure means nothing in real life."

Aaron looked to Asher and he shrugged, hopefully equally confused.

"What's happening to your skin?" Raile said, pointing at the tattoo-like pictures on the skin Amber chose to show.

"It's a very long story. But they are not cosmic horror tattoos."

"I can tell they're not tattoos. Is this because of Zo?"

Amber nodded as a secret.

"Amber, **look at me**," Raile said with a tone that hushed gods. With the grip of rebellion, Raile's hands became one with Amber's

The Antagonist's Prison

forearms.

"Ouch."

Raile's jaws of life grip crushing Amber's arms to marble dust. She tried to pull away, but Raile didn't budge. "Look at everyone at this table. You know you deserve to be at this table. At any table. Amber, you did not deserve what happened to you. But you came out here, with us. And we got you."

The light in Amber's house clicked on. Someone moved in and cleared cobwebs and swept up the joint. Nodded in approval of this forgotten and unused space.

The waiter carefully placed five mud and grease-trap milkshakes on the table. Her eyes stared out at a middle distance. There were little umbrellas on top like they were in a cabana and not at their wit's end.

"Chug these, you do not want them to sit," the waitress said. She floated away on a cloud.

They placed the umbrellas on the table. The two supposedly grown men made a competition out of it. Finished at the same time. Raile finished next, followed by the unskilled chugging of Midge. Amber's mud flowed down her chest, but she did not seem concerned. It wasn't the worst thing ever tasted. Hurray for that. Almost immediately, vision zoomed in and out. Aaron was sucked into the grain of the table.

Bar gone. Mind feral.

Crimes and a Billowing Scarf

Wait. Noose. Widow in Yellow. Pleasure. Red-skinned man. Dwelling dark. Blinds closed. Little light. Man cried on couch. Eyes pinned open. Yes...

"Do you know why I'm here?" Widow in Yellow. Man not answer. "Children are horrid things. But to kill one, that is quite the transgression. I know from experience. And you thought you got away with it, did you not?"

Lip twitch beneath leather. Widow in Yellow ask to bring Man's children.

No noose.

Top of stairs. End of hallway. Two doors. No more doors. Infant in crib. It screeched. Carry by stomach. Other room. Girl beneath covers. She cried. Not bogeyman! Smile. Drag girl by arm. Screams remind. Thrown on couch. Arm pieces on floor.

Infant not survive landing. Widow in Yellow pick up. Limp in arms. Cooed at it. Instructed find wife. Listen. In basement. Door locked. Door gone. Splinters. Bottom of stairs. Wife hold doll against her. She apologized. I grip hair. She bled. Warmth ecstatic. Up stairs. Wife's eyes pinned open.

Wait. Noose.

"And you thought you could get away with your sin. I found

The Antagonist's Prison

your dark secret, I am the horseman, the inquisitor. Critch is my weapon. The Antagonist is your reckoning. How do you kill people who can't be killed because they've set up endless contingencies? You send Critch because nothing can stop him. He is an armageddon. This is pro bono work. For The Antagonist's self-esteem more than anything. It suits his preferences."

Bored. Tear dead infant in two pieces. Blood-drenched parents. Noose tugs. Wait. Husband and wife holler. Yes....

Girl run. Snap neck. Widow in Yellow instruct kill wife.
No noose. I take womb. Wife not create more of me.
Wait. Noose.

Mr. Bennett returned to the table, lungs burnt to a crisp. For the first time in recollection, he was anxious, absolutely terrified of what waited behind his eyes. The way space bent to relocate to wherever he wanted. How gingerly he touched everything before it catastrophically fell to pieces. How movements came from all angles as a slow, undeniable bolt of lightning down the middle.

Reality tried with all its rules to reject him, only to roll off like the blood of those children.

Raile scowled at whispers behind her. When she noticed Aaron was back, she questioned with a look. He lit a clove and smoke smothered the table.

"Not a chance," he said.

Raile smiled as if she already knew what he saw. Pleased Aaron was finally on board.

Amber, Asher, and Midge stared at the ceiling, their heads held back in a prolonged moment of clarity. Amber's eyes shimmered when she was within the current reality. Immediately threw up a mixture of blood and mucus.

Asher came out, world shattered. Raile held his shoulder. He cried as Raile's godlike empathy washed over him.

"It's like in DotA," Amber said. "When the carries on the other

Crimes and a Billowing Scarf

team are fed and you can't take them in a five-man fight, you have to farm and smoke gank until you kill one or two of their supports, then out-number them in the next team fight."

Hell if Aaron knew what Amber was talking about.

Midge came back next. Blood oozed out of her swollen eyes and down her cheeks. Midge smiled. Whatever happened quelled something within her. Raile reached down into the purse strapped to her thigh like a holster and handed Midge a rag to clean up with.

Amber starried serious at Tyler's player and realized she was quite late. She puked blood against the wall and half fell out of the store. Raile handed Amber a cloth to clean up.

"It's probably going to be fine," Amber said as if it was going to be.

The shaded ink smudges now had hard lines of abstract watercolor tattoos of non-euclidean geometry.

"Everything doesn't always have to be fine for you to keep going," Raile said. "Run riot."

"Raise hell," Amber said before sprinting out of the shake shop.

"Did anyone else not understand a word she said, but actually did understand it?" Asher said.

They nodded, sort of.

"I'm more concerned that Amber seems very sick," Raile said. "Do any of you know what's happening to her?"

"No, but it is a little late to help her," Mr. Bennett said.

"You saw what was necessary for you to see," the waitress said as she cleaned up their mucky glasses. She came from a distant introspection from whence she'd never return. "We can't guarantee what you saw is true, but, from my own experience and investigation of others, there's meaning within the revelation."

"We need to get going. How much?" Not Currently Mentioning Critch said. Dammit.

"Seventy-five each."

"Dollars?!" Raile said.

The waiter smiled with denial. Seventy-five grand.

"Fuck me," Asher said.

The Antagonist's Prison

The table knew what he was thinking. They all lived like him for a long while. Money was not something to be wasted on anything, it was something to be terrified of. Every dollar out of their account put them that much closer to starvation and/or no shelter. Spending three dollars on that cup of coffee filled them with dread and exigent guilt.

Still Not Referring To Aaron As That Thing reached into his jacket pocket and pulled out a Favor. The waiter took it and left.

"Are you fucking kidding me!?" Midge said. "What's the actual value of those? That's three hundred and seventy-five grand."

"I said before, it's a separate currency."

"How many of those do you have in there?" Raile said.

"Dunno...Around twenty-five. I brought thirty."

"THIRTY!" Asher screamed.

"I have another two hundred Topside."

Raile and Asher's skin emptied of color.

"What has The Antagonist done..." Asher said.

The spaced waiter snapped to reality for a second to judge Mr. Bennett when Asher said Who Knows Who. People were going to start recognizing him if they kept throwing that name around.

"Theories no one wants to confirm," Raile said. "No one deserves Critch, that's the going mantra I'm hearing."

"Correct," Midge said.

"Why did you obey The Widow In Yellow?" Raile said.

"I don't remember. I do remember a want to be contained. And then a knowing of being understood for once."

"Oh, fuck a god," Midge said. "That gluttonous wretch of a woman understands him now."

"Would you date yourself four years ago?" Raile said.

"Hell no," Midge said. Then pursed her lips out. "Point taken."

The Underground had a sparse populace, typically rich degenerates getting their quick fix of whatever cursed them before their

Crimes and a Billowing Scarf

sad ride home. But this part of The Underground shone with an abandoned spook. No one was supposed to be here.

Asher stopped and bent low, failing to hide in plain sight, though he tried desperately. This group could not hide anywhere. Aaron's height and lank, Midge's colors, Asher's dark-haired version of a Barbie doll's metal-music-man friend, and Raile's heart-shattering beauty. If they walked into a party, the music would scratch.

"Alright, we gotta be quiet," Asher said hypocritically. "The Knights are too large to fit down the alleys. And the Men have horrible night vision. If we keep to the alleyways, we should be fine."

"Why are you hunched over?" Raile said.

"I'm trying to stealth," he said.

The corner of Raile's mouth curled up only a little bit. Her half smirk demeaned Asher to his core mortification.

"You don't go into hiding by stepping light and ducking. You change the way your feet hit the ground. Instead of heel-toe, it's your whole foot with a rebalance from back to front. Instead of ducking, you change your attitude to being ignored. Not hiding, but as if you aren't looking for anyone and they aren't looking for you."

Raile flickered and disappeared. Never there.

"Vanishing," she said, behind them.

They did a few practice runs. Aaron found it easy enough. Midge couldn't seem to figure out how to be ignored. Asher understood the theory, but the execution was lacking.

The three of them hurried through the twisting alleyways. Took strange sharp turns that lost Mr. Bennet, so he followed Asher.

"How far do we need to go?" Raile said.

They all jumped. Forgot she was the fourth one with them. Raile stood three feet from Aaron, but her whisper seemed like they were cheek to cheek in the middle of a masquerade. Aaron always knew Raile was skilled at subterfuge. This was at his tier of society.

"You're a scary chick," Midge said. "I forgot you were there."

Which was incredible, considering how Midge's mind worked.

"No, you knew I was here, but your brain just excused me as

The Antagonist's Prison

normal environment, instead of a person."

"Mr. Kinns has cleared out most of the area," Asher said. "So there are no alleyways like these to hide in. There is a half destroyed building on the border of his territory, I've used it to spy on the enemy. I've heard what you're capable of, but I don't know what could survive an ambush by a pack of Knights."

"A monster," A Monster said.

Midge gave him a terrible teacher's glare.

"What'd he say?" Asher said.

"Nothing," Midge said.

"They say the sharpest swords need the thickest sheaths," Raile said.

"The fuck are you talking about, homegirl?" Midge whispered. She definitely didn't have Raile's whisper skills.

"**Now is not the time to be having this conversation**," Raile said. Her tone not necessarily scary or intimidating. It made the situation utterly stark. We were right here, right now. Work it out.

Midge grumbled something or other. A cat fight cometh. Raile's smirk mocked again.

"And Asher, where the fuck are we going?" Raile said.

"I usually just wander the alleyways until I find my way to the other side," Asher said.

Raile slowly shook her head. Her yellow eyes intensified and finally gave away her full smile. She was now in charge. Where she liked to be and where she belonged.

"Follow me," Raile said. The power of life Aaron loved about her ignited and warmed them in her hearth.

She led them directly through the twisting alleyways. The Miscreant Royalty lived and traversed the in-between areas, cutting through the streets and sidewalks. Raile did not walk, she advanced, and with so little noise it made everyone else's footfalls echo. She blurred as she navigated the needlessly complicated alleyway, made it exceedingly difficult to keep track of her.

Once they finally approached a corner, Raile pointed.

Please Not Again glanced around and had just enough time

Crimes and a Billowing Scarf

to see a behemoth cat scaled with blue stone plates instead of fur. Critch's mind seared and sent himself to shudder in the corner.

Aaron came out kneeling and gripping his chest as his heart's bpm came out of warp. The readjustment of bones hadn't finished yet. The rhino cat lay decapitated on the ground. Midge sprinted around the corner and hugged Not Her Other Half from behind. Her bloody tears beaded on his jacket and ran down his arm.

"Are you alright?" he asked.

Midge's smirk curled against his neck. "Really? Goddamnit, Aaron. You're dying on the ground!"

Aaron grabbed the cat by the bloody neck and struggled it into the alleyway. Raile and Asher still dumbfounded. Aaron *Vanished* as he dashed across the street into a deserted building. The only light came from the entrance and the top of a stairwell. A fluttering sound beyond. A motherfucking fairy swooped out onto the landing and perched. It peered hard into the dark house, and flew away when it did not see The Antagonist trying not so hard to loom in the gloom. He grabbed a piece of rubble, tip-toed to the top and fastballed it into the bobbing creature. It screamed, then popped into ash like a balloon floating over a wildfire wreckage.

Midge's scuffed academic walk came up the stairs.

"What was that?" she said.

"A fairy."

"A what?"

"Just say 'what the fuck?' and move on."

"Don't question insanity," Midge said.

He raised an eyebrow at her. "Fair enough."

From their second-story vantage was their first full view of what lay ahead. Mr. Kinns laid waste to this part of The Underground. The ground dropped beneath the buildings and piled the debris into the lake. He used the rubble and trash to create a gray badland of flies and whisperings that stretched to the cave

The Antagonist's Prison

wall, where he carved out a castle. The windows glowed yellow like little jack-o'-lanterns in the distance. Across the desolation, creations lumbered about, erecting towers and barriers.

A cloud of fairies swirled above. At least a hundred knights labored and fortified already formidable barricades. Even his demonic side doubted himself. It scared him. His body groaned. He burned and ached. Bones drilled out, and any extra weight pressed would splinter them. Blood ran thin.

"Now's that time to make a joke," Midge said.

"I don't have one. You know those movies where the hero stands on a little hill and the army across from him stands ready but nervous that they must face this hero of the people? Has a billowing scarf or cape to blow in inexplicable wind?"

"Sure?"

"I feel like this is that moment for me. I don't own a large enough scarf to make up for my inability."

"You're also fucking fearless...and...wise? You might be the most sapient person I've ever met. But I know what you mean, I don't know what I'm looking at here, let alone what to do about it. But I do know we need to do this, and if we can affect this god forsaken place, to make it more...moral? I'd feel productive."

"And to think, I'm doing this because that bastard burned my shop down, an eye for an eye. But look at this. I'm overly vindictive. It sucks being a hero. I have to deal with all kinds of bullshit."

"There's the joke," Midge said. She hugged Our Relentless Shadow. Somehow making light of the situation again.

Their two compatriots came around the corner to see them holding each other. Asher nodded, understanding how crushed their egos had become. Raile led them back to The Heathens House. Cut through the ziggered and zaggered alleys and made it back in half the time.

Crimes and a Billowing Scarf

The Heathen House reminded of younger times. Surrounded by people with shallow beliefs and unstructured doctrines. Bullshit and arrogance without justification. The people in this house slung in lack of experience. Poor Raile and Aaron were too old for this level of bravado. Academia-exclusive bravado. As soon as she saw her friends, Raile pivoted into the kitchen and grabbed a cup of coffee from a convoluted dispenser on the counter.

"You have a problem with impossibility, don't you?" Midge was saying to a presumptively nerdy kid. He refused to accept the reality he was in with Raile's art. Her deeds. And Charlie hiding between the cushions after the kid screamed bloody hell at him. "Even after all that's happened to you on your way down here. You're clearly holding onto an antiquated schema. How do you expect to get anywhere in life if you keep trying to hammer what you've seen into a parochial, super-annotated paradigm?"

Aaron saw no use in learning the kid's name, but his mouth fell open, staring at the small woman who just destroyed his worldview with a vocabulary nobody but them could understand. His glistening young eyes gave Aaron the old up down. The dust of his imploding mind aggravated The Antagonist's nose hair.

"You're here to rescue Jazz, right?" Raile said. Sometimes The Antagonist forgot the why of what he was doing. For so long, that was other people's responsibility.

Raile had a plan. It wasn't even a plan. She just told the future how to act.

"That's the plan yeah," Midge said.

"I met a woman on the way down here, hidden away in a tunnel. That woman was extraordinarily beautiful, people who call themselves E-Zealots, worshiped her perfection. Long story short, people died while gazing upon her. She's not like a Medusa, simply looking at her will not kill you. People die voluntarily, they starve to death because they can't bear the thought of tearing their eyes off her."

"She might not be Medusa," Midge said. "Though she might have a power similar to whomever Medusa was modeled from.

The Antagonist's Prison

The original Medusa probably didn't have snake hair and a glare that turned you to stone, but I bet there was a beautiful woman that the Medusa myth came from. Perhaps her stare froze men in their tracks. Historically speaking, she might have been African."

"The gorgon won't kill anyone anymore. I kicked her teeth out. I have a theory, though," Raile said, ignoring the fact that Midge just described what she was going to say. "I think Jazz is a weaker version of the woman I met in the E-Zealot's cave. It's the only way I can explain her history. My knowledge says Jazz betrayed lots of guys, gals, and nonbinary pals in the last four months since she's gotten into Indigo Bay. Some of them could be lying, of course, small caliber tend to lie, so the statistics are wildly inaccurate." Raile thought upon her coffee. "Yet whenever people talk of Jazz, there's nothing but good news. You are the first to give negative word on her, Aaron. An example of your caliber."

"That's exactly what I've always said!" Midge said, leaning forward and engaging Raile in one of her retina-burning glares. Aaron picked up a cushion and lightly smacked Midge's head. She threw her arms up at him, nostrils flared, but she worked it out after she saw his expression.

"I have important concrete details to back it up," Raile said, continuing the antagonism.

"You can go fuck yourself, Raile!" Midge said, standing up. "I've been saying that about her for years. It doesn't matter what she does to people, she always comes out in a good light."

"Validation is toxic," Raile said.

The Lady Made Of Dark's Bump In The Night took out a clove and poked the exposed flesh of Midge's hips with it. She grabbed it and flopped on the couch. He drew another.

"Can you guys not smoke inside, please? It makes me cough," Cassie said.

"Then go outside, or don't breathe," Aaron said.

Jeff laughed and asked for one. Jeff only smoked around The One Who Stares Back From The Void, but that's how it begins. You start off being a social smoker, bumming off people, then you start

Crimes and a Billowing Scarf

buying your own packs, then budgeting your income to make sure you have enough. Midge dared him to continue shutting Cassie down with a subtle nod.

"If you're going to be a part of this community, smokers and their smoke are something you're going to have to build a tolerance for. Unless you're dealing with addiction. Which you're clearly not."

"Anyways," Raile said, directing the conversation away from that route. "I've noticed a lot of terrible people are being called powerful and smart these days. Have a black heart of gold," Raile said, stopping him from ruining Cassie's week again. "And some people who are exclusively toxic are called sweet and considerate. Not just by the people that like them, but by the people who have every reason not to like them. These people have Charisma. That's with a capital C."

Not Learned Name was about to well-actually in with some exception.

"Listen to words before you find exceptions," Raile said "Pay attention to the bell curve, not the interesting bits at the edges.

"Creative name," Midge said.

"Capital, like when a word is at the beginning of a sentence," Raile said, finishing with her mocking bemused smile. She slurped the remainder of her coffee for longer than necessary.

"Ok, I get it, you're fucking with me. Continue working on your revelation."

"Thank you. I name things with the most simple, direct description. However, with the magnitude of people that Jazz has hurt, and the zero bad news about her, there's something amiss."

"My friend Naomi does the same thing. She's a huge run-around like that?" Aaron said.

"No, she isn't. Sexual history means nothing. We are here now. And there's loads of bad news about Naomi. This makes me think that Jazz has a ton of Charisma."

"So that's what Mr. Kinns wants with her?" Asher said.

"Hmm?" Raile said.

The Antagonist's Prison

"Well, Mr. Kinns is looking to make perfect beings," Asher said. "Manipulating specific qualities into people to make them into the creatures you've seen. The Knights have strength, the Men have agility. He must want Jazz for her Charisma."

"This is becoming a little too sci-fi," Your Imminent Unforewarned Reckoning said.

"This coming from you...The Lady Made of Dark's Bump In the Night?" Asher said.

"There's magic in this world, maybe not fireballs, or magic missiles. But there are people out there who have interesting talents," Midge said.

"Far ends of the spectrum," Raile said.

"Exactly," Asher was going to continue, but Raile stole the words from him, said it better than he would have anyhow.

"Why didn't he go after Gradick," Aaron said. "He has more Charisma than anyone."

"Probably because Jazz was female and the First Lust was female," Raile said.

"Mr. Kinns is sexist then?" Midge said.

"It's hard to tell with this bullshit," Raile said. "But I would suspect that a man who's presumably straight would look for Charisma in feminine, not masculine, certainly not in the middle. That means he's not looking for the best of the best, he's just looking for the best he can define from his narrow point of view."

"I don't see how this matters for what we are trying to accomplish," Critch said. "I don't really care why Mr. Kinns has Jaslynn. That's not why I'm going after him. You need my help with the Cult?"

"Then why are we doing this?" Midge said.

"Because despite the damage it's caused," Mr. Bennett said. "I'm more in control. I'm coming out of the berserks quicker. I'm disgusted with Critch's carnage. Appalled at the devastation. I came down here to save Jaslynn, get revenge or something or other, now I'm here to show Critch that I can stand up."

Midge smiled.

Crimes and a Billowing Scarf

"Is everyone ready to continue this horrorshow?" Raile said.

Her students nodded and stood in unison.

"Thank you, everyone, for housing us," Mr. Bennett said. They were pleased he was leaving. As always, tentative acceptance shifted to familiar rejection.

"You guys are awesome," Raile said, hugging everyone. "If you all are ever Topside, I have two hundred couches for you to sleep tight."

"'PDA,' Interpol," Midge said.

"Fuck, she beat me to it," Jeff said.

Youths and a Shrieking God

Asher took them from the Heathen House toward the heavily populated area of the Cultists. Last Aaron was here, it was filled with Wiccans and Cthulhu worshippers. He was not sure why the Brotherhood of Einingar branched off on their own. Maybe their numbers got too large and they split from the hive like bees. Or they actually believed, versus were-in-a-cult. Another split was happening soon, because the only people roaming the Cultist area were all in white t-shirts with shitty silkscreened rainbows on the front. Purple sweat pants. Somewhere between a hundred and a hundred-and-fifty cultists hurled themselves around, determined, yet utterly confused. Told to act and do things without reasons or goals with often conflicting orders. The smell of frustration of never doing it right and not being told why.

Asher stopped and pointed Midge and Aaron down a street, then he pointed the Queen and company down an alley.

"It was good to see you. Be safe," The Antagonist said.

"Revel in knowing you are never safe," Raile said. She tied her black bandana with the simple gold heart around her face. Her students did the same. "Aaron, I appreciate this, really, but I don't think you know what you're up against. I saw what these cultists can do."

The terror of Raile's memory gripped and shrank her. Aaron

The Antagonist's Prison

put his hand on her shoulder and smiled, but that didn't help, it only deepened her terror. He took his hand away.

"Good luck. See you soon," Oh No Those Are Kids said.

"Run riot. Raise hell," Raile said. Her yellow eyes brighter than a lighthouse spotlight.

"Have a black heart of gold," Midge said.

"Scatter like a savage," Jeff said monotone.

Her Dear Apocalypse turned back one last time. The five of them dematerialized the moment they entered the alleyway. Bandanas around their faces.

Every cultist stopped and tried to stare them out. Midge uncomfortable with the countless angry eyes of teenagers.

"I don't want you to berserk here," Midge said. "Some of them look barely twelve."

"It's never Plan A to kill everyone. I'll leave that up to them if they want a fight."

"Of course they'll want to fight. Kids like these always get contentious..."

He found a cluster. A boy preached to his younger group, holding up a cast iron black pot. They silenced as Aaron and Midge trespassed on their congregation. They stared, thinking the power of their glare would stop them. Midge scooted behind Our Relentless Shadow.

"Hello, everyone, my name is Aaron. This is Midge. Sorry to interrupt, but we're looking for your leader. Do you know where we can find her?"

"Diane has passed the rainbow, found the treasure, and has come back to show the worthy her path."

"Fantastic, great for her and all of you. And she's here, excellent. Can you take us to her? That'd be best for all involved."

The rainbow children continued to stare.

"Fuck a god, you're really bad at this," Midge said, looking at him horrified. "Hi, guys, is Diane taking visitors?"

"You must ascend from violet to indigo before you are worthy to speak with her. You are still Uncolored."

Youths and a Shrieking God

A mass of white shirts surrounded them. Two dozen or more crowded up in everyone's involved businesses. The Antagonist towered over the children too young to understand the true horror of him. He reached around Midge's waist. She looked up, concerned for Aaron or the rainbows, His Unflinching Grin didn't know. This would end badly.

"Trouble is not what you or I want. I'm sure Diane can see us for a moment," Aaron said to the rainbow who still held up the black pot. "It's an Underground Mediation. I have no problem with what y'all are doing. What I have to talk to Diane about is neutral."

"Underground Mediation?" Midge said. "Is that what we've been doing?"

"What it's conventionally known as, yes."

"I dunno, it could have just as likely been called a Beneath Conversation."

"I enjoy that one more."

"You shame us with your presence! Diane would never see an unworthy Uncolored. Leave us!"

"Nope. Not gonna happen," Aaron said. "I need her permission to move on Mr. Kinns."

"You're an arrogant fool. You think that being nice is enough to Color Shift. In order to be here, you must be useful. You are not useful."

There were maybe fifty kids now.

"Now you're assuming things. If this escalates, it will end poorly."

"You are grossly outnumbered," another white shirt said from behind Did-They-Think-They-Stood-A-Chance.

"Numbers never matter."

"Take them away," the boy with the pot said.

Seven people ripped Midge away from The Antagonist. She screamed before she flailed and bit arms. Mr. Bennett waited for the flush, but it didn't come. Fine. The shirts pulling Where'd He Go? didn't have a chance against his strength. He ripped away from them, decking the one in front of him. Grabbed the hair of

The Antagonist's Prison

another and kneed him in the face.

The whole mob jumped on top of Lowly Human, and he fell beneath their awkward tonnage. Midge fought back and cursed at her abusers. Aaron snarled and growled and tried to pull his way out. Making more movement than the twenty children on top of him expected. A metal strip cinched his throat. Vision faded from asphyxiation.

Midge shrieked the same noise Raile made in the Arena. Critch's smile splintered the cobbles as children mushroom clouded above him.

Aaron expected his bed. The pain in his chest purple. His vision throbbed. Bruises and cuts all jumped up to meet the fuck out of poor Mr. Bennett. His nerves the sizzle of water poured on coals. His tear glands shriveled to husks long ago. He tried to stand, but Midge was holding him. The broken corpses of teenagers laid waste. Pieces slid down blue walls. The cobbles flowed heavy with frothy blood disturbing his boots. The smell of blood burned his smoker lungs.

"Aaron?" Midge said. Her white seal fur tank top spattered with remnants of his atrocity. Critch picked up a dented cauldron. This'd do as the token from The Cult. He didn't want to be here anymore. His traditional reaction to keep moving further from his past.

"Aaron!" Midge said, using her teacher voice. Hints of his evil smile twitched his cheeks. Blood cascaded off his clawed hands. Some of the blood his. Most of it the poor children.

Charlie hopscotched over the cobblestones. His Unflinching Grin knelt to pick him up. He nuzzled into his red right hand.

"You really want to talk about this?" he said, gesturing to the hundreds of dead bodies and red walls surrounding. November once said to count heads. Like broken bottles in a wine shop, count the corks. Keep up with inventory. Charlie copied his gesture with his front leg. "What's talking going to do? Look around us, it's a

Youths and a Shrieking God

playground massacre. How do you think this makes me feel? Do you really think talking is going to remedy? Just accept my sins and move on."

The Antagonist placed Charlie on his shoulder. Wiped off the blood and scraps from his hands and wrung out his shirt. Flicked pieces of flesh away. Futile as he darkened his hands with each flick.

Midge pounded the cobbles with angry steps, splashing up blood like harmless puddles. She grabbed his arms and pointed at the bleeding bludgeons and seeping gashes.

"Fuck you! Yes, what you did was terrible. I don't care about the gore anymore. I care about you and I see the pain in your face, even if you don't feel it. You're going to die if this keeps going."

"I've taken worse."

"Shut your goddamn mouth! Fuck a god! You know that's not how it works!"

Midge started crying. It was time to go.

"We have to go to the Seekers of the Initial Noise," Aaron said. "We can discuss this later."

"Fine! Just keep going Aaron, it's so admirable," Midge said hiccuping.

"What do you want me to do? Join Berserker's Anonymous? You know what? I'm not having this discussion at this time in this place."

She was pissed. His Unflinching Grin shook his head and walked, sort of, limped was more apt, perhaps shuffled. He stopped fifteen steps later, nodding for Midge to follow. She sighed. Wiped her nose. Cleared her eyes. She jogged up to him and wedged herself under his arm to help support.

"I don't like watching someone I care about die in front of me. I already watched my brother die."

"I'm not going to die yet."

"You can't spare a dollop of worry?"

"I'm only going to say this once. I'm not afraid of dying. But with that said, I have no intention of doing so at this time."

They paused and hugged before following the sound of atrocious guitars.

The Antagonist's Prison

A boy and a girl crouched outside The Seeker's with electric guitars. Thin and sort of clothed. Aged around eighteen. Their maturity fluctuated between eight and eighty depending on the topic. The girl wore a partially-buttoned denim vest with nothing beneath. The boy across from her inferentially her brother, although, instead of blonde, his hair was blacked out.

They both jangled unpleasant, atonal music on their guitars, staring at each other with intense lust. When they saw the It's Okay To Be Friends they stopped their avant garde foreplay.

"Critch..." the boy said, standing and backing away. His girlfriend stood in front of him.

"It'll probably be fine," Precedent Says Probably Not said.

"You've been making a lot of enemies and friends," the girl said, shaking terror frequency. "All in places that you don't want to have friends or enemies. My name is Didds. This is my twin brother, Neil."

"We know your employee, Amber," Neil said. "Talented girl, after Zo broke her."

"Broke her?" The Antagonist said like the gates of Mordor opening.

"Yeah...Please don't kill us."

"You didn't hurt Amber, why would I kill you?"

"Zo tortured her to break her bulwark and allow Amber to channel Initial Noise."

"You seem awfully nonchalant about the harm caused to my employee."

They scooted away by micrometers and little foot pivots.

"That fucking cunt!" Midge said. "Where the fuck is she? I need to tear her a new asshole. She deserves an episiotomy!" She thrust out her pinched fingers as if performing the procedure with the gesture.

"Good, you hate her, too. Unfortunately, you need to pass a test to come inside. We will give you three songs. Tell us the names, and

Youths and a Shrieking God

you can go inside. You only get one guess at each song, so be careful."

They played unplugged white electric guitars. They sounded amped. Best not to ask how people achieved the impossible down here.

Neil let out a primal yell. Both of them went off on their guitars, a fast punk-inspired thing. Didds sang backup during the chorus, sounding definitively male. They stopped one minute in and, knowing punk music, that was about half-way through the song. Aaron had no clue what it was.

"Not too fast, Midge. You know the song, and the band, but the trick is to name who's featured in the song. Who was Didds impersonating?"

"Well, I know it was, A.F.I., 'A Single Second.' I'm going to venture a guess and say Didds was Nick 13, from Tiger Army."

"Very good. Try this one."

Didds played a slow bass line. It was simple, like a heartbeat, with upbeats of optimism. Neil sang about selfless gestures of affection given without any carnal award. Naive sort of way to win affection from a woman. The song built, and he looked increasingly frustrated until he made his guitar wail with rage. Midge smiled, but The Lady Made Of Dark's Bump In The Night had her beat. When they stopped, they looked up at Midge.

"'No Pussy Blues,' by Grinderman," Still Remember He's Critch said. Midge and the deviants perplexed by his lucky knowledge.

"I thought you didn't listen to music?" Midge said.

"Never said that. Just don't listen to much. Love Nick Cave, though."

As the musicians played and listened to their banter, their fear dissipated. In turn, it made Critch more at ease. The walk on eggshells worked both ways. The constant easing of other's fear was necessary but time-consuming and stressful.

"Good," Neil said. "Last song."

Neil and Didds did not seem interested in performing these tests. They acted as if they were unimportant and bored.

Didds plucked up and down her notes, and Neil would blast

The Antagonist's Prison

a chord whenever Didds was done with the plicky pattern. They could get five or six different instruments out of their guitars and trip the hell out of their audience. There was no message to the song. After the bullshit lyrics, Neil screamed out "Sail!"

"I don't understand," Midge said. "I thought you guys were testing our hipster cards."

"No, we're testing your knowledge of music with Initial Qualities. It's sad when, to hear this kind of music you have to dig a lot to find it. But every once in a while Initial Music sneaks into the mainstream collective."

The siblings strapped their guitars and led them inside.

"'Sail,' by AWOLNATION, by the way," Midge said. She couldn't help herself.

"Amber talked about Initial Music just the other day, when she showed up naked at my store, drugged off her rocker."

"She wasn't drugged. Zo stole her from a show the night before and tortured her with Initial Music until she broke. Zo's been using her and us."

Critch's irises spun. Neil and Didds backed up unconsciously. The fear returned. Ruined reparation. If Aaron had a white knight syndrome, it'd be flaring.

"So are you going to let Zo get away with hurting my employee?" he said like the dread of a snowstorm.

"She uses everyone," Midge said. "She used me a long time ago. Zo will burn anyone who can further her path. Shoots them in the head when they are no longer useful to her."

Midge pantomimed shooting Didds with her cocked finger. Didds nodded.

"What's your plan, then?" Aaron said, horrifically headcocked.

"There is no plan. When we get the chance, we're pushing her in front of the train. Amber's going to do it," Didds said.

"Sounds like you're just going to let Zo get away with it. I'm not a fan."

"We still need her," Neil said.

They were not shaking from fear then. More withdrawal.

Youths and a Shrieking God

Whatever drug Zo had them on was potent. Clever, in a truly evil way, to keep people you'd burned from leaving.

The walls of the blue stone drywalled and full wall display screens mounted. On each four-foot section were sound waves of various iconic songs. Dozens of waves vibrated next to their siblings. At the back of the viewing grounds, a full wall dedicated to one song, 'Don't Stop Believing,' by Journey. It was an important song for some reason. Above the Journey sound wave, a forty-foot bay window reigned over the main floor. In the center of the room, a stage had a simple drum set, two guitar stands and a microphone. There was to be a show here shortly.

The room rammed with all walks of people. Different subcultures coming together under one banner. But every person had the same expression in their eyes, that of a fanatic. The faded, unquestioning angry stare, and the constant, comfortable smug smile. Their conversations were interesting if very scripted and full of code-speech jargon. Aaron blocked out their words.

Amber came out from a side room upset, broken and refugee. She grabbed a bottle of amber and took a long drag off the bottle. Still in her tasteful three-quarter-length sleeve button-up, black slacks and black suspenders. The only clothes which neither hid her body dysmorphia, nor elevated it.

Peter appeared, as those men do, and put his hands on Amber's shoulders in a manner Critch did not approve of. Bits torn from his scalp. Claw marks all around his face. Black bruises around his head from Critch's grip. He often crushed craniums. The Failed Antagonist Hunter favored his left side. A wound underneath his clavicle. Aaron often didn't know how he hurt his victims.

The crowd parted as the mob of Initial Music worshippers felt Critch's presence approach. Amber spun and shattered the whiskey bottle across Peter's temple. An Antagonist Hunter could've been stabbed in the heart and kept going. The type of person who could fight in the Arena couldn't be stopped by a silly whiskey bottle. Aaron loomed behind Peter as he readied to lunge.

"I wouldn't do that, good sir," Your Imminent Unforewarned

The Antagonist's Prison

Reckoning said.

Peter turned to retch horror just from the sound of Aaron's voice. Amber embraced him with all the power of her bones and not much else. When she released, some of the blood still in Aaron's clothing dusted her white top.

"Be a dear and fetch Zo for us?" Midge said to the fighter.

Aaron recognized the way the man walked, his body unspun, his mind in tatters. The Antagonist felt no guilt, though. Well, maybe a tad, no one should face him. He was intrigued by the shift from the proud fighter on the Arena floor to the empty tomb in front of him. Insanity whistling innocent through his caverns.

"How are you, Amber?" The Antagonist said with true concern. "You seem ill at ease."

Amber's wounded Aryan features analyzed her boss's damage. Her prismatic marks now fully realized images of insanity. Spiraled out madness of prehensile tongues from geometric mouths. Fingernails piercing eyeballs. Mouths chewing flesh. A slug crawling out of a mouth into an eye. A moth with its proboscis sucking in a dead woman's vagina. All shiny new tattoos Amber would never get. Few would ever get.

"Compared to you? I'm fine."

"Me? I'm good, always good. Just tired of this place. Seems like when people learn I'm Critch, all they want to do is meet him. And I get bloody knuckles."

"Oh yeah, like our travels have totally been a stroll down the beach, Aaron. We've been through hell, Amber. And Aaron is not ok, he's dying in front of us," Midge said.

The dark trails down Midge's cheeks like she cried dirty tears. Amber's eyes faded between awareness and Initial Music fanatic.

"You're looking at me all funny, Amber. Let's go have a chat outside," Aaron said.

Her irises slowly changed from her typical clear brown, to green, to blue and back as she followed Aaron. Her Dear Apocalypse flicked out three cloves for the group. Amber had ash on her and reeked of cloves.

Youths and a Shrieking God

"You look like everyone else in this building. You have mirror eyes, like a cultist. And trust me, I know what a cultist looks like."

Midge snorted from his gallows humor. "That might be the most fucked up joke I've ever heard."

"Are you a follower of Initial Music?" Aaron said, for once, maybe a tish threateningly.

"I'm well on my way, albeit against my will," she said.

A girl with a colorful patchwork hoodie came out with Zo. The patchwork Indian girl's hair recolored so many times there was no primary theme. Zo's clean dreads and handmade clothing were still impressive.

"I hear the flutter of wings," Midge said loudly, with her hand to her ear before she faced her.

"That never does get old, does it, Midge?"

"Aaron!" Midge said, hand on his shoulder.

His vision fuzzed in. His Unflinching Grin held Zo high against the wall by her stomach, about to break skin. She howled desperate as she flailed against Your Imminent Unforewarned Reckoning's arm holding her aloft.

Amber's whole body sunk into her feet. Disappointed despair. The girl with way too many colors no longer around. Supposedly Aaron lowered Zo. Didds held Neil as they both faced away crying.

"I'm sorry," Aaron said.

"Me too," Zo said, trying her best to compose herself. It didn't work. She fell to her knees. Stomach in hands. "No one deserves Critch..."

"No one deserves Critch," The One Who Was Never Deserved said.

"She fucking does!" Midge said.

"I do," Zo said.

"No one deserves...Critch," Amber said. "That...That was not to be spoken of."

The Antagonist's Prison

"Follow me, please..." Zo said. Straightened her sweater, flicked her dreads over her left shoulder. "I'm a busy woman."

"Even after almost dying to the motherfucking Antagonist, you're still a monster. Bitch, be humble," Midge said.

They followed Zo inside. Amber remained outside, chatting with Neil and Didds. Through an empty white room with writing scrawled across the walls in a colorful graffiti array. Midge took pictures with her eyes. Zo unlocked a door leading upstairs.

"You need my approval to advance with your plans to overthrow Mr. Kinns," Zo said. "I want to show you a few things, Critch."

Aaron chose not to correct her. There was nothing to correct at this point.

Upstairs to a blank office with a green bean bag chair in the middle of a red carpet. On the far side was a desk with tapes, CD's and records stacked. Peter waited for Zo to come in the door. He held a pair of wireless headphones.

"We haven't been properly introduced, Critch," he said, holding out his hand. His head already bandaged around Amber's wound. His clammy hand trembled, barely able to grip.

Okay, now the guilt panged. This demeanor used to be so common around Mr. Bennett. Great shame drenched. "I'm truly sorry."

Peter didn't respond. He handed Midge the headphones.

A knock on the door. Peter opened it, and Carly stood there holding a missive for him.

"Critch..." Carly said before sprinting away.

"I'm really tired of people saying my name like that when they see me," The Scariest Person In The Vicinity said.

"Can't blame them," Midge said.

"Another client needs my services." The relief in Peter's voice made Aaron gulp.

"You can't do anything with Critch here anyway," Zo said in blasphemous condescension.

"I've been made aware," he said, then slid out of the room.

Zo stood in front of a window overlooking the main area. The forced, hard silence, a result of soundproofing. Downstairs, Amber

Youths and a Shrieking God

was onstage with Neil, Didds, and the colorful girl.

"You ripped a rib out of Peter, then stabbed him with it," Zo said. She held her greening stomach and shuddered. "Grabbed him by the head and killed a few Firemimes with his body. It was horrific."

Amber belted across heaven, earth, and the space betwixt the stars. Unblinkingly hypnotic. Threw her body raw into the lyrics. The way the band blurred as they played. The pit stood paralyzed. All of them did. The song stopped. Aaron hadn't heard a single note of it, and even muted, his eyes hurt as he blinked.

"Crazy right?" Zo said. "You may not believe in Initial Noise. But if you don't? Explain that. Now. Neil, Didds, and Beebee were all talented musicians before I awoke them. Then I learned of Amber. I found my singer..."

Aaron emerged with the soundproof panes of glass in pieces flying across the room below. Thick jagged shards floated away from him. Zo hung from his outstretched arm. Midge nowhere near him. His bones cracked and popped as he reformed. Held her with intent to kill but brought himself out.

"I want you to understand something, Zo" he said, holding Zo aloft by her throat. "A notion with my expertise. Good things brought about by wicked acts are wicked and not anything more. Great things have been done by inhuman evil. Reckoning comes for you, but it will not be by my hand. That right is reserved for them."

Zo nodded in his angry gaze. Hung twelve feet up. Her face blued. The crowd huddled protection on the other side of the room.

"Let's get this over with," Midge said, quietly.

He stepped back from the ledge. Finally let Zo go. She crumpled, holding her throat and coughing. "No one deserves Critch."

Zo shook as she placed the headphones on Midge, who now sat on the green bean bag cross-legged. Zo's back blued from the thick glass she impacted.

"When Neil sings he sounds like Mike Patton," Zo said, ner-

The Antagonist's Prison

vously muted. "But when Amber sings she sounds like Adele, Florence, Emily Armstrong, Nico Vega, Alison Mosshart, Greta Van Fleet, and Meg Myers all got shoved down her throat, it's goddamned impressive. Finally, the world will hear another Freddie Mercury. But I can see you all don't care."

"I care," Midge said. "I've never seen anything like them."

Zo watched Aaron as she carefully approached her A&R stacked desk and pressed a button.

"This plays a clip of Initial Music. It's not a song with Initial Qualities, it's an...it's an actual clip of Initial Noise. If you can hear it I'll give you my approval," Zo said rapidly.

Cult speak to Aaron, but the air tingled.

"I want to hear this," Midge said. She squeezed the headphones closer and hunkered on the bean bag. She clamped her eyes shut and concentrated like what she was hearing was hard to make out.

"What's it take to hear Initial Music?" Aaron said.

"Mostly just awareness, you've got to have good senses. You think Midge can hear it?"

The band restarted their set on stage. The Antagonist had no idea what he heard, but it was amazing. Everything he could like in a song, not that he was an expert. As a man who felt little toward music, he wanted to get their whole catalog and never listen to anything else.

"I have no doubt that she can. How will you be able to tell if she hears it?" Aaron kept looking over his shoulder, expecting someone to be there. Waiting for a tap that never came.

"Depends on the person!" Zo yelled over the jaw drop below. "Most people get a wide-eyed expression! Others throw the headphones off and scream! When I hear it, there's a deafening pop, like a gunshot by my ear!"

"So if you hear and see everything perfectly, what would happen?" He swore the world quieted from moment to moment.

"I don't know, something big!"

The One Who Stares Back's ears refused to pop. The sudden pressure swallowed him. The silence in the room went away, left

Youths and a Shrieking God

nothing. Midge stood up, holding tight to the headphones. Her unhinged mouth screamed silence into the void. Blood fountained from her nonexistent eyes, down to the red carpet floor. She threw herself into full crucifixion. The spray slowed to a standstill as her head jerked skyward. The Antagonist was able to move with only labored effort toward her.

The pressure vanished. The world about to implode on them like a supernova condensing on Midge. Aaron moved in strobe.

A whispering shriek rushed up. The sound of god split the building in half as Aaron tackled Midge, throwing off the headphones. The walls billowed out, then disintegrated.

Chatters and a Desperate Suggestion

He Who Smiles Back From The Void pulled Midge out of the dust the building had turned into. It wasn't as if a bomb or an earthquake struck the building, there was no rubble to pick through. The blue stone was immaterial, all that remained was the foundation. The mob of people nothing more than settling powder.

Mr. Bennett offered Midge a cigarette, but she refused. She lost ten pounds. The energy of what she listened to vacated her. Her ears and eyes bled. Amber and hers climbed out from their dust mound.

"How are you okay after that?" Midge said. Her voice had trouble getting into the world.

"I'm resilient," Her Dear Apocalypse said.

"Clearly," she said, sitting down in the dust. Now was not the time to have this discussion once again. Amber ran into Aaron crying. Her eyes slowly cascaded through the conventional pigmentations.

"If you're alive make a noise?" he said to potential survivors. There were no calls for help or gurgling from beneath a rock. There was no rock to be crushed under. Only Midge and Aaron, along with Amber and her band. Charlie rocketed out of a pile and scurried next to them. He celebrated. It was not the comic relief he had hoped for.

"Fucking damn, is that all?" Aaron said.

"Why are we the only ones?" The drummer said. All of them

The Antagonist's Prison

were covered in fine dust. Their empathy tears traced lines down their faces.

"I watched Zo turn to dust..." Midge said. She knew now was not the time to be confused. That came later, now was about gathering survivors.

Amber coughed and sadly lit a clove. The One Who Will Make You Undone didn't know why her choice to smoke cloves made him uncomfortable. Her thinking was loud. Amber's group judged The Antagonist.

"Critch..." Neil said. He snarled.

"What? You thought I'd be taller, built like a Semi?" Critch said.

"I thought you'd have more teeth," the drummer said. Aaron couldn't remember her name. He didn't say anything to that. His Unflinching Grin didn't have the willpower to answer morbid curiosity.

Neil ran in to tackle him. But he might as well have shoulder blasted a tree. Blame-shifting, most likely.

"Check yourself," Aaron said.

"I saw you on the beach once. You have no idea what the sight of you has done to me!"

"I'm sorry you had to witness me. I'm afraid I can't offer any reconciliation for that. No one deserves Critch."

Mr. Bennett rubbed his hands, then arms and stopped before he went to his whole body. The awkward came onto his radar. This drama was not what he wanted to deal with right now. The Antagonist had done the required politics, they had every Head's approval. Now it was time to go back to Asher, then to Madam Ava, so he could have support for the approach on Mr. Kinns. Then get to die trying.

"I've been scared for so long now that I don't know if I'd react appropriately if something truly scary came along," Amber said. "At this point, would I just shrug?"

"Amber, you have instincts," Aaron said. "You always know when to run. It's the people who hesitate that die. Just listen to yourself and you'll know what to do."

"I just don't know what to do with this new world I'm being thrust up through," Amber said.

Chatters and a Desperate Suggestion

Midge chuckled briefly.

"What, did I say something wrong?" Amber said.

"Only for gutterminds," Midge said. "Don't worry about it."

"I keep trying to step up," Amber said. "Try to expect the unexpected. Yet every time I bolster myself. The world smudges me out with another atrocity I could not prepare for. It's fucking impossible."

"I hate to tell you this, Amber, but that's kind of what life is like," Midge said with gravity of an adult truth. "I get knocked down, but I get up again, you're never gonna keep me down," Midge sang with a strange jolty dance. Charlie popped up and down in time with her on Aaron's shoulder. Our Relentless Shadow and Amber raised their eyebrows at them. "Well, Amber. Your struggle to stand up again is not unique. It is all our struggle."

"Is that like some Fight Club reference," Neil said, coming unwelcome into the conversation. "You know he was anti that kind of shit."

"I don't matter, neither do you," Aaron said. "And there is a sublime beauty in realizing that. I'm not jealous of those who matter. I pity them because they have to care. They're too big to be selfish. Because if they are too selfish the world burns. You all aren't, you are insignificant, and there is a perfect freedom to that, something to treasure. There is no greater thing to be a part of, you are by yourself and for some reason that is terrifying instead of happy. It's all about you understanding yourself and being okay with your differences from others. It's an Occam's Razor sense of reassurance and absolute liberty."

Amber and band. Hardened and bitter. Faces dropped.

"Holy crap, Aaron, where did that come from?" Midge said. "That is not the usual one-liner of vague philosophy. That was...I dunno, coming from a mind I knew you had."

"No matter where it came from, we have all made proper clusterfucks of our lives down here. Raile is well on her way to finishing up, and I will be damned if I finish last. Zo is gone, and none of you are done with whatever surreality you've been twisting in. Have at it."

The Antagonist's Prison

Critch walked away, covering leagues with his cock-eyed stride. Midge caught up. He put an arm around her shoulders, careful not to put too much pressure on her back.

"I don't think either of us has the right to say what's possible or impossible anymore. Did you see Amber's eyes?" Midge said.

"Fuck her eyes, I've killed a fairy, giants, and a smilodon."

"Touche," Midge said.

They stopped before rounding the corner to the Heathen House, something was amiss. Rumbled grunts, snarls and cracking.

They peeked around the corner. Giants and cats ripped apart bodies and gnawed on bones. Your Imminent Unforewarned Reckoning's heart sank. He wasn't too hurt about the rest of the Heathens, but he liked Asher. Aaron resorted to believing he made it out alive.

Mr. Kinns watched his carnage. He was just far enough away not to sneak up on. He turned around and saw the Friendship Out Of Trauma, his face contorted into rage not unlike Critch. His squad of creatures dropped their current snacks to snarl at them, dripping with Heathen gore.

"Aaron?" Midge said. "Remember what you said to Amber about knowing when to run?"

"Yeah, let's get the fuck outta here."

More of Mr. Kinns' giants lumbered up behind them. They dribbled ooze on the ground, leaving a snail trail behind them. Critch called to himself, but he was nowhere. Fear shivered through his body.

"I love a good ambush!" Mr. Kinns said, delightfully chipper, with a proud smile on his face. "Where is Critch, Mr. Bennett?"

Midge looked him up and down. Aaron shrugged.

"Not the time to be having doubts, now is it?" Mr. Kinns said, doing the Charleston across the cobblestones, twirling his cane between his fingers.

The giants broke from their slow lumber and charged, their spittle sprayed everywhere from molared mouths. Aaron pushed Midge into the alleyway next to them and dove in after her. Asher

Chatters and a Desperate Suggestion

was right, Mr. Kinns' creatures couldn't fit down here. Bad planning on his part.

The giants reached into the alleyway. They ran deeper in, but Aaron was sure Mr. Kinns had blocked all the exits. Midge placed a hand on his chest. An eight-foot-tall superhero landed in front of them. He stood and spread out black and white butterfly wings behind him. They twitched there.

"The ambush worked exactly as planned," he said.

Aaron shoved Midge to the ground so hard she bounced, and Not Remotely Ready For This charged the giant fairy. He tried to catch Aaron's punch. Mr. Bennett pulled back and went to kick his knee in. The Fairy God's uppercut sent Behold! A Flimsy Human flying up. He landed on the roof of a building. Then the giant Fairy rocketed out of the alleyway carrying Midge by her hair.

She screamed Critch's name as the imprecisely sized fairy flew toward Mr. Kinns' fortress. Aaron's breathing went heavy. Skin flushed and Critch erupted from him in catastrophic glory.

Aaron woke up in chains, cross-legged. Tried to lift his head, but his neck was attached to his hands manacled to his feet and in turn bolted to the floor. He could still wiggle his tingling toes, though his knees killed. He hadn't been out long. This was a pretty common position to wake up in. The Widow in Yellow used to tie him down with braided aircraft cable. Aaron could hop around a bit.

The dark room, from the sound of his breathing, was not large. Light came from underneath the door. A thin light line burned his retinas as he blinked.

A ripping sound, like sucking through a thick straw with holes, came from somewhere above him. There was someone else in the room. They were standing, clanking chains as they shifted around.

"Wowee, look here everyone! Tha behemoth, tha legend, tha mighty Critch! He's here, live and in person. How ya feel, brah?" a slurred voice said through gritted teeth.

The Antagonist's Prison

"Like shit," The Antagonist said.

"Don't we all. I had my mouth fuck'n ripped open by a demon. Oh wait, that was you! Remember that, brah?" Ramn said.

"Yeah, you chewed on my fingers. Hopefully they aren't getting infected."

"Seriously? Don't be a dick, dude. Not cool, I'm chained in this room too. Equals amiright? Well, I guess not. Fuck man, I've talked to other berserkers. We made fun of you, man. The way you make fun of some hot as shit pop singer who can't sing but gets all the fame."

"Are you drunk?"

"Always man, been drunk for months. Gets me close to berserk. Ramn here ta smash! Well, that's the story. Our fucking function in this junction. Ha! That was a joke. What's the matter, Critch? Don't you laugh?"

"So, what's going on?" Aaron asked. Drunks, you needed to keep them focused.

"Naw, man. Then I saw you. Fuck. No one deserves Critch. I dunno. They haven't needed us yet. How're you not dead yet, man? I mean, really, I need to know. Because I'll fucking kill you right here and now."

"Berserking, right?"

"Naw, naw, man. Dude, ok, check it. So, the guy before me, and the guy before that dude died. Like, they are dead. They were killed by that dude, Peter, that crazy chick Zo uses as her Arena man. They bled out, man! So the black bitch, you know, the Dom in charge, had to scale back her whole operation, all far back, for me. Do you know what it's like being able to do what I do? But all anyone ever says is that I'm no you. And I ain't even close. I get no recognition, man!" Ramn said, a little teary-throated. "It ain't fair! I was a football player. Good as shit, too, getting scouted out all kinds. But then I killed a dude in the locker room, you know, disrespect, you can't have that shit stand. Ruined that school's shit, man, I went to juvie and all. Madam Ava heard about it, got me outta that sitch, brah. And here I am, mouth ripped open by the motherfucking all star."

Chatters and a Desperate Suggestion

There was a pause. He hiccuped. Dejection seeped up through the dark. "Fuck you man, I could've been playing in a bowl game! Think of the pussy, brah, you think I'm getting any of that here?"

"You can't keep thinking about what you could've been. Nobody expects this, we certainly don't want it. I got myself out. You gotta look forward," The One Who Will Make You Undone said. While he could empathize, he wanted more from his first fellow berserker conversation.

"No shit, I don't want this. I got it from my dad, bro. He was a monster, that shit head. I'll kill him," Ramn said. He shook his chains and maybe got bigger.

"At least you know where it came from."

"Dude, you gotta know where it came from. You aren't born like this. It's from broken shit in your head, brah. You know, trauma."

"I don't remember anything. Just bad dreams."

"You ain't so bright are you, dude? Something bad happened to you, man. Like real bad. See, I remember what happened to me. Dad locked me up in my room so he could skin my mom alive for three days outside my fucking door. I near starved to death. Compete with that, man! No way you could end up normal after that shit! Naw, if you don't remember, it happened before you could remember. Like, you musta been real little, man." Ramn started to cry. "Man, I felt so goddamn powerless. Couldn't do shit. And there she was, screaming for someone to help...Three days!"

His breathing went hard and deep. Aaron knew what that meant.

He struggled hell-bent against his chains. The wind from his flails tousled Aaron's hair and knocked off his iconic hat. Ramn's yell rained spit and blood over Critch.

The door swung open. Firemimes stormed in.

"Good, meeting Critch got him raging," Madam Ava said.

Ramn was eight feet tall and six-hundred pounds of calves and biceps. Freight train chest with twelve-pack abs. The Firemimes baited him out. His thudded footfalls and crashings into walls as he maneuvered his way outside. Madam Ava and November appeared outside the door.

The Antagonist's Prison

"You're having trouble berserking, aren't you?" November said, kneeling down to unlock Aaron's chains. Violet perfume and smoke drowned him.

"Where's Midge?" Oblivious Man said. November helped him stand. There was no need for her cheek to brush his. Madam Ava raised an eyebrow at her. Aaron tried to wipe off some of the paint. There was none. How much sunscreen did she have to wear?

"I don't know," she said. She refused to look at him. Her hat tilted low. Aaron didn't know what she was playing at. Knowing her as an associate of Madam Ava, The Antagonist knew not to look into the game. For that was all it could be.

"Mr. Kinns has her," Madam Ava said.

His lip twitched. Lassos fell from Madam Ava's and The Widow's waists by instinct, they weren't aircraft cable and therefore not effective against him, perhaps the climber's rope was good enough for Ramn.

"I'm fine," Your Imminent Unforewarned Reckoning said.

"Well, that's a shame. Because Mr. Kinns has moved on The Underground. News is sparse from the other Factions. The Heathens and The Divorce have fallen. Raile is making her move against Diane. The Seekers all but evaporated. Haven't heard from The Smugglers or The Brotherhood," Madam Ava said.

"My Firemimes are holding them off, for now. But not for long," November said matter of factly. Numbers in a machine calculated for simulations.

A bloodied and oozed-on Firemime appeared around the corner. "We got that wave, but Kinns is regrouping. Ramn's down. He ain't breathing."

November helped Mr. Bennett follow Madam Ava and the Firemime outside. Like everything in Madam Ava's world, her back areas were labyrinthine and filled with closed, locked doors. Her architect must have had a thing for the least efficient way to move around a building. They backtracked, opened doors, walked into rooms, waited and went out through the same door.

Outside, Ramn was no longer eight feet tall, maybe six five. In

Chatters and a Desperate Suggestion

his non-berserk, he was a well-built personal trainer, instead of the Mr. Universe six-hundred-pound titan known as Ramn. Contusions from blunt impacts patterned his body, more blood on the ground than inside. He twitched and bounced, refusing to believe he was dead like severed octopus legs. Twentyish Knights dissolved on the ground. At least forty dead Firemimes in their wake.

"Gather around, everyone, now is the time to push back," Madam Ava said.

The feeling returned to Aaron's feet by the time they reached the wasteland in front of Mr. Kinns' fortress. November insisted on supporting him as he limped along, doing well despite her stiletto six-inch heels, which did not seem appropriate for battle. Neither did her long black gown and ornate Firemime jacket. More a nun than a warrior. Madam Ava more suited for the battle in her thick leather dress covering every inch of her. She pulled up the pleats, and through a miracle of loops and knots managed to tie it around her pelvis. She dragged a gruesome cat o' nine tails behind her.

They totaled out at only five Firemimes plus the three of them. Hardly an army, especially against the two lines of at least fifty Knights and blue smilodons facing toward them. The Fairy King fluttered a few feet off the ground in front of his ranks.

"Is that all you have?" he said with a general's bellow.

Fifteen Norsemen jogged up in formation, like they waited for the Fairy King's mock. Asher hustled alongside Oscar.

"I ran to recruit the Brotherhood after I escaped," he said, hands on his knees, breathing heavily.

Oscar bowed before Madam Ava, then picked Her Dear Apocalypse up in a huge hug.

"Where is your witch, berserker?" Oscar said, elated.

Aaron pointed at the fortress.

"That was a poor decision on that little man's part. How is it you haven't already made your way in there?" Oscar said, still holding him.

"Critch has been unreliable as of late." Aaron's back popped under Oscar's force.

The Antagonist's Prison

"This isn't the time to be doubting your abilities, Critch! That's why witches find berserkers, to help them in their trials!" Oscar roared two inches from his face.

"Fuck you, now is the exact right time to be doubtful. Look at what we're up against," he said, half-gesturing to everything. Not moving his upper arms much. "I'm still going to fight, but I can have my doubts."

"No one needs or deserves Critch," November said.

"We shall see if that is the case," Oscar said.

"You were saying you need a witch, Critch?" Luciana said as she approached alone, the more the merrier. "That came out more lyrical than intended."

"Enough!" The Fairy King echoed. His butterfly wings flickered. He zipped ahead of the ensuing army.

No hesitation as their diminutive squadron charged down the hill. Underground at War! Midge would have been miffed at the name for it.

Aaron was a lucid dreamer. Treaded the line between becoming too conscious of the absurdity. Doing something to wake yourself up was difficult for him. He was light and distant. A step ahead of reality. That was his mindset as he led the charge. Rose up in his body. Weight shifted into his head where it steamed out into the cloud of fairies above. As he lightened, he pulled ahead of his enthusiastic but doomed squad with a red scarf billowing behind.

Charlie stood proudly on Aaron's shoulder and shook a leg at their enemies. Fun fact, the end of his leg looked like a cat paw.

They hit the wall of impossible creatures. The Firemimes fought with drunken mastery, the Norsemen swung hard. No one knew what the fuck Asher was trying to accomplish with his ineffectual slingshot. Knights fell to Luciana's Stills. However, they all knew that without his berserk, they stood no chance.

A circle formed around the Fairy King and Nonexistent Grin With A Black Heart Of Gold. He never understood why the generals got a little arena to fight in.

In his lightness, he dodged the speedy blows. Sighing, The

Chatters and a Desperate Suggestion

Mockery Of Oberon grabbed The Antagonist with hands that wrapped from his chest to the middle of his spine and flew up into the swarming cloud of fairies pelting him with paintball pebbles. He dropped The One Who Will Make You Undone. Critch grabbed hold of a leg to shatter his knee. The King of Court barrel-rolled and hurled him to the ground. The terrain zoomed into focus. Aaron hit feet first. Fell into a roll over the debris and things he refused to think about, like tiny human skulls with sutures not quite sealed.

His left leg took too much of the impact. It didn't work anymore. He stood on the right, not looking down to assess the damage. Brushed off the sticks and stones sticking out of his scarred skin. For the first time ever, he needed a weapon. The Fairy King smiled from above, then smashed into the ground, sending up a wave of wasteland. The shock signals from his leg couldn't quite breach his newfound lightness. The Fairy King's claws slashed across Aaron's face. Mr. Bennett rolled sideways as it skimmed his nose, eye, and cheek. He couldn't get up from the roll. Faded in and out from blood loss and shock.

The One Who Stares Back From The Void wished he could recall little things about Midge in the blackouts, but they really hadn't been together all that long. He didn't even know her smell. Instead, Aaron was overpowered by violet and expensive cigarettes. Kept returning to Critch's awful memory brought on by that milkshake.

Purple fish swam inside his eyes. In the next lucid moment, fifty or more white figures swirled around. Someone clicked over in echoing high heels.

He was lifted. His face pressed against an old shirt smelling firmly of man and blood. No one moved. They examined him with disquietude dribbling out their lips. Five white shirts with rainbows, four heavily damaged Firemimes, Asher, Oscar, and two Norsemen all starried at Critch from bodies nearly as wrecked as his. Madam Ava stood proud next to him, her skin glistened, not hurt at all. November fanned herself as she faced away. Luciana holding a limp arm.

Gradick smiled down. Raile and their Circle stood behind.

The Antagonist's Prison

Gradick shook him. He stabilized.

"You don't shake a dying man, fucker," He Who Smiles Back said with a smile. He thought it was a friendly smile. No smiles from him were good at this point.

"Wipe that smile off your face, old friend, it does not suit you. It belongs to a side of you you no longer need."

The smile fell off Aaron's face, melting into the terrain of skulls, bodies, and slag.

"There, much better," Gradick said.

Everyone stared in horror at the left side of Aaron's face. He opened that eye, and wetness spilled down his shirt. Cassie threw up. Don't think about it.

"You're a wreck," Raile said.

"It's good to see you're still alive, Gradick," Our Relentless Shadow said.

"You're barely alive though," Raile said. "We need to get you to a hospital, you should be dead from the blood loss alone."

"Can I call myself a tough guy yet?" Teeth fell out.

Madam Ava leaned over to check him.

"How do we get him out of here?" Jeff said.

"We need The Adumbration, Madam Ava. Now!" Raile said.

"No, not yet," Madam Ava said. The Widow in Yellow dropped her fan and clicked away angry.

"Where's Midge? Raile said.

"Mr. Kinns has her," Madam Ava said. November whispered something to Madam Ava. "The locks are broken, Miscreant King and Queen."

"Not anymore! Scatter like a savage," Raile said.

"It's true, we need to get him out of here, Lady Made of Dark. This is how berserkers die," Oscar said, spitting out a tooth. "The strength with which that winged fella hit my men, well, we lost three with each blow. I saw you flying around, berserker, but you kept standing up."

"He's not gonna be standing soon. What the fuck is wrong with all of you?" Raile said. "Ok, guys, we'll carry him out."

Chatters and a Desperate Suggestion

Aaron vaguely did not understand that he was no longer saying the right words.

"No, I have to get Midge," Aaron Bennett said.

Gradick tried to grab him, but Madam Ava snapped her cat o'nine tails.

"Stop. Do not disrupt him out of this mindset, it's the only thing that's saved him before."

Aaron spun on his good foot and assessed at the stretch before him. You just gotta keep going, never stop. His head wouldn't stay still but managed to stay upright. With the next step, he crumpled. Got back up. Lifted shredded corduroys. Jagged bone popped through his thigh. About right.

"Come on, Aaron..." Gradick said. His god-like empathy choked him. So much worry for a corpse. "We need to save you... You're dying. You're not making sense anymore. Why are you so concerned with Midge? She isn't worth it. Scatter like a savage, please..." Coulda been Raile saying it too. Either could say either.

Their concern was motivating and heartwarming.

Stupid question though. He couldn't feel anything, pain, fear, anger. A mind in an armored shell. He felt alone and far away. "I can't feel pain, I don't hurt..."

Raile or Gradick wiped some of the blood off his face. "I don't know what's going on with you, but don't worry about it. It's your greatest boon right now. Your body won't keep this up for long. You're on a time schedule and time's almost up. Run riot. Raise hell."

Aaron shrugged and endured toward the cave wall. Charlie ran bravely ahead, then turned back to check on him. You hadn't won yet, Mr. Kinns. Well, basically you'd won. But Aaron was still here and he had more blood to spill. Just, you know, not a lot.

"His white wolf has taken over," Oscar said. "I'm worried about its endurance."

Mocks and a Relinquishment

The One Who Stares Back From the Void fell against the cave wall, glad to no longer support himself on his shattered leg. Inside we go. The cave lit by harsh red chemical torches, creating opaque shadows that messed with depth.

He didn't know how long he had leaned there. The lightness in his head drained. The pain of his body crawled up with hope. He didn't have much time before he went into shock. This might be shock, for all he knew.

Frozen air billowed. Through the mist, in an icy freezer the size of an airplane hanger. Crystallizing blood trailed behind him. The white light reflected harshly off the freezer's distant walls. Felt Charlie shiver in his coat pocket.

Uncounted yards ahead were two stone pillars, spaced suspiciously far apart. Between them, a chained naked man's head looked up. Thick, rusted chains hung from elastic bands around his wrists. He could easily escape his bonds but seemed content standing in the chattering cold.

"Hello Critch, my name is Leba. That's Abel backward."

"Good to know, Leba. I don't have much time left. What do I have to do?"

"Mr. Kinns captured me, he uses me for the creation of his Knights. Will you be my Cain today?"

The Antagonist's Prison

Must be his tagline. Good for him.

"Mr. Kinns told me that he would've much rather had Critch for his machinations. That's hurtful," Leba said.

"I wouldn't count yourself out just because I'm perceived better." Aaron had no idea what he was talking about, but had no time for clarification.

Leba cocked his head. "What? Whatever. You're not the only berserker out there, Critch. Many of us are better, and many of us have terrible consequences when we berserk."

Mr. Bennett was not going to be able to have a conversation with this guy. He didn't even seem to be listening. Fortunately, he clearly had a speech prepared.

"Teach me a lesson, then."

"You're speaking nonsense, Critch. You have all the infamy, yet those of your kind mock you."

"I'm sure you all could easily outmatch me."

Leba's body pulsed and he doubled in size. Heat rushed by like a fireplace igniting.

"Speak English! I don't want to kill you. I don't want to berserk at all," he said as if just hit in the ribs.

Aaron stood taller than him before. Now he was four feet taller than Aaron. The once-loose shackles stretched to contain him. The Antagonist wiggled back, putting two and two together. The high ceiling and the thick pillars.

Your Relentless Shadow stumbled over what to say, knowing nothing would help at this point. He couldn't ask him to calm down. Nor could he say he understood his predicament, his berserk didn't do this. Maybe if Ramn was here.

"Say something!" Leba twitched as his bones readjusted and popped into place after the expansion.

His Unflinching Grin wanted to ask what he wanted to talk about. Couldn't ask about the weather, his job, what he was studying, philosophy, music.

"I wish I could help you. But it appears no other options have been explored."

Mocks and a Relinquishment

"I still can't understand you! This is the end for the two of us! Our kind die!"

Aaron swallowed a giggle. "We haven't yet."

Leba doubled again with a burning hillside heat. This wave pushed Aaron back. Well, that didn't work. The pop and rip of his body sickened. His muscles convulsed.

"Now fight me, Critch. I will show you how worthless you are!"

"I'm not going to fight you. If you wish to kill me, fine. But I don't think that will fix either of us."

Leba doubled again and The One Who Will Make You Undone had to stagger away from his behemoth. Aaron's pain, and Leba's heat, became unbearable. He blurred out, each thought getting washed away in tides of Aaron retching. Leba grew again out of frustration. Now close to fifty feet tall. His quakes shook the floor. His eyes swelled and the vessels inside burst. Doubtful he could see anymore.

"You lucky shit," he said with a last rumble. He sagged against the chains, his huge red eyes staring at Aaron. His death rattle shook the barely-standing person of interest.

Aaron didn't know how he found the will to stand. Didn't know he fell. He wished to say it came from wanting to save Midge. Indeed, the thought of getting to her and somehow stopping Mr. Kinns urged him once he was standing. But to get off the ground, to keep moving, was another matter. Charlie jumped down and ran ahead. Turned around and twitched his leg at Aaron to come on.

He Who Stares Back fell. Which was fine. The slouched and dead gargantuan behind. He'd remember him. He knew he was here. He'd find out where he came from and let his loved ones know he died. If he had any left. Charlie jumped up and scratched at Aaron's nose. Thank you, good little friend.

Drowsy. Her Apocalypse was dying. Bothersome as that was. The ground wet from Leba's heat defrosting the place, but the powerful freezer worked hard to cool his corpse. The hum of the fans soothed Critch. This was good, keep observing things. The door was over there. Get to the door. Was it the door he came through?

The Antagonist's Prison

No, he was leaving a trail. Unless Mr. Kinns was fooling him. No, come on Aaron, you're delusional, not stupid. Keep in this world, that'd be a good mantra.

Nope, keep changing the topic.

Don't go anywhere else, stay out of your head. Notice something. Here's a hall. Blue stone. Painfully rough.

"Still alive, I see? But just barely," a man's voice said.

Aaron recognized it as someone he was going after. Midge! Right, Midge. He saw her against a chair, a phantom parasol twirling over her head. Silly umbrella, you were not there. Aaron hacked up black stuff. Looking ravishing, indeed.

Man approached to kick.

"I beat Critch. No one could beat Critch!" Terrible kick. "But I did! Me!"

The kind who lived behind others because he couldn't suffer the world himself. Aaron stopped his leg with a ruined black hand. He pulled, and the man fell over. The well-dressed man scrambled up. Took a teetered step back, spotted a large red spider and stepped on it with a light pop.

Someone screamed. Aaron heard sobs. Saw a naked and tortured black and blue cut on Jaslynn. Her whole body an expression of released hysterics.

"No," Aaron Bennett, Critch said.

"What? I can't hear you, Mr. Bennett! Too much blood in your mouth."

"No, you didn't beat Critch," His Unflinching Grin, Her Dear Apocalypse, The One Who Stares Back From The Void, The One Who Will Make You Undone, Your Imminent Unforewarned Reckoning coughed up more blood as he stood. Red rivulets fell. "I'm Critch. And I stand in front of those who cannot."

The world condensed and his mind popped like a high altitude yawn. Aaron was back. Midge mid-episode. The impossible effort needed to move in Midge's Still was negligible. He knew she was thinking about her brother, and how she couldn't lose another person she cared about. Mr. Kinns frozen in place about to garrote Aaron.

Mocks and a Relinquishment

Jaslynn's restraints were not all that secure and in Midge's Still, Jaslynn's frozen eyes burned with rage. Aaron couldn't kill Mr. Kinns, not in his condition. But she could. And she deserved it.

The Antagonist used her body to pull himself up and loosened her ropes. Midge's Episode ended on cue, as though she willed herself out of it. Aaron listened as Jaslynn and Mr. Kinns struggled.

"I am the Second Lust," Jaslynn snarled murderously.

Mr. Bennett didn't care. Midge hopped over, still strapped to her chair crying. He focused hard, using what blood he had left to untie her.

Hearing came back. Midge launched from her chair and caught him as the final blackness consumed everything. That last focus was a bad idea.

"Stay with me, Aaron!"

But he was gone. No more dealing with this useless reality.

Exsanguinations and a Bittersweet Reunion

Walking next to a short person of indeterminate anything. Their head hooded, and Aaron assumed they were desensitized in other ways. Earplugs, gloves and thick clothing. All to mute the outside world. Of course, all of the accouterments were black.

The disconcerting figure was leashed to the waist of a six-foot-some woman. She was close to Aaron's age, held herself well. Jet black hair almost out of the bottle. Six-inch heels with red soles, open-backed black dress. Huge black hat. Brim tilted low. When she noticed him examining his surroundings, the loud rhythmic snare clack from her heels ceased, turned to Mr. Bennett, hips popped out with a powerful leg freed from the high slit. He smelled violet.

"Hello, Aaron. Do you remember me?" she said, using a flat sultry blues voice he recognized from their many passing moments.

"November?"

"Yes," she said, more akin to a posh New York. A flat wealthy way of speaking. Hard to tell where she was from because that royal accent was never taught from birth. It was earned. "I have something I wish to get off my chest. So, please, let me say my peace and I'll leave you to think on it. And I request, call me Emily from here on out."

The Antagonist's Prison

Aaron shrugged, not knowing where this headed. Her grayed-out blue eyes poured out an insane, unfathomable calm. He'd never seen the color of her eyes. They commenced a sprint-walk toward a hospital that was not in Indigo Bay, but when Aaron tried to read the name, it was indecipherable. The world took on an amorphous quality. It wasn't real but tried really hard to be. Aaron didn't want reality to feel self-conscious, so instead he walked lock-step with Emily. Mayhaps that's why he walked so quickly. Their blistering pace must have been an odd sight to witness.

The hooded figure struggled hard to keep up with a bounding, blind trot.

"Do not worry," Emily said. "This is how they prefer to traverse the world. It also keeps questions down as we travel through Strange Town."

Like the hooded person, Aaron didn't care about whatever Strange Town meant. Emily seemed to know where she was going. Though to be fair, in the deepest marrow of his bones, Mr. Bennett felt a knowing that she always knew where she was going. Something he knew intrinsically about her and from vague deja vu impressions from blocked memories.

Inside, the hospital was orderly, but the residents regarded them as a waste of time. A disdain mixed with a *no not again* vibe.

"It is best if you ignore them, they are not real," Emily said as they ran-marched past them. "This appears to be a short one, so I will try to make this brief. I know quite a bit about you. More than you know about yourself."

The Antagonist chose to let her speak and felt no need to question why he felt as healthy and normal as he did not a few days ago. Mostly not in pain. He remembered passing out but not waking up. Mayhaps this was his dream.

"I was never a part of The Fetishes. Madam Ava drafted my Firemimes to tend to Critch so she could focus on the multitudes of other things dividing her attention. Because of my position, I know almost everything about you. You and I aspire to achieve very similar lives. I have always wanted a quiet life away from most any-

Exsanguinations and a Bittersweet Reunion

one, instead of managing things as I am. I followed my calling, and it has made me all of the money and all of the power, but I dislike it a great deal. In honesty, it bores me. I believed having all the power and all the influence would be invigorating, if at least stimulating."

"Do you always speak in paragraphs?"

"Do you have any questions or comments? You do not typically, I apologize if assumed incorrectly."

"No, not particularly. Maybe it was a social obligation that I felt I should be participating? This is not a conversation."

"It could be, if you so desired. But if I know you like I know I do, then you do not. You always preferred listening instead of speaking. May I continue? Madam Ava agrees that this is not my proverbial career."

Inside the rooms there were no residents. All beds lay empty. No doctors or nurses. No speakers buzzed out information.

"Why is there no one here?"

"Because this part of Strange Town is part of the mayor's psyche that cannot be populated. At least that would be my hypothesis given the nature of our Dreamer." Normally, someone would nod their heads toward who they were referring to. Emily chose not to do that. Correctly assuming Aaron's inference.

"Do you know why I choose violet as my perfume? It is because the smell of violet has a chemical called ionone. It resets its smell. It renews itself. That is why when wearing it you will occasionally smell it again, unlike other smells which you forget about once you get used to them. That resurrection is something I cherish. Midge is an amazing woman. However, Madam Ava and I both agree she is not right for you. I am," Emily said with lowered drama while still flat. Maybe through timbre. Aaron didn't know.

"I wish for you to keep something in mind. When Midge defended you in The Underground, she said that she would fan your flames, make you a forest fire. I did not believe it. You are not a fire, that description is reserved for The Miscreant King and Queen. No, you are a lava flow. Fires leave nothing but ash, lava leaves hard, tempered, and fertile ground. Miss Estire will hinder

The Antagonist's Prison

you soon enough. She'll politely request for you to change, for you to become nicer, go back to school, become what she wants her partner to be. I do not want that to happen. I wish to remind you that an argumentative person is a sign of insecurity. Midge never stops arguing, not to understand, but to mold, to create everyone in her own image. After I have left my position, I hope to seek you out, and I would be devastated to find that you had been smothered to crackling embers, poked at by an obnoxious redhead. It would crush me."

They stopped just short of a service entrance to the hospital. Out the window, workers unloaded straight-jacketed person after straight-jacketed person with care and ceremony.

"One of the more important things I learned from Madam Ava is that normal people have a luxury that we do not when it comes to finding a partner. Normal people can settle for what they have, or can reach for more, following that romantic comedy façade. Normal people can find love from a large pool, as they have many options. People like you and I, well, we do not have many options. We need a very specific kind of person, one with the same background, the same learned philosophy. Without such specific compatibilities, there will be a void that grows and consumes. Patient understanding, academic approaches, and armchair relations are not enough for us. We need more. You need more."

Emily opened the back door and ushered Aaron through. "Do not make the same mistake I did with my first husband."

Paused in the frame, she smiled at him and that was the first expression anyone had ever seen from her.

Aaron was bewildered. Not sure what to think about her monologue or the setting of it. Midge had been nothing but supportive, and thus far, allowed Aaron to be Critch. The Antagonist didn't understand where Emily was coming from, so he dropped it. Tried not to sniff for trace violet clouds as he stepped through the door.

Exsanguinations and a Bittersweet Reunion

Aaron woke up. How odd. He didn't think he would. Aaron didn't see a white light, nor did he dream, or maybe he did. It's happened before, Aaron came out of a dead sleep with no feeling of rejuvenation and realized never waking up again wouldn't be so bad. It's not like he'd know that he'd never be awake again. He'd be dead.

Aaron had no idea what time it was, and that bothered him more than the plastic medical structure strung up around him. His leg suspended and stitched, with a little metal contraption to pinch bones in place. Based on all the hardware, the reconstruction must have been a nightmare. He couldn't see out of his left eye. Bandages down his cheek. Needles poked into both hands and the pits of both elbows. Lots of machines reported doctor-useful information.

Midge wrapped up in the corner, surrounded by tablets and laptops, doing academics like a pro. She noticed him stir, and looked over casual, like movement from a corpse was normal. Her bagged eyes hadn't slept in some time. She saw that he was awake and flew to his side to embrace. No strappings, barriers, hollow medicine cords, or wires could prevent her from crying and mumbling tearful happiness into his hospital gown.

"Ow," he said instinctively. He was under too much for anything to hurt or even be real. "How are you, Midge? How long was I out? Entertain me."

"The doctors weren't sure if you'd wake up. There was such a slim chance after all your trauma. You should've been dead before you even got here. Putting that much donor blood into you, there was a high chance you'd reject it. They pumped five liters into you! Do you know what that means? A man your size has less than six liters of blood total! You were alive, sort of, with only one liter! Do you realize that humans die after losing only one-third of their blood? Papers will be written on you."

"Take a breath," he said. She sobbed mid breath. Shuddered. "So, we're Topside?"

"Uh, yeah...? You are a little fuzzy, aren't you?"

A doctor came in. Handsome chap, around Aaron's age. Good for him. This room seemed fancy.

The Antagonist's Prison

"Mr. Bennett, my name is Dr. Michaels, it's a pleasure to meet you. You're a lucky man."

"I'm not at Indigo Bay General, am I?" Thinking he might be at the hospital in his dreams.

"You're at a Medical Center. If you know what I mean. How are you feeling?"

"Got it. Out of it. Is it the meds?"

"Most likely. You could be reacting to any number of things, the pain medication, antibiotics, or blood transfusions. Would you like to hear the damage?"

"Let's do it."

"Let's see." He flipped a page over on his clipboard. "When you arrived at the trauma center, you were in stage four hypovolemic shock from severe blood loss. The hemorrhaging caused cardiac arrest and renal failure. You are lucky, Mr. Bennett, to have not suffered any permanent brain damage due to lack of blood flow and oxygen deprivation. However, your kidneys became ischemic, resulting in acute renal failure. We were able to effectively treat one kidney but had to remove the other due to what appeared to be severe damage from blunt force trauma. I am happy to tell you that you will not be needing further dialysis.

"Additionally, you sustained a depressed skull fracture, where the cranial bones are displaced inward into brain tissue. Cerebrovascular hemorrhaging occurred in your temporal lobe, but, luckily, you arrived just in time before you again sustained permanent brain damage.

"Next verse same as the first, you've sustained a supracondylar femur fracture with an associated separate femoral shaft fracture. A Less Invasive Stabilization System Fixator was inserted submuscularly, and attached with distal screws," he sighed, flipping another page of the chart.

"Jesus. Sounds like you guys were busy. Thank you for your trouble," Mr. Bennett said.

"One last thing. You sustained penetrating trauma to your left eye. We couldn't save it."

Exsanguinations and a Bittersweet Reunion

"Does that mean I get an eye patch?"

"We can give you a glass eye if you'd prefer."

"I think I'd prefer a patch."

"We'll get you one once the wound has healed. Unfortunately, your recovery is going to require a bit more time here at the hospital."

"As long as I don't get those bedsores everyone speaks about."

"Unlikely. Now that you're awake, physical therapy will want to get you out of bed and moving."

"Sounds exhausting."

"Yep, it will be. I have to say, I am so curious about what happened to you. Apparently, I can't legally ask you those questions, someone higher up protects you. I digress. Do you have any questions?"

"Not really." He waved a hand and jiggled the tubes around.

"You've become quite a celebrity here at the hospital. I'll send my PA in to check up on you in a few hours. I'll see you tomorrow, Mr. Bennett."

Midge grabbed his bandaged hand. "Thank you for coming after me."

"Almost didn't make it. Thank you for getting me out."

"Now that was a motherfucking ordeal. Jazz and I dragged you out where everyone was waiting. Raile and Gradick took you from us and we ran you to Madam Ava's yacht. We took a rainbow elevator out of The Underground, and you fucking disappeared before we got to the surface! The doctors said there is no way for you to be alive."

"How did I get to the hospital?"

Midge clutched her head from an apparently sudden headache. "Gah! By boat maybe. Just not the yacht. Must've been a dingy of some sort. I didn't see you leave."

"Dunno if my superpower is worth it." He yawned, suddenly exhausted.

"You should go to sleep."

"You look like you need a nap," Aaron said.

"I get a few hours here and there. Don't worry about me. I've

The Antagonist's Prison

got stuff to keep me occupied while you're sleeping. If I'm not here when you wake up, I'll be back soon enough. I have to go to the coffee shop down the street, hospital coffee sucks."

Over the next few days, all manner of people came in to talk to Aaron. Important doctors asked questions he didn't know how to answer. Madam Ava sent a lawyer to brief him on his story.

John and Kat visited frequently, and they exchanged stories and happenings. The titles of Raile and Gradick had been passed. Jeff and Wren had taken the names Basilio and Sloan. Kat and Midge became friends again under the radar, and they seemed happy. John and Aaron played chess and talked contacts. Aaron was going to be drunk for weeks with the amount of drinks promised him. A larger contact web than Aaron realized he had.

Jaslynn was committed to a mental health institution. No amount of psychological fortitude could sustain whatever she went through.

Midge brought him lots of eye patches Tyler made at the store. Artists Aaron didn't know knew him created fancy canes, carved or painted.

The Widow in Yellow came in on behalf of Madam Ava. She kissed his cheek and let her hand brush from his chest down his arm. The conversation was awkward.

The only person who didn't visit in the couple of days was Amber. Aaron worried about her. No one knew where she was, or if she even got out of The Underground. Mr. Bennett hoped she didn't die trying to finish her Magical Mystery Tour.

Kat, or more accurately Katarina, came in one day for a visit. Amber showed up at their house in the middle of the night, starved and ravaged. John and Kat stayed up to take care of her while she told them of her adventures in The Underground. But she never came to see Aaron. Katarina said something about feeling unsettled.

Exsanguinations and a Bittersweet Reunion

They sat on Midge's couch a few weeks after the dust settled. His cane rested to the side. A new compulsion to check its whereabouts at all times. Aaron's leg could barely support weight anymore and the pain buckled him. Southern Gothic Music, Midge's favorite music genre, crooned in the otherwise quiet studio. The takeout cooled on the table. Neither of them a fan of screen media, so she listened to the music while endlessly studying and tippy-tapping at her laptop covered in stickers.

A full glass of whiskey in his hand as he stared across the room, having a grand ole time within the moments passing from one to the next. Some seemed to need constant stimulation. That was great for them, but he was not that sort. He did not mind the pressing sound of the world preoccupying him.

Midge stared at him.

"Yes, indeed I'm still here," he said.

"That's weird, you seemed all spaced out."

"I don't really space out. Dunno if I could if I wanted to."

"But you certainly don't mind doing nothing for hours."

"You're just noticing this?"

"I mean, no. I just find it odd. You don't read. You only take out your phone when you get a call or text. Otherwise you just sit there like you're waiting."

"Wouldn't describe it as waiting, either. I assure you I am having a good time."

"But you're not doing anything! What are you thinking?"

"Fleeting thoughts. Don't really keep track of them."

"Then like clockwork, you get up every half an hour on the dot to smoke. Don't even check the time."

"You're getting it."

"Dunno, it's just weird." She gently pet a new flash tarantula tattoo on the side of her neck. The eyes larger than Charlie's, but memories of him always had large eyes. "You could be more than a screen shop owner, yet that's all you do. Then you come home and do literally nothing but stare at a point on the wall until you've had your fill of whiskey, which never gets you drunk, and then go

The Antagonist's Prison

to bed for like a wink and go back to work for fourteen hours."

"Where is this going?"

"Every single day. Do you want to plan a vacation or something? Maybe we could get away and do something?"

"Sure, I'd be down."

"Any suggestions?"

"Not really."

She sighed before getting up for whatever new Hazy IPA they sold wherever. New four-pack twenty dollars a bunch. The IPA bubble had to burst soon. She skipped the song by tapping her earbud.

"Did you know bisexuals feel pansexuals are pushing them out of the queer community?"

"Seems like an infight in a community that absolutely should not be fighting each other. There shouldn't be any fight over any designation of how not hetero they are. Tiny villages bickering with each other against the fucking patriarchy? Seems the wrong fight."

Midge kneed, faced him. A tired alarm sounded.

"What's the matter?" he said.

"I love your mind, Aaron. But I so rarely hear what's going on up there."

"Never saw a need to spout out what I'm thinking."

"But I want to hear your thoughts. I want you to participate in this friendship."

"I feel like I just did."

"But that's not how I feel. And you cannot tell me how I feel."

"True enough. I apologize."

"And...?"

"You're gonna have to prompt me. I don't really want or need to voice my opinions out of the blue. Silence has always been a nice blanket for me."

"But you have an active listener now. You don't have to be afraid."

"Not afraid. Is that what you think? I'm afraid to voice my thoughts because of pushback against them?"

Exsanguinations and a Bittersweet Reunion

"I don't know! You never tell me anything."

"Well, I suppose, that's the question you should be asking? Why must you know what I'm thinking, when you already know me?"

"Because I enjoy you."

"Why is that not enough?"

"I don't know..."

Midge went back to dejectedly send drafts of papers to people. Opened a journal to peer review. She shudder-sighed. He went out to smoke at one-thirty in the morning. Just as he finished his sixth glass of whiskey. The randomly chosen cue to leave and go to bed.

The halfway house came recommended. When Aaron asked if the City Beneath would fund it, the City refused. Madness caused by the Underground was common and part of the schtick. Aaron funded the treatment himself. He'd visited several times, but Jaslynn wasn't ready. When he was informed that she was now verbal, Aaron dropped what he was doing and drove out.

It was outside of town in an industrial zone where constant manufacturing happened. Cars drove by the tanks and towers and sneered at the ugly necessity. It was odd that smoke always came out of stacks but no one was there, and workers from the area were never hired to the gray location. Occasionally a semi truck would roll through, but it was a mostly excused place.

Aaron knocked on the supervisor trailer with a series of knuckles and palms. A kindly couple opened the door and smiled at the reaper man. Happily invited him in. Their fashion of an ultra specific generic. Everyone's rich relative who says very little of their business but are a joy at gatherings. Make the best potato salad.

"Mr. and Mrs Williams, how are you two doing?" Aaron said. His small talk even more unnecessary than for most.

"Fantastic, Mr. Bennett. Can we get you anything?"

"A coffee would be much appreciated."

The Antagonist's Prison

"Oh, how convenient, my husband just whipped up a new pot." Because of course he did. "Now, please sit."

Aaron sat like an omen on the couch. The coffee was good. Served in a #1 Grandpa mug. The Williamses sat smiling at the same time with His and Hers mugs, polite sips. The talk was pleasant, predictable, and for the requisite amount of time.

"She's doing well by the way," Mr. Williams said after a time. "Come a long way I would say, yes."

"That's good to hear. Would it be possible to see Miss Philips?"

"Oh yes. I believe that would be a wonderful idea. She asked to see you. Oh, this will be wonderful."

Mr. Williams rolled an iconic catalog rug up and put it in the same spot he always put it. Then he popped up a pressure latch on the hardwood and lifted the floor to a staircase down. The space opened into a larger space. Cozy, clean, and warm with soft lighting. Open but not an open floor plan. Little knicks on the wood, wallpaper, and brick. A place where imperfections were expected, and that added to the charm.

Painting, gardening, a work-out space and recording studio. Only a few trained workers lived here full time and rarely left the facility. They were fine with that part of the contract. The Williamses were calculating in who they hired.

Their clients were few in number and they liked it that way. There's no wait list because they reached out to the clients, not the other way around. Aaron was an exception. As he was not wont to be.

Jaslynn sat in a fluffy chair made of meticulous comfortable. Her clothes loose and free. She sat with a toy that played back lights in the same sequence as the buttons pressed. She looked up at Aaron as he approached and smiled. It was a genuine smile, not one of manipulation. He chose to stand. All the nearby chairs were short, and a person of his height and lank wasn't right on a little stool. Aaron was not the sort to sit on the floor.

"You're looking much better than when I saw you last. Welcome back."

"Thank you, Aaron." Jaslynn's voice relaxed, with less urgency.

Exsanguinations and a Bittersweet Reunion

"And thank you for this place. They told me you're funding it."

"It's the least I can do."

"Thank you for coming for me. I've been going over and over what I was going to say when I could get words out." Eyes rimmed red, voice shaking. "And that's what I came to. Thank you for coming for me."

"There were varying opinions on my motivations. But I keep my own counsel for most of my decisions."

"People can be cruel and selfish, I suppose. I didn't know who you were when we met at that party. But if there was ever a man who could stand up to Mr. Kinns. You fit the fucking part, I'll tell you what."

Mr. Bennett let a little smile out. It was also a real smile. "In the end, you saved yourself, don't lessen that fact."

"I know." She went thoughtful for a minute. "How long do you think I'll be here?"

"Quite some time, but not forever. Coming from me, this sort of thing never really resolves itself."

"Your name isn't Aaron is it?" Still Jaslynn.

"Depends on your perspective. It is my name as much as any name isn't. I don't know my birth name. I don't know my family. No memory of my past. So even though it was not given in a traditional manner, I'm a fan of my name."

"But why Aaron Bennett? You could have chosen anything."

"I have my reasons. But I think more than anything the name suits me."

Jaslynn unfolded to stand up. "Thank you for insisting they call me Jaslynn. I don't think I'm much of a Jazz anymore."

"Seasons of life remark. Names mean a great deal. I don't take what people want to be called and referred to lightly."

There was awkward.

"How about a handshake?" Aaron said, proferring his fully healed hand. Jaslynn took it happily. "I'll visit often, no worries."

"Please." A blinked-away tear.

"And please don't say thank you any more. You've said it

The Antagonist's Prison

enough."

Mr. Bennett left the facility soon after, followed by a trail of 'y'all come back nows.' In ways he would never admit, he wished he got this treatment instead of Madam Ava's employ. Alas, it was not Mr. Bennett's way to long for what he could not have. It would have been a waste of his time.

It was three in the afternoon. Aaron drank on his porch. It had been three months since Midge had been reliable. Flaked more and more until they both stopped. Miss Peach cooked her foul-smelling food inside. Tuna, brussel sprouts, kale, and curry all in a concoction the neighbors hated. Miss Peach still regarded him as a foster child. Worried and all that. Every once in a long while Aaron would think of Charlie's capricion fondly.

A woman walked along the sidewalk with a gait of absolutism. Champagne hair. A sea-spray-blue dress made from one square piece of fabric wrapped meticulously to accentuate her robust frame. A gaudy black metal belt around her waist and over her torso. Beneath the strange dress unyielding legs supported by low purple Converse crop tops.

The woman stopped in front of the walkway, took out a cigarette holder and twisted a hand-rolled cigarette into it. Untied Critch's noose around her waist and let it drop to the walkway with a thud.

Aaron met her at the top of the stairs. She stopped at the bottom and blew out her drag. Her coruscating blue eyes, primed by her blue dress, shone out their sockets.

"Hello, Aaron," Emily said. "Do you remember me?"

"Of course, care to join me?"

"I would love to."

Aaron sat on one side of the swing, Emily sat in close proximity. His left side tingled. His neck burned from past associated abrasions. Aaron paused Amber's music. They smoked for a bit without talking. Miss Peach came out to see who Emily was. They

Exsanguinations and a Bittersweet Reunion

both glared. She went inside. Unlike her.

"I am no longer The Widow in Yellow."

"As you said, you'd find me after."

"It pleases me you remembered. I am still on retainer. But free to be who I desire."

"As we are both."

"It was unfortunate about you and Midge never developing more than a friendship that faded."

"You're the only one."

"I suppose, but that's the kind of person I am. Others first, me always."

"A good summation of both of us."

They watched the sky turn orange. Emily opened the second bottle of whiskey, drank from it, put another cigarette in her holder.

"We're going to have to go to the liquor store if you're going to drink that one," Aaron said.

"I look forward to it."

"So are you a widow?"

"Does that bother you?"

"Not in the slightest."

"I killed my first husband when I was twenty. He deserved it, I'd love to tell you about it, I think you'll agree he deserved it," Emily said.

"So then did I give you the name The Widow in Yellow?"

"Yes, Madam Ava loved using all of your descriptions for us as our titles. She owes you everything."

"I guess we both understand murderers well."

"I propose we are slightly different than those who kill out of a need."

On their way to the liquor store, "Deria said I have five years to live."

"Deria's science is pseudo. That was before, when Critch influenced your biomechanics. I think you have a long life ahead of you."

"Why didn't you make a move before now?"

The Antagonist's Prison

"The Antagonist worked on guilt. He pulled it out of you. He made you realize what you did until you begged for punishment. He then stretched out the sentence until you wished for anything but what you were being put through. Then Critch killed them, almost always as a mercy kill. A facet of him Madam Ava disliked."

"That doesn't answer my question," Aaron said as they meandered to the shop's counter.

"Two bottles of Glendorach, 15 year," Emily said.

They walked back toward the porch at the same unnecessary pace.

"I'm guilty," November said, lighting yet another high-end rolled cigarette. "Critch hated me. I have done a lot of evil things. But, with Critch in the way, I could not make a move. When I delivered those letters, my hands shook so awfully I surprised myself when I was able to keep composure. I only felt fear in your presence. Rightly so. We killed over a thousand people together."

"Does that mean you're terrified of Critch?"

"Of course I am terrified of what you used to be. Him and quite literally nothing else. You understood me once, you will again soon. I know you are no longer The Antagonist."

"Do I need to know anything you haven't resolved?"

"No. That is the beauty of it. We have encountered each other at a crux. You are perfect. I am perfect. I do not require you to do anything, I have no goals for you or us. What I want is a partner, not a tool, not a servant, not an anchor. I have had all those and disliked it. What I want is a partner I can live with and see me as I am and love me for the atrocity I am and nothing more. Just a person who makes me happy to be around and alive."

"So what do you make of Kat saying the sharpest swords need the thickest sheathes."

"That sounds like Katrina suggesting to you that you should have thought about what was happening. You disagreed with the Miscreant Queen. If I were to conjecture, that was her plan all along. To answer your question, I say a sword has no use in a sheath. But two people using two swords is better than one sword

Exsanguinations and a Bittersweet Reunion

hidden from the world by someone trying to protect the blade."

"Even for their own protection?" Mr. Bennett said.

"I do not need you. You do not need me. I want you. I want you by my side. Not protected for my own gratitude. John and Katarina's marriage bodes ill tidings for people of our world."

"In what way?"

"The Miscreant Royalty finally understand their roles as cultural assassins. Madam Ava quashed them, for she was afraid. Now that Katarina has met Hatch's, sorry, John's level. People like the Lady Made of Dark do not have a place in their new world order. Madam Ava will not even see them coming."

"What about us? If we're to do this. I don't think either of us...what did you call them, The Black Hearts of Gold? Are we in trouble?"

They resumed their seats on the swing.

"No, I would like to think we are on their side. But I think I am worthy of you. Are you worthy of me?"

"I'll strive to be."

Emily smiled. A quiet, minute twitch of a thing, just as unemotive as he remembered her. "And I hope that I'll always be striving to deserve you as well."

Emily slowly placed her head on his shoulder. Touch a rare thing for both of them and an ultimate sign of affection.

Aaron kicked the rocks of Critch's cage. Not sad that part of him was gone. But he did wonder where it went because he never watched it go. For trauma never leaves. It licks its wounds over elsewhere, sometimes for years. For now, he found his cheeks hurt by the end of the night. They were tired of smiling.

Acknowledgements

This was the first book I ever wrote, and I will be forever indebted to my first beta readers. Especially Kevin McAuliff and Daniel LeMelle. Thank you for your enthusiasm for the work. You kept me motivated to finish. I am so grateful to finally be able to share it.

I wouldn't have been able to publish this book without my editor, Britta. Not only is Britta insanely talented at what she does, but she was one of the few who gets it. She enthusiastically pushed the book to its fullest potential. A huge thanks to my book cover editor, Jennifer. She created the cover I didn't even know I wanted. I am indebted to her true artistic talent.

And finally, my deepest gratitude will always go to my wife, Camille Jones. You have been my champion through all the ups and downs. You are the reason this book happened.